'Riotously funny, charming, and nostalgic, *Seven Exes* is a truly optimistic look at turn[...] all the mess that can c[...]

Laura [...]

'Fun, playful and warm, *Seven [...] whirlwind* of book. Riotous yet sincere, lighthearted yet [...]thoughtful, this book is absurdly entertaining and will make you laugh like you're with old friends'

Caroline Hulse

'I really enjoyed *Seven Exes*! It was like a therapy session cleverly wrapped up in rom-com packaging. A bright, sparky rom-com that will make you question your relationship with the past, for sure!'

Justin Myers/*The Guyliner*

'Lucy Vine always knocks it out of the park and *Seven Exes* is no exception. I couldn't put it down! It's so smart, so funny, and so warts-and-all real. A nostalgic, comforting romcom. I loved it!'

Lia Louis

'Funny, hopeful and agonisingly relatable, Esther is all of us. Lucy Vine writes with such compelling honesty, *Seven Exes* made me laugh, made me cry and made me want to call all my friends to tell them I loved them, then call my exes to apologize/punch them in the nuts. Equal parts rom-com and life lesson, it's a must-read'

Lindsey Kelk

'*Seven Exes* is a bit of me! A shimmering rom-com with plenty of gorgeous romance and even more achingly funny comedy. I loved the nostalgia, I loved the tenderness and I absolutely adored the friendship between Esther and her best pals. This is a joyous must-read'

Hannah Doyle

'Bursting with sparky humour. Esther and her female friends are a joy and Esther's search for the boy from her past who may or may not have got away is both funny & moving'

Jill Mansell

'Hilarious, relatable, heart-warming, extremely binge-able'

Kate Weston-Brookes

Also by Lucy Vine

Hot Mess
What Fresh Hell?
Are We Nearly There Yet?
Bad Choices

Lucy Vine is a writer, editor and the bestselling author of novels *Hot Mess, What Fresh Hell, Are We Nearly There Yet?* and *Bad Choices*. Her books have been translated into sixteen languages around the world, with *Hot Mess* optioned for a TV series in America. She's also the host of a podcast and live event series, the Hot Mess Clubhouse, celebrating funny women. Her writing has appeared in the likes of *Grazia, Stylist, Heat, Fabulous, New, Now, Marie Claire, Cosmopolitan, Daily Telegraph, Sun* and *Mirror*.

Lucy Vine

SEVEN EXES

**SIMON &
SCHUSTER**

London · New York · Sydney · Toronto · New Delhi

First published in Great Britain by Simon & Schuster UK Ltd, 2023

1 3 5 7 9 10 8 6 4 2

Simon & Schuster UK Ltd
1st Floor
222 Gray's Inn Road
London WC1X 8HB

Simon & Schuster Australia, Sydney
Simon & Schuster India, New Delhi

www.simonandschuster.co.uk
www.simonandschuster.com.au
www.simonandschuster.co.in

A CIP catalogue record for this book
is available from the British Library

Paperback ISBN: 978-1-3985-1532-1
eBook ISBN: 978-1-3985-1533-8

Typeset in Bembo by M Rules
Printed and Bound in the UK using 100% Renewable
Electricity at CPI Group (UK) Ltd

SEVEN EXES

PROLOGUE

Are you my person?

Are you him? Are you the person I will finally, somehow, be fully *me* with?

Imagine if you were that person! Imagine if you were someone I could just *let go* with. Someone I could stop worrying about holding it all together in front of. Imagine if I could be all of the *me* I hate so much; if you were the one person in the world who wouldn't judge me for it. Imagine if I didn't have to say sorry when I let those parts I don't like leak out of me. If you just held me close when I was anxious for no reason. If you stroked my head through hangovers without judgement, if you brought me tea with three sugars in the morning without being asked, if you left the towels in the specific way I like them. Imagine if you were someone I could show my saggy stomach and boobs to, and you only fancied me *more*. Imagine if you pretended you weren't awake when I farted in my sleep, or bought more chocolate without saying anything when I ate all our supplies for breakfast a week before my period. Imagine if you were him.

Are you the person I'll be able to talk to about all the things I feel sad about? Will I be able to cry in front of you about everything that's happened, without feeling embarrassed and ashamed of myself? Can I get too drunk with you and talk nonsense too loudly, and obsess about that girl I hated at school who has her own cake business on Facebook that seems to be doing annoyingly well now – and *not* wake up at 2am, heart thudding with horror that I have alienated and disgusted you with the real me? Are you him?

I look into those beautiful big eyes, examining the long, dark eyelashes – so much nicer than mine – and wonder silently: are you The One?

You take my hand, kissing the throbby, veiny bit on the inside of my wrist and finally – after seconds that feel like a lifetime – move closer to kiss me on the mouth.

Fuck. I think you might be.

CHAPTER ONE

THREE MONTHS EARLIER

'So then we took his dog for a walk, and it turned out he'd forgotten to bring any of those tiny poop bags.' I grimace, remembering the horror. 'So we had to pick up dog shit with' – I pause dramatically to check they're listening – 'a condom.'

'Jesus.' Bibi shifts above me as she covers her face with a hand.

'Wait.' From her position on my lap, Louise turns to see me better. 'What does that mean?' Her lovely face is screwed up in confusion. 'Like, a *used* condom?'

'No, no,' I say and stroke her arm reassuringly. 'New. But yeah, in front of a bunch of old ladies and a postman – all angrily watching from across the road to make sure we picked up the dog's mess – he tore open a brand new condom he happened to have in his back pocket and scooped the whole thing up.'

'Why did he have a condom with him?' Bibi is still hiding behind her hand. 'Did he think you were going to have sex with him on a *dog walk*? Like, is this a thing now? Is this what dating has come to?' She shudders.

The three of us are lying like a human centipede on my bed. Bibi is at the top, our house alpha propped up against the pillows, while I'm sprawled across her with my head on her lap. Louise lies on me, squashing my thighs and stretching her toes over the end of my bed. It is oddly comfortable and oddly comforting to be so entwined with these people I love – particularly when pulsing, as I am, with a truly awful hangover.

'Why are condom packets always so purple and metallic?' Bibi muses, idly picking up the remote control and turning the sound up on the TV. *BBC Breakfast* gets vaguely louder, but still beige and easily ignored. 'Do you think a bunch of condom manufacturers were sitting around in a condom marketing meeting one day, and some junior condom exec – looking for his big condom break – leaned forward with intensity and said, "Has anyone considered just how *sexy* shiny purple foil is?"'

'I'm sure that's exactly what happened,' I nod earnestly. 'Oh, hey, maybe you should get a job in condom marketing, Beeb?' Bibi currently works as a barmaid, but she used to do marketing for a big firm before getting made redundant last year. She's tried for ages to get another job in the same field, but it turns out her many years of training and that MA in psychology were all an expensive and useless waste of time.

All it's apparently good for is a job in a pub. Poor old Bibi and her pointless £25k of degree debt.

Actually, I nearly made the same mistake at eighteen – starting a degree in history before quitting only a term into it. Oh, except I failed to let the finance department know, and managed to spend an entire year's student loan before they stopped depositing funds into my account. It's fine, though, because a term of history studies I'm still paying for is *super* handy for my job as an events planner, I can tell you. Louise – an actress who never works and lives on baked beans with the occasional, decadent slice of bread – is carefully straight-faced whenever we moan about the student loan letters sent only to mock us. We are suckers; the by-product of our parents' generation who got it all for free and pushed us to do what they did but without all their fun consequence-free drugs. Or the £35k houses waiting on the other side.

But sure, scold us some more for not having any direction.

'Nah.' I feel Bibi's body shrug again beneath me. 'I think condoms are probably over. Nobody uses them anymore – even STDs are more fun than using condoms. I might as well get a job promoting CDs or floppy discs.'

'Is floppy discs a euphemism?' I murmur, as Louise sits up straight, taking her body heat with her. My legs feel suddenly cold and lonely.

'Do you think condoms are really bad for the environment?' Louise looks anxious. 'They're very plasticky and I can't imagine they rot away very easily.'

Louise is, like, properly pure. She's always trying to be a

better person, always worrying about the world and society; wanting to learn and teach – although that mostly means reciting things she's memorized from Florence Given's Instagram page.

'If they are, Esther is personally responsible for a lot of climate change,' Bibi sniggers. 'They should bring up her sex life at the next G7 Summit.' I sit up so I can give her a full-faced scowl.

'It's not my fault dating people is so terrible,' I say. 'I only have sex with them because it's the best way to speed up boring dates.' Bibi nods, accepting the truth of it, even though she never really goes on dates. She's been single for a few years now, but she doesn't mind. The fucking bitch actually genuinely *likes* being single.

I used to be like that. I didn't used to mind.

'I got through a hell of a lot of condoms before I met Sven.' Louise still looks concerned. 'Maybe I should go vegan to compensate for my carbon vaginaprint? I need to be more Greta Thunberg.'

'Oh fuck, please *don't*.' Bibi collapses forward on the bed, burying her face in my duvet. 'I know she's doing super important stuff, Lou' – Bibi's voice is muffled in the foul sheets – 'but GOD, imagine how tedious it would be hanging around her. No one wants to be *friends* with Greta Thunberg.'

I nod emphatically. 'Yeah, Lou, by all means try veganism. But do it because Beyoncé was vegan for half a minute, not to be a good person – boring.'

'Oh, OK.' Louise still looks worried. 'I didn't eat beef for a week after I saw *Cowspiracy* – that probably helped the environment, didn't it? And I only eat bacon when I'm *really* hung-over, or when I'm comfort-eating after another failed audition or an argument with Sven.'

I hold back an eye roll because – the truth is – she and Sven never fucking argue. They're both too nice.

Louise has been dating Sven for nearly three years now, and they're, like, the most gorgeous, sweet couple ever – everyone says so.

But they're not exactly perfect, I remind myself. We all know their sex life is dull AF. But they're close enough to make my whole body surge with a jealous fury I hate, whenever I walk in on them giggling together in the living room in that soul-contented, intimate way only long-term couples have. Obviously I'm happy for them and I love to see my friend happy, but also, ugh, fuck them both for finding something that has proved so impossible for me.

'So you slept with him and stayed over for a morning walk, but there will definitely be no second date for this . . .' Bibi smoothly changes the subject. She knows of my vein-deep petty-bitchery when it comes to other people's joy. ' . . . what was his name again?'

'Andrew,' I confirm. 'Although, he spent much of the date trying to persuade me to call him *And.*' I make a face. 'Not Andy or Drew, or some other fairly standard Andrew derivation – but *And.*'

'Imagine' – Bibi can't hide her smile – 'when you

guys introduced yourselves, you'd be all, "Hello, we're Esther *and And*!" Try saying that out loud without having a seizure.'

'It's not a name, it's a conjunction!' I am outraged. 'But you can talk, *Belinda*.' I raise an eyebrow at Bibi and she laughs.

'Wrong. My name is *definitely* not Belinda.'

'Damn you.' I shake my fist. 'Er, Brianna?' She shakes her head.

When Bibi moved in here a few years ago, she made the mistake of confirming Bibi is actually a nickname. She wouldn't tell us her real name, and we've been trying to guess it ever since – without success.

Louise shuffles in even closer. She smells familiar and warm and I let myself be parented in this small way. If Bibi is the stern voice of reason in our flat, then Louise is my emotional support animal. 'I'm really sorry, Esty, I know you had high hopes for this date.'

Despite myself, I start to well up.

'I'm just so sick of it, you guys.' I use her dressing gown cord to dab at my watery eyes. 'I feel like I get my hopes up every time, even though I promise myself I won't and know it's idiotic to keep believing. I exchange a few messages with someone's photos and they seem so amazing. Until I show up to a dude who looks and acts like Fred West's much older and much creepier uncle. It makes me feel so stupid and so *disappointed* every time. I'm drained by it all.'

Bibi gives me an uncharacteristically kind stroke through the robe. She's not usually one for overt sympathy; things *must* be bad. 'Ah, love, you *have* had a bit of a rough time of it on the romance front recently.'

'I really have!' I say, feeling ennobled by their sympathy. 'Remember that lad who wouldn't stop touching my hair? Or the foot fetishist who spent the whole time complaining that I hadn't worn sandals for our date? Or the anti-vaxxer who kept trying to put fridge magnets on me to prove I've become magnetized since my Covid jab? Oh, or that dick who said he didn't need to wear a condom because Febreze had made him immune to STDs?' I sniff dramatically. 'Then there was that bloke who turned out to be working for a multilevel marketing scheme and Tinder was where he found customers slash victims.'

'Don't forget that man who put porn on the telly within five minutes of you going home with him,' Louise adds helpfully.

'How could I?' I sigh. 'Never mind the two years of options I missed out on thanks to the pandemic.'

Bibi tuts. 'I told you, you should've Zoom-dated like everyone else.'

'I never understood the point.' I shake my head. 'If you couldn't meet up and check for a deformed penis, what was the point in months of video chat? Plus, Zoom felt too much like work.' I look down at my own lap. 'I mean, I'm doing everything they tell you to do – I'm *putting myself out there*. I'm staying *open*. I'm experimenting with men who don't necessarily seem like they'd be my type. I'm *lowering my standards*. I'm agreeing to a second date even after they leave a massive immoveable shit in our toilet.'

Louise looks suddenly alert. 'I think he was the one who broke our loo, y'know! It hasn't worked right since.'

'He was a fucking treat,' Bibi mutters but it doesn't slow me down.

'I swear being twenty-nine changes everything when you're dating. Men think you must be horrified by the prospect of turning thirty and that your biological clock is now a bomb, so you will now accept any kind of shitty bull-type bullshit from them. And the sad thing is that I secretly kinda think I *might*.' I blink hard, looking at my two best friends. 'But none of these epic losers even like me!'

They've heard this speech before, but I keep giving it because *I know* they don't get it. Not really. Bibi is happy on her own and Louise has Sven. They can make all the right tutting and hmming noises they like, but they don't know how frustrating it is to be me. They don't know how much I hate myself for not feeling complete on my own. How much I hate that I'm not strong enough to do all this without a Someone. How much I hate that I used to love being single and dating and laughing at the awfulness of it. They can't understand how much I hate that the last year of my twenties has changed something in me; how my stomach churns at the sight of babies. How my eyes follow elderly couples along the road wondering if I will die alone. How it physically hurts to see all my friends pair off, one by one. They don't know that I've applied for *Dinner Date*, *Take Me Out*, *First Dates*, *Married at First Sight*, the *Guardian*'s *Blind Date*, and even *Love Island* in a moment of desperation.

Sometimes I wish so hard that I could have a quick – the briefest! – look five years into my future. If I could just see that I've met someone great and am happily settled down, then I think I could relax. I could enjoy my life for what it is now, without going about with this constant gnawing worry in my stomach. The worry that it won't work out for me. That I *will* be the one person who never meets anyone.

A depressing silence falls over us. The *BBC Breakfast* presenters introduce yet another segment about some kid raising money for attention (charity) and I study the yellow damp stain on the ceiling. It's spreading – getting bigger every day – but I'm too scared of our bully landlord to do anything about it.

I feel haunted this morning. I have that kind of hangover you can't really call a proper hangover because I don't actually feel *that* ill. There is no headache or sickness, but there is the ever-present feeling of despair that keeps sweeping over me in waves. Lou, Bibi and I prefer the term *pangover* to *beer fear*, because a) it hits you in pangs all day, and b) we don't drink beer, we only drink pink wine with insulting novelty labels that call us 'Wine slut' or 'Basic bitch'. Either way, I feel like my life is over – that I've ruined everything – and I can't pinpoint any particular reason why.

Aside from the obvious, of course: that I am departing my twenties in a few months with what feels like nothing to show for it. I haven't had a proper boyfriend in ages, I live in a rotting old flat, and I cannot, for the life of me, get my eyebrows to fucking match.

I know I should be happy being single; *I know that.* I'm an adult woman with a fun job and friends I adore, but something in me keeps wondering. Wondering what if there *is* something I'm missing out on? What if all the Netflix romcoms starring Vanessa Hudgens that I totally watch every time the algorithm tells me to are right? That you can't have a fulfilling life without a partner? Sometimes at night, when I'm lying in my big bed alone, I remind myself how good this is; how nice it is to have the whole mattress to myself and how fewer pubes you have to deal with when you're single. But but but. Something in me keeps wanting and hoping. Because sometimes it'd be nice to find a pube that isn't mine.

'This is fucking depressing.' Bibi shoves me off. 'And I have the solution.'

Both Louise and I turn to face her, eyes wide and hopeful. Bibi always has the answer, she is so wise and all-knowing. She will solve my pitiful life for me.

She holds the room for a moment, leaving an overly dramatic pause as she looks between the pair of us. And then she reveals her solution and it is exactly the right answer.

'We shall get 10am day-drunk.'

CHAPTER TWO

By midday we are already pissed and staggering into The Swan – our grotty local pub – five minutes from our front door.

God, we love this place. I mean, if you happen to be in bed at 11pm, trying to sleep as swarms of drunken idiots shout outside your window, it's a nightmare living so near a pub. But luckily we're usually here, the ones *being* the nightmare.

It's not that it's a nice bar. Actually it's fully gross. We tend to refer to it as *The Swab* instead of The Swan, because honestly, you'll need a whole range of tests at your local free clinic after consuming anything on the premises. But familiarity breeds contempt – and contentment. It is *our* disgusting disease hub and we won't hear a bad word said against it. Unless it comes from us.

Bibi gets us drinks – pink and insulting wine as per – and we settle into a corner booth. We are the first and only people here, a fact we are drunk enough to be proud of.

'I HATE DATING,' I scream into the empty room and

a frightened-looking Franco – the pub manager – cowers a little behind the bar. He knows us. He knows we are messy and confrontational when drunk. Poor guy also once accidentally saw me naked, but that's a whoooooole other story.

'I DID TOOOOOO BEFORE SVEN,' Louise shouts and we both giggle.

'I HAVE NO STRONG OPINIONS ON IT REALLY BECAUSE I NEVER DO IT,' Bibi yells and we all collapse across the booth.

'What is this?' A groggy Louise reaches beneath her, pulling out a magazine lodged beneath the lurid pink corner cushions. She lobs it at Bibi, who throws it at me.

It lands in my lap and I peer at it through watery, drunk eyes. It's a battered old copy of *Cosmour*, the best mag of the nineties and noughties. I was a subscriber until it died a death a few years ago and it stirs up all kinds of feelings in me, seeing one again. Curious, I study the folded edges and shouty coverlines about orgasms and the Taliban. I don't recognize this issue.

'Oh, no way, I used to love *Cosmour*!' Louise shouts, shuffling closer in the booth to look over my shoulder.

'Me too,' I laugh, flicking through the pages. So much fun and nostalgia reflects back at me. I pause about halfway through on a brightly illustrated feature with an eye-catching headline.

'Read it to us!' Louise claps her hands and even cynical old Bibi gives me an unguarded, encouraging smile.

I clear my throat and begin in my best grown-up voice.

The Seven Relationships Every Woman
Has in Her Quest to Find the One

Research says we all endure the same kind of love stories
in life. Here, *Cosmour* writer Demi Doris breaks them down

'Er, Bibi, are you going to actually work today?' An anxious-
sounding voice interrupts my reading and we turn as one to
glower at Franco.

Technically, Bibi works here.

'Maybe, Franco,' she slurs, very obviously – as my grand-
mother would say – pissed as a fart.

'Erm, well.' He purses his lips, unable to follow through
with any kind of authority. 'OK, but five minutes, all right?'

'Fuck you very much, Franco, that's really decent of you,'
Bibi gushes, breezing over the insult. She stares him out until
he shuffles away, looking scared.

'Aw, you should be nicer to him,' Louise says, always the
best of us.

'He's a dick,' Bibi pronounces, as Lou giggles, turning
back to me in the booth. 'Keep reading,' she says urgently,
looking excited.

The Seven Relationships Every Woman
Has in Her Quest to Find the One

Research says we all endure the same kind of love stories
in life. Here, *Cosmour* writer Demi Doris breaks them down

There are plenty of depressing things women have in common: periods, weird nipple hair, earning much less than men for doing the same work (ugh, let's not even right now). And now we get to add one more thing to the list: our relationship patterns. New research has found that we all – more or less – endure the same kinds of relationships before we settle on The One. But, whether they're the friend you shagged just because they were there, or the guy at work you were so sure was a mistake, your big love is in there somewhere – FACT.

Intrigued, I skip down, scanning the seven boxes detailing the different relationship types: The First Love; The Work Mistake; The Overlap; The Friend With Benefits; The Missed Chance; The Bastard; and The Serious One.

'Ha!' Louise is still reading over my shoulder. 'I've had some of those. Do you remember that guy Gabriel from the pantomime I was in years ago? Who told me his penis was allergic to condoms and then gave me syphilis? Talk about work mistakes!' She laughs and leans her head on my shoulder affectionately, but I'm not really listening. I'm thinking; counting.

The First Love
The Work Mistake
The Overlap
The Friend With Benefits
The Missed Chance

The Bastard
The Serious One

A roaring sound begins in my ears as I read the words again and again. I read the boxes in full now, drinking in the words; the detailed descriptions. I'm vaguely aware of Bibi leaving and returning, slamming another bright pink bottle she definitely didn't pay for down on the table. She takes a seat across from us, ignoring the looks from Franco on the other side of the room.

'You pour it.' She shoves the wine at Louise who happily takes the reins, sloshing more liquid into our glasses.

Alistair, Carl, Alex, Paul, Idris, Will and Rich.

All my relationships, all the connections – real, stupid, intense, absurd, horrible, heartbreaking, illuminating, silly, sexy – they're all there on the page. *The First Love, The Work Mistake, The Overlap, The Friend With Benefits, The Missed Chance, The Bastard, The Serious One: Alistair, Carl, Alex, Paul, Idris, Will and Rich.* Maybe not in the right order but all there. I read the details of each one again and the roaring sound in my ears becomes a drumbeat, filling my head with all their voices shouting at once: begging, laughing, hating, fucking, dumping me, being dumped. It's awful.

I tug at Louise's sleeve but she barely looks up. She's Instagramming the wine label. 'You can really taste the basic bitch,' she says solemnly to Bibi as they clink glasses.

'Guys,' I say quietly, and then again, louder: '*GUYS.*' They both turn, looking alarmed by my tone. I jab at the page, feeling panicked. 'I've had all these relationships – *all of them*. Every last one.' They look blank so I add desperately, 'And that's all you get!'

'What are you talking about?' Bibi squints at me, looking irritated. 'What do you mean "that's all you get"?'

'I *mean*,' I glare at her, 'this is why I've spent the last six months going on beyond-terrible dates. This is why the universe keeps sending me men who think wearing an indoor scarf is a personality trait. It's because I've had all seven of these relationships – *these exact relationships!* – every single one, and one of them was meant to be *The* One. I've used them all up! I've used up my share of partners, now I won't ever find The One. Oh god.' I put my head in my hands and wail. 'I've had my love allocation and discarded them all!'

'That can't be right.' Louise laughs nervously and takes the magazine from me, eyeing the page warily. She looks shaken.

'No, really, you guys.' I look between them, feeling wide-eyed but suddenly very sober and sure of myself. 'You don't get it. These were my chances – my only chances.' I pause as something tickles at the back of my brain; the beginnings of an idea. What if I . . . no, that would be terrible. An awful, stupid, traumatizing, nonsense thing to do.

But what if it's the only option?

What if this is the only way I'll ever find The One? What if *not* doing it will doom me to years of dread every time wedding season approaches? Of begging Bibi to be my plus one at work parties? Of seventy-eight-year-old Auntie June on my dad's side still asking in every Christmas and birthday card if I've 'finally' settled down? That cow still has *years* of spiteful life left in her.

I look back down at the pages of the glossy magazine. It's there, in black and white. Research says you only get these seven chances at love. That means scientists have looked into it. People with degrees who wear white coats and look like Chris Whitty. They *must* know what they're talking about.

I know what I have to do. It's the only thing I *can* do.

Louise waits intently, eyes wide, for my next words. Bibi picks some gum off the edge of the table, totally disinterested.

I take another breath. 'Lou, Bibi. I think I have to find my exes.'

'Which one?' Louise says, confused.

I look down at the article again, the vivid pictures blurring into one.

I swallow. 'All of them.'

She gapes at me as I take the magazine from her and shut it.

This is it. This is what I have to do, this is the answer; this is why I can't find my husband – because I've already found him. I just need to re-find him.

And I know exactly who to start with. The only one I could start with.

Alistair Morris.

EX 1: ALISTAIR MORRIS

AKA The First Love

PART ONE

St Jude's Comprehensive School

The bike sheds

12.40pm

'OI, FANNY ADAMS, ALISTAIR MORRIS SAYS YOU'RE PROPER FIT.'

I spit Apple Tango onto the tarmac, spinning around and landing in a sort of half squat. Usually the sound of my name — or that variant of my name used by most of Year Ten — is accompanied by someone kicking a football at my head. I have learned to duck.

Louise takes a step forward, assuming her role as my co-best friend and spokesperson. 'YOU WOT?' she screams back at 10PT's Nick Wilde from inside her huge, metallic grey puffer jacket. Lou fancies Nick because his mum – Mrs Wilde – is our drama teacher, and that's her favourite lesson. She says she wants to marry Nick so she can do improv with Mrs Wilde every weekend.

Shelley joins in with enthusiasm. 'YEAH, HEY, NICK WILDE?' she shouts in her distinctive Aussie tang. 'WOT YOU SAYIN' ABOUT ESTHER?'

From the other side of the playground, Nick Wilde – surrounded by three or four spikey-haired lads from the football A-team – laughs like this is hysterical. Cupping his mouth he tries again.

'I SAIIIIIIIIIIIDDDD' – exasperated emphasis on the D – 'THAT ALISTAIR' – brief pause to point at one of the group cowering at the back – 'FANCIES FANNY ADAMS!'

My whole body flushes red. I rise up and out of my skin, looking down at my horribly awkward fifteen-year-old self in my market-stall-bought, knock-off Ellesse jacket. This is an unprecedented situation. We never attract this kind of attention. The three of us – me, Shelley and Louise – we're always trying to be seen and always trying to be invisible.

Louise glances back at me, pure astonishment naked on her face. She has no neck in that coat, she is just a thumb head, frozen with indecision.

'Did you hear that?' Shelley hisses through chewing gum. 'Alistair Morris from the football team, Esther! From the *A-team*, Esther!'

This kind of thing doesn't happen to me. It doesn't happen to Shelley or Louise either. It just doesn't. The three of us

21

have been joint best friends with each other since Year Seven, predominantly because no one else likes us. United by our outsider status, we spend most of our time down here near the bike sheds, perpetually pretending to smoke a single cigarette we stole from Lou's older brother a month ago.

'It must be a joke,' I whisper, but I am shaking with some kind of unfamiliar feeling under my school uniform. Alistair Morris is so fit. He looks like Charlie Simpson from Busted.

Louise turns back to Nick, who is now distracted in a shove war with another of the football lads.

'OI, NICK WILDE,' she screams and he turns back. 'ARE YOU MESSIN'?'

He laughs and mutters something to one of the other boys before replying. 'NAH! FOR REAL, ALISTAIR WELL FANCIES YOUR MATE. TELL HER TO COME OVER HERE. HE WANTS TO, LIKE, ASK HER SOMETHING, YEAH?'

Louise and Shelley both stare at me and I stare back. We have no clue how to handle this. The closest thing to attention we've had before this was last term, when Jodie Matthews from 11BG heard my grandpa calling me Fanny Adams at drop-off. It's just a stupid pet name he has for me because my middle name is Annie, but Jodie and Janey Thompson really ran with it. They looked it up online and it turns out the nickname actually comes from the murder of an eight-year-old girl in the 1800s. Fanny Adams was chopped up so bad that sailors later started referring to their meat stew as Sweet Fanny Adams. So then everyone started calling me

Fanny Adams, which is such a cute little nickname, I totally don't mind at all. It's fine.

'Should we go over there?' Shelley hisses again and I shrug a little maniacally.

'I don't know!' My heart is racing. 'Do you think it's a prank? Are they going to pull our tops up or twang our bra straps if we go?'

We all glance down at the oversized, padded jackets we're wearing. There is not much opportunity for access there.

'I think we should do it,' Lou nods, full of bravado, but I spot her bottom lip wavering. 'If it *is* a prank, they can prank us any time, right? So we might as well get it over with? And' – she moves closer so her hot breath is in my face – 'what if it's true? What if Alistair Morris *actually* fancies you?' We all look over again. The group of boys are laughing and kicking each other's backpacks like footballs. Alistair stands slightly apart, nervously glancing in our direction and then away again, quickly.

'OK.' I breathe out and the three of us link arms with intent. Moving slowly and cautiously, like we're going over the trenches and into battle, we make our way across the playground. A hundred interested eyes from our year watch and I feel myself growing fainter with every step. Only Lou on my right and Shelley on my left, both standing tall and strong, keep me moving. About twenty feet away from the boys, we stop, decisively throwing our bags on the ground like we just – y'know – decided on a whim to choose a new lunchtime spot today.

Nick turns to us. 'Oi, Fanny Adams, do you fancy Alistair or wot?'

'Shut UP, Nick!' Alistair hisses at him and Nick scoffs. The boys start shoving Alistair until he is forced up front. He resists only minimally, going limp as he's abandoned at my feet by laughing friends.

'GO ON, MY SON,' one of the boys yells and I resist every impulse inside screaming at me to run away. At my side, I can feel Louise shaking with fear, while Shelley quivers excitedly with the attention. The year watches; a playground silenced by Something Happening.

'All right, Esther?' Alistair Morris says in a low voice. 'All right, Louise? All right, Shelley?'

'Oh my god, Alistair Morris knows our names,' Louise says at a volume that was probably meant to be under her breath.

'Shut up, Lou,' Shelley snaps, always the coolest under pressure.

I clear my throat, desperately praying my voice doesn't squeak. 'Hey, Alistair,' I squeak.

'I've added you on Bebo,' he mutters, kicking at the ground and my vision swims before me. Mum doesn't let me use the internet at home except on Saturdays – how will I accept his add?

'Cool,' I say, unable to manage anything else.

'Do you want a Monster Munch?' He offers me the half-eaten bag. It crinkles in his hand and it is the sexiest sound I've ever heard.

'Nah,' I reply in a faint voice. 'I've got some Apple Tango. I really, really love Apple Tango.'

'Cool,' he nods and I think he *gets* how great Apple Tango is.

There is a proper circle of onlookers now, all watching and waiting. The anticipation is thick in the air and I catch a muttered Borat impression from someone: 'Alistair Morris thinks Fanny Adams *is niiiice!*'

'I, um . . .' he trails off and I hold my breath, taking in the potent aroma of Lynx Africa aftershave and his hair, so slick with gel. 'Um, I wondered if you wanted to maybe go to the cinema or something?' He clears his throat, quickly adding, 'With me, I mean.'

Louise cannot help herself and a low hum of squeal leaks out. I elbow her sharply. 'Ermmmm, OK, yeah,' I say at last and my voice sounds a thousand miles away. My heart is racing and I can feel sweat dribbling down my back under the school uniform and coat layers. Shelley tightens her arm in mine supportively. I think about dissecting all of this with both of them at my house after school. Is it even real? Am I really here?

'Sweet.' He nods a lot, and then offers up a half smile. His incisor is crooked and I decide this will be my favourite thing about him. My favourite thing about Alistair Morris. When I talk to Louise and Shelley later, I'll be like, 'He has the fittest smile, I love his crooked tooth, it's my fave thing about him, y'know?'

I'm going out with Alistair Morris, Alistair Morris is going to be my boyfriend.

He bites his lip and smiles my new favourite smile again. 'Can I have your number?'

'Cool, yes, sure.' I am flustered as I hand Shelley my Apple Tango. I pull out my flip phone and read the number aloud from my contacts.

We are going to fall in love – I basically love him already. We are going to be the envy of everyone in the year. We will speak every day, all day every day, learning everything about the other. We'll be madly in love and then get married – not too old, like twenty – and I will tell people at our wedding that my favourite thing has always been his smile.

'I'll text you,' he says, hitching his backpack further up his shoulder. 'See ya later.' He nods formally at Louise, then Shelley, before wandering over to his group again. They greet him with a cheer and some back slapping. Someone in the crowd does another Borat impression.

I can't believe it. Me and Alistair Morris, together forever.

CHAPTER THREE

Bibi nods encouragingly as I sketch out a Dickhead Tree of my exes on the back of the magazine. I hand it over and she studies it, trying to make out the details I've written across an advert for Kardashian make-up.

She takes a drag on her vape. The stink of raspberry-flavoured smoke is worse than normal smoke. 'So, will you start at the beginning? With your first boyfriend?'

Louise jumps up and down in her seat. 'Aaaaah, Alistair Morris! Oh my god, that whole thing seems like a lifetime ago!'

Bibi gives her a dark look. She doesn't like any overt reference being made to the fact that Louise and I have known each other longer; that Louise is the – unspoken – OG; that Bibi fills a hole left behind by Shelley dumping us. I gulp hard at the thought.

'He was so nice and you had such a sweet relationship.' Louise pauses, grinning impishly at Bibi. 'They were snogging *constantly*, Bibi, you cannot even imagine the saliva wastage. Esther was dangerously dehydrated throughout most of Years Ten and Eleven.' She turns back to me as Bibi barks a laugh. 'How will you find him, Est?'

I scoff. 'Same as everyone else finds anyone from school.' She looks at me blankly, so I add, 'Facebook.'

My hands shaking, I pull up Facebook Messenger, searching for his name.

There he is.

Alistair Morris was the one bright spot in my time at school. He was much, much more popular than Lou, Shelley and me – the star of the football team – but he was more than an idiot sports star. He was kind, funny, and a bit of a dork who had to pretend not to be as clever as he really was, in order to maintain his place in the cool kid gang. And when he noticed me – when he actually liked me – I assumed it would change my entire existence.

Maybe he still could?

He is – at the very least – a decent place to start in this mission. A safe, lovely person who it will be genuinely nice to reconnect with.

I start typing.

Esther Adamsonline
Hi Alistair, I'm sorry to get in touch like this
after all these years ... random I know!

I pause.

'Should I do a LOL there?' I ask anxiously. Louise and Bibi answer simultaneously.

'Absolutely yes!'

'Definitely not!'

They regard each other crossly.

'Maybe a smiley face emoji?' I suggest cautiously and they both nod gravely back.

> **Esther Adamsonline**
>
> Hi Alistair, I'm sorry to get in touch like this after all these years … random I know! 😌 I wondered how you are and whether life is good. I'd love to get a drink and catch up properly at some point, if you're up for it? Esther

I stop again.

'I know it's not my best opening ever, but it's to the point, right?'

They both shrug.

'It's good,' Louise says, nodding encouragingly.

'Yes,' Bibi agrees confidently. 'You can't start cracking jokes until you know who he is these days. You haven't spoken to him in, like, ten years. He might be entirely humourless as an adult.'

'Should I add a kiss?' I ask but Bibi has already reached across me and hit send. The three of us stare at the screen, horror dawning in my stomach as I watch his name light up with a green dot. He is online.

Oh god oh god oh god.

His reply is almost instant and Louise gasps dramatically at the words as they appear.

Alistair Morrisonline
Fuck off, Esther

Oh.

Maybe this whole thing won't be as straightforward as I thought.

EX 1: ALISTAIR MORRIS

AKA The First Love

PART TWO

My parents' house

My bedroom

11.45pm

'Just fucking shush, OK?' I hiss, pulling the covers over my head. 'My parents are only down the corridor and you know Dad will murder us both in cold blood if he finds us.'

'Try YouTube,' Alistair suggests, pulling in closer. 'They're bound to have instructional videos.'

I open the search box and type: 'P u t t i n g o n a c o n d o m s o t h e r e a r e d e f i n i t e l y n o b a b i e s'. Return.

'Phew, there are loads.' I scan the search results and click on the second from the top. Someone once told me a grown-up thing to do in restaurants is to order the second-cheapest wine on a menu – instead of automatically asking for the cheapest – and I apply the same philosophy to search results. After all, I am seventeen in fourteen minutes, so it's high time I started doing grown-up shit.

Including sex at long last with Alistair Morris.

We watch the video and I try not to cringe at the slimy thing in the woman's hands. It's mega minging and I am appalled I have to use one of these things during this super romantic night.

I still can't believe I'm finally going to lose my virginity.

'Didn't Mr Havana teach you all this in biology?' Alistair says after another minute of watching. His voice is unreadable.

'Ewwww.' I shift under the covers. It's getting hot under here. 'As IF I could look at him when he explained this stuff! Shelley had to tell me about it afterwards. Apparently he got a condom out but then couldn't get it on the banana. It pinged off into his face – the whole class went mad. Plus, I bet Mr Havana's never had sex in his life – he's got *ear hair* for god's sake, Alistair. That's probably why he was so bad with the condom.' I shudder under the hot covers. 'Anyway, I'm not taking any chances with getting up the duff or catching one of those sex diseases.'

In the dark, I feel Alistair look at me. 'Esther, you know I'm a virgin, too.'

'So?'

'So I don't have any sex diseases. You're not *born* with them.'

I don't know if that's right, so I say nothing.

The YouTube video ends and I look again at the small square packet lying between us; so much like a sweet wrapper. We lie in silence for a minute.

'OK,' I say at last. 'I think that's all pretty straightforward. Shall we, er, do it then?'

'Um, do you think I could come out from under the covers first – just for a minute?' Alistair asks nicely. 'I'm bloody boiling under here.'

'Fine,' I say slightly impatiently. 'But you have sex under the covers, that's how it works. Plus, it'll muffle the wild animal noises I will apparently be making.'

We are both red-faced in the dim light of my bedside lamp.

'Should we kiss?' he asks tentatively and I nod authoritatively. I am, after all, the one in charge of all this. I am the one who has decided I'm ready for sex at long last, and I'm the one who has done all the research.

'Yes' – my tone is professional – 'foreplay is apparently very important.'

He leans over, the weight of him heavy across my body. It makes me feel better; familiar. This is the easy part. We've kissed a lot – I mean, *a lot a lot.* Louise and Shelley are constantly getting at us to stop doing it in front of them, but I can't help it. I fancy him so much.

His hand is on my boob. That's OK, too. We've done that before – and other stuff! We have touched each other's private parts, and I've even put his willy in my mouth a few times. It tasted like soap the first time, then sweat the times after that.

He's gone down on me, too.

'Shall we take our pants off?' He is still whispering but I shush him again just in case.

'Yes, OK.' I yank at my knickers, reaching them over my knees and feet, while Alistair does the same. I am now as naked as I've ever been with him; wearing just a new bra and a half-shaved vagina. I was going to shave it all off, but I gave up after one too many cuts. I really hope I got off all the bits of tissue I used to stem the bleeding.

'Shall I climb on?' He gestures in the semi-dark and I nod. I've seen all the different positions on the internet, but I don't want to try them. Not yet. Missionary is fine for this.

He shifts himself on top of me and I can feel his willy hard against my thigh. This is romantic, I remind myself. We love each other, it's natural and normal – something everyone does! I'm going to love it! Totally love it! It's going to hurt at the start, but then it's going to be amazing and we'll both have multiple orgasms.

Plus, he's going to leave me if I don't put out soon. He's waited so long and been so nice and patient, while everyone else in our year has done it with, like, twenty-five people each.

I can feel his hand fiddling around our parts and then a pushing sensation, like I'm doing the opposite of a poo.

'Is it in?' he whispers and I nod, discomfort radiating from my groin.

'Yes, I think so.'

Afterwards, I feel sore, but elated and grown-up. He holds

my hand really tightly and says he loves me so much. I know he means it, but I'm also picturing the beautiful girl he will dump me for one day soon.

Alistair rolls away to dispose of the used condom in a plastic Tesco bag. He hides it in his backpack and turns back to me. 'You won't run off with some other lad when you go to uni next year, will you?' He smiles in the dark, his silhouette visible as he climbs into bed again.

'Of course not,' I scoff, squeezing his hand tightly. As *if* I would ever leave him, I love him so, so much. He's the one who'll leave me. I've known that all along.

CHAPTER FOUR

You know when you take that first bite of something sweet and your whole mouth fills with saliva? The same thing happens when I hear his voice behind me.

'Is it still a Malibu and Coke then?' I spin around in my chair, nearly toppling it over, and my stomach drops at the sight of him.

Alistair Morris.

It's really him. He looks so much the same as he did ten years ago, but more like his own big brother, if that makes sense? And that's if he had a big brother, which he didn't – only sisters who ignored me. He looks older in a completely undefinable way. It's all still the same old Alistair, always half smiling with that cute crooked tooth. Always slightly overdressed – particularly for this dirty pub in the middle of Soho – and always a tiny bit adorably gawky with too-long limbs he doesn't know what to do with. There is nothing discernibly different about him and yet he is different. He's a grown-up now.

I laugh, understanding his question. 'I've mostly moved onto wine these days,' I say, standing up and instinctively reaching for a hug. 'Malibu is a tiny bit noughties teen, don't you think?' Our hug lasts a fraction of a second too long and I pull away, the smell of him still on me. It makes my skin tingle and I fight the urge to lick my lips.

'Actually, I got us a bottle.' I gesture at the table. 'But obviously I can get you something else if you're not a wine person?' I laugh nervously at the oddness of asking someone I once knew every inch of – inside and out – whether they like wine.

Certainly he drank wine back when we were teenagers. But only when it was two bottles for £4 and only when one of us remembered to bring a corkscrew to the park. Which neither of us ever did. The Malibu and Cokes came later, when we were both closing in on eighteen and able to get into bars. Our last year together.

'Wine sounds good,' he grins, flashing the infamous snaggle tooth again that I loved so dearly. We sit down across from each other. 'I'm glad you didn't get red,' he continues. 'These days it gives me such awful hangovers!'

I smile nicely and take a long swig of my drink feeling a wave of irritation. I wanted to feel like a teenager again tonight – a teenager who thought a hangover was puking green liquid over someone I still then snogged half an hour later, and waking up the next day raring to go again. I don't want a reminder that we're old people now. Old people who get bad hangovers from wine.

There is a lengthy silence between us as we both drink slowly from our glasses, avoiding eye contact. The moment of frisson when he walked in – of memories and long hugs – has gone. We are now just two strangers with nothing in common but a shared loss of virginity. I feel a bead of sweat run down my back and I'm suddenly far too aware of the fake leather on the seat sticking to the backs of my thighs. I will not be able to go to the loo without ripping myself free.

'Oh, hey, sorry for telling you to fuck off on Facebook,' he says with a laugh, but the nerves make it a strange, jangly sound. 'I thought I was being funny, but realized right away how bad it sounded. I guess I forgot for a moment that we don't actually know each other these days.'

I nod. 'Don't apologize.' I blink, remembering the horror in my stomach at his words, until the follow-up laughy face emoji. 'Although you're right, I guess. Ten years is a long time and people change. But not that much – I still love swearing!' He titters politely at this and silence descends once more.

'So, what have you been up to in the last decade?' he says at last, his voice too high. I match his pitch, my own voice unrecognizable.

'Ha!' It is a squeak. 'Big question!' I laugh awkwardly. 'So, um, I'm an events planner these days. I spent a bit of time working as a chef after I quit university, before moving into events. I work for the Norris Museum in south London – do you know it?' He shakes his head. 'It has exhibitions open to the public during the day, but they rent it out as a cool space in the evenings and across weekends. It's a really small events team, basically just me and my lovely assistant, Katie, but it's great. We host weddings, birthday parties, corporate launches, business conferences ... We even did a product launch for a new line of novelty candles recently. One of them was the scent of cat litter box!' I bark a small laugh. 'Anyway, it's really, er, fun and there's always something new to do every day ...' I trail off. 'So that's, er, my work ...' Aaaaaand I cannot think of a single other thing I have done in the last ten years. Maybe I have done nothing? What has been the point of my life? Why haven't I got kids or pets or hobbies? I've got the cat litter candle, maybe that's like having a cat? Oh, and I've got a fake cactus in the bathroom! Should I mention that? Oh god, I have no life.

I give myself a shake. It's OK. It's O-very-K. Because this is part of what I'm doing here. The Seven Exes Mission is about finding more. About finding a life. Alistair can be the other thing I do with my life. We can get married and have plants and kids and a real-life cat litter tray *together*.

'Um, so what about you?' I finish lamely. 'What do you do?'

'I'm a police officer, actually.' He smiles and my first thought is of the pot brownies in my freezer. My second thought is of him in the uniform and it makes me even more nervous.

'Wow!' I try weakly. 'That must be so interesting?'

'It can be, but it's also a lot of paperwork,' he shrugs, grimacing.

The silence descends again.

'And, um, how about Louise and Shelley?' He reaches for something safe, without knowing it's not safe. 'I've been meaning to organize a school reunion, it's been so long since we all saw each other! Wouldn't that be fun? Are you still in touch with them? You guys were so close around the playground.'

I nod, smiling tightly. 'We really were!' I clear my throat. 'Well, yeah, um, yes, we . . .' I take a deep breath, composing myself. 'Lou and I are still best friends. We actually live together these days, along with our friend Bibi. But, um, Shelley . . . we, um . . . we ended up, well, er, a bit . . . and she . . .' I trail off and he studies me. His brown eyes are kind.

When I don't continue, he picks up the thread, his voice soft. 'People drift apart a bit after school, don't they? You can be so close to a person and then life takes you in different directions. I still see a few people from the football team, but I wouldn't say we're close these days.' He pauses. 'It's OK, though, it doesn't mean you can't think back fondly to those times you shared. It doesn't mean you can't still care about them from a distance.'

His familiar kindness flicks a switch in me and I find myself smiling widely. I feel the knot in my stomach loosening and relaxing.

'I think fondly of you – of us,' I say a little shyly and he brightens.

'You do?'

I nod and he smiles. 'We shared a lot together, huh?' He

laughs. 'Hey, do you remember when you took me skiing with your family and I nearly died on a red slope because I'd claimed to be an expert?'

'And you'd actually never been skiing in your life!' I cover my mouth.

'But I was really good at ice skating!' he cries. 'I thought it would be the same kind of thing!'

As I top up our glasses, we begin to speak more easily, reliving old memories and creating new ones. I find myself studying him; studying his pores and the newer freckle smattering across his nose. I try to be objective: if I didn't know him, would I think he was handsome? It's hard to differentiate this adult Alistair Morris from the School Hero Alistair Morris, Captain of the Football Team, Leader of the Cool Boy Pack.

But he is handsome, I think.

I realize with an internal duh that I still fancy him. A lot.

'Do you remember that house party I had in Year Eleven' – he leans in, smiling easily – 'where Louise was sick in my cutlery drawer? It was impossible to clean fully. I swear the reason my parents ended up moving a few years later was because Mum was still finding teaspoons glued together with congealed chunks.'

'That was my fault,' I confess. 'I fed her a highly toxic combination of nine Blue WKDs and an entire tube of salt and vinegar Pringles.'

He laughs easily, maintaining seriously sexy eye contact. 'Or that time you, Shelley and Lou were all in the Christmas pantomime directed by the drama teacher, Mrs Wilde – do you remember, she was Nick Wilde from the football team's mum?'

I join in eagerly. 'Yes! I was Friend No. Two of the Wicked Stepsisters, which was a totally made-up part and I felt very patronized. Shelley and I only auditioned because Lou made us.'

'Which explains why you didn't know any of your words on the night,' he snorts. 'Louise kept shouting all your lines for you, and then you and Shelley disappeared for the second half altogether.'

'In the interval Mrs Wilde told us to go the fuck home,' I grin. 'It was the first time a teacher had ever sworn in front of us.' I pause, drinking him in. 'Lou is still acting.' I clear my throat, looking away. 'Sort of, anyway. She has an agent and goes out on auditions.'

'That's great,' he says warmly.

'And she's all loved up with her boyfriend, Sven,' I add, wondering even as I say it why I feel the need to tell him this. 'They've been together for years, they're, y'know, *sorted*. They'll probably get married and have kids soon.' I look down at the table, trying to keep the jealousy out of my voice.

Alistair misses my tone as he continues down our memory lane. 'Do you remember when Louise had that massive argument with Nick in the playground?' I nod, remembering the days-long drama all too well. 'She was so insistent that the expression wasn't *The simple fact of the matter*, but *The simple fucked of the matter*. She was so sure it was rude.'

'I'm still not sure which one is right?' I muse dryly.

He laughs heartily, we both do. 'I remember Shelley backing her up when they were squaring off, but then telling everyone on the playground that Lou was wrong.' He tops up my glass, his long arm reaching easily across the table. 'You lot were always such a tight-knit gang. Always so fucking great – such cool girls,' he says when we calm down enough to speak.

'What?' I almost snort wine back into my glass. 'I don't think you could ever accuse us of being *cool*.' I laugh again and he cocks his head, his brow furrowing.

'Of course you were.' His voice is playful but serious. 'You three were the coolest girls in our year. You were a bit of a scary clique, if I'm being honest. All the other girls were afraid of you. *I* was a little afraid of you.'

I shake my head, baffled. 'Have you rewritten history? Me, Shelley and Lou were absolute *losers*. No one wanted to hang out with us, that's why we hid out down the bike sheds every day.'

'Er' – he smirks an all-knowing smirk – 'I think *you* might be the one who's rewritten history. You hung out in the out-of-bounds area, smoking your cigarettes, blanking the rest of the year because *you were the cool girls*. How did you miss this?'

I close my mouth, trying to find some of this apparent coolness in my memory banks. I thought we were rejects at school – did everyone else feel like we were rejecting *them*?

Alistair continues. 'Yeah, you were always so pretty and clever, while Shelley was brave and naughty – plus, being

Australian and always chewing gum really gave her a cool, outsider edge – and then Lou was really sweet and cute. All the girls wanted to be in your group or be like you.' I shake my head, still flabbergasted by this news. Alistair smiles. 'I still remember the day I asked you out. I was way too chicken to approach you myself. Nick was the only one brave enough to shout you over. We thought you would tell him to fuck off, or that Shelley would.'

Shelley did tell people to fuck off a lot. But it didn't seem that offensive in her Aussie twang.

'Well, I'm glad you did. Asked me out, I mean,' I say and there is another silence. But this time it is not awkward. If anything, it's charged.

Alistair is the first to speak. 'So you haven't met anyone special since, er,' he laughs, 'well, *me*?'

I pause, thinking of the other relationships, each import-ant and special in different ways. But I know what he wants to hear.

'Nah.' I hold his eye contact and something in my chest flutters a little.

'So I'm still your best boyfriend ever, then?' He sits up straighter, chest puffing out a bit as he grins.

'Ha, well, it's hard to judge. It was all a bit silly, wasn't it?' I giggle and swig from my wine. My head is swimming a little. 'We were just children back then really, weren't we?'

I assume he will laugh but instead something dark crosses his face. I can't quite gauge the mood shift so I gesture at the almost-empty bottle. 'Would you like another drink?' I suggest nervously into the silence. 'Wine or Malibu? Grown-up drink or daft, teen-us drink?'

'Oh Esther—' he begins, but stops himself. He looks like he will say something else but instead pushes back in his chair, his face contorted with some unreadable emotion, and leaves without another word.

For a moment, I sit still, stunned.

'Whoa!' I mutter to myself after another moment. What just happened?! I sneak a look to my left to find the formerly rowdy group at the next table now sitting in silence, looking over at me with a mixture of pity, amusement and accusatory glares.

I guess he'd had enough? Surely he wasn't offended by the offer of more wine? Was it because I didn't say he was my best boyfriend? Even though he probably was.

I swallow down a lump in my throat. I will *not* cry.

Seriously, what just happened? We were talking about the old days, it was all fun and laughter. And then he . . . why did he . . . what happened?

I mustn't cry.

Does it matter what happened? He's gone and I just need to get out of here. He's obviously just a weirdo who had a strop for no reason. I'll just get my stuff and go home.

But I don't. I keep sitting there, feeling eyes watching me, wondering what I did wrong.

EX 1: ALISTAIR MORRIS

AKA The First Love

PART THREE

Durham University

College room

6.31pm

'Go on then, bloody do it!' My roommate rolls her eyes. 'Happy Hour starts in half an hour and they've got five Snakebites for a fiver on special offer.'

'I'm scaaaaaaared, though,' I bray, already half cut. 'I know I have to do it but it's horrible, isn't it? We've been together for years. I still care about him a lot, y'know?'

'Oh come off it.' She rolls them again. 'Every single person comes to uni with a boyfriend or girlfriend, and every single one of them dumps or gets dumped in the first year. You have to get in there first before he dumps you. It's what uni was made for! It's where we go to start anew and have some adventures.' She stomps her foot a bit impatiently. 'Seriously, Ellie, the Snakebites are waiting.' She's been calling me Ellie since we met a few weeks ago, and I don't know how to correct her. Particularly since I haven't got the faintest idea what her name is.

It's weird when you're sharing a room with a stranger. You sort of have to throw yourself in and act like you're best friends right from the start. And if you miss the big stuff early on – like, er, names – then you kind of have to just pretend.

I grit my teeth and pick up my phone, hitting speed dial one.

'Hey baby,' he answers quickly. 'Finally returning my calls! How's uni life? Enjoying it so far?' He laughs but doesn't stop for any answers. 'I feel like I've barely heard from you. Not calling to dump me, are you?'

Oh god. Why did he say that?

He stops laughing when I don't join in.

'Alistair,' I begin slowly, feeling horrendous. My room-mate shoves another glass of green liquid in my face and I quickly knock it back. 'Alistair, I know this is a shit way to do this but—'

'Jesus, you're not being serious, are you, Esther?' His voice suddenly sounds horrified. 'Are you *actually* breaking up with me? Are you really?'

I open my mouth, and shut it again. 'I'm so sorry.'

There is a long silence as guilt crushes down on my head. Am I doing the right thing? This random girl is right, isn't she? Everyone breaks up when they go to university, don't they? There are so many new people here, so many parties, so many wild experiences to try. I want to have adventures, I want to experiment with who I am, I want to snog countless boys and girls. Plus, Alistair's my first love, it's not like it was going to last, right? Especially not long distance for three years while I'm in Durham! I've always known Alistair would leave me at some point so I might as well do it for him.

'Out of nowhere? *Over the fucking phone?*' He sounds so hurt. I thought avoiding him this past week would lessen the blow — that's what Roommate suggested — but it's clear he had no idea this was coming.

'Um . . .' I feel dizzy. What if I'm making the wrong decision? 'I mean, I had thought we should maybe talk about a few things — about where we are, or—'

'I can't believe this.' His voice sounds crackly and far away. 'I really can't believe this. You're actually dumping me. After three years together. You've only been there a few weeks, is university that fucking compelling?'

I don't know what to say. There's a sticky sweet lump in my throat: part emotion, part cheap shots.

'You swore you wouldn't do this,' he says in a devastated whisper. 'You promised me we wouldn't break up when you went to university. You haven't even given this a chance. It's barely been half a term.'

'I'm so sorry, Alistair.' My voice dries up again. 'I didn't want to do it like this and I know it seems sudden but—'

Across the room, my impatient roommate mimes a drinking action. 'Hurry the fuck up,' she mouths aggressively before adding in a much louder voice, 'IT'S HAPPY HOUR, ESTHER!! The lads from down the corridor are waiting for us!!'

'It's clear you're in the middle of something.' Alistair's voice is suddenly cold. 'I'll let you go.'

'Look, can we talk more about this later?' I plead, feeling wretched. I thought breaking up with my first boyfriend would feel grown up but it feels awful and cruel. 'Like, maybe I can come back to visit at the weekend? We – oh, actually I have plans this weekend, there's a balloon party in college – but maybe the weekend after or the one after that? We can go through everything properly and I can explain? I'm so sorry, Alistair.'

Instead of answering, he hangs up and I drop my phone onto the sofa beside me, my stomach and chest empty and raw.

'Finally!' Across the room, my new friend laughs meanly, and I suddenly miss Louise and Shelley so intensely. They feel a long way off, just when I need them so much. Louise is back at home, having a gap year and taking a few acting classes. Apparently she wants to make a career out of it, which I'm guessing won't last. Shelley's gone off to study computer programming at Warwick Uni. She's been a bit distant lately, and I've been worried about her replacing us. I swear now, as I watch my roommate collecting her bag and coat, that I won't lose Shelley as well. I can't lose her or Louise. Not now I've let Alistair go.

It hits me suddenly that I will probably never see or speak to my boyfriend again. My *ex*-boyfriend. My first love, my only love. What have I done? I run to the loo, where I throw up vile green liquid that burns my throat for days afterwards.

CHAPTER FIVE

No, fuck this. I'm not letting him do this to me. He can't just run out of here on me. I deserve better! Or if not better, I at least deserve answers.

Casually, I grab my bag, smiling blandly – as if this is how drinks with pals always end! Y'know, my friend and I just leave a few minutes apart, doesn't everyone? I hitch the strap up my shoulder, give a fake yawn to show how at ease I am with this situation, then turn for the door. Moving fast but also a kind of studied slow.

The cold air outside hits me and I realize that I am tipsier than I'd meant to get. Did I say something stupid and drunken that I've already forgotten? Why did he leave like that? I search frantically left and right, before spotting his head, far off but taller than everyone else – just like always – heading in the direction of the tube station.

'Alistair!' My voice is strained as I shout after him. I can't tell if he heard, but he doesn't turn around.

What the fuck happened? What I said about our

relationship wasn't *that* bad, was it? I thought we were having a nice time, I was even starting to think … maybe. But I guess that could've been the wine. No, it *was* nice, we *were* having fun, and he doesn't get to stomp off like that. We're adults, not kids anymore. Temper tantrums and stropping off are sooo fifteen years ago.

I take off after him, weaving between the late commuter crowds.

'ALISTAIR!' I try again now I'm closer. A few people turn towards me but not the person I need. 'ALISTAAAAAAAAAAAIR!' I take off after him again, nearly bowling over a chugger and a few confused tourists. When I catch him at last, just before he reaches the steps down into the underground, I grab his arm. He doesn't resist.

'Alistair!' I yank him around to face me but he looks up at the sky. 'Dude, what the fuck? Why did you leave? Why are you so angry? What did I do?'

He sighs now and looks down, at last, into my eyes.

'I just—' Someone shoulder-barges him, muttering about 'bloody tourists', and Alistair leads me away from the busy entrance. We stand in front of a towering glass window of a huge department store and I wait, cross now.

'Look, Esther … I'm sorry I left like that, but I couldn't listen to you sitting there doing the same thing you always did back then. It's always the same with you, even after all this time.'

I'm baffled. 'What? What did I do? What are you talking about?'

He looks up at the sky again, clearly uncomfortable.

'You ... well, you always made out like our relationship was nothing. Just some silly little thing that didn't matter. Like we were kids playing a game.'

I say nothing, taking this in. Is that true? I do remember telling myself back then not to get carried away in the relationship. It was like a mantra: this is your first love and he is too good for you, it will not last. He will leave you for someone better. I made sure to remind myself how unimportant this romance was and that it would be OK when it ended because it was just a first love.

But I don't remember saying it to Alistair. Not *that* much. And even if I did, he always had so much confidence, I assumed he knew he could have me for as long as he wanted me. Then I'd get dumped for some other much prettier and smarter girl, who he'd probably end up marrying and they would giggle about his trivial little school girlfriend who had the audacity to think she could keep him.

'We were together for *years*, Esther, years!' He whispers the next part. 'You were my first love, we lost our virginity to each other. It was important and meaningful and I adored you. But you were always pushing me away or playing down what we had. You never had any idea how much I liked you, even though I told you constantly. When you agreed to go out with me, I couldn't even speak to you for, like, two weeks because I was so nervous. Nick had to force me into going to speak to you!'

I think back to those early days. How we barely made eye contact in the weeks after he asked me out. We would stand near each other in the playground – him kicking a ball, me drinking Apple Tango – and not exchange one word. It took us ages to start acting like a couple.

He sighs and continues. 'We – you – made so many promises about us staying together when you went off to university. We were going to make it work, and I believed it. But then you went away and hardly called me. When you ended it, you acted like it barely mattered. Like *we* barely mattered. I was fucking heartbroken.' He sighs again, like it still hurts. 'It took me bloody ages to get over you. And then you casually drop back into my life – or my Facebook Messenger app at least – and act like none of it was a big deal. Esther, it *was* a big deal. I loved you. I thought we were going to be together forever.' He kicks the ground with his shoe. 'I just don't want you telling me it didn't matter.'

In the silence that follows, surrounded by the noise of London, I feel shame rain down on my head. Because he's right – I did end it like that. I acted like he wouldn't care because I really thought he wouldn't. I had brainwashed myself into thinking it was a silly little teen romance that he didn't really care that much about. And I cut him off so cruelly. I did it over the phone one night, in a two-minute call, goaded on by that mean girl I shared a room with, whose name I never knew. And then I got dressed up and went to a student night in a local bar where I flirted with a bunch of boys and pretended I was fine. I blocked out any sadness I felt by snogging the hordes on offer without a second thought. In hindsight, it was deeply unfair.

'You wouldn't speak to me after you dumped me.' He takes a deep breath. 'And I only had Nick to report back to me from uni.'

'Nick Wilde from school? What did he tell you?' I reel. Nick and I were the only ones from our sixth form to go north, up to Durham University, but we barely had anything to do with one another. We both wanted to escape our school personas, eager to start anew with different identities.

'Not much,' he shrugs. 'Just that you'd moved on and you seemed happy. It wasn't exactly what I wanted to hear.' He laughs now, a little uneasily, and I hang my head.

'I'm so sorry,' I say quietly, meaning it.

'Hey,' he shrugs again, but this time like he's shaking off his old pain. 'It is what it is. And I'm sorry, too. Like you say, we were kids.' He laughs again, this time a little more easily. 'I overreacted before, sorry. It was stupid. It was just a bit triggering, hearing you dismissing what we had – the eighteen-year-old me clearly hasn't quite let it go! But twenty-nine-year-old Alistair understands a little more.'

'No, you were right.' I shake my head and someone tuts in my direction, barging past and shoving me closer to Alistair. We are suddenly within breathing distance and he looks at me intently. For a moment I think he will kiss me, and a big part of me wants him to. There is still so much between us, and there could be even more if I just leaned in two more inches.

But.

There is a lot attached to a kiss with Alistair Morris,

especially after so much time spent *not* kissing him. There are a thousand emotions and memories attached, so much meaning. So many old wounds and school insecurities I thought I'd let go of. It could all come flooding back so quickly.

And what would it mean if we kissed? Especially after his speech about how much our relationship meant to him. How much more might I hurt him? He doesn't deserve that.

He looks down and laughs in the sweetest way. It makes my heart hurt for him, as I lightly step back; the spell broken.

Maybe I'm not ready for a kiss, but I want to see him again, I really do.

'Can we do this again sometime?' I aim for casual and miss. It sounds embarrassingly earnest. 'Like maybe we could go on a real . . .' I pause, embarrassed ' . . . date?'

He seems taken aback. 'Oh?' He rubs his face with the back of his hand and there is a pause that stretches from here until eternity as I die a thousand humiliated deaths. Is this so out of left field? I thought it had been a relatively flirty few hours.

At last he looks down again, clearly embarrassed for me. 'Shit, I'm really sorry, Esther, I think I've fucked up here. I – I have a girlfriend.'

I swallow hard, trying to control my reaction but I feel my face flame red-hot. 'Right.' I swallow again. 'God, sorry! I didn't . . . I had no idea . . . I mean . . . fuck.'

He puts a too-nice hand on my shoulder. I feel the warmth of his palm through my thick coat. 'It's my fault, I'm really sorry. I should've mentioned her earlier in the evening but it was so much fun catching up. I didn't . . . think.' He pauses. 'I know people say this all the time and don't mean it, but I really would like us to be friends. Can we? You're still so brilliant and funny, I'd love to have a sort of *mates trial* if you're up for it? It would be awesome to see Shelley and Louise again, too.' He quickly realizes his mistake. 'I mean, just Lou. I'd love to see Louise.' He waits, a little nervously, and I nod, my head heavy.

'Of course.' I am still nodding, unable to stop. 'I'd really love that, Alistair, it's been . . . great to see you.'

'Definitely then,' he says, satisfied.

We say our goodbyes, and my chest is tight and painful. I don't think I'll ever see Alistair Morris again. But then, I've thought that before.

CHAPTER SIX

'So he's not The One?' Bibi's face is screwed up in confusion. 'Or he is?'

'Ugghhhhhhhh!' I throw myself onto the bed. 'How many times? It doesn't matter either way. It was a waste of time – he's got a girlfriend.'

She gives me a look. A very Bibi look.

'OK, fine, there was *something* there,' I declare. 'Even as we said goodbye, there was all this mad sexual tension between us, I'm sure I wasn't imagining it. But he made it very clear he's not interested in anything more. Plus, I'm not here for any home-wrecking, thank you.' I pause, then add, 'Barbara?'

'Fair enough, and wrong.' Bibi looks amused by my latest guess at her name, and we fall silent, lying side by side on her bed. Through the wall, we listen disinterestedly to Louise and Sven having tedious sex.

'Ugh, you got crumbs on my face,' Lou is telling him faintly, sounding annoyed. 'Can you give yourself a shake down after eating biscuits in bed, please? Especially when you're going on top. There are bits of biscuit in my eye now.'

Sven's voice mumbles an apology.

'Is *that* really what you want?' Bibi asks, half turning to look at me with a cocked eyebrow.

I laugh, then sigh. 'Actually, yes, it kind of really is,' I admit. 'I really want that boring intimacy. I want to know someone so well that I can discuss their lactose-intolerant shits. I want to be so comfy with a person that we can share our Tesco deliveries login. I want a partner who'll moan about getting my hair in their bum crack and wrapped around the end of their penis. And yes, I want to eat biscuits in bed together and then complain about the crumbs ruining our standard, weekly missionary sex.'

Bibi rolls away. 'Sounds fucking dreadful to me.'

'But they love each other, even with the boring sex!' I exclaim. 'I can put up with lame sex. I'd probably *prefer* it to be honest. God, I hate giving blowjobs. You'd think all those LFTs men had to do during the pandemic would've made them realize how awful it is. Like, mate, if you're choking and gagging, with eyes streaming for ten minutes over a *cotton bud*, maybe it's time for a rethink.' Bibi smirks beside me and I put a hand on my hip. 'Ooh, I know what your name is,' I laugh, giving her a shove. 'It was so obvious all along, *Bridget*. You're so single and you've even got the giant pants.'

She shakes her head. 'Nope.'

Louise is suddenly at the door in her dressing gown. She

is all glowy and post-coital. Apparently even boring sex is still worth having.

'Esty! You're back!'

'I'm back.' I open my arms and she throws herself into me. She smells like sex, but I don't mind. It's the closest thing I can get to intimacy right now.

'Was it magical?' She looks up at me hopefully. 'Are you back in love with Alistair? Or has he aged horribly and is now the kind of person who shares fifty memes a day on Facebook?'

'Oh Christ.' I sit up and she falls off me. 'I didn't even check that stuff. I don't *think* so, but you can't tell just from looking at someone whether they share memes on Facebook.' Lou giggles, then regards me more seriously.

'Are you OK? You look a bit shattered.'

'I am,' I admit, the weight of tonight's emotions hitting me all at once. Seeing someone I loved so much after all this time . . . it's exhausting. 'And it was all pointless anyway. He has a girlfriend and he didn't propose or *anything*.'

Bibi shakes her head. 'I can't believe the rudeness.'

'Right!' I reply, outraged, then lie back down, resigned. 'Oh well, onwards and upwards to the next ex.'

Lou looks thoughtful. 'Esther,' she begins slowly. 'Do you really, really think this is going to be worth it? I mean, it didn't work out with these guys the first time, why should it work this time?'

I consider her question carefully. After all, it's not like the same thoughts haven't crossed my mind. 'But I *want* it more now,' I tell her earnestly. 'I'm ready for something that I wasn't ready for when I first knew Alistair, or Paul or Idris, or any of them. I don't think I gave any of my relationships a fair crack actually. I was too quick to dismiss them at the first sign of trouble. I was too young. Not ready. I wanted to be single and I was immature about it.' I pause. 'Plus, it's super romantic, isn't it! Reuniting with a long-lost love! Think of the wedding speech. It'll be so *romantic*! Like you and Sven have!'

'Humph,' Bibi grunts. 'It's all downhill after the first year.'

Louise looks affronted. 'It's not downhill!' she cries. 'If anything, it feels very much uphill!'

'That's not a good thing either,' Bibi points out but Louise continues, oblivious.

'Sven is so thoughtful and sweet,' she beams at me. 'He still leaves me love notes.'

'I prefer fifty-pound notes,' Bibi mutters dryly as Louise does a little happy dance, knocking over a lamp that lands with a harmless thump on the carpet. 'Oops!' She covers her mouth.

From the floor below, there is a loud bang.

'Fuck off, Mr Heckles,' Bibi half shouts.

'Don't call him that,' Louise pouts. She's close to her grandma, so she is extra respectful towards older people. Even dickhead older people. 'His name is Ivan. Or Mr Walsh to you, rude people. And I don't think he means it when he bangs the ceiling at us. I think he just wants to say hi.'

We live in the middle flat of an old, three-storey Victorian house in south-east London. The top floor is rented by a former dancer called Sofia who moved in about a year ago. She's cool, we like Sofia. She gives us food and reminds us to pay our bills. And if it were just us and her in the building, it would be the dream! But the ground-floor flat below us is occupied by grumpy old Ivan. A name Louise only really knows because of nosing through his post. He bangs on his ceiling a lot, usually when I'm stomping or Louise is having boring sex. Bibi and I have long since given up trying to be friendly with him, but Lou is determined to win him over. She hates it when people don't like her. It's why she wants to act, I think. She wants the whole world's love. She even made him *biscuits* the other day, leaving them on his doorstep, and he's still being a shit to us.

'So anyway, are you going to continue to do the mission in relationship order?' Bibi asks. She's examining the Dickhead Tree. 'Is it . . . Carl next?'

Louise and I look at each other and she makes a face.

'Yes, he *would* be next – I met him when I was just twenty-one,' I hedge.

'You sure you want to see him?' Lou asks nicely and I take a deep breath.

'Ummm . . .' I think about this. 'Yes, I am sure. But not yet. I know who I want to see next.' I give them both a big smile. 'My Harry.'

Louise looks mystified while Bibi grimaces. She re-examines the Dickhead Tree. 'What? Who the fuck is *Harry*? He's not on here.'

I sigh a little dreamily. 'Paul. My friend, my former co-worker, my lost love. The Harry to my Sally.' They exchange a look, so I add, 'My Missed Chance!'

Bibi and Louise swap another glance but I don't care. If Alistair isn't The One, it *has* to be Paul. Surely.

CHAPTER SEVEN

'Duck!' Everyone except Bibi simultaneously dives for the floor, as the entire café turns to look at our group. We've spent a week planning this, but it's really not turning out to be the covert operation I'd hoped for.

'OK, un-duck,' I mutter, embarrassed as I sit back up in my seat. Louise emerges sheepishly from Bibi's lap, her dark sunglasses now skew-whiff.

'What the fuck are you all doing?' Bibi asks, unfazed as she sips her tea.

'I thought I saw him coming out,' I admit and Bibi glances past me, out of the window, to look at our object of interest.

'You mean that very elderly woman with no hair, who just left the restaurant?' She regards me with amusement. 'You thought that was Paul?'

'Well,' I pout, 'it has been five years, I wasn't sure.'

'IS IT SAFE TO COME OUT?' Under our table, our upstairs neighbour, Sofia, is crouched on her haunches, clinging to one of the wooden legs.

'Yes, Sofia, come on out. False alarm,' Louise tells her gently, offering a hand that gets ignored. Sofia unfolds gracefully, smoothly retaking her seat, not a hair out of place.

'So what now?' She huddles in, conspiratorially.

Our upstairs neighbour has been permitted to join our mission this afternoon because – it turns out – she had all the equipment one might require for spying on one's ex. Bibi asked her on a whim if she had any dark glasses handy, and she arrived on our doorstep as we were leaving, armed with binoculars, kid walkie-talkies and three super MI5-y trench coats. Louise was trying to get the loo to flush at the time so she missed out on the coats and toys – so she's sulkily wearing a boring old bomber jacket and fiddling with a plastic cup on a string.

Anyway, Sofia's proving to be the best spy among us – for a seventy-seven year old, she sure is spry.

'Um' – to be honest, I'm not sure what now – 'I don't really know. We wait?'

Bibi rolls her eyes. 'Dude, why can't you just text him?'

Louise leans in. 'Yeah, why not?' Her eagerness is obvious. 'You didn't leave on bad terms, did you? I'm sure he'd love to hear from you. He's your Harry, Esther!'

'What the hell is a Harry?' I catch Sofia muttering but choose to ignore.

'Ohh,' I moan helplessly. 'I know I could! I just want to get a good look at him first. Y'know, get some clues about his life now. We were so close all those years ago – our friendship was so intense – and then he started dating that woman, *Celeste*, and we started to drift . . .'

'Are you nervous because of what happened with Alistair?' Louise asks softly.

I look down at my feet. 'Maybe.' I take a deep breath. 'I went in so hard with him.' I hear the sulk in my voice. 'And I really thought there was something between us! Until he casually mentions his girlfriend, ugh!' I throw my hands in the air, almost knocking over Sofia's cup of tea. 'I just want to know what I'm getting into with Paul. I don't want to get my hopes up. I liked him so much.'

Bibi looks amused. 'Well, unless it's take your partner to work day, you're not going to be able to tell if he's still dating Celeste by watching his place of business all afternoon.'

We collectively jump in our seats as the waitress appears from nowhere. 'Would you ladies like anything else?' She regards the four of us with amusement and I suddenly realize how absurd we must look. A group of grown women in sunglasses and trench coats – except pouty Louise – all hunkered down in a café watching a restaurant across the road.

'No, we're fine,' Bibi says breezily as Louise adds a grateful, 'Thanks ever so.'

'On a stakeout, are we?' The waitress is not leaving, and neither is her amused look.

'Indeed we are!' Sofia sounds thrilled. 'We are trying to track down the great lost love of Esther here.' She gestures at me and I redden further.

'Oh,' I bluster, 'I don't know if he's a *great love* exactly . . .'

'What?' Sofia is outraged, the waitress extra amused. 'Who is he then?'

66

'He's, um …' I feel stupid. 'He's someone I was good friends with for years in my early twenties. We met when I was working in a kitchen—'

'You were a chef?' Sofia looks even more confused. 'I thought you did parties for work?'

'I was, yes' – I frown at *parties* to describe my big-ass job – 'and I loved it, but the hours are horrendous. You work for sometimes sixteen, seventeen hours a day … I couldn't handle it in the end.'

The waitress shifts from one foot to another. She's starting to look less amused, more bored.

'Anyway,' I move on quickly, 'Paul and I worked together, he was one of the only people in that restaurant who was actually nice to me. We always had this brilliant, flirty friendship that never went anywhere, even though it was so obvious we were mad about each other. First I was dating someone, then he was. You know how it is. We lost touch a few years ago, but god I fancied him like *mad* back then. Every time we were together I wanted to kiss him.'

Sofia peers at me a bit crossly. She's never looked more French. 'If he is not a great love, what is it we are doing here?'

I stare at my hands. This had seemed like such a good idea at home. The first step of the many-point plan. A covert spying operation! We never should've brought Sofia along. She's far too good at rooting out flaws in perfectly good strategies.

Louise jumps in. 'It's a *mission*, Sofia!' She glances at me reassuringly. 'It's to help Esther find The One. She's retracing her boyfriend–steps. It's the Seven Exes Mission. This guy was her Missed Chance – Paul.'

Sofia laughs. 'I would not like to see all my exes, they are mostly awful.' She pauses. 'Or dead now.' She looks directly at me. 'But you had true feelings for this *Paul* man, *oui*? And you think they could be rekindled?'

I shift uncomfortably in my chair and then look out the window again, across the road at the place he works these days, as a head chef.

Did I have true feelings for Paul?

EX 4: PAUL D'SILVA

AKA The Missed Chance

PART ONE

A'Diva Restaurant

The doorstep

7.40am

Being the new person is always the absolute worst.

I mean, I knew this already. It's *always* the worst. But I thought starting at this new place already *knowing* it would be the absolute worst would mean I'd be better prepared for it to be the absolute worst. But no such luck. It's the absolute worst.

There's always that first few days where a new situation is kind of OK. Where the excitement and the novelty carry you through and you think, 'Hey, actually maybe this won't be shit!' But then that passes and you realize you have no friends and no idea what you're doing and nobody really cares if you live or die.

And you remember that being new is the absolute worst.

It's my second week working in the kitchen at A'Diva as a commis chef – basically one up from a trainee – and after a few days of people being vaguely friendly and interested in who I was – and whether I'd be potentially fuckable – I'm being completely ignored. Today is the worst of it so far.

I worked until two o'shitting clock last night! Two in the morning, after starting at 8am. And as I left, one of the snotty, superior sous chefs informed me he needed me here early. I was to arrive by seven at the latest, or I'd be fired.

It genuinely nearly killed me, dragging myself out of bed at that ungodly hour after so little sleep. But I got here! I bloody well made it here for 6.58am! Only to find the restaurant all locked up, exactly the way I left it, with no one around to let me in.

I'm so unbelievably cold, it's down into my bones.

What's most annoying about this situation is that I know a couple of the chefs live upstairs, above the restaurant. So I *know* they're in there. They're inside, snoring away under their big, cosy duvets while I freeze out here. And of course they've ignored all my attempts at ringing the bell and banging frantically.

I don't know if this is some kind of rite of passage – some kind of frat initiation – or if they're just running late today, but either way, I've been hovering on this doorstep, freezing my arse off for forty minutes now. I can't even sit down because I've got my chef whites on and will be sent home to change if I mess them up.

'All right?' I start at the sound after so much silence. It's one of the chefs de partie, Paul. I memorized everyone's names so carefully on my first day last week, desperate to impress. Not that it made a blind bit of difference.

'Have you got a key?' I snarl, too cold for a greeting and already too over this job to care what he thinks.

He nods, looking at me closely. 'You OK? You're the new commis, right? Emma, is it?'

'It's Esther,' I snap. 'Thanks, *Saul*.'

'Sorry,' he smiles winningly, retrieving the key from under a stupidly obvious flowerpot. 'And you can call me Saul if you like.'

I hang my head, feeling bad. 'Sorry. I've been sitting out here in the cold for ages. I feel like I'm dying. And I'm so tired.'

'Don't worry about it.' He opens the door, standing back to let me in. The warmth from inside hits me and melts away some of my frostiness. Especially when he adds, 'I know it's the absolute worst being new.'

I stop just inside the doorway and look at him properly, taking him in. He's good-looking – but not necessarily conventionally so. He's quite short and hairy, but stocky in a dependable way. He's got that triangle thing going on, typical of men who seriously work out. He's also tanned and glowy, which is hard to put together in my head. The chefs I've worked with tend to be more apple shape, from years of tasting their own food, and sickly pale, thanks to long hours spent hidden away from the world in basement kitchens. Honestly, it's not a healthy profession.

In the kitchen, I watch Paul and his clearly often-squatted bum move to fill the kettle.

'So, *Esther*, what brings you to A'Diva? It's not our famously handsome and talented new head chef, is it?' He winks and I laugh because I'm too embarrassed to admit that, yes, the head chef is why I'm here. Not that he's given me the time of day since I started. Our last full conversation was in a car park on the day of my job interview, and I clearly blew him away because he hasn't looked in my direction even once since.

'No.' I take a steaming cup of tea from him. It looks rank – like watery milk – but I take a sip anyway. 'It was all about the chef de partie. The food world is abuzz with talk of you, Saul.'

Paul laughs openly and it is like having a drink of water when you wake up from a fever dream. It's been such a lonely time here at the restaurant, having no one to acknowledge my existence. I've felt so rejected since I arrived, and the sixteen-hour days mean I haven't even been able to vent to Shelley or Lou about it. Genuinely, no one's shouted more than two words in my direction in this kitchen, and there's been so much to do. There were moments cleaning worktops and prepping ingredients all alone when I wondered if I was maybe dead and this was purgatory.

But Paul is real, so I must be. And he's so *nice*.

'Where were you before here?' He takes a seat next to me and I sip my gross tea again. Actually, it's not that bad. He's added a lot of sugar and the sweetness soothes me.

'A little family-run Italian restaurant,' I explain. 'It was a lot lower stakes. Not like this place.' I wave a hand at the freshly tiled walls of the swish new west London eatery. It's very clear money has been lavished and the owners are hoping to make it the go-to place for the London elite. I should feel lucky to be here. I mean . . . I do. Don't I?

'I started off as the kitchen porter,' I continue. 'Actually' – for some reason I decide to launch into the whole thing – 'I was at uni studying history and got the job as a part-time thing after spending my entire student loan in the first week.' I pause to shrug apologetically. 'I thought I could buy friends with alcohol, which it turns out, you absolutely can!' He laughs politely as I keep going. 'Anyway, the only place that would look at my CV – or lack thereof – was La Rita's near my college. I was washing dishes for twelve hours at a time, but for some reason I was immediately mad about the whole thing and desperate to become a chef. I quit after a term of uni, having missed just about every single lecture and seminar, and that little Italian promoted me to a trainee and set me to work.'

'That's a nice story,' he smiles teasingly and I bask in his attention. 'But A'Diva must be pretty different from what you're used to.'

I nod. 'In hindsight, I feel slightly tricked by my last bosses. They were so sweet and kind. They always insisted everyone went home at a decent hour and had proper days off. This place has been quite a shock to the system.'

'I think you've got what it takes, though,' Paul tells me generously and I feel instantly better. He has a calming, reassuring presence. It's good to be around. 'We haven't been open long, but the staff turnover has been insane.' He grins. 'If you've lasted a week, you're already doing a whole lot better than most.'

The sound of the outer door opening jolts me out of our intimate conversation. Loud voices begin their arrival down the corridor towards us.

Paul turns to me quickly. 'Can I take you out for a drink some time? It would be nice to get to know you more. I'll even buy you a sherry.'

I frown. 'A sherry?'

He smiles broadly. 'It's a brilliant drink! Very underrated. You get very drunk *very* quickly and it's like a shot of Haribo straight to the veins.'

'I don't know if I *want* a shot of Haribo.' I try to picture it. 'And isn't sherry a bit . . . grandparents? No? And y'know, a bit . . . feminine?'

He looks mock-appalled. 'That is very gender-normative of you, Esther. If girls can be astronauts and murderers, I can drink sherry and talk about my feelings, OK?' I nod, shame-faced, as he continues proudly. 'You cannot undermine my masculinity. I am incredibly confident with my sherry choices and will not be embarrassed by you or anyone, thank you.' He pauses. 'Plus, you'll see, it's delicious. You'll be a convert in no time.' I laugh and he leans in, eagerly. 'So? Do you want to go out some time?'

I open my mouth to answer, just as the air vacates the room. It's him.

The head chef has arrived. He's never been here this early before! He sweeps in, his presence instantly filling the space around us. The smells around him are richer, the sounds clearer, the colours all brighter.

Poor, eager, kind Paul is suddenly no more to me than a vague outline in my peripheral vision.

My hero and leader zooms in on me out of nowhere. He has barely glanced in my direction and he's suddenly in my face. So close. My breath catches in my chest.

'Esther Adams!' He smiles an insanely sexy smile and I hold back a gasp. He knows my name. The head chef knows my name! How is this possible?

'Yes, Chef?' I try to say through my thick, swollen tongue, trying not to look at his huge arms and shoulders.

There is a rumour that he once lifted a commis chef clear off his feet – with only one hand! – and threw him across a prep counter. All because he'd drizzled dressing on the wrong side of a plate.

I want him to throw me across a counter. Oh god, I want that so badly.

'Little Esther Adams,' he booms again, his eyes flashing as he tastes my name. 'I need you on salads today. Get me a coffee and I'll talk you through it. You know where the French press is, don't you?'

'The French press?' I reply like an idiot child with a head injury. He looks at me, amused, and I add quickly, 'Of course, Chef, sorry, Chef!' I leap up as he glides away to get his whites.

As I head for the cafetière, I at last remember Paul.

'Shit.' I am flustered, turning back to him. 'Sorry, Paul, um, what were you saying, er, mate?'

The light has gone from his eyes as he answers. 'Never mind. Good luck with the salads. You'll do great. I believe in you.'

CHAPTER EIGHT

'OK, enough of this!' Sofia stands up, stretching herself to her full height. 'We can't see anything over here. We must get closer.'

'What?' I shrink down in my seat. 'Absolutely not! No! Sit back down, Sofia!' She doesn't. In fact she's leaving, and so are my traitorous friends, Bibi and Louise, both scrambling to follow our elderly neighbour as she heads out of the café door.

'You must take risks in life!' She is already sailing away and into the road. 'As long as people won't get hurt, you must *try*!'

'But people might get hurt!' I cry, leaping up to follow.

She does not stop, but waves her hand in the air dismissively. 'Bof! What people would get hurt?'

'ME PEOPLE!' I shout, but she is already out of earshot.

Dodging traffic, we somehow cross the road, settling into a tight huddle a building down from the restaurant. We hover stealthily on the corner, four excitable heads poking out to watch the now-too-close shopfront. A few people sit outside, chatting as they eat.

We watch in silence for a minute before Bibi gets bored.

'Is this really worth it?' she sighs. 'I mean, maybe you should see where things go with Alistair before you get too caught up in stalking your other exes.'

'Not stalking,' I object. 'And there's no point in starting a whole mission if I start and stop with my first love.'

'My mum says you never really fall out of love with your first love,' Louise sighs dreamily. 'It's something to do with the mad hormones you're experiencing back then, plus those chemicals firing for the first time.'

'Huh.' Bibi looks intrigued. 'Like how MDMA is never as good after that first time you take it?'

'What is MDMs? Is that a rapper?' Sofia looks curious.

'It's a drug,' Bibi tells her smoothly. 'Speed, ecstasy – y'know?'

'How exciting!' Sofia claps her hands. 'Can we get some? It might liven up this boring spying day?'

Keen not to get too off-topic – and also keen not to kill my elderly neighbour with a fashionable recreational drug – I clear my throat. 'Sofia, who was your first love?'

Her eyes go all faraway. 'I have never been in love.'

Louise gasps dramatically. 'Never?'

Sofia shakes her head quite cheerfully. 'I have had many dalliances and much lust, but love has eluded me.' She bites her lip playfully. 'But you know, I have the most awful crush on the man downstairs. I've always had a thing for younger men.'

'Ivan!' Bibi is horrified. 'But he's so grumpy and mean! And you're so cool!'

'No, he's not!' Lou defends Ivan. 'He finally spoke to me the other day; I think it was the biscuits I left for him that did it.'

'The hallway biscuits?' Sofia enquires. 'No, I ate those, my darling. They were OK this time, you're getting better at baking. Still a little dry but better.' She pats Louise kindly, who looks furious but says nothing.

'Ugh, Lou, stop trying to bond with Ivan!' Bibi rolls her eyes. 'He doesn't want to be our friend, stop trying to befriend him. Stop trying to make fetch happen.'

'I can break him,' she mutters.

'What did you and Ivan talk about?' I ask Louise, genuinely curious.

'Mostly his, er, teeth,' she says, looking a bit embarrassed. 'He was telling me how expensive his veneers were.'

'Ooh,' Sofia jumps in. 'Aren't they just marvellous? So white and straight.'

'Have you asked him out?' I lean in, delighted by the possibility of an in-house romance.

'No, I have made eyes with him, but I've not yet done the flirting chat.' Sofia pauses. 'You think I should ask?'

Louise and I nod excitedly as she says encouragingly, 'You should definitely ask him out! We can help?'

Bibi looks a bit uncertain. 'Don't we have enough of these love missions to be going on with?'

'Well, yeees.' Louise looks torn. 'But finding love is so important!' Bibi rolls her eyes again.

'You have a long-term beau, no?' Sofia turns to Lou. 'I've seen him come and go many times. Unless he is a casual friend?'

Lou's face darkens. 'Yes, Sven is my boyfriend. But I don't want to talk about Sven right now.'

'Oh, right,' Sofia nods, and the group returns to staring en masse over at Paul's workplace.

'OK, I'll tell you.' Louise sounds put out by our disinterest, then sighs dramatically. 'Right, so listen to this.' She has her prosecutorial opening statement prepared. 'Sven comes over last night and he asks me within, like, five minutes, if I'm "OK".' She looks between us all, eyes wide. 'Can you believe it, you guys? Am I "OK"? he asks me in this really soft, kindly voice. Like I'm sooo fragile and about to explode. But I *was* totally OK! I wasn't being weird or anything at all, I was actually being super nice, and he asks me if I'm "OK"! So I say of course I'm fine, and he gives me this hug like he doesn't believe me, and then says, "Are you sure?"' She throws her hands up, looking to me for support, so I try my best to look horrified. 'What even *is* that?! Am I *sure* I'm OK, because clearly I'm being so weird and difficult. I was being nice, I swear! The dickhead! So then I got really passive-aggressive and asked him if *he* was OK and he said yes, all cheerfully. Then of course I got in a huff and wasn't actually OK – but did he ask me again after that if I was OK?'

Her eyes get wider, awaiting an answer and I offer a hesitant, 'No?'

'Obviously not.' She tuts furiously. 'He's so out of order.'

I nod supportively, while Sofia looks underwhelmed. 'This is not an argument,' she says gravely. 'I once threw a chair through a window.'

'Cool,' Bibi murmurs.

'So anyway,' Lou sighs. 'Now we're in a stalemate where I maliciously do nice things for him so he has to say a resentful thank you even though we're in a bad mood with each other.'

'Aha, the faux high ground,' Bibi says, and we smirk at each other.

'I usually love him, though,' Louise adds to Sofia, as an afterthought. 'Mostly, like, loads!'

Sofia has lost interest – in Louise's underwhelming long-term bickering and in our spying. She flounces dramatically and says, 'Cannot we just go in?'

'We'll have to,' Bibi pronounces. 'How likely is it that he's just going to wander out in the middle of Saturday lunch for us to get a look at him?'

'Does he definitely even work here?' Louise asks unhelpfully.

'I will google him,' Sofia says, pulling out her phone with a flourish. 'What is his surname?'

Louise scrunches up her face. 'What is it again, Esther? It's a posh-sounding surname, right?'

'Paul D'Silva,' I say in a serious voice. 'Ooh, imagine if I was Esther D'Silva – that's quite something isn't it?'

'Ugh!' Sofia spits. 'You would change your name if you got married? Why would you do such a thing? How can you spend your whole life with a name and an identity and then throw it away to blend into a man's life? To assume his identity instead? It is grotesque!'

I squirm, embarrassed by my lapse in feminism. 'Um, I don't know. I guess I'd only do it if it was a super cool new name like Esther D'Silva.'

'Humph!' Sofia says, glaring at me, and Bibi moves closer to the older woman.

'Sofia,' she begins slowly. 'No disrespect meant, because we know your generation began the feminism journey for us. But our lot understand that feminism is about having choices. It's about having the freedom – literal and societal – to make your own way without a vagina forcing you down just one path. If Esther wants to change her name or stay at home in an apron baking pies, she can do that. As long as she doesn't feel obliged or pressured into it by society or a partner. She gets to choose.'

'Fine.' Sofia waves her hand. 'But remember, I did not wear a bra for a decade on your behalf, OK?' We nod gratefully. 'My boobies are down around my vulva, OK?' she carries on and we bow our heads, suitably humbled. 'My nipples point at my feet.'

'I'm so sorry,' Louise whispers. 'Thank you.'

'You're welcome,' Sofia says nobly.

'So I can be Mrs Paul D'Silva?' I crow, delightedly.

And it's not until I feel a tap on my shoulder that I realize we've not only got very loud in the last few minutes, but we're standing out on the pavement, right by the restaurant.

EX 4: PAUL D'SILVA

AKA *The Missed Chance*

PART TWO

The ~~Swan~~ Swab

Table in the corner

10.23pm

'Honestly, it's driving me bananas,' I wail, head in hands. 'I keep thinking they've gone, and then it happens again.' I hiccup so loudly, people at the next table look over. A small child up way past its bedtime points at me and starts crying. I give its parents a weak wave and mouth, 'Sorry.'

'They're pretty dramatic,' Paul agrees, sipping his sherry.

'HICCUP,' I go again, feeling like crying. 'The weird thing is that I also have "Defying Gravity" from *Wicked* stuck in my head. Every time I hiccup, my brain reaches the crescendo bit where she's flying.'

He shrugs. 'Never seen it.'

'Fuck off-EEEEEP.' My hiccup turns the 'off' into a disturbing screech that sets the kid off again. It's gone ten, I should be able to hiccup if I want. I might report the parents to social services.

'What causes hiccups? Is it stress?' he asks with concern.

'Is that right? Because I am super stressed out, Paul,' I sigh.

'Aw, Esther, are you really?' He reaches out a hand to take mine. He's always so tactile, it gives me a tingle every time. I really miss being touched. But I mustn't read anything into it. 'What is it? Don't you like your restaurant? Are the team not nice?'

'No, it's not that,' I say with a shake of my head. 'I guess I do like it – and everyone's nice. It took me a while to stop feeling like the hopeless new girl, but it's been nearly two years since I left A'Diva.'

'Wow, that's gone fast!' He breathes out and then looks at me closer. 'So what is it?' He looks so concerned I want to cry. 'You can talk to me if you want?'

Oh, but that's the trouble! I don't know if I want to talk about what's on my mind. And if I start, I won't be able to stop. I stare down at the table.

'At least you don't have to deal with the dickhead's demands anymore,' Paul adds mildly, referring to our old boss. 'You got out just in time. The guy's out of control.'

I don't know how much Paul knows about what happened to me at A'Diva – how I left in disgrace, under such a dark, horrible cloud. Paul never brought it up with me then – or since – so I would hope very little. I just told him I'd had enough and quit without notice. He never questioned it. Enough people left like that, it was plausible.

'Yeah, *this* head chef is actually very nice,' I say. 'And I love being a sous. The hours are still so long and exhausting though, dude, I don't know how much longer I can do it for. It's endless and I feel like I get no life outside of it.'

'Tell me about it!' He rolls his eyes. 'I can't believe we managed to get the same night off, it's like some kind of miracle! I barely see any of my friends, never mind having a second to do any dating.'

'Cheers to that.' I clink my glass of wine to his sherry.

Paul looks at me a bit impishly. 'No blokes on the scene then?' He gives me a wide, hopeful smile.

'Definitely not,' I confirm, burying my face in my large drink and – predictably – hiccupping into it.

I can't talk to Paul about Alex. I just can't. Mostly because I will cry and I can't let him see me cry. I'm a hideous crier.

I still can't believe we ended that way last month; I'm still in shock. It was all so out of the blue, so nasty. I didn't know Alex was capable of any of it.

HICCUP.

'Right.' Paul puts down his sherry, looking determined. 'I know how to get rid of your hiccups. I'm coming over there.' He stands up and comes to my side of the table, where he grabs me around the shoulders. I fizz a little through my clothes as he repositions me to face him. We are suddenly closer than we've ever been and I can hardly stand it.

Staring at me intently, inches from my face, he reaches up and covers my ears with his hands. A blank, roaring sound replaces the noise of the pub and I instinctively swallow as if my ears have popped.

'You OK?' he mouths at me and I nod, feeling oddly vulnerable. We're so close. I can smell the sweetness of the sherry on his breath. 'Right, now count to fifty in your head, and open your eyes as wide as you can, without blinking.' I read the words on his mouth, unable to hear much of anything. His bottom lip is a little chafed, as if from chewing, and I want to burst from the impulse to bite it.

One, two, three, four, five—

He leans in closer now and I fight the urge to blink.

—six, seven, eight, nine, ten—

I feel, rather than see, his mouth curl into a smile, an inch from mine.

—eleven, twelve, thirteen, fourteen, fifteen, sixteen, seventeen—

I can feel his warmth on my cheeks as my heart begins to race.

—eighteen, nineteen, twenty, twenty-one, twenty-two, twenty-three, twenty-four—

When he gently starts to blow across my skin, the smell of him intense, I honestly feel like my whole body lifts up off the ground. I can see nothing but him. I can smell nothing but his smell.

—twenty-five, twenty-six, twenty-seven, twenty-eight, twenty-nine, thirty—

I have never wanted to touch someone more in my life. The desire to grab him is turning me inside out – every finger, every toe – and burning like I'm on fire.

—thirty-one, thirty-two, thirty-three, thirty-four—

The blowing stops and I ache for it. I ache for him to kiss me.

—thirty-five, thirty-six, thirty-seven, thirty-eight, thirty-nine, forty, forty-one—

It feels like I will die if he doesn't kiss me now. I lean into him and feel his lips against my cheek. He lets it linger there for a moment before pulling gently back and continuing to blow gently.

—forty-two, forty-three, forty-four—

I have to stop this.

I can't risk my heart again. Not after everything that's happened with Alex. How can I even be contemplating kissing Paul? How much of a fucking idiot must I be? To be flirting so outrageously? It would ruin everything if I kissed him now. We'd never be the same. I'd lose him, just like I've lost Alex. I can't do it. I have to stop. Right now. STOP IT.

I shut my eyes and turn my head.

'Hey!' He pulls away and the spell is broken. 'You weren't supposed to shut your eyes! It probably won't have worked now.'

I swallow carefully, waiting nervously for the catch in my chest.

'No,' I say, smiling warily, 'I think it did work. That was

very ... distracting. Thank you, Paul. I can imagine that's always a very effective way of getting rid of— HIC – OH FOR FUCK'S SAKE.'

Across from us, the kid starts crying again.

CHAPTER NINE

'Did you just say Paul D'Silva?' A handsome, middle-aged man is peering at us with confusion. Shame burns my face. There is no question; he heard me shouting about marrying Paul. He clearly knows him; this is the worst possible outcome of the mission within a mission. We are not good spies.

I stare at him, my mouth hanging open. After a moment of silence, the man looks awkward. 'I'm sorry,' he mumbles, turning away. 'I thought you said . . .' he trails off, shuffling away and I find my voice.

'Do you, um, know him?' I ask, my voice strangled.

He turns back. 'Yeah.' He gestures at the restaurant behind him. 'I work for him. He's my head chef.'

'Is he in there?' Louise asks excitedly.

'Why bother with Paul? This one is quite handsome,' Sofia says, moving closer and giving him a once-over.

The guy ignores Sofia and shakes his head. 'He's actually away for a couple of months. The bosses have him on an intensive new training course up north somewhere. Do you need me to pass along a message or something?'

He's not in there. He's not even in London. I can't see him.

This was a waste of time. I feel my shoulders slump and my head nod forward. Another disappointment.

'Er, no,' I answer in a low voice. 'No message. Thanks, though; we ...' I don't have any more words and he nods slowly.

'No problem.' He scratches his head. 'Er, take care.' He turns to leave and Bibi shouts after him, 'Is he still dating Celeste?'

The man turns back again, and this time he's squinting at us. 'Who?'

'Or anyone?' Lou adds eagerly. 'Does he have a girlfriend at all? Is he married, divorced, dating? Or is he single?'

Sofia adds, 'And are *you* married?'

Something like fear settles on the man's face. It's akin to someone realizing they've just walked into a lion's den. 'Er, how did you say you knew Paul?' he asks nervously.

'We're not stalkers,' I say far too quickly, sounding very much like a stalker. 'We're really not.'

'*Tu es un peu,*' Sofia whispers.

'I mean,' I stutter, 'I know we were, like, hiding here on this corner, watching the restaurant, but we're definitely not weirdos.'

The man takes a full step back, reaching inside his pocket.

'You don't need to call anyone.' My voice gets high and scary. 'Definitely not, like, the police!' I titter a staccato, frightening noise. 'You can take your hand out of your pocket, my friend, because we are just *normal* people, asking normal questions' – I said *normal* too weirdly – 'and there is no reason to be scared or call the authorities or—'

'Fuck it,' Bibi interrupts my terrifying monologue with a shout, 'RUN!'

We all take off at a lick, Sofia way out in front, running like an elk, all muscled thighs and elegance.

I glance back as we reach a corner, just long enough to see a look of utter bafflement on the man's face.

That went really well.

EX 4: PAUL D'SILVA

Aka The Missed Chance

PART THREE

Wetherspoons

The worst table

10.14pm

'C'mon, let me see those boobs,' he says, leering down my top. 'You've been leading me on all night. Just let me have a little look at those milkies.'

Gagging slightly, I stand up. 'I'm going now,' I say as calmly as I can manage. 'And I'd suggest for future Tinder dates that you steer clear of calling breasts *milkies*. Unless you're on a date with a dairy cow.'

I don't wait to hear his reply before I walk away and out the door of the pub.

God, the cold air feels so good on my face.

What a miserable, horrible date. What a sad excuse for a night. Ugh, I'm just so sick of dating. I've had one good date in a year – and that wasn't really a date. More of a frenzied encounter in a disabled toilet. But let's not think about *that* right now.

Around me, it starts to rain and I stop to search my bag for an umbrella. My phone lights up and I reach for it instead.

There's a voicemail. Voicemails always give me a bit of a thrill. It feels exciting, somehow. But today, it's more exciting than usual. Is this what I've been waiting for all week?

Ignoring the rain, I press the phone to my ear.

'Good evening, Ms Adams, apologies for the late call. It's Anjan Cochran here from the Norris Museum. I'm delighted to be in a position to offer you the role as events co-ordinator, we loved your interview. Please give me a call back when you get this – tomorrow is fine – so we can discuss terms. Hopefully this is good news!' He laughs a little at this. 'Right, enjoy your night, speak soon.'

I put my phone away. My hands are shaking.

I got the job. I got it, I actually got it.

Who should I call? My fingers hover over the phone screen, ready to hit the speed dial for Bibi or Louise. But a small, powerful jolt hits me as I realize who it is I really want to tell first. The person I want to scream my news to and dance around the room with. The person I want to celebrate with. And do other stuff with.

I'm finally done with cooking. I'm done with the mad hours and the hot, sweaty kitchens full of dismissive, angry men. This is my chance for a new life. A life that actually has stuff in it that includes things that are not work. I can actually enjoy myself. I could have a boyfriend.

It's Paul I want to call. It's Paul I want to kiss. It's Paul I think about all the time.

For so long, he and I have danced around our attraction. We are so clearly mad about each other, I fancy him so much, and we *work*. We're good together! Everyone says so! For ages I denied it to myself, while I was working alongside him. Partly because of the awful drama at A'Diva, and partly because it seemed stupid to get involved with him. Then I was so worried about getting into something again after what happened with Alex. I didn't want to ruin my friendship with Paul.

But I realize now that having a decent friendship as a foundation is vital for a relationship. It's the basis of any proper love. Being best friends who fancy each other is the best kind of love there is! Paul and I could have that. We could have the best thing ever and it has to be worth the risk.

I put my phone in my bag. He'll be working tonight, but I have to see him. I have to tell him all of this face-to-face. I have to fucking let myself kiss him at long last.

I find myself on a bus heading towards the gastro pub where he now works as a senior sous chef, and as I jump off outside, I still don't know what I'm going to say. Maybe I won't say anything, maybe I will just finally snog his face off.

They're locking up when I walk in but the bar manager grins when I mention I'm here to see Paul.

'He's in the back, go on through.' He gives me an odd smile. Almost amused. And I realize why when I open the kitchen door.

Paul is in the midst of a passionate kiss with one of the hottest women I've ever seen. My insides crumble and I find myself leaning on the cold kitchen wall to keep from falling. I want to leave before he can see me but the sickness bubbling up inside me wins out.

I gag noisily and they leap apart.

'I'm really sorry.' I cough now, trying not to be sick. 'I'm so sorry, I've interrupted. I didn't mean—' I turn to leave, the mortification burning my cheeks and the stomach acid burning my throat.

'Esther!' I hear Paul's voice chasing me as I leg it back out the way I came. He catches up with me at the bar, looking confused. 'What are you doing here?'

I gulp. 'I don't really know. I was passing and I had some . . . news.' I am breathing too heavily to be clear. 'I had a terrible date and then I heard I got the events job and I—'

'What?!' He hugs me. 'That's amazing news, dude! Congratulations.'

I am limp in his arms. 'Who was that?' I murmur.

'Who?' He pulls away, examining my face. 'Oh, that's Celeste. I was going to tell you about her when we had our drink next week. We've just started seeing each other.' For a moment, a look of anxiety flashes in his eyes. 'Would you, er, like to meet her? She's great.'

He knows. He knows this is horrible and awkward and

that I'm heartbroken. He can see it, we can both see it, but we have to pretend it's fine. Because officially we've never been anything more than friends. If anything, I'm the one who's been holding us back all these years. I can't be upset or annoyed he's moved on. Not when I've kept him waiting for three long years.

'I'll meet her another time,' I say and gulp down the solid lump of tears in my throat. 'I would love that. But I am exhausted and have to get my milkies home for the night.'

'Your what?' he says with a frown, but I ignore the question.

'I'm so happy for you, though; she seems . . . I mean, she looks so beautiful!' Tears start blurring my eyes so I turn for the door, walking away as fast as my wobbly legs will carry me. 'Really, really, really happy for you, Paul! REALLY!' My voice is starting to choke and I clock the bar manager watching us from across the room. 'It's brilliant news! I'll speak to you soon, yeah? Byeeeeeeeee.'

I take off, running in the rain, and I don't stop until I get home, crying harder than I can ever remember. We had so many opportunities, so many times we could've tried it. And now we've missed our chance.

CHAPTER TEN

As we open the door to our building, a kind of intense weariness settles over me, making my bones feel heavy and sore. I can hardly even face the stairs up to our first-floor flat. We wave goodbye to Sofia, watching her leap up the remaining stairs with a former ballerina's agility.

Inside, I mutter an excuse and head for my room, immediately collapsing on my bed. I sigh deeply into the duvet, wondering whether this is all worth it. Is this mission just going to be humiliation after humiliation? So far it's been a total letdown with Alistair and his girlfriend, then the Paul stalking. I'm sure it'll get back to him that a group of women were shouting about marrying him, then demanded to know his whereabouts and relationship status. I can't ever message him *now*! Even if I were willing to wait months until he's back in the city.

Beside me, I pick up the Dickhead Tree and examine it. There are five names left: Carl, Alex, Idris, Will and Rich. Above their names, I've doodled a list of B names to ask

Bibi about. Is she a Belle, Betty, Billie, Bernadette, Bianca? Ooooh, Bertha! She sort of looks like a Bertha. I reach for my pen to write it down.

My phone vibrates on the bed and I check it automatically. The name sends something through me that I can't quite put my finger on.

Alistair Morris (school)
Hey there pal! Good week?
12.20

Absolutely fucking not. Terrible week, actually, Alistair Morris (school). But that's not what you want to hear.

My finger hovers over the reply box.

Why is he texting? It's been a couple of weeks since our weird, intense, climactic and anti-climactic evening together and I wasn't really expecting to hear from him. Did he actually mean it about being friends? How strange, I've never had a boy mean that before. Come to think of it, I've never meant it when I've said it either.

I run into the living room, phone still in hand. Bibi and Lou are sitting close on the sofa, drinking tea. They stop abruptly, looking guilty as I rush in, but I'm feeling too panicky and sweaty to care that they were obviously gossiping about me and my embarrassing encounter.

'Guys!' I am high-pitched and Lou sits up straighter. 'Alistair just messaged.'

'Let us see!' Lou leaps up as Bibi claps happily.

I hand over my phone and there is a long, twenty-second silence while they read and compute.

'OK ...' Bibi is first to speak, her voice full of uncertainty. 'OK, so. Um, he's asking how your week was. That's a ... good sign?'

'Yes, but it's a bit nothingy, isn't it?' I am anxious. 'Like, if there was more to it, he'd have more to say, wouldn't he? Especially after the way we left things. And that fucking *pal*,' I seethe. '*Someone* is being very careful to make sure I know where he stands.'

'Maybe he's just working out how you feel before launching into some big confession of love?' Lou sounds hopeful. 'Or maybe this is him nudging you to make a move? So then he can dump his girlfriend and you guys can run off into the sunset together?'

'But shouldn't I feel bad about that? Shouldn't I be ignoring anything like this out of respect to her?'

'Maybe,' Louise nods half-heartedly, looking worried.

'You had him first,' Bibi says petulantly. 'And maybe he's not that serious about her. Did he say how long they'd been together?'

I shake my head. 'He told me nothing about her, nothing at all.' I re-read the message. 'And obviously I didn't ask.' I throw my hands up. 'Oh god, I don't know. What about that exclamation mark? What does that mean?'

As we continue to dissect the spaces and the lack of an x, the phone – in Lou's hands now – vibrates again. We look at it like it's magic, and then at one another.

'It's him again,' Lou says in a shaky voice. 'He says, "Would you fancy a drink on Friday?"'

'Oh my god,' Bibi replies quietly, like we are discussing nuclear codes. 'Oh my *god.*'

'What does it mean?' I wail, hands in the air. 'What does it meeeeeeeean?'

'I think it's a date,' Lou says, her voice quivering. 'I think he's asking you out on a date!'

'Or it could be a friendly group thing,' Bibi counters, looking concerned. 'Do you think it's a group thing?'

'Brenda, you know what I know!' I tell Bibi a little impatiently. 'It's vague! Vague I tell you! And he called me *pal* so pointedly in the previous message!'

'Yes, he called you *pal*' – Louise looks confident – 'but he's also inviting you out on a Friday. Everyone knows Fridays are inherently romantic. Fridays are sexy, everyone feels sexy on a Friday! It's a date night!'

'OK, well, you should say yes,' Bibi continues smoothly. 'And then ask casually if it's a group thing or not? And I'm not called Brenda.'

I look at her aghast. 'I can't just *ask* that! What are we, *normal people*? Of course I can't just *ask*, Bibi! If I question whether it's a group thing, he might panic and invite a bunch of people. And if I ask whether it's just us, he might laugh at me for thinking this could be a date. I can't *ask*, Bibi. Jesus.'

She has the good grace to look ashamed.

Lou nods. 'Esther's right. OK, so you just say yes, and then be prepared for both eventualities.'

'But I have an event I'm supposed to be working on Friday night,' I tell her anxiously. 'Katie and I have been planning it for weeks.' They look at me helplessly and I groan. 'Sod it, I'll tell her she has to look after it on her own. She'll be OK, I'm sure. Finding the father of my children is more important than a sanitary towel brand showing journalists their new period pant range, right?'

'That sounds right,' Louise says, looking unsure.

I nod. 'So if I turn up and it *is* a group thing, you guys have to be ready to come join us. You can be stationed at a local bar or whatever, ready to come, yes?' They nod in unison.

'If it *is* a date,' Lou begins carefully, 'and you love each other again, will you continue with the Seven Exes Mission?'

I think about this. 'Um, well,' I reply slowly. 'If he's, like, fully dumped his girlfriend and confesses undying feelings, which I also feel in the moment, then I guess no, I'd sack it off. But if it's all still up in the air, then I think I should probably keep going as long as I need to. I can't quit, I've hardly started.'

'Gotcha,' Lou nods, looking surer now.

'But, I mean . . .' I pause, looking at Bibi so I don't have to look at Louise. 'I've been thinking about it and maybe I can just skip Alex anyway. It would be fucking awkward – probably more awkward than any of the others – and I don't need to see *all* my exes, do I?'

There is a brief silence before Bibi nods.

'I think that might be a good idea,' she says and I smile at her gratefully.

101

Lou shakes her head. 'Uh, I don't really agree, sorry. I think seeing Alex is important. If you're going to do this mission properly, you need to see it through. And if Rich the Bastard is on the list, surely Alex has to be, too.'

My chin comes down. 'Hmm,' I hedge. 'Maybe. Let's get this reply to Alistair written and my outfit ready – then I'll figure out what I'm going to do next.'

Bibi and Lou exchange a pointed glance that I choose to ignore.

CHAPTER ELEVEN

Friday arrives and I find myself outside the bar, leaning against a wall and breathing heavily. Something big feels like it's about to happen. Something potentially life-changing. After all, the man I'm meant to be with could very well be waiting for me inside. Everything might change this evening. I might have sex. I might have sex with the first and last person I ever have sex with. Do I want that to be Alistair? He had a lovely penis, and our sex life was . . . enthusiastic. Plus, he's bound to have learned a whole bunch of tricks in the last ten years. I sure have. But is *his* the last penis I ever want to have inside me?

I pull at the hem of my dress, feeling self-conscious. Lou convinced me to wear a sexy number that defied every rule about only showing off one of your assets at a time. All the leg and all the tit are currently available for anyone's viewing pleasure. And, unfortunately, the one shot of back-of-cupboard whisky I had before leaving the flat hasn't been enough to dismiss my insecurities about it.

For a minute, I picture Alistair sitting nervously at a table inside, bottle of wine already waiting. He was always so thoughtful like that, always considering what might make me smile. He'll hug me properly this time – he was always a hugger – and then we'll sit down. We'll look at each other across the table and sparks will fly.

I pull out my compact to reapply yet more lipstick. I have to look perfect, I don't want a hair out of place.

Then, when we've got a drink, he'll tell me he's broken up with his girlfriend in a way that won't make me feel bad – maybe she'd also met someone else and is desperately relieved by him ending things. And then he'll reach across the table and—

'ESTHERRRRRR!' My name is shrieked in a way that immediately shatters any romantic illusions I might have had.

Alistair is here and Alistair is drunk. He runs over, scooping me up and into his arms, spinning me around. I laugh and he whispers, hot breath on my ear, 'I'm sorry, I've had a few.'

'I can see that!' I snort again as he puts me down.

'They made me!' he cries accusatorily, waving behind him. In slow motion, I take in the array of familiar faces, all smiling and waving.

Fuck.

School people. People from school. Folks I haven't seen in over a decade. This isn't just a group drink, this is a fuck-ing *reunion*.

There is a collective chorus of lazy hellos as older versions of people I never spoke to but knew intimately file past me.

'Hiya!' I manage, urgently feeling for my phone as I follow everyone in. Barely looking and using my fastest fingers, I panic-text Lou and Bibi:

> EMERGENCY. COME RIGHT NOW, IT'S
> DEFO A GROUP THING. A *SCHOOL*
> GROUP THING. FCKIN EMERGENCY.

Inside the bar, Alistair is back in my personal space.

'Can you believe everyone's here? I told you I was going to sort out a reunion, didn't I? Isn't this the best?' He beams at me expectantly and I feel a rush of affection for my boyish, excitable, happy-go-lucky first love. I want so much to grab his face and kiss it all over. He leans closer. 'Can I get you a drink? It's my round.'

'Sure!' I say enthusiastically, trying to get a hold of myself. Ugh, rounds, they're the worst. Why can't we all just pay for our own drinks? 'I'd love a white wine, thanks.'

'Come with me.' He circles an arm around my back and his hand hovers for a moment before landing. It's positioned carefully – not too high on my shoulders so it feels like I'm a mate he's challenged to a game of darts, not too low that I feel groped. But still, I feel the warmth of his body against me and it sends something undefinable through my stomach.

We wait in the crowds by the bar, hoping for a tiny space

to dive into, and I clear my throat. 'So, er, will I get to meet your girlfriend tonight? Is she here?' I try to keep the tension out of my voice and fail. But the fuzzy coat of booze Alistair is wearing saves me.

'Er, no, no, just some old faces from school.' His answer sounds nervous and I wonder if he'd noticed the tightness in my voice. 'I sent out a mass email about meeting up and everyone was super excited. I mentioned I'd seen you recently and a few of them insisted I invite you, too.'

Oh. Not a date and not even his choice to have me here.

He is oblivious to my pain. 'I thought you'd like to catch up with everyone!' He smiles widely. 'It's been so long.'

'Oh, yeahhhhh, it's amazing! Sooooo nice to see them.' I grin back, remembering how he used to be able to tell when I was lying.

'And of course, I wanted to see you again,' he adds quickly, grinning goofily down at me. Maybe he senses my disappointment with the situation because he presses a little closer to my side. 'And I wanted to say—' He breaks off as a gap opens up at the bar. The crowds heave forward together and we lurch simultaneously. Alistair lands neatly at the bar while I land in someone's arse crack.

'Jesus twat fuck!' I shout, trying to stand up and only succeeding in elbowing several people around me. One of the elbow victims helps me up as I apologize wildly. 'Sorry, lads, all my fault.'

I finally right myself, turning towards my saviour. It is a familiar face and I find myself audibly gasping.

Nick Wilde from school. And also technically from uni, since we went to the same place for that one term.

'Esther Adams!' he says with a smile as I gape. It is somehow more bizarre to see Nick in the flesh again than it was to see Alistair. He was such a weird-looking boy in the playground; short, scrappy, forever crowing in science lessons about his Puma jacket as Louise googly-eyed over him across the classroom. He's so different as a grown-up: tall, dark, with thick-rimmed glasses and a somewhat unkempt beard he definitely didn't have the last time I saw him.

'Hello,' I say with forced joviality. 'How are you, Nick Wilde? Still yelling at girls across playgrounds when they're trying to drink their Apple Tango in peace?'

He laughs nicely. 'Yes indeed. I do that constantly. It's why they've put me on that register. Playgrounds are a no-go for me now, it's a terrible shame.'

We nod seriously at one another, acknowledging how quickly we've descended into darkness.

From the bar Alistair yells over at us. 'Nick, you're here! Nice to see you!'

'I've actually been here ages,' he yells back. 'Where have you lot been?'

Alistair gives him a helpless sorry shrug. 'Drink, mate?'

Nick gives him a thumbs up. 'Apple Tango please,' he shouts as I cover my mouth, amused.

Alistair looks confused. 'What?! I can't hear you very well.'

'Lager, please.'

Alistair nods and turns back to the barman.

'So' – Nick's gaze returns to me – 'you and Alistair again, eh?'

I feel prickly. 'What do you mean me and Alistair? There's nothing going on, we're just friends. Friends who haven't seen each other for ages – years! That's it.'

He puts his hands up in surrender. 'OK! I just meant you've met up again after a long time apart.'

'Right.' I smile brightly, trying to dial back my defensiveness. After all, it's true, isn't it? This is clearly a friends thing I've come along to. There's nothing more in it than that. And what if there had been? Was I really going to try something, knowing Alistair has a girlfriend at home? It makes me feel guilty even considering it. I don't think being a man-stealing predator would really suit me.

'And you guys are still close after all these years then?' I make polite small talk, counting down the minutes until I can pretend I need the loo and excuse myself to hide.

Nick shrugs. 'Not massively. I haven't seen him in years myself. We were close for a while after school but you drift apart a bit, don't you?'

'Sometimes,' I acknowledge, thinking of Shelley.

'But an occasional nostalgia trip isn't so bad, is it?' He grins and I look away, thinking that nostalgia isn't always that fun.

A memory of a recent Instagram post hits me and I grab for the conversation starter. 'You got a dog, right?'

He looks mildly surprised, but pleased. 'I did!' He pushes

his glasses further up his nose and it suddenly makes him seem schoolboyish again. 'She's called Jackie and she's the absolute best.'

'Jackie the dog?' I confirm hesitantly and he throws back his head laughing.

'I know it's stupid,' he answers after a moment. 'But I've always had a bit of a thing for dogs with human names. Plus, she has Jackie Weaver vibes about her – grey hair and ears shaped like a bob around her face.' I can't help myself and lean in, enthralled as he continues in a delighted voice. 'I shout across the park, "YOU HAVE NO AUTHORITY HERE, JACKIE WEAVER." She always comes running back when she hears that – and you should see the looks we get.' He stops to laugh again and I join in, laughing mostly at how much he's laughing.

'What kind of dog is she?' I ask at last, fighting through the mirth.

He shrugs. 'God knows. She was a rescue. One of those lockdown impulse purchases that didn't work out once the world resumed normality.'

'What passes for normality these days, you mean,' I point out wryly.

'Quite,' he nods, looking at me curiously. 'Esther,' he begins slowly, glancing over at Alistair at the bar. I move closer, holding my breath – just as we're interrupted.

'OOOOH, is this the famous Alistair then?' I jump at the sound of Bibi's voice suddenly in my ear. She slings a heavy arm over my shoulder as Lou appears at my other side, leaning in to kiss my cheek like we are long-lost family. Their breath smells like wine – they've clearly been drinking without me and I feel a familiar pang of jealousy.

'Of course it's not Alistair!' Lou sings. 'This is Nick Wilde! Nick from Mr Snelling's science class. *Nicky* from the football team! Mrs Wilde the drama teacher's son. We all went to school together, didn't we?' She hugs him and mutters to me too loudly, 'God, he smells really good.'

'She's drunk,' I tell him by way of explanation and he grins.

'I'll take any compliment I can get.'

'So where *is* Alistair?' Bibi looks irritated. 'I want to meet him.'

Nick glances at me, amused.

'This is our flatmate, Bibi,' I explain, a little embarrassed.

'That's not her real name, though!' Louise gets too close to Nick's face. She seems to be studying it. 'It's Bethany or Bailey.' She veers back to Bibi, who is shaking her head. 'Or Bobbie?'

'Alistair's at the bar.' A bemused Nick points Bibi in Alistair's direction. 'If you hurry, you might get a drink out of him.' She leaps to attention, bounding eagerly through the crowds.

'So, how are you, Louise?' Nick grins widely as they regard each other. 'Is life good?'

'Really good.' She bats her eyelashes, drinking him in, and I give her an elbow. I know she had a big crush on him at school, but has she forgotten about a certain long-term relationship?

'Er, Louise, have you made up with Sven yet?' I ask pointedly before adding as an aside to Nick, 'Lou's boyfriend.'

She pouts. 'Kind of. But not really.'

'Oh no.' I turn more towards her. 'Is it the *are you OK* argument still?' adding quickly to Nick, 'He asked her if she was OK. The twat.'

Nick nods with faux understanding, his eyes twinkling. 'I see.'

Lou takes a deep breath. 'Right, so I stewed for a few days, but last night I decided I was over the argument – totally over it – and ready to be the bigger person. Y'know' – she narrows her eyes at Nick – 'forgive and forget. So when he got to our place last night, I sat him down on the bed and said, "Look, Sven, I'm sorry for how I acted the other night."'

'That was so good of you,' I tell her and she glows.

'I know, right!' Then her face darkens. 'But you will *never* guess what he said.'

Nick leans in, blinking hard behind his glasses. 'What did he say?'

'Uh oh,' I offer, wary.

Louise takes a big, deep inhale before answering. 'He said, "*Don't worry about it.*"' She looks at me and Nick with naked astonishment. 'He said I shouldn't worry about it because I was tired and he was happy to just forget about it.'

I shake my head slowly, not sure what she needs from me right now.

'Can you *believe* that?' She joins me in the slow shake. 'He didn't say sorry back, he said not to worry about it – as if I really, actually had something to say sorry for! I was only saying sorry to be a good person. I expected him to go, "Oh, babe, no, you have nothing to be sorry for, it was all my fault!" And then apologize a lot, y'know?'

'Heinous,' Nick says, joining in with the head shaking and the three of us shake our heads some more.

She beams at him, pleased to see he gets it. 'So anyway,' she sighs, 'it felt petty to tell him I take back the sorry and he can sod off, so I got into bed fully clothed and went to sleep without another word. Hopefully he had a good long think about his bloody *don't worry about it.*'

'Quite right,' Nick says, nodding now instead of shaking his head. 'But if you'll excuse me, I'm going to pop to the loo. Great to see you both.' He pauses before adding to me, brow arched, 'Good that you and Alistair are back in touch.'

'Right,' I say, feeling weird. 'And best of luck with Jackie Weaver. I hope you give her plenty of authority.'

Louise launches at him for another hug and I pull her back. Nick gives us a little wave as he heads for the gents' and Lou watches him leave, a thoughtful expression on her face. 'Jesus, Nick looks *so* fit, doesn't he? I can't believe how much he's changed since Year Eleven. He's such a . . . *man*, y'know? What was that about a Jackie? Is that his girlfriend?'

'So you didn't think you'd invite Sven tonight after the *don't worry about it* incident?' I ask loudly, ignoring her question. Her head snaps back to me.

'Definitely not!' she pouts. 'Forget Sven, what did you and Nick talk about before I got here? He seems so charming and sweet. I love his glasses. Remember him in the playground? Always playing football and being annoying.'

'That was all the boys,' I remind her and she nods. 'And nothing really, just small talk. He's got a dog, she's got a people name.'

'Nothing else?' Louise looks exasperated. 'You didn't find out if he's dating or married or anything at all?'

'Why would you care about that, Lou?' I narrow my eyes and she waves me away breezily.

'What's going on with the mission anyway?' Her gaze wanders off again, back over in Nick's direction. 'Bibi said you've messaged Alex! That's so great. I know that would've been tough, so well done.'

'It was, but' – I sigh, a little frustrated – 'it was an old number and I don't think it's right. Or maybe I'm still blocked? I've had no reply anyway.' I lick my lips. 'In fact, I was thinking of messaging someone else on my list – maybe Will or Idris? Or getting over my humiliation and sending Paul a text to see if he wants to meet up when he's back in town?'

Lou frowns. 'But you won't give up on Alex, right? There must be other options you can try, other than an old phone number.'

'Maybe,' I say dismissively. 'But I don't want to lose momentum with all this. Especially now it seems increasingly clear that Alistair's never going to happen.' At the bar, my first love is paying for the biggest round in human history while Bibi shouts in his ear.

Lou sighs deeply. 'Do you really think he's a no-go?' She rests a heavy head on my shoulder. 'I'm so sad, I was rooting for you two.'

I squeeze her arm. 'Me too. But this is the whole point of exploring all seven exes. Maybe I'll text Paul tonight – you never know, he might be popping down to London in the coming weeks, maybe he'd be free for a drink.'

She turns to face me, nodding carefully. 'OK. But don't give up on Alistair just yet, promise? There's clearly something there between you that needs exploring.' We both look over at him now, as he pays for the drinks. He fumbles trying to tap his credit card and giggles awkwardly as he misses. His arms are too long, I remember how they were always getting in the way. It made him clumsy. He looks adorable now as the long-suffering bartender gets annoyed and Alistair – so hopeless and goofy – tries again for a third time. It makes me want to squeeze him and do things for him forever.

'I promise,' I smile widely at Lou.

She nods again, more authoritatively now. 'Good. Now let's go to the loo, we might pass Nick on the way. We really should talk to him more, don't you think?' She side-eyes me. 'That beard really suits him. There's something about men with a beard and glasses. It's like they're wearing a sexy disguise.'

I roll my eyes but she adds, 'Plus, we need to go to the loo because you have, like, a LOT of lipstick on your teeth.'

My face drains of all colour as I count up the people I've greeted in the last half an hour since applying it outside. 'WHAT?'

CHAPTER TWELVE

'Explain to me again how this has happened?' Bibi is hissing in my ear, her elbow grinding into my ribcage.

'I'm honestly not sure,' I murmur, my confusion all too real.

'I think it's exciting!' Lou declares, wrapping her coat closer around her body against the gusts of cold wind knocking us about.

We're standing outside our building while I await collection by football A-team's Alistair Morris and Nick Wilde for a road trip up to Milton Keynes. My fifteen-year-old self would've been utterly bewildered by this turn of events. And, actually, my twenty-nine-year-old self is, too.

'Show me the texts from last week,' Bibi says, still perplexed, and I hand her the phone.

Paul D'Silva (work)
Friday
Estheeeeeeeeeeer! Hello there my

favourite MIA pal, how are you? I know it's
been years and sorry for messaging out of
the blue but – and this will sound mad as
anything if I'm wrong – were you outside my
work last week?!! One of my chefs said a
group of women were asking after me and
his description sounded a little like you?!!!
Random, I know. Either way, it would be so
nice to catch up soon? I fucking miss you. It's
been far too long and I'm dying to see that
gorgeous face. Paul (Saul) xx
9.12pm

OMG PAULLLLLLL! I have
9.13pm

Sorr, quiet drunk, didn't ean to sen
9.14pm

Just owt with old schoo fiends
9.15pm

Anywaay, ssooo nice to hear fom u!
No that defo wastn me or bibi or Sofia
or Loulou outside your restaurant &
he rilly overrreacteded by getting all
scarred and weird
9.16pm

117

I want to c u toooooo!!!!!!!
Wen are u back in London?
9.17pm

Not that I know ur not in London.
You're porbably in Lonndn becos why
woultdn you be in London right???
9.18pm

Lol, Esther, you are still hilarious. I'm
in Milton Keynes for a bit, doing some
training for work.
9.20pm

Hey, why don't you come up here?!!!
We could hang out for the day, it would
be so fun!!
9.21pm

Go on, say yes. Be spontaneous. I have next
weekend off, come up next Saturday?!
9.22pm

OMG YES! I'M BLOODY WELL IN.
9.30pm

PS. I puked
9.31pm

Over her shoulder, I jab at the screen, whispering to Bibi, 'See, that's when I drunkenly asked Alistair if he had a car and fancied a day trip to Milton Keynes.'

She shakes her head. 'I remember.' Her voice is low and solemn. 'He said yes, and then you both jumped around screaming excitedly like it was the best idea ever.'

'Yep,' I nod. 'Then everyone did shots and tried to get a conga going.'

Bibi is nodding now, too. 'That was a low point.'

'But, obviously, I assumed slash *hoped* he'd forgotten because I didn't hear from him all week!' My hair blows into my face and I pause to disentangle myself. 'Then he messaged this morning to ask what time he should be here to pick me up. I should've said no, I could've just got on the train.'

'Yes,' says Bibi at the same time as Louise shouts, 'No!' Honestly, at times it's like having an angel and a devil on each shoulder. Only, I don't know which is which.

'Nooo,' Lou repeats. 'It's a great plan! This way, you can bond on a mini road trip! Listening to music together, playing I Spy, falling in love over the other idiot drivers going too fast.' She checks her watch and scans the road anxiously. Alistair is late. 'Plus, you can feel out more details about this girlfriend of his. By the time you see Paul, you'll probably know if Alistair is the one for you.'

'But how are you going to get rid of him when you get up there? I assume you're not taking him along to meet your Missed Chance?' Bibi's voice is almost lost in a gust of wind that whips up our fringes in formation. Hairography.

'I told him I was going to meet a friend,' I explain. 'And he said he'd go shopping and we could meet up in the evening to drive back.'

'So, wait, how come Nick Wilde is coming, too?' Louise asks, her face screwed up.

'That,' I sigh dramatically, 'I have no idea. Alistair dropped that information into a text ten minutes ago.'

A silver Alfa Romeo takes a left onto our road and judders to a stop in front of our house. I bend down to peer in and meet the eyes of a tired-looking Nick behind the wheel. He turns off the engine as Alistair leaps out the passenger side, swooping in to hug each of us in turn. I feel better, his energy infectious.

'Road trip!' Alistair yells happily, every inch – in that moment – the fifteen-year-old I loved. He pulls me close and his familiar, delicious smell overwhelms me. I don't want to let go.

'Bloody hell, it's windy, isn't it?' Nick laughs awkwardly, appearing behind Alistair and breaking the spell.

'How are you, Nick?' I'm trying not to ask why he's tagging along. He'd said he and Alistair weren't even close anymore.

Lou shoulder-barges me out the way before he can answer. 'Hi, Nick!' she says, breathlessly batting her eyelashes. He smiles warmly and they hug, which strikes me as strange. Did they bond *that* much at the drinks last week?

'Sorry about this,' Alistair murmurs in my ear and I turn too quickly, almost brushing cheek to lips. He blushes and retreats a step, continuing in a low voice, 'Nick's parents actually live in Milton Keynes these days and he mentioned visiting them this weekend. I thought we could cadge a lift.' A few feet away, I notice Nick laughing easily with Lou. He removes his glasses as they chat, cleaning them thoughtlessly on his woollen jumper. 'He's also the only person I know with a car in London.'

I shout over the wind, 'Right, right!' I nod a lot. 'Very nice of him! Shall we go?'

Alistair scolds me kindly as I try to get in the back, directing me instead to the front passenger seat. As I protest about his need for leg room, he winks. 'Believe me, I'm getting the better deal. You have to cope with a very enthusiastic travelling companion up front.'

I wonder if he means Nick as I climb in and almost land a heavy bum cheek on . . . Jackie Weaver the dog.

'Whoops, sorry!' Nick laughs, climbing in the other side. 'Forgot to warn you. She loves a car journey and I didn't want to leave her on her own for the day. My parents haven't met her yet either, so they insisted I bring her.'

I grin. Two hours with a cute, fluffy dog? This is turning out to be the best road trip ever. 'A big moment, introducing your new lady to the folks,' I comment dryly, stroking her soft head. Jackie regards me intently, but seems content as I shift her into position on my lap. Nick chuckles as he fiddles with the stereo, jabbing at the controls until he finds some seventies bangers.

'I really hope they approve.' He checks the mirrors. 'I'm so nervous, I've never introduced them to a woman before.'

'You should be,' I tell him sternly, stroking Jackie Weaver's long grey body. She looks up at me again, so much wisdom in those big, black eyes. 'If they don't like her, you might have to choose between love and family. I'm *constantly* cutting my family off because they don't like the cute animal pictures I send in our WhatsApp group.'

Nick snorts as he starts the engine. The car growls disturbingly and he makes an apologetic noise. 'Sorry, Esther, this car is older than the internet.'

'It's OK, girl,' I whisper to Jackie as the wind howls outside. It occurs to me that I should be nervous; sitting in this ancient car with the apocalypse outside and an unknown entity driver heading for the motorway. But I feel oddly safe.

'We really appreciate this, man!' Behind Nick in the back seat, Alistair gives him a friendly mini shoulder punch as he plugs in his seatbelt.

'We really do,' I add and Nick turns to smile at me warmly. For a moment I think he will say something else, but instead he begins singing along to Abba, very loudly and incredibly tunelessly. It's funny seeing this serious-looking man singing with such a lack of self-consciousness.

I wave at Bibi and Louise out of the window as we begin the slow trundle away, music blaring. I'm still wondering what I've got myself into as we turn the corner but – as Jackie nuzzles her little head into me and Abba croons about being seventeen – I suddenly feel . . . hopeful?

CHAPTER THIRTEEN

We're meeting outside Paul's hotel and for a moment, as I pull at my jacket awkwardly, I feel like I'm on a Tinder date. What if I don't recognize him? It's been five years since we last saw each other. What if some stranger says hi and I can't tell if it's Paul? What do I do then?

I turn this way and that, my head swivelling for a glimpse of my old friend.

'Guess who?' His voice from behind is smooth and oh-so-familiar as I turn to face him. 'I was going to do the classic thing from films, where I cover your eyes with my hands? But I thought you might elbow me in the groin.' He pauses. 'Which would be fair enough.'

'I don't know how more movie stars don't get kicked in the penis,' I grin. 'Taking such a risk like that.'

'They would deserve it,' he nods solemnly.

For a moment we look at each other. It's really Paul. It really is him. And Jesus effing Christ, he's still so *fit*. In fact, he seems hotter than ever. Is that possible? I think the history and nostalgia and years of longing have made him even better-looking. That, and the gym. The man looks *hench*.

'You look absolutely gorgeous, Esther.' He grins happily, and I suck in my gut instinctively. 'Really, I mean it. You haven't aged at all, you little fuck.'

I laugh, my insides flipping like mad. 'I have, you total liar. And you can talk – you look great.'

He shakes his head sadly. 'I'm old now, it's devastating to admit. I'll be thirty-four in December, it's pitiful. I blame the kitchens. You got out when you should. Any longer and you'd be as broken and decrepit as me. Thank god we saved you and your lovely face.'

All the compliments are getting to me. 'Shall we head to a pub?' I suggest, the nerves jangling in my voice.

'Let's do something more exciting first!' Paul replies, sounding more at ease than I'd like. 'If we walk for a bit, we might come across something that excites us. I know we're not in London, but there must be fun stuff on offer in Milton Keynes, surely!'

'OK, sounds like a plan!' I reply, deeply resentful that I won't be able to calm my nerves with booze just yet.

We begin to walk in companionable silence, my arm linked through his. It feels like no time has passed as we walk, huddled together side by side. But that thought makes me feel suddenly a little nauseous. I stare down at the arms of his coat, dying to look up at him. I want to see him properly, to drink it all in. To look for the grey hairs or extra wrinkles. I want the missing years to be documented somehow. Otherwise where did they go?

This feels so different to Alistair. Alistair, who treats me almost like a sister. Who is attentive and fun and sweet, while Paul is intense and open and adoring.

I spent a lot of the car journey here staring in the side mirror at Alistair in the back, trying to figure out what I felt; what all of this meant. And whether I had any right to be spending all this time with him, when I fancy him so much and he has a partner waiting at home. I don't know what to make of it.

'So what made you look me up after all this time?' Paul's tone is light, a little playful. 'I *know* that was you outside my restaurant.'

I bite my lip and decide not to deny it. 'I'm, well' – how much do I say? – 'I'm kind of in the midst of doing a . . . er, *review* of my life.' I pause to gauge a reaction. I get none, he's just listening intently. 'And I remembered how much fun we used to have together, *Saul*.' He laughs at this. 'Either way, I wanted to catch up and see how you are. We used to be so close, I fucking miss you.'

'I miss you, too.' He puts an arm around my shoulder like it's the easiest thing in the world. 'And I want to know everything. How are things going with – sorry – what was the boyfriend's name? Idris?'

'Oh!' I laugh for no reason.

I suppose the last time I spoke properly to Paul – beyond 'HAPPY BIRTHDAY!!!!!! Hope all is well!!!!!' – was when

I was still dating my serious boyfriend, Idris. He was part of why Paul and I drifted. Not that Iddy banned us from hanging out or anything – it just happened, I guess. Paul was dating Celeste, I was all caught up with Idris, and the inevitable drift ended up with us on different friend-continents. I don't think I've even messaged him on his birthday for the last couple of years. I suppose, with both of us taken, it seemed odd to maintain a friendship that was so obviously much more than a friendship.

'Idris and I are ovahhh!' I explain. '*So* over. We broke up a couple of years ago and it couldn't be more dead and do—' I stop short, remembering that Idris is still on my list to speak to. Fuck.

'Ah, right.' He looks at me sideways and smiles. 'Sorry to hear that.'

'And what about you and Celeste?' I say, sounding a little more tetchy than I meant to. 'Are you guys still going strong?'

He shakes his head. 'Celeste didn't stick around,' he says with a shrug. 'I'm verrrrry single.'

'I'm sorry.' The nausea is back, and I instinctively reach to stroke my stomach through my coat.

He grins sideways at me. 'Don't be sorry. I'm happy.'

'Oh.' I swallow some sick. 'Jolly fine then.'

He stops in his tracks, turning to me. 'What did you just say?'

'Nothing.' I stare into his eyes. So pretty.

He smirks. 'You said *jolly fine*. You can't say that. It's *jolly good* or – ideally – no jollys at all.'

'Why wouldn't jolly fine be acceptable?' I argue, trying not to laugh. 'Fine is pretty much a synonym for good, so why wouldn't jolly fine make sense?'

'It definitely doesn't.' He shakes his head seriously.

'We found out the other day,' I begin, 'that my friend Louise has spent her whole life saying "I'm playing ketchup", instead of "playing catch-up".'

He snorts at this. 'I love that. My brother is still convinced unconscious people are coma-toast, instead of comatose. He reckons it makes sense because we refer to dead people as being toast.' He squints at me. 'Like, y'know, you're toast, buddy! So when you're halfway there, you're coma-toast!'

'You're coma-toast, dude!' I yell and a few people look over.

The smile on Paul's face fades for a second and he takes my hand in his. 'I was very sad when you stopped messaging me much.' He sounds it. 'And then it dried up altogether. I felt a bit like you didn't want me around once you met your boyfriend.'

I squeeze his hand, feeling desperate and regretful. 'I felt like *you* stopped messaging as much! Once you started dating Celeste, I felt a bit awkward bothering you with my silly life updates. And then I met Idris and it seemed funny to message you all the time, like we used to. A bit disloyal maybe.'

He smiles shyly. 'Well, I'm glad we're messaging again now.'

'Me too,' I whisper.

We start walking again, passing a small market full of

hideous-smelling cheeses that waft into our path. 'Ooh, shall we?' He raises an eyebrow.

I love cheese. There's nothing better than a truly stinky, gone-off-looking cheese. But it's not very romantic, is it? Maybe Paul just wants to be friends after all.

'They have wine,' he adds and I nod, very much sold.

CHAPTER FOURTEEN

In the room next door, Louise and Sven – for maybe the first time ever – are having some really interesting sex. And as usual, Bibi and I are listening.

'OK, so now you call me Althea the magic one,' Louise is telling him in a sultry voice. 'And I shall call you Ambrose the elf!'

'Yes, my beloved Althea!' a muffled voice obediently replies. 'I come bearing a magical staff to take away your troubles!'

'Ooh, I love your staff, Ambrose,' she says. 'And I need some of your magical potion to help soothe my ails.'

The other side of the thin wall, Bibi and I make eye contact and nearly die. I cover my mouth to stop from laughing too loudly, while Bibi finds an empty pint glass by my bed to press against the wall.

'This is fucking amazing!' she mouths at me and I nod back, delighted.

This is exciting new territory for our Louise and Sven. Usually it's standard missionary once a week. In fact, before

129

today's drastic change in tone, basically every time they had sex, we would hear the following through the wall:

'Can you at least lick it?'

'Ughhhh, but I gave you a blowjob a couple of months ago.'

'I know, but I really love it, and I did go down on you for ages last week.'

'Hmm, when did you last wash it?'

long silence

'Um, this morning?'

'Properly?'

long silence

'Yes.'

'OK, I'll lick it and see.'

unenthusiastic slurping noises

'Can I stop now?'

'But it's not hard yet!'

'It's sort of semi–hard! It's fine, I'll just thumb it in.'

'OK. Ow. Owwwww. Ooh. Oh yes, Louise, YES.'

'You like that?'

'Ohhhhhh yes, yesssssssssss! YESSSSSSSS.'

'Are you done?'

'Yes, I love you so much, Louise.'

'OK, I don't want to get cystitis so I'm going to the loo now to empty this out.'

'Love you.'

'Yep.'

I wonder what's inspired this new twist on their sex life?

Maybe it's a part Louise is auditioning for. But I thought the *Game of Thrones* hype was over. She hasn't mentioned anything specific, but she's been super busy with meetings this past week or so. She said she doesn't want to jinx anything by telling us any more about it, but she's buzzing all the same. Honestly, the range of 'acting jobs' she goes for is so broad, it could be anything. Being an actor out on auditions seems to mean anything from starring in a West End show to being someone's fake girlfriend at a bar mitzvah.

'We should probably stop listening,' I mouth at Bibi as they reach a bit of a romantic/disgusting point in proceedings. The magic staff is preparing its potion.

She frowns. 'Is that *definitely* Sven?' she whispers and I mirror her frown.

'Of course it is.'

Bibi shakes her head. 'It just doesn't sound like him at all.'

'You can hardly hear him,' I snort, adding, 'And who else would it be?!' She nods thoughtfully, then breaks away, flopping onto my bed.

I join her. 'So how's your life going, Barry?'

She perks up a little. 'That's not my name, but hey, I've got *two* job interviews next week. For actual real-life marketing jobs! I might be able to tell Franco to stuff his fucking bar job soon.'

'That's so exciting!' I say as encouragingly as I can.

The trouble is, Bibi has constant, never-ending interviews for jobs, and they never seem to go anywhere. It's so dispiriting for her. And for me, if I'm honest. I rally some enthusiasm and say, 'Tell me about them. What are they for?'

She waves her hands dismissively. 'If I get a second interview, I'll tell you all about it, promise.'

'Ugh,' I harumph. 'You and Lou are so secretive about your projects these days.' I eye her. 'Meanwhile, I tell you every pathetic detail of my existence. At least you weren't actually there in person to witness my humiliation in the car last week.'

She laughs. 'It wasn't that bad,' she lies. 'I'm sure Alistair wasn't toooo horrified.'

It's been a week since my road trip to Milton Keynes with Alistair, followed by the cheese and wine reunion with Paul. On the way home – slightly drunk and horny – I basically wrestled Alistair into the back seat, so he'd be sitting next to me. Jackie stayed in the front next to Nick, which left us finally able to talk.

Except – it turns out – trying to bond romantically with your ex when his mate from school is singing Run–DMC in the front as his dog whines along is, er, an impossibility.

And then, about twenty minutes into the drive, as boiling hot, stale air blasted from vents that were fused open, and the slightly broken seatbelt pierced my side, the cheese and red wine caught up with me. In a big, epic, disgusting way.

At the service station, I tried to clean up the smell of Stinking Bishop and Gorgonzola as best I could, but it was fairly hopeless. Nick was very kind, saying I shouldn't worry, and that the car had seen worse, but I didn't dare look at

Alistair for the rest of the journey as we all hung out the windows. I haven't heard from him since.

'At least it went well with Paul, though, right?' Bibi clears her throat, speaking louder to cover the noise of busy magicians next door. I nod, trying to dismiss images of undigested cheese in Alistair's lap.

'It was amazing,' I sigh. 'It was the same as it ever was between us – or better actually. I think I really like him, Beeb. Everything feels so easy and fun with him. And the chemistry is really intense between us, you should see how hard we flirt.' I smile, thinking about how great it was, hanging out with Paul, talking nonsense. Bantering endlessly like we always used to.

'But you didn't snog?' She winks at me. 'Another missed chance with your Missed Chance.'

I hit her with a pillow. 'No. It was all very chaste. But when he gets back to London in a few weeks, we're going to meet up again. And I hope there will be kissing next time. Lots of it. And probably other stuff, too.' I feel a tingle as Bibi faux retches. When she recovers she turns back to me.

'So is that it then? You and Paul? Done and done? End of the Seven Exes Mission?'

I shake my head. 'No! It's not like it's a sure thing. I want to keep going. Plus' – I cover my eyes, taking a deep breath – 'I didn't hear back from that phone number when I texted Alex, so I've tried Instagram. I can see the message was read, so there's no plausible deniability when it comes to ignoring me now. If I don't hear back, at least I'll know for sure I'm being officially rejected.'

There is an odd silence before Bibi speaks.

'Well, I think it's a bad idea,' she says shortly.

'What?' I am perplexed. 'Why is it a bad idea? You never even met Alex.' She doesn't reply. 'Why are you being funny about this?' I ask, as non-confrontationally as possible, and she turns away on the bed. But that's OK. It's how Bibi opens up – she can't be looking at you directly when she's feeling emotional. Not that she ever is.

'You know I just feel a bit weird about Alex,' she says at last, in a quiet voice. 'You and me never would've met or become friends if you two hadn't broken up. If you hadn't had your whole friends with benefits thing. You wouldn't even know me. What if you become mates again, and don't want me around anymore?'

'That would never happen!' I exclaim, lying down to spoon her across my bed. I nestle my face into her neck as she remains stiff in my arms. 'Honestly, Bibi, you are my friend because of who you are and I am so lucky to have you in my life. Nothing will change that. We were so lucky you came along when you did. You're no one's second choice or replacement. I love you so much – both me and Althea the magic one love you.'

She sniggers against me and I feel her body relax a little.

'OK,' she says at last in a small voice. But I'm not sure if it totally is. Bibi's always had a problem with Alex; that's not suddenly going to change after one conversation.

Through the wall we hear the familiar sound of a male orgasm, and the less-familiar sound of Lou having one, too.

'Good for them!' Bibi says smiling.

'I know!' I am relieved we have moved away from trickier subjects. 'Maybe this is the start of some decent sex for them. They'd have the actual perfect relationship then, the fuckers. I hate them.'

'You never know,' she laughs and I pull her in for a proper hug. Surprisingly for Bibi, she lets me.

CHAPTER FIFTEEN

'Toilet's fucked again.' Bibi bounces a little as she lands heavily on my bed. I'm straightening my hair and turn back to the mirror.

'You're kidding, the overflowy thing *again*?' I sigh. 'This seems to be every weekend lately. Have you rung the landlord?'

'Yip and yip,' Bibi confirms. 'The arsehole has promised to send his dippy son-in-law over with a plunger again. Because that obviously worked so well last time. Louise is currently on duty in there, bailing out water, but she's going out with Sven later. Can you take the next shift or shall I?'

I turn to face her. 'I don't know. I might be able to do the last shift, but I'm going out myself in a sec. Sorry.'

Bibi sits up straight. 'Going where?' She sounds outraged. 'What are you doing without consulting us?'

I turn back, staring resolutely in the mirror. I don't want to face Bibi when I say this.

'Alex finally replied.' I tug my hair tightly with the

straighteners until it hurts. 'We're meeting in a few minutes at The Swab.'

There is silence and I don't turn around. Instead, I stare down, unable to even look at myself.

'What's happening?' Louise arrives in the doorway. I can hear in her voice the anxiety that something is going on without her. The FOMO is strong with this one.

There is a beat of silence and I pick up my hairbrush, swallowing hard to push back tears.

'What?' Louise sounds scared now. 'Where are you going, Esther? Have I done something? It wasn't me who broke the toilet again, I swear. Maybe it was Sven? He had onions again.'

'No,' Bibi snaps, standing up. 'Of course *you* haven't done anything.' She makes the *you* sound like an accusation.

I check the clock on my phone; it's time to go.

I pick up my bag, steeling my nerves and giving myself another anxious lookover in the mirror. No lipstick on my teeth this time.

Bibi quietly clears her throat. 'She's going to meet Alex,' she tells Louise in a low voice.

'Oh!' I don't need to see Lou to know the expression she currently has on her face.

'See you guys in a bit,' I mutter, exiting without looking at either. As I close the flat door behind me and head down the entrance hall, I hear their hushed worried voices.

The few minutes from front door to pub are brutal, with every step bringing a whole new set of nerves. I don't know if I've ever felt this nervous. It's way worse than it was with Alistair and Paul. This is *Alex*. My Friend with Benefits, Alex. My lover, Alex. My friend. This could be very bad – awful really.

I reach for the door of the pub, wondering if I can quickly cram in a couple of shots to steady myself. It's then I hear my name.

'Esther.'

It is a statement, not a question, and for a moment I can't bring myself to look. This has been a long time coming – seven years – and I don't really know if I have the strength to handle it.

As if in slow motion, I turn and look into the eyes of someone I loved so, so much for so long. But – ultimately – not in the right way.

'Hey, Shelley,' I say shyly, taking in my oldest friend and how she has changed – and all the ways she hasn't.

EX 3: ALEX SHELLEY

AKA The Friend With Benefits

PART ONE

St Jude's Comprehensive School

7QT form room

9.34am

'Miranda George?'
  'Here, Miss.'
  'Louise Hickman?'
  'Here, Miss.'
  'Alistair Morris?
  'Present, Miss.'
  'Kelechi Musa?'
  'Here.'
  'Annalise Price?'
  'Here, Miss.'

'Alexandra Shelley? Alexandra? Alex?'

'Yeah, I'm here, Miss, but you can just call me Shelley, yeah?'

En masse, the room turns, wide-eyed, in the direction of the rebellious voice with an intriguing accent. A bright-eyed blonde girl with a tan smiles cockily from the back row. She sits slouched in her plastic chair, her left arm flung across its back like every cool girl in every teen film. She half smiles at our collective astonishment, looking more sure of herself in this moment than I've ever felt in my life.

The rest of the class turn swiftly back to the teacher to gauge her reaction but I stay staring at this compelling creature. Mum bought me a dictionary over the summer, as part of a confused attempt at prepping me for my first day of secondary school. I've just got to the word 'audacious'. This girl is *audacious*.

We make eye contact. She smiles.

'Right ...' The teacher's weary-sounding reaction makes me turn back. 'Fine, whatever. Shelley it is.'

As the class ends, I make sure to be standing next to Alex Shelley as we file out. I make my opening approach as coolly and casually as I'm capable.

'Yo, Shelley,' I offer, looking down at my timetable, printed on a piece of card in my hand. 'So are you, like, American or something?'

'Australian,' she drawls, sounding the perfect amount of bored. 'My family just moved here because of my dad's dumb job. It's cold in England.'

'It sure is!' I agree with all my soul, even though it's actually very warm today. 'And that's sooo cool you're Australian. I watch *Home and Away* a lot, it's the best.' She shrugs, so I try another tack. 'So, um, what class do you have next? Science?'

'Yeah,' she says through chewing gum, and I feel her eyes on me, taking me in – judging me. 'I totally hate science.'

'Oh god, yeah, me too!!!' I am too loud and I shake myself. Dial down the eagerness to please, I internally instruct – *be cool*. 'I mean, yeah, it's totes rubbish and I'm sooo dreading it.'

'What's your name?' She kicks at a stone as we walk and even that seems awesome.

'Esther Adams,' I tell her as we walk in the direction of the science block. 'But you can call me Adams if you want?'

She looks scornful. 'Going by a surname is kind of *my* thing, OK, Esther? Don't copy me, yeah?'

'Yeah totally!' I immediately copy her scornful tone. 'Yeah, and Esther is fine. There's an Adam in our form anyway, so it could get confusing, yeah?' I bark a laugh.

Arriving at our science lesson, we file to the back in silent agreement, selecting a table together in the corner. Another girl takes a seat beside us and introduces herself as Louise. She seems lame but kinda funny. Everyone seems lame next to Alex. Sorry, *Shelley*. The three of us giggle as a group for no reason over the randomness of sinks on every table.

A girl I knew from primary school asks if she can sit with us and I give her a *withering* look. I have a *crew* now, I don't need the people I went to kid-school with.

'Right.' The teacher sweeps in, tall with a booming voice.

141

'Welcome, Year Sevens, I'm Mr Havana and I'll be teaching you biology. Let's get to know each other by taking the register.' He looks down at the folder before him as Louise and I turn to watch Shelley in action.

She slouches down in her seat and prepares for her name to be called.

CHAPTER SIXTEEN

The silence has stretched on for aeons. Empty, empty emptiness is all around us as we sit here, unable to form words.

The Swab is busier than usual, so we've gone outside in the cold. We're sitting as far away from everyone else as possible, on a splintery picnic bench next to the pub's large, overgrown pond full of ducks. The uncomfortable seating is matched only by the discomfort of this situation. I'm regretting moving away from the cover of other people's noise. I didn't want anyone to be able to hear us talk, but it turns out we have nothing to say.

Alex is the one to finally break the interminable nothingness.

'Jesus, it kind of hurts to look at you.' She smiles through the painful words and I frown, looking down at the wooden table between us.

'Because of ... because of the way things ended, or because of the friendship we lost?'

'Oh,' she laughs softly. 'Maybe a tiny bit of the first, but mostly the second.'

'I'm really, really, fucking sorry,' I whisper and we fall back into silence.

More silence follows.

I cough lightly, turning towards the large pond. 'It's nice, isn't it?' I say lamely, even though it's not. It's a mess of algae, gnats and weird smells. She nods, staring off into the distance.

A duck quacks and a few others join her.

'Sweet!' Alex comments at long last in a strangled voice. 'Ducks are cool.'

It's been about seven years since I last saw her in person, and her Australian accent is still as strong as ever.

We continue to stare desperately and awkwardly at the pond. A male duck begins to swim beside a female, like they are courting. It is almost romantic.

That is, until he forcibly mounts her. The girl duck tries to pull away, desperate to escape, but it's utterly futile. She goes under the water, trying to shake him off, duck-screaming for help. It is the most awful thing and god save us the noise is horrifying. It is loud and brutal and too much.

Alex and I look at each other.

She opens her mouth and says in a very solemn voice, 'Nature is healing.'

We start laughing and don't stop for a full two minutes, even as the sound of animal screams continues to fill the air around us.

'That poor creature,' she says through watery eyes. 'Should we do something?'

'I mean, I'm not sure what we can do?' I snigger. 'I could shout *DUCK RAPE* until someone comes to help?'

'Oh but' – Alex looks thoughtful – 'you're not supposed to shout rape if you're being raped, though, are you? You're supposed to shout *fire* because people don't care that much about women being brutalized.'

'That's true,' I add. 'And they'd only point out that the duck wasn't wearing a long enough skirt, so she must've wanted it.'

'And that she smiled at the boy duck a week ago,' Alex nods. 'Led him on.'

'DUCK FIRE,' I yell across the garden and a few curious heads turn in our direction.

'It's not funny,' she protests but starts cracking up again. 'Mother Nature is an absolute bastard, isn't she?'

'Bloody hell, it's a good job this wasn't meant to be some romantic date, isn't it!' I burst out laughing, and then stop, realizing what a stupid thing it was to say.

'It's OK,' she says smiling after a second. 'I never thought you were asking to meet up so you could make some kind of love confession after all this time. And if I had any doubts at all, I knew for sure it wasn't a date when you suggested The Swab. I can't believe you and Lou still come here. It was bad enough when I lived with you guys, but it's actually somehow worse now.'

I laugh heartily as a hurt Franco slinks by, collecting glasses. 'Our flatmate Bibi actually works here these days.' I feel strange talking about Bibi – the person we found to fill

Alex's space in the flat after she left. No wonder Bibi is so weird about Alex. 'I think she's actively working to make it a worse pub.'

'She sounds fun,' Alex smiles warmly, no hint of awkwardness. She pulls out some gum, offering me a piece, and I shake my head. She looks down for a moment, as if gathering herself. 'Hey, Esther, I'm really sorry.'

I sit up straighter. '*You're* sorry?! No, I'm the sorry one, Alex. Really.'

She sighs. 'Honestly, I don't think you have to be.' She looks up now with big, familiar blue eyes. 'I knew what we were doing but I convinced myself there was more to it. It was all just hurt ego and a bruised heart. Then, once that had faded, I was too embarrassed to get in touch. The thought of "unblocking" you and reaching out felt so horrible and humiliating. I couldn't face it, my pride wouldn't let me.' She bites her lip. 'I acted like a child, throwing all my toys not just out of the pram but *at you* as much as possible.'

'I understood.' I hang my head, not quite willing to let go of my guilt in all this. 'And I was in the wrong. I should've valued our friendship too much to let sex get in the way. I never should've risked it. You were too important.'

She nods. 'I'm so sad we had to stop being friends. And I'm so sorry I rejected all your attempts at making up. I would like to make up now, if it's not too late?'

'Oh my god, yes!' I burst into tears out of nowhere. 'I really do want to make up. It could never be too late!' She starts crying too, so I head to her side of the table for a hug. It's familiar and lovely and I want to stay there crying together for as long as possible.

I finally pull away because there is something I want to say; something I've wanted to say ever since we broke up. 'Alex' – we regard each other with watery eyes – 'I need you to know that I did honestly have real feelings for you back then. I might've played them down and pretended it was all meaningless sex, but I do understand now that it *was* real. At the end, I think I made you feel like you were mad to think there was something special between us, but there was, there really was.' I pause. 'There were so many confusing, blurred lines between the friendship and the love I felt for you already, but I know that what we had meant something. It was wrong and unbelievably shitty to deny it.' I squeeze her hand. 'I'm really sorry.' She nods slowly and I circle my arms around her again, knowing she hears me.

My phone vibrates. It's Lou.

> **Louise Hickman (school)**
> Message: Babe, how's it going? Tell Shelley
> that I still love her and really miss her.
> Message: *Alex!
> Message: or whatever she's going by
> these days
> **5.45pm**

Also, when do you reckon you'll be back?
Bibi is over guarding the loo and says it's
your turn.
5.45pm

I dry my face with my sleeve while Alex does the same.

'Um, Shelley – I mean Alex – would you fancy coming back to the flat to see Lou and meet Bibi? We kinda have a toilet situation that I need to oversee.'

'A *shit-uation* you mean?' she grins.

I grimace. 'Not quite, but it needs monitoring until our twat landlord turns up.'

'That would actually be lovely.' Alex stands up. 'I owe Louise an apology anyway. She did nothing wrong in any of this and I hurt her too.'

I get up and we watch the ducks for a few more seconds. A group of girl ducks arrive en masse and the rapist duck reluctantly climbs off and slinks away.

'I bet it was when you shouted *duck fire*,' Alex says in an awed voice. 'The other female ducks knew what that meant and they came to save their friend.'

I nod. 'They'll probably start a spreadsheet of bad ducks to watch out for now, including him.'

We high-five for girl power – human and animal – before heading for the pub exit.

EX 3: ALEX SHELLEY

AKA The Friend With Benefits

PART TWO

Sky Lounge

Dance floor

1.34am

'Oh my god, I don't think I've ever been this awake,' I scream over the music and Lou gives me a thumbs-up, sweat plastering hair across her forehead.

'BEST NIGHT EVER,' she screams back, jumping up and down to the music.

'I CAN'T BELIEVE WE'VE NEVER TRIED COKE BEFORE, IT'S SO GREAT!' I do some little boxes with my hands knowing with absolute certainty that I look super cool.

'I KNOW, RIGHT! WE SHOULD DO THIS ALL THE TIME!' She grins maniacally. 'LET'S DO IT EVERY DAY!'

'I MEAN ...' I consider this option. 'MAYBE NOT *EVERY* DAY BECAUSE THAT MIGHT BECOME AN ISSUE, BUT SURE, LET'S TOTALLY DO THIS AGAIN, IT'S GREAT, MY GUMS FEEL WEIRD.'

Louise nods, accepting this. 'MINE TOO. DO YOU THINK WE'RE DOING THAT GURNING THING?'

I shrug, still dancing. Maybe I will try big boxes with my hands now.

Lou looks anxious at my lack of interest in gurning. 'SHALL WE ASK SHELLEY? SHE GOT US THE COKE, SHE'LL KNOW IF WE'RE GURNING AND IF IT'S NORMAL GURNING OR IF WE NEED TO GO TO THE HOSPITAL.'

I look around. 'WHERE *IS* SHELLEY?' The club we're in is heaving with sexy, sweaty people dancing. They're all women.

'MAYBE WE SHOULD GO TO THE HOSPITAL ANYWAY?' Lou has stopped dancing and looks pale now. 'WHAT IF IT WAS BAD COKE AND ACTUALLY WE HAD WASHING POWDER OR RAT POISON AND BLOOD WILL START COMING OUT OF OUR EYES IN A MINUTE?'

'LAST TIME I SAW HER SHE WAS CHATTING UP THE DJ.' I ignore Lou's wild speculation, still looking around the room.

'I'M CALLING 999,' Lou tells me as I spot Shelley, swigging a drink in a booth on her own, and wander off in her direction. I take a seat next to her.

'Lou's calling herself an ambulance,' I say conversationally. Shelley nods back, chewing on her usual gum, even while clubbing.

'Any particular reason why?'

'She's having a panic about the drugs you got us.'

'For god's sake.' Shelley rolls her eyes. 'I gave the pair of you a bit of sugar from the tea cupboard. I didn't think either of you could handle actual drugs, and clearly I was right. Plus, you both only put about three specks on your gums anyway. Even if it had been actual coke, it wouldn't have been enough to do anything.'

'Oh.' I am disappointed. 'But I feel so high!'

She looks rueful. 'Er, that might be all the booze? We've been drinking since midday.'

'And much of said booze was shots,' I nod, understanding the sense of it all. 'So Lou and I are still the losers who've never done drugs?'

'Yes,' Shelley confirms, taking out her gum and disposing of it in a tissue.

'Ugh!' I sink lower into the seat. 'I'm so pathetic. No drugs, no boyfriend, a kitchen full of cliquey men at work who make it very clear they think I'll never make it as a real chef. *And* I haven't had sex in an age! I can't believe it.' I roll over in the booth to face her. 'You know the last time I had sex was Carl? I mean, it was really, really hot and everything.' I pause to check she believes me. 'I totally, definitely enjoyed the whole experience with him – definitely. But it was nearly a year ago now! I'm twenty-two, shouldn't I be banging everyone around me and doing lots of things I regret?'

'Absolutely,' she agrees. 'I'm constantly regretful – it should be the way of things.'

'The trouble is,' I sigh deeply, 'I never have any time off. This has been my first Saturday not working in – how many months? Fucking loads. I work from eight in the morning until one in the morning. When exactly am I supposed to find people to have sex with?'

'Oh mate.' Shelley looks sympathetic and I reach out for a hug. She's so warm and smells so good.

'Honestly, Shell, I'm starting to think maybe I don't want to be a chef after all. I'm working such insane hours and it's become my whole life. I barely even see you and Lou – and I live with you guys.' Over her shoulder, I spot Louise in the corner looking sulky as she's scolded by two furious-looking paramedics.

Shelley squeezes me tighter. 'But mate, you've trained so long for it! You can't let those dickheads you work with win.'

'Ugh, I know.' I look up at her big blue eyes. She is so beautiful and I love her so much. 'I really do love cooking but it's taking over everything. And I don't think I'll even be a sous chef for at least another year.'

'I guess you have to figure out if it's all worth it then,' she says sweetly and I watch her mouth as she speaks. She has these gorgeous, straight white teeth I've always envied. God, I love Shelley, she's so pretty and sarcastic and funny. I wish I was like her.

'I think I just need to get laid,' I whisper. 'I think that will relieve the pressure and I'll be able to think straight again.'

She's looking back at me now. We're looking at each other.

'If you think that will help?' she says slowly, her plump lips moving with the words. Her breath smells like lovely mint.

'I think it really will,' I whisper again, unable to tear my eyes away from hers. How have I never noticed before how incredibly sexy she is? I've always worshipped her, always wanted to be close to her, but I didn't consider anything beyond a friendship before tonight. I'm realizing now that the distance between adoring someone – loving them to death – and wanting to kiss them isn't as far away as I thought. In fact, I'm already there and it only took me half a step.

'Do you want to go back to the flat?' My voice trembles and she takes my hand, entwining our fingers, meshing them together. It feels amazing and I suddenly want to touch the rest of her so much.

We get an Uber home, abandoning Lou to her fate. It's an expense we normally wouldn't dare spare but we can't wait. And it's worth it because back at ours, I'm treated to the best orgasm of my life. Afterwards, we collapse in a sweaty heap on my bed.

'Holy crap, Shelley, you're so good, I had no idea.'

She looks pleased, then thoughtful. 'Esther, can you call me Alex? I've been thinking for a while that I don't want to be Shelley anymore. It's so juvenile. It was the pre-teen me, trying to stand out and seem cool. I don't want to be Shelley now, and I especially don't want to be Shelley with you, in these moments.'

'OK,' I nod in understanding, then pause. 'Moments – plural?'

She looks shy. 'Well, have a think about it, but I was thinking we could do this on a very casual basis, if you want. I know you're too busy with work for anything real or serious, and I'm having a lot of fun out there dating. But we could provide each other with a few orgasms from time to time. A release, if you will. If you wanted?'

'Like a friends with benefits type situation?' I sit up straight in her bed.

'Exactly,' she nods happily.

'But what about us living together, Shell – um, *Alex*?' I pull the duvet up around me. 'Won't it fuck everything up and get messy?'

She turns to me, tracing a finger along my jaw and sending tingles through my whole body. 'We won't let it.'

I kiss her again, believing her words completely. Because I want to.

CHAPTER SEVENTEEN

When we arrive at the flat, Bibi and Louise are both outside on the doorstep, chatting to two Jehovah's Witnesses.

'I saw a black squirrel the other day,' Louise is saying, looking fascinated. 'Was it a sign of the apocalypse?'

'Er . . .' The men glance at each other. 'We're here to discuss the scriptural command given to Jesus and his followers.'

'Well, I still don't get it,' Bibi is saying. 'But it's all very interesting and I respect your views, dudes.'

'Let me just read you Matthew 24:14 again, young lady,' the taller man says, leaning closer.

'OH MY FUCKING GOD, SHELLEY!' Louise interrupts his flow at the sight of us. Bursting past the evangelists, she throws herself into Alex's arms. 'You're hereeeeee! And I mean Alex, sorry.'

Alex laughs and wraps herself around Lou. 'I am! And I'm so sorry, Lou. I've been such a horrible prick for so long. Can you forgive me?'

With her face still buried inside Alex's coat, we make out

Louise crying as she squeals, 'Of course! You don't even have to ask.'

'God' – Alex looks over at me from inside Lou's squeeze – 'I thought this apology thing was going to be harder – or, at least, take longer. If I'd known it would be this easy, I'd have done it years ago.'

'I wish you had,' I tell her, my voice thick.

We all move to go inside, squeezing past the Jehovah's lads who are reading another Bible passage. Bibi is pouting, but I can't tell if it's at the pushy preachers who won't leave, or at Alex's arrival.

Inside, I head to make tea, while Louise and Alex's long-running hug migrates to the sofa. Bibi hovers jealously in the doorway.

Released momentarily, Alex smiles brightly up at Bibi. 'Sorry, I haven't said a proper hello yet. I'm Alex. You must be Bibi.'

'I must be,' Bibi replies shortly. 'You're back then, are you?'

Alex glances over at me, a little confused. '*Back* sounds a bit dramatic, but I guess this whole thing is a bit dramatic. Yeah, I guess I am.' There is an awkward silence before she adds, 'Er, is that OK?'

Bibi shrugs and I shoot her an angry look. I get that she feels threatened by Alex but she could be polite.

'So, tell me everything I've missed!' Alex turns away from Bibi, as I hand over a steaming cup of tea. I hope she still takes it the same way. 'Seven years of dramas and nonsense, fill me in. Does Esther still get her tits out whenever she's had too much House of Virtue gin? Does Louise still bring cutlery on nights out for her kebab? Is that lost satsuma still under this sofa?' She laughs and we join in. But I find myself somewhat horrified that we've moved on so very little in all this time. I'm still in the same flat, still single, still getting my tits out.

To be fair, they're nice tits and I want to share that joy with people.

'Yes, yes, and yes,' Louise confirms. 'And I know you can get those wooden forks for free in the kebab shop, but it doesn't seem sanitary. What if they're just rinsing off used ones at the end of the night and putting them back in the pot? Or what if I got splinters in my food?'

'A good point!' Alex confirms.

'But I have a boyfriend now!' Louise says proudly. 'He's called Sven.'

'A boyfriend you have rubbish sex with,' Bibi mutters and Lou looks embarrassed.

'Er, can you just give us a second?' I paste on a grin for Alex as I grab Bibi by the elbow and hustle her out of the room, heading towards the loo. Door shut behind us, I turn my sternest face on Bibi. 'Look, I know this is weird for you, but no one is replacing you!' I tell her crossly. 'Not unless you keep up this mean girl shit. Alex is great, so can you just play nice and smile for the rest of the day? Please?'

She looks down sulkily.

'Bibi,' I say in a low warning voice, 'I love you, you're very important to me, but Alex is really important to me, too. I've known her since I was eleven. I fucked things up between us years ago and this is my second chance. Please don't ruin things for me. *Please.*'

She looks up, worried. 'Are you getting back together?'

'What? No!' I shake my head. 'I meant a second chance at our friendship. I would never *ever* risk things with Alex like that again. It's taken seven years to rebuild what sex ruined. If *anyone* has sex with Alex again, I'll get pissed off.' I laugh as I put a hand on Bibi's shoulder. 'Look, Beeb, Lou and I really want Alex back in our lives and we need you to understand that. She's not pushing you out! We don't have a one-in one-out policy over here. In fact, we'd love it if you could be friends with Alex, too. Can you make an effort? I think if you do, you'll realize she's fucking wonderful. She's funny and clever and brave. She makes all of us more fun, you'll see.'

Bibi sighs dramatically. 'OK, fine.'

I return to the living room, a sheepish Bibi at my heels, and clap loudly.

'Right! Back to the pub? You guys missed some mad duck rape.'

Alex looks at me sternly.

'Sorry.' I dip my head. 'Some mad duck fire.'

EX 3: ALEX SHELLEY

AKA The Friend With Benefits

PART THREE

Our flat

Sitting room

10.44am

'What are you doing down there?'

'Dropped a satsuma, didn't I?' Her voice is muffled, half buried under the sofa.

'What?' I am flummoxed.

Alex emerges, red-faced and cross. 'I was trying to have a relaxing satsuma in our living room like a normal person, and I dropped it. It rolled under the bloody sofa and I can't reach it. I can't leave it under there to rot forever.' She pauses then looks up at me hopefully. 'Can I?'

'Definitely not,' I say sternly. 'Shall I help? I've got quite small arms.'

'They're small but they're not spindly like we need,' Alex says thoughtfully.

'Oh cheers.' I am miffed. 'So I'm a fucking T-rex, am I? With my short little stumpy arms constantly clawing at you.'

She snorts and reaches for me from her place on the floor. 'I love you clawing at me, T-rex. Do you fancy a quick claw now?'

'No,' I scold. 'I have to go to work in a few minutes.'

Lou bounds in. 'What we doin'?' She doesn't wait for an answer before throwing herself down on the carpet and staring under the sofa. 'Looking for monsters?'

'Satsuma monsters,' I mutter but she seems undeterred.

'I always check under my bed at night,' she says, still straining to see in the darkness under there. 'Because you never know. I wish I could meet someone nice to protect me from the under-bed monsters.' She sighs dramatically. 'It's very annoying that you two are dating each other – usually I'd ask if your partners knew anyone they could set me up with.'

Alex laughs at the same time as I say, 'We're not dating, Lou! We're friends with benefits.' Her laugh stops short but she says nothing.

'Whatever.' Lou waves her hand at me. 'It's been, like, a year of you two banging and it's killing my dating life. Don't you know *anyone* you might be able to set me up with?!'

I consider this. 'Actually, there's that guy I used to work with, Paul—'

'Ooh, I remember him! Sexy name!' Lou squeals.

'I saw him for some drinks the other night and it was quite flirty.' I think about it. 'There was always a bit of something between us but I was seeing Carl when we met. I bet he has loads of hot mates. Shall I set up a double date drinks thing?'

'Yesssss!' Louise stands up, punching the air. 'Yes please.' She runs out shrieking about making a hair appointment and I laugh. But when I turn to Alex, she is cold-faced.

'What?'

'What the fuck was that?' Alex asks, clearly angry.

I am suddenly afraid. 'What do you mean? I'm sorry, did you want to do a triple date? I guess I can see if Paul knows any hot women who—'

'What the hell is wrong with you?' She stands up, satsuma forgotten. 'We've been seeing each other for nearly a year and you think it's OK to just casually mention other people you fancy in front of me?'

'But ... but ...' I am lost for words. We've talked about fancying other people before. Not for a while, I guess, but this thing between us was always casual. That was the agreement. That was what we said: friends with benefits. 'I'm so sorry, Alex,' I say, stammering. 'I didn't realize ...' What didn't I realize? Have the rules changed?

'You have no idea, do you?' she says quietly, the anger gone. 'You don't even realize.'

'What?' I say again, feeling helpless and afraid.

There is a long silence. 'I'm in love with you, you fucking idiot,' she says at last. 'I thought it was obvious. And I thought you were starting to feel the same.'

I feel my mouth gape open, but I am powerless to close it.

In love with me? No, this doesn't make any sense at all. Why would she ... but we're *friends*, we've always been friends. That's what we agreed. It was never about love, how can ...

'Fuck, Alex ...' I trail off; the words I have are no good.

She stares me down, waiting, until she can't stand it anymore. 'So you don't love me?' It's said in such a sad, broken-down way that I nearly start crying. But the truth is I don't. Not like that.

I can't say it. I don't know how to admit that.

Reading my mind she says impatiently, 'Just fucking say it, Esther. Tell me. If you don't love me, just say it.'

'But I do love you,' I reply weakly. 'You're my best friend, Alex Shelley, I love you so so much.'

'Not as a girlfriend, though?' she confirms, her voice limp.

I hang my head and whisper, 'No.'

She starts to cry and I pull her in for a hug. She sobs against my shoulder for a few minutes as I tell her I'm sorry, over and over.

She stops at last and murmurs something against my shoulder. It's too muffled to make out so I move my ear closer.

'What?' I whisper and this time I can hear.

'You've used me.' I feel myself go cold at her words. 'You've fucking used me. You never cared about me at all, you fucking *cow*.' She pulls away properly now and her tanned face is contorted with rage.

'No, Alex, that's not true.' My voice is high and pleading. 'I thought we were on the same page about all this, I'm so sorry. Please don't say I used you, it wasn't like that! I thought we were both having a good time. I thought it was OK.'

'You let me think you loved me!' Her voice is louder now, full of fury. 'You held me and stroked my hair and told me I was beautiful.'

I feel shame fill me but I try again. 'Alex! It was your idea to do this – you suggested being friends with benefits! You can't change the rules and then get angry at me about it. You should've spoken to me – told me how you were feeling – I had no idea you had feelings for me!'

Lies.

Something in me knew how she felt, and ignored it. I could feel something changing on her side in recent months and I let it happen, all the while pretending it was fine. I *have* used her. I am a scumbag and I deserve the hatred pouring out of her right now.

'You're a liar and a user. We're done!' She screams this, her face purple. 'We're not friends anymore, we're not *anything* anymore. I'm moving out and I don't want you to contact me again. We're so over.' She storms out of the room and I hear her bedroom door slam shut and lock, leaving me in shock.

By the next morning, she's gone. Her dad comes for all her stuff later that week and gives me such an awful, hateful look, I cry for four hours straight. Alex won't take my calls or messages. She won't take Lou's calls or messages. She blocks me on Facebook and Twitter, and a letter I send to her mum's house gets returned to sender.

She's gone from our lives after twelve years of friendship, just so I could get laid. We're over, just like that, because I was bored and lonely.

I've never hated myself more.

CHAPTER EIGHTEEN

'Is Key West different to Kanye West?' My assistant Katie pauses, her young face contorted with confusion. 'Or is it one of his old names? Like, he's Ye some of the time and Kanye others, but he used to be Key West?'

We have American clients arriving this week for a big event at the Norris Museum and it turns out the UK education system has failed my young protégée.

'Er, different things,' I hedge, not wanting to embarrass her too much – but then unable to resist. 'Key West is a city in Florida, babe.'

She flushes and ducks her head as I smile affectionately at the top of her scalp.

'Don't worry about it,' I tell her magnanimously. 'Geography was never my strong suit either. For ages I thought they spoke Hollandaise in Holland.'

She perks up. 'Didn't you used to be a chef?' she grins. 'I bet that was a fun conversation when someone asked you for Hollandaise sauce on their Eggs Benedict.'

I laugh loudly and people walking by glance over.

It's been another long day at work, planning for this event. The Florida couple are celebrating their thirtieth wedding anniversary and wanted to have it at the Norris because it's where they had their first date. Which is both incredibly romantic and also very WTF – what kind of tedious monster has a first date at a museum? Either way, Katie's popping back to mine to grab some paperwork she wants to get done tonight. I feel vaguely guilty over the prospect of making her work this evening, but I'm also enjoying the power trip. Plus, it really does urgently need doing and I've been so distracted lately.

Lucky Katie's so brill.

I study her for a moment as she fiddles on her phone. Katie's one of those cool people who can casually wear eyeliner every day without it a) looking like she's due at a rave any minute and b) turning her face into some kind of asymmetrical Picasso mockery. She is fabulous and I feel fortunate to have her on my team. She's only about twenty-three but has so much conviction and certainty over who she is. She – and all of her generation – seem to be so much braver than I was at her age. It gives me hope for the future of feminism. There's an extra injection of who-the-fuck-cares about her – something I'm sorely lacking. As we approach my house, I close my eyes for a microsecond, trying to let her confidence wash over me. I want her feminism to seep into my pores, somehow, so I can be stronger and braver . . .

And that is when we're catcalled.

'HEYYYYYYYYYY,' comes a voice from inside a car, suddenly dawdling along threateningly beside us.

I glance at Katie, wondering if I can get away with minimal outrage. This is my chance to prove my credentials but I find that I increasingly don't have the energy for confrontation. Her brow furrows as she stops and bends down, glaring into the car.

'ESTHERRRRRRRR!' the creep in the car says now, and I realize that I recognize the battered, silver Alfa Romeo and its non-creep occupant.

'Nick Wilde!' I say with some surprise – and relief. 'Katie, this is a guy I knew from school,' I tell her, watching her hackles come down. I pause before adding lamely, 'His mum was our drama teacher.'

'Oh right,' Katie says a little uncertainly. 'I, er, had a drama teacher.' Nick and I regard her blankly and she clears her throat. 'Nice to, um, meet you!' The stone-cool feminist is gone. 'I just need to, er, text my flatmate about something . . .' She backs away from us, looking panicked, and I wonder briefly if she is this awkward with our clients.

'Sorry to shout at you from the road,' Nick apologizes as I turn back to him. 'It was clearly a hangover from my playground days. I thought I'd left that shouting-at-girls career behind me long ago.' Beside him on the seat, Jackie the dog looks delighted to see me, clambering across his lap so she can enthusiastically lick my hand.

'You're lucky I didn't have an Apple Tango to hand to throw in your face,' I tell him serenely, stroking Jackie's lovely head. A thought occurs to me. 'What are you doing driving around here?'

He laughs, leaning casually on the window. 'I live around the corner!' He points vaguely down the road and I shake my head.

'How did I not know that?'

'You didn't ask.'

I clear my throat, feeling guilty. We had that whole car journey to Milton Keynes together, and I was too busy glancing in the side mirror at Alistair in the back seat.

'Sorry,' I mutter and he waves an unconcerned hand. The car stutters and stalls, as he curses and restarts the engine.

'I better get this stupid thing home.' He glances up and I notice his glasses are smudged. It makes his eyes look all misty, like he's a character from an old-timey movie. 'See you around?' he smiles and I give a tiny wave as he drives off, Jackie leaping up on her seat to watch me well into the distance.

Katie returns to my side, breathing heavily. 'Oh my god, I'm so sorry I was so embarrassing! Fit men make me so awkward, I forget all words. Did I actually say I had a drama teacher?' She cringes. 'Esther, I nearly asked him his thoughts on Kanye West!' She turns to me. 'What's his deal anyway? Is he single?'

Another question I haven't asked him. But if he lives around here and hasn't popped up on my Tinder, he's surely taken.

Why is Nick Wilde suddenly back in my life? The reunion

drinks, the Milton Keynes road trip, and now he happens to be driving by? As if I don't have enough ghosts from my past haunting me right now.

'No idea,' I tell Katie dismissively, and turn the conversation back to something safe: helium balloons for the party – how many is too many?

CHAPTER NINETEEN

'Can I use the loo, Sofia?' I ask politely and she hands me a candle, wick flickering.

'Go carefully,' she warns. 'There are many things in the way between here and my bathroom.' I nod seriously and pick my way out of her front room in the pitch darkness.

We're in the midst of a power cut. The whole bloody building is out – the whole row! It's outrageous and we would definitely complain to someone if any of us in the flat knew who our supplier is. We had a massive argument in the dark about where the bills were kept before giving up and heading upstairs to Sofia's flat. We knew she, at least, has candles. Because all grown-ups have candles and she is definitely a grown-up.

Plus, she's probably been through a bunch of wars, right? So she'll have all that wartime spirit and know-how. She'll know how to rip up sheets to deliver a baby and how to cook food without a hob. I don't exactly know which wars or when – I only did a term of history at uni – but there have been a whole bunch, right?

I have my wee in the dark and it's as weird as you'd think. Afterwards I move the candle close to the loo seat to inspect for drips before flushing – delighting in the functioning facilities – and head back to the living room.

I stop in the hallway when I spot Louise.

She's hunched over her phone, typing frantically. Her lovely face is lit up only by the screen and she's wearing an expression I don't recognize. There is something odd about her whole body language. Something secretive and guilty. Why would she be texting out here anyway? It's not like we'd all demand to know what she was doing on her phone.

Maybe I should demand to know what she's doing on her phone.

'All right, Lou?' I whisper into the dark and she jumps a clean five inches in the air.

'God, Esther, you scared me!' She shoves her phone into her pocket so fast her hands blur, even in the candlelight.

'What are you doing?' I ask, sounding innocent.

'What do you mean?' she replies, guilt pulsing in her voice.

'Estherrrrrr!' Sofia shouts from the living room. 'Hurry up! I want to hear the latest with your mission!' Louise grabs the opportunity to head back in without answering my question, and I follow, flopping back down on the sofa and wondering. Is something going on with her? She'd tell us, wouldn't she? Maybe a family member is ill or something?

'Come on!' Sofia's face is impatient in the flickering candlelight. 'Tell me what's happening with you stalking all these dreadful exes!'

'I wouldn't quite describe it like that—' I protest but she continues, oblivious.

'Tell me, how is it going? Have you found a great love yet? Have any more of them called the police on you?'

'Nobody called the police on me,' I correct impatiently. 'And for your information, that actually worked out well in the end. I met up with Paul – the guy we were trying to find – and it was so lovely.'

'So he is The One!' Sofia cries happily.

'Maybe,' I beam confidently.

'*Maybe?*' She screws up her face. 'How can he *maybe* be The One?'

'Well, this other guy, Alistair, might also be The One,' Louise explains helpfully.

'Or it might be Will, Idris, Carl or Rich,' Bibi chips in with a snort from somewhere in the dark.

'I mean, my true *One* in all this might end up being my renewed friendship with Alex,' I add in my wisest voice.

'*What are you TALKING about?*' Sofia shrieks and we all jump. 'You are all speaking nonsense!'

'I know, sorry, Sofia,' I agree humbly. 'I'm a mess.'

'Hey!' Bibi's tone is full of rebuke. 'You're not a mess. You're being really brave with all this, confronting your past and who you were back then.' She looks at me encouragingly and I smile back.

Bibi's trying her best to be a bit warmer at the moment. Ever since a couple of weeks ago when I told her off in the bathroom. Ooh, maybe I should tell people off a bit more? I'm obviously great at it.

'Genuinely, though,' I begin. 'If nothing else comes of this mission, I'm so happy I've been able to mend fences with Alex.' I stop because I feel suddenly quite emotional. 'She was a childhood friend, Sofia,' I explain. 'And I fucked everything up by sleeping with her for a while. But we talked it all through and it's OK now, it's really OK. Maybe better than ever.'

I can't see her very well but I sense Sofia softening. 'That is beautiful,' she smiles.

'It is,' I grin back. 'She's been over to the flat almost every day these last couple of weeks, catching up on everything. It's like old times, like nothing's really changed.'

'I think that is the test of a true friendship,' Sofia says grandly. 'If you can go without seeing one another for a long time, but when you do, everything is how it was.' I nod heartily even though she can't see me do it.

Beside me, my phone rings. It's Katie from work. I stare at it, a feeling of fear squirming through my stomach.

'Are you not going to answer?' Louise asks gently and I shake my head. I can't face talking to Katie right now. There have been two massive events at the Norris in the last few weeks that I've totally ignored. My poor assistant has been doing everything and I know she wants to talk about an upcoming fiftieth birthday party we haven't even begun to prep for. We need to discuss budget, caterers, how many waiting staff we'll need, what the colour scheme is – all the little details I'm usually buzzing with around a big event. But my head is too busy already; too full of Alistair and Paul and Alex – not to mention all the other exes I've yet to see.

'I can't concentrate on the office at the moment,' I tell the room, guilt pulsing through my voice. Katie can figure it out for now; she's great and I'm sure she can cope.

A silence descends before Bibi turns to our host and asks, 'How are things going with *your* mission, Sofia? With Ivan downstairs, I mean?'

'Ooh, maybe we should invite him up here?' I suggest hopefully. 'He can join in our power cut club. It could be quite romantic for you guys, sitting in the darkness. And then we could bugger off if you start snogging!'

'I don't think there's any point,' Sofia sighs. 'I tried the other night. I invited him up here for tea – I am a shameless hussy! – and he said no! Very nicely, but still no.'

'Hmmm, errr . . .' Louise makes a slightly strangled noise in the dark and I feel the rest of us turn in her direction.

'What?' Bibi sounds accusing.

'Huh?' Louise sounds guilty. 'Um, oh nothing! Well . . . no, nothing!'

Beside me on the settee, Sofia leans in. 'Darling Louise, what? Just say it. Don't worry, I have heard it all, it is impossible to shock me.'

'Ohhh I don't want to say!' she wails and we wait, giving her a moment. 'OK, fine. Um, I'm really sorry, Sofia, but I'm pretty sure Ivan has a girlfriend.'

'What?' I gasp.

'I was chatting to him out the front the other day,' she begins hesitantly. 'He's really warmed up to me at last.' Half in a whisper she adds an aside to me: 'I made a new batch of biscuits and made sure he got them this time.' Her voice returns to a normal volume as she continues. 'Anyway, as we said goodbye, he said he was off to take care of his darling Pearl.'

'Maybe it's his cat,' I suggest a bit lamely.

'It could be!' Bibi jumps in. 'There *is* a cat that hangs around in the garden, I've seen it. A brownish one?'

'Yes, I've seen it too!' I join in enthusiastically. 'Pearl is definitely Ivan's cat.'

There is a long, sad silence and, at last, Sofia sighs. 'You're all terribly sweet, but I'd know if there was a cat living in this house. I'm so allergic, I'd be sneezing even walking past his door.'

'Or maybe he has a literal pearl!' Louise offers half-heartedly. 'He might have a very expensive pearl in his jewellery collection that he loves to polish at night?'

'That sounds very euphemistic,' Bibi mutters but no one laughs.

'Well!' Sofia claps her hands. 'Girlfriend or no, he does not seem interested. *C'est la vie.*'

We fall into sympathetic silence once more.

'At least Esther is falling in love!' Sofia tries to bring the mood back up. 'With Paul, is it? Or Alistair?' She giggles. 'It is good to have options.'

'Alistair's my favourite,' Louise crows from the corner, her face barely visible in the low light. 'He was Esty's first love and I want them to be together sooo much.'

I look down, feeling shy. 'He has a girlfriend, Lou,' I scold lightly. 'And I did throw up all over him, if you remember.'

There is a traumatized silence as Lou and Bibi relive it. 'But'– I breathe in dramatically – 'he did finally message me this morning, and there was no mention of vomit. He wants to grab a coffee soon.' I sigh loudly. 'I don't know, I think he's just enjoying being friends again. Maybe I'm just some sad ego boost for him. The first love who dumped him all those years ago, returning to beg for another chance while he's madly in love with someone else.' I pause. 'Or maybe he really *does* want to be mates.'

'Pfft.' Sofia waves her hand. 'You *have* friends, you don't need more friends.'

'Good point, no more friends,' Bibi says archly. She's not totally over her paranoia or jealousy then. She continues the briefing. 'Then there is Paul, but he's still away on his dumb work trip. Who is next then, Esther? If it was in order, after Paul came Idris, right?' She glances at Sofia. 'That was her serious boyfriend. They were together for three years.'

'Ooof.' I cover my eyes with hot hands. 'I'm not ready for Idris yet, I don't think.'

'Who then?' Louise asks curiously.

'I think,' I say slowly, 'it's time for The Overlap.' Sofia peers at me curiously in the gloom, so I add his name: 'Will.'

EX 6: WILL AKUFFO

AKA The Overlap

PART ONE

The internet

Twitter.com

9.40pm

Will Akuffo @losingthewill · June 10
Genuine question, has anyone ever – literally
ever in the history of wearing clothes – made
use of the spare buttons they put on your
inside label?

Esther Adams @SweetFannyAdams · June 10
I used them once to throw at someone.

Will Akuffo @losingthewill · June 10
Was it effective? Should I inform Bush we finally
discovered some weapons of mass destruction?

Esther Adams @SweetFannyAdams · June 10
What an incredibly up-to-date joke!

Will Akuffo @losingthewill · June 10
Wassssssssssupppppp! Is niiiiiice. Who ya
gonna call?

Esther Adams @SweetFannyAdams · June 10
I stand corrected, you are the very embodiment
of current references.

CHAPTER TWENTY

I'm going to hit her, I'm honestly going to hit her.

'But wheeeeeeeeeeeen are they going to seeeeeeeeee me?' Bibi wails at the ceiling and the entire waiting room turns to look. Or *glare* to be more accurate.

'Probably any minute, babe,' Louise says reassuringly, the patience of a saint.

Bibi lolls onto my lap, looking up at me pleadingly. 'It huuuuuuuuurts, Essssssstheeeeerrrrr!'

'Yes I fucking know,' I hiss. She has been saying the same things for three hours straight, as we wait to be seen by the doctor.

She has what we think is a broken little finger. Which is extra frustrating because – from what we've seen online – there's not even anything the docs can do about it. They'll just strap it up and send her on her way. But she insisted we come all the same, wailing like a banshee for the whole car ride over here.

Nick drove us.

Personally, I was ready to waste money on an Uber, but Louise – embarrassingly – called Nick, claiming it made sense because he's the only person we know with a car and only lives around the corner. He very kindly obliged, turning up looking more dishevelled than ever and – hilariously – in his pyjamas. Which is why he's now waiting outside in the car instead of in here with us. That, and the fact that he understandably didn't want to pay the £65-ish car park charges.

It's the broken toilet's fault. It started doing its stupid overflowing thing again, and while Louise was back on the phone with Lord of the Pricks, AKA our landlord, Bibi decided to take it upon herself to try to fix it once and for all.

Of course, she immediately dropped the hefty ceramic cistern lid on her hand. After a lot of screaming and crying, we got Sofia out of bed to ask her opinion. She gave Bibi the only drugs in the house – some heavy duty Night Nurse – and said we should all go to A&E. We didn't realize until too late that Bibi was secretly downing the entire bottle in the car, and she's been semi-conscious and talking gibberish ever since.

'It huurrrrrrrts, Louiiiiiiiiiiiise,' Bibi starts again. 'Why don't we go see a doctor?'

'We are, love,' Lou shushes her kindly. 'We're just waiting to see someone, it's taking a while.' The receptionist looks over at us disapprovingly and Lou adds quickly, 'Which is not the fault of the NHS! Not at all. It's all those bloody cuts, isn't it!' She tsks loudly before continuing, 'The doctors and nurses and, er, receptionists are all doing brilliant jobs and it makes you proud to be British, doesn't it? Well done, the NHS!'

She glances around for applause from the other waiting room occupants and looks disappointed when she finds none.

'Whasshetalkinbout?' Bibi screws up her face, looking to me but I have no answers. 'When are they going to seeeeee meeeeee?'

I give her a light shove off my lap and back into her own seat. She lollops over us both and seems to pass out.

'Thank god,' I say with a sigh of relief. 'She is such an annoying ill person.'

'I think we probably all are,' Louise says wisely. 'Sorry your night got ruined. What were you up to?'

'I was composing a message to Will, actually,' I admit. 'So much of our relationship was joking about and flirting online, I needed it to be really funny and brilliant, y'know? I sent him a quick something in the end, but it was decidedly *not* funny or brilliant.'

'You met on Facebook or somewhere, right?' Louise squints at me across Bibi's prone body.

I shake my head. 'Twitter. He was just some random funny account I followed, but there was something about him. All I knew about him was that he was clever with 140 characters, and his fuzzy little avatar photo looked handsome.' I sigh. 'At first it was just a bit of silly fun, replying to his hilarious tweets, but then he DM'd me. We started talking a lot after that.'

'It's easy to get carried away with a flirtation like that,' Louise says, a faraway look in her eyes.

I regard her carefully. Lou has been weirdly busy lately; she's hardly been home, and even when she is, she's been locked away in her bedroom.

'GIRLIIIIIIIIIES?' Sofia flounces across the waiting room towards us, accompanied by a half-asleep-looking Nick. They've both been sitting in the car outside for hours, and I feel a sudden shot of horrible guilt over this poor guy, dragged into our dumb drama. Again.

He yawns, covering his unkempt beard with a hand. 'Any news? Has Bibi been in to see the doctors yet?'

Lou and I shake our heads.

'Sofia? Nick?' Bibi blinks up at them before passing out again. It occurs to me this could be the perfect opportunity to find out her real name. All those tall walls are down thanks to the Night Nurse; surely she'd tell me.

But that feels cruel. To take advantage of someone when they're so very vulnerable ... I mean, I wouldn't care but she *is* unconscious.

'*Merde!*' Sofia shouts, stamping a dainty foot. Nick and a few of the patients smirk at her excessive Frenchness. 'Fine,' she yells. 'I'm going back to the car. I have been swiping on Tinder! This hospital is full of men in their seventies. I'm getting hundreds of matches!' She struts out as Lou and I try not to laugh. I guess that means she's over Ivan and good riddance to that.

'Does anyone want a coffee?' Nick asks and I leap out of my seat, my legs creaking from hours sat still.

'Oh god, I do,' I say loudly and he seems amused by my enthusiasm.

Louise looks down anxiously at Bibi in her lap. 'I suppose I'd better stay with Bibi,' she says. 'Please may I have a cappuccino, Nick?' Her voice is high and sweet. He grins and nods goofily at her, pulling his coat tighter over his navy blue plaid PJs. I glance between them for a moment before striding off towards the coffee machine.

'God, it's nearly four,' Nick says as he falls into step with me, sounding a little breathless. 'I don't think I've been up this late since uni.' He smirks, adding, 'You remember?' I feel myself go red – we only really spoke, like, once at Durham and I'm still vaguely embarrassed about quitting the course so early on.

'Not really,' I tell him breezily, feeling a bit hot and cross. 'How's Jackie? You didn't think you'd bring her on this middle-of-the-night excursion?'

He shakes his head. 'Nah, she loves her sleep and gets very grumpy when woken up prematurely. She won't even notice I'm gone.'

'Well, tell her I said hi,' I say, pressing some buttons on the yellowing machine and setting up Lou's paper cup. 'Did your parents approve of her in the end?'

'Adored her,' he confirms, breaking out into a gooey smile. 'I think they officially love her more than they love me now.'

'Quite right,' I nod, handing him his coffee.

He shows me dog photos as we head back, sipping from the molten coffees in a sleepy trance.

'Right, I'm going back out to the car,' he says as we rejoin Lou and a still-unconscious Bibi. 'Call if you need anything.

I'll be asleep on the back seat, but I'll have my phone.' He winks at me. 'The smell of Stilton is almost completely gone now.'

He's left before my face can turn its usual full-throated beetroot.

Louise stares after him and then glances at me, a strange look in her eyes.

'So,' she begins smoothly, 'you were saying about Will? How it started off as just some flirty messages?'

'Yeah,' I nod slowly. 'I was telling myself the whole time that I had no reason to feel bad. This guy was a stranger and it was just some harmless banter! It wasn't like I was cheating on Idris! But something in me knew it wasn't right.' I pause, remembering the first night of DM'ing with Will, where I realized the flirting was getting out of hand. 'Do you remember when Idris had just moved into my room in the flat?' I ask Lou and she nods. 'We'd been together about two and a half years by that point. Things seemed great, he was wonderful, and you and Bibi both adored him.'

'Oh, he was the loveliest flatmate,' she beams. 'He always put the loo seat down and did his washing up. He was great.'

'Better than me,' I agree, feeling sad. 'Anyway, there was a night not long after I'd started flirting with Will, when I heard Iddy arriving home from work. I checked the time and realized I'd been chatting – flirting – with this stranger for literally six hours straight. I remember being shocked and horrified at myself. Like, I knew that wasn't cool or fair to my boyfriend!' I watch Bibi's breathing for a moment. 'And then, when Idris fell asleep, I went right back online and carried on chatting to Will. I hated myself but I couldn't stop.'

Louise doesn't reply for a minute. 'It's understandable,' she says at last.

'But it's not really!' I argue, looking at her askance. 'It was really shitty! I told myself I'd block Will after that – I told myself that so many times – but I didn't. It ended up being just the start of things. Just the start of my awful behaviour.'

In Louise's lap her phone vibrates with a text. She checks, but puts it back quickly, this time face down. I wait for her to say something but she doesn't. She just stares down. 'What were you up to before Bibi ruined everyone's night?' I ask politely.

'Oh, er, nothing,' she says in an odd voice. I glance over again but she's still looking away, taking in the other patients dotted around the waiting room. 'Just chatting to Sven on Zoom.'

'How are things between you guys?' I am genuinely curious.

'Great!' she says too quickly. 'So what are we going to do about Bibi and Alex, eh?'

The distraction works.

Alex has been over a lot in the month or so since we resolved things, and it's been fucking excellent. We're all good friends again. The only problem has been Bibi. She's still being openly hostile and awkward around Alex. Alex tries to make an effort and seems completely bewildered by Bibi's attitude towards her, but hasn't said anything directly to me. I guess she's afraid to rock the boat, same as us. To be honest, Lou and I are at our wit's end.

'I really don't know,' I sigh. 'I've tried really hard to talk to Bibi about it, but she's just so threatened and pissed off about everything. She thinks we're going to be *stolen* by Alex or something. Which would make sense if Alex was being a bitch back, but she's been nothing but lovely to Bibi! It's really juvenile, we're not toys to bicker over.' Between us, Bibi suddenly snores very loudly. 'Do you think maybe she just needs to get some sex, or something?'

'Maybe.' Louise thinks about it for a moment. 'But she's so stubborn about being single. Always insisting she loves it.'

'Maybe we could fix her up with a hot doctor or nurse tonight,' I cackle. 'Might as well make use of the time while we're stuck here.'

'Or maybe we just lock her and Alex in a room together!' Lou sits up eagerly and it knocks her phone in my direction. Before she grabs it, putting it firmly in her bag, I spot what looks like a familiar name on the screen. It was upside down and only a glimpse but it looked a lot like 'Nick'. I only know one Nick, but it couldn't be *that* Nick, not the Nick sitting outside in the car, surely . . .

Bibi wakes with a start. 'I DIDN'T GET THE JOB,' she slur-shouts into the room, before falling asleep again.

'What?' Lou blinks before looking up at me.

'Her job interview last week,' I realize with some sadness.

'Do you think that was true?' Lou asks. 'She didn't tell us that she'd heard anything?' Her phone vibrates in her bag again.

'Me neither,' I say, feeling suddenly so miserable for Bibi. I know she was really hopeful with this one. 'Maybe it's not true. She has drunk a fuck ton of Night Nurse.' I pause. 'But if it is, I really don't know what to say. This job search of hers seems endless, it must be really dragging her down.'

'Even more reason to get her some sex,' Lou smiles, before turning to me thoughtfully. 'Speaking of sex, any word from Paul? And how's your "friendship" with Alistair going?' She giggles impishly, stroking Bibi's arm affectionately as I consider how I will answer her question.

'Paul is still away, but he's texting a lot,' I tell her. 'We'll definitely meet up when he's back. I can't wait, honestly.'

'And Alistair?' she prompts impatiently.

I picture Alistair's lovely face and try not to feel guilty about the feelings it brings up. 'We had a coffee the other day during my lunch break at work. He was telling me about this guy he'd arrested for stealing a milk float and joyriding it all over Hackney.'

Louise gapes. 'Milk floats still exist?' She recovers her composure.

'They deliver artisan cheese,' I say as explanation.

'Did you talk about seeing each other again?'

We did, and I feel a wave of guilt about it and then another at how much I want to see him again. There is something between us, but I'm afraid of what might happen, and how terrible I'd feel if it did, knowing he has someone at home.

Maybe Louise is right, maybe I should stop the mission

now. What if I'm messing with too many lives here? Too many lives and too many emotions.

My own life seems to be crumbling a bit, as well, to be honest. Not one of my exes has confessed their undying love to me, my friends are both acting weirdly, and work is terrible. I've been trying to get my head back in the game, but I know it's obvious to my colleagues that I'm not really as invested as I was before all this. I am handing more and more off to my assistant, who I can tell is getting increasingly pissed off with me.

But you have to break eggs to make an omelette or whatever, right?

And so what if I don't like omelettes?

'BIBI COLMER?' A nurse appears before us.

'Yes, that's us!' I leap up, waving, while Lou tries to resurrect our unconscious patient. Bibi stirs but waves us away.

'Come with me, please, Ms Colmer,' the nurse instructs, looking disapprovingly at his messy patient.

Bibi wakes up a little more, looking around and taking in her surroundings.

'Where's Sofia?' she slurs sleepily. 'And Nick?'

'Waiting for us in the car.' I try not to sound too annoyed. 'Come on, time to see the doctor you demanded.'

'No.' Bibi wakes up properly at last, eyeballing the nurse. 'Thanks for your service, Mr Medical Professional, but I don't need to see anyone. It doesn't hurt anymore.' She wiggles her supposedly broken finger for us. 'We're going home.'

Without another word, she breaks free from our helping

hands, staggering off towards the exit and leaving Lou and I to apologize. Typical.

In my bag my phone vibrates twice in a row. Two messages at once! I feel abuzz with dopamine.

One is from Paul. He's back in London at long last next week and wants to meet.

And the other? The other is from Will.

EX 6: WILL AKUFFO

AKA The Overlap

PART TWO

The flat

My bed

6.10pm

I have never really seen Idris angry before. Which is why I
don't immediately recognize it as such.

'What is this?' He's standing over the bed, his eyebrows
knotted together.

'What's what?' I sigh, exhausted from a long day of work.
Although this kind of exhaustion doesn't even come close to
the way I felt coming home from those long days in the kitchen. I throw my bag down, already wondering if the CVs in
there can wait until the morning. I'm looking for an assistant,
mandated by the bosses who have finally acknowledged my

need for one. I've never had an assistant before – unless you count the kitchen porters who generally told me to fuck off if I asked them to do anything. I'm so excited! I cannot wait for the interview stages so I can be really stern and ask pointless power trip questions about where they see themselves in five years. I'm going to be the best boss.

Flopping onto the bed, I turn and reach for Idris. I want a hug. He moves away and it's my turn to frown.

'What's wrong, baby?' I sit back up, worried now.

He nudges the laptop I hadn't noticed between us on the bed. 'Who is *Will*?' He turns to watch my face and I try not to react. Stay blank. I've done nothing wrong. Nothing wrong *technically*.

'Will?' I screw up my brow as if trying to identify the name. 'What Will?'

'@ Losing the Will!' Idris looks impatient. 'The guy you follow on Twitter! You've been messaging each other on direct message, flirting non-stop for weeks.'

'What?' I match his angry tone. 'What are you talking about? And what the hell are you doing, going through my computer?'

'The laptop was open when I came in.' He waves this away. 'All your messages to each other were right there on the screen.' He starts pacing up and down the room and I feel cold. 'What the hell is going on with this guy, Esther? You message each other constantly. And please don't try to pretend it's not flirtatious.' He stops and puts a hand over his mouth before mumbling the next part. 'Are you sleeping with him?'

I leap up off the bed, the offending laptop bouncing lightly on the covers. 'Jesus, Idris, *no*. I've never even met him!' I put my hand on his arm and he shakes it off, still unable to look at me. 'I swear to you. He's just a mate, honestly. It's a bit of silliness online but I don't even really know him. We're just online friends who chat a bit. It's nothing, really!' I pull at Idris's sleeve and see him take a big, shuddery breath in.

When he finally looks up, his eyes are a little red.

'You swear nothing's happened between you?' He looks deeply into my eyes and I nod emphatically.

'On my life, I swear we're just friends. Really really. And I'm allowed to have male friends, aren't I?' I sound defensive now but it works. Idris looks alarmed.

'Of course you are!'

He clenches his jaw. 'I just ... I don't know, I just felt like some of those messages crossed the line.' He pauses, looking worried. 'But maybe I'm overreacting. And I know I shouldn't have read your private messages ... I'm sorry, Est, I don't—'

My heart is pounding. 'It was nothing more than what you saw there on Twitter.' Apart from the texts and photos.

'Please believe me, baby.' I reach for his arm, touching him lightly. 'I wouldn't cheat on you. I would *never* cheat on you, it's horrible. I promise I haven't and wouldn't. I swear it's completely platonic!'

He nods after a moment and I pull him in for a hug. We hold each other for the next few minutes, not speaking, just squeezing and smelling. Our breathing falls in sync, slowing down together, but my heart continues to pump loudly, roaring in my ears.

I feel like I'm standing on the edge of a cliff, and I don't want to jump, but I also know I'm going to keep edging forward until there is no other choice.

CHAPTER TWENTY-ONE

'So you're saying you want to start a doggy daycare' – he's laughing so hard – 'that's based on a boat and it'll be called ...'

'Noah's Bark!' I finish for him, delightedly. 'Yes, we'll sail around, picking up your dogs every morning, and then return them at night. Of course, a person would have to live near the river to use our services ...'

'Of course,' he nods, eyes bright.

'Isn't it brilliant?' I ask eagerly. 'Do you want to invest in Noah's Bark? We're open to investors but we're not going to be sharing literally any of the profits.'

'Who is *we*?' Laughing, Paul raises an eyebrow at me, and the action is so unbelievably sexy that for a moment I can't remember what I was saying.

'Um,' I swallow. 'Ahem, er, well, *we* is me and my board of directors.'

'Your board of directors?' He wipes his eyes a little and takes another sip of his sherry.

'Yes,' I nod. 'They're not entirely real, but they make me and my business sound way more profesh.'

'Oh my god, you make me laugh so much.' He sits back in his chair, looking at me hard. He has this knack of looking at a person like there is no one else in the entire world. No one that matters as much as me, at least. 'How are you *this* hot, Esther Adams, and yet also so funny and great?'

I shrug. 'Obviously I had a huge trust fund that hit my bank account at twenty-one, which enabled me to have every available cosmetic surgery on the market. And a few from the black market too.'

'Any from the farmers' market?' he asks seriously and I crack up.

I ponder this. 'Actually, they probably have all kinds of cool goat gall bladder-type stuff the A-listers would eat whole for younger-looking skin. Gwyneth would snap that shit up for Goop in a second. We should've searched harder in Milton Keynes!'

He bursts out laughing again.

Somehow, I am *funny* around Paul. Properly funny. He makes me funny. And I know it's hot – even *I* fancy me.

'God, you're so fucking cool and sexy,' he tells me again.

The chemistry between us is palpable, everything in me is reacting to him. I should be wearing a Tena Light right now.

After what seems like a lifetime of waiting for him to get back from his trip, Paul and I are finally out for our much-waited-for second meet-up. And we've been celebrating with an intense bar crawl, finally settling on this pub two hours ago. The whole thing has been ... well, magic. There's no other word for it. There's been no lull in conversation, no awkwardness, just endless flirty, silly, fun chat. And a *lot* of staring at each other longingly. We could power the national grid with the electricity crackling between us.

A part of me feels weird, sitting here, liking this man so much, when I'm also messaging Alistair and Will. Is it OK? Is it unfair on Paul? Or unfair on all of them? Is it a form of cheating? The blurred line is getting finer and fainter all the time.

The texts with Will have been flying thick and fast since the other day in A&E. Back and forth easy banter. It's exactly like old times. But now I don't have a boyfriend to distract me, it's easier, and even more intense. I looked up @losingthewill on Twitter last night. He's still on there and his charm and intellect felt all too familiar and seductive.

There was no mention of a partner, but then there probably wouldn't be. Twitter isn't the place you share your engagement photos, it's where you ruin jokes for strangers by pointing out how problematic everything is.

'Ah Esther, you'll laugh at me.' Paul covers his eyes, shy all of a sudden. 'I've just realized how much you look like a classic Hollywood film star called Greta Garbo. Obviously I mean back when she was young and glamorous.'

That's weird, I'm sure he said that last time. I remember because the only thing I know about Greta Garbo is that she had very thin, nineties eyebrows. He said it exactly like that, too – all shy and sweet. We talked about it for ages, it's strange he forgot.

But we're all repeating the same shit every time we open our mouths really, aren't we? Half of my relationship with Idris was just nodding nicely when he told me the same story yet again. And I expect he'd say the same about my chat.

Paul reaches to take my hand across the table. His skin on mine sends something undefinable running through my whole body. With his thumb he rubs the back of my hand, all the while looking at me like I'm the only person who ever existed. The blood roars in my ears. I fancy him *so* much.

Will and I don't have anything like this. This, with Paul, *this* is real. And if I have to sacrifice the mission – Will included – to get a chance of love with Paul, that's a decent price to pay.

Fuck it, I'm going to be brave. I'm going to say it. We've already lost so much time. So many years of date nights we could've had; so many dinners, so many cinema visits, all that sex we've missed out on, all that lying around in bed, teasing each other and bickering over who's going to get up to make tea. We've missed so much together through bad timing, I can't let us miss another chance now.

'Paul' – I gulp down some air – 'I have to just say this. I think we both know there's something between us. It's obvious to anyone that we fancy each other like mad, but it's more than that. We get on so well and have so much fun. I think we should give things a go, don't you? A few dates, a few snogs — let's see if this thing between us can become something real and amazing?'

There is a silence, potent with anticipation. I try to read his expression, wondering whether he is going to kiss me or speak first. God, I hope he kisses me, I've wanted to kiss him for so long.

His mouth opens and I smile sweetly until I understand the words.

'I'm really sorry, Esther, I don't feel like that. I don't want to date you.'

What.

'I'm sorry if I gave you the wrong impression,' he stutters, looking down at the table. 'I just thought we were good friends.' What what what. No, what?

The crushing humiliation piles down on me and I feel my face burn as he continues. 'Sure, we flirt a tiny bit sometimes, but I didn't realize you thought it was more than that. It's just the way we are together, isn't it? We're both flirts, it's just some fun.'

Oh my god oh my god oh my god this is so embarrassing. How could I . . .? I'm so dumb, so stupid. My throat is dry and I grab at my drink for something to do. My hands shake as I throw back sour wine. How could I have got this so fucking wrong? Have I completely lied to myself? Made up all those moments? Read something into the way he flirted and complimented and constantly touched me?

Something tickles at the back of my mind. Something vague and unformed.

He regards me anxiously. 'I honestly had no idea you felt like that, Esther, I'm sorry. But I really, really don't want to lose this friendship. Please can we forget this? Pretend the last few minutes never happened and go back to having fun? You mean so much to me. Please?' He grabs for my hand again, squeezing it. That's not a friend thing, is it?

Ah. There it is. The click.

'Um, Paul.' I swallow another large mouthful of acidic wine, extracting my hand. 'Do you have a lot of female friends?'

He frowns. 'I guess so, sure.'

'And are they mostly single?'

His forehead creases further. 'Well, er, yeah, mostly.'

'And' – I lean in – 'are they, like, mates with each other, or do you mostly just meet up with them one-on-one?'

He shifts in his seat, looking uncomfortable. 'Er, one-on-one, but what does that matter? What's it got to do with anything?'

I nod, the truth hitting me way too hard. He's a Collector. He's a fucking Collector. I have been so blind, of *course* he's a Collector. He's one of those boys who likes to keep a harem of women around him, all half in love with him, to worship at his feet. But he doesn't want to actually *be* with them, that's too much bother. He'll see them each individually, making them feel so special and loved. He'll have the thrill of a one-evening girlfriend, without any of the commitment or the in-laws or the birthday present buying. He might even *have* a girlfriend on the side, but she'll never meet any of his 'female friends', and they'll never meet her. But she'll be wielded as a weapon if any of them forget their place and ask for more from him. And that's why it feels like he's reusing the same lines sometimes – because he *does*. He probably has a bloody filing system to keep track of all his women.

I feel like such a fool. Because I should know better – I've seen Collectors around, loads of them. I remember Lou being in thrall to one many years ago and it took us ages to get her away from him. But I hadn't realized Paul was one! I guess because there were always legitimate reasons for us not to get together until now.

He doesn't want to date me, he doesn't want to date any of these women he flirts with and keeps on a string. But he wants the *option* of it. He wants to know that in every direction is another lovelorn female who hangs on his every word. Oh my god, I can't believe I was one of them. For *ages*! What an idiot.

'Please can we keep being friends, Esther?' He reaches to take my hands in his again but the electricity is gone now. I recognize him for what he is and it has freed me. Suddenly he's not so dazzling, not so attractive. He's just a little man in need of an ego stroke. He made me feel wanted and fancied for so long, but I wasn't wanted or fancied. Now I know the truth, his big shoulders have lost their lustre.

'Esther?' He looks anxious. 'Really, I adore you, and nothing has to change. We can still have fun and flirt, it doesn't have to change. I really don't want to lose you.'

'Obviously you don't,' I say pleasantly. 'I'm sure I've been one of your most ardent fans. One of your most prized collector's items.'

He frowns. 'What do you mean?'

'Never mind,' I say breezily. 'Right, no harm done. To me, at least. Your poor other collectibles, I hope they're released one day, too.' I wave at the table server. 'Shall we get the bill? I just realized I paid the whole bill last time – and the few times before, actually – so how about you get this one?' He looks alarmed and I give him a friendly pat on the shoulder. 'Bye, Paul, it's been nice to see you, if only because I got to realize that you were never a Missed Chance. You never would've happened. *We* never would've happened.' I stand up, feeling powerful and sure of myself at long last. 'Thanks for all the laughs. Although they were mostly provided by me, actually.' I pause. 'But you did boost my ego from time to time, so I can be grateful to you for that.' His mouth hangs open as I give him a small wave. 'See ya, don't message me again.' I sail out the door, just as the bill lands on our table.

CHAPTER TWENTY-TWO

'I'm actually feeling weirdly cheerful!' I stick the vase in the loo, letting it fill with water and then emptying the whole thing into the bath. Lou watches me with interest.

'You're serious? After everything that happened with Paul? All that build-up, only to realize he's a big old user?' She looks anxious as I fill the vase up again with over-flowing water.

The toilet is doing its usual thing and Louise and I are in a stalemate over who will call the landlord. Bibi is the only one who can make him listen but she's MIA.

'Yes,' I nod, really meaning it. 'For real! I am sort of sad it didn't work out and I know I should be humiliated by the rejection, but for some reason I don't feel that way.'

She blinks at me, clearly baffled. After all, we are people who are usually humiliated by the smallest thing.

'It was always hanging over me – the Paul question,' I try to explain. 'Like, I always blamed myself for it never happening between us. And even if I'd met someone and they were my soulmate, I think a small part of my brain would've always wondered if Paul was even more of a soulmate, you know what I mean? I actually rejected a great guy once because I was so sure things were about to happen with Paul. Now I know!' I beam at Lou across the toilet. 'And I genuinely feel like I've had a bit of a lucky escape. Imagine dating Paul! All those women pals he cultivates to be half in love with him! It would be a constant power struggle, with him always gaslighting me about his "friends". Making out like I was nuts for worrying about it being more than that.'

'Like you did with Idris about Will!' It's out of her mouth as the thought occurs, and her face falls immediately. 'Oh god, sorry, Esther. I didn't mean that. I'm really sorry. Obviously you're nothing like Collector Paul. He's a game player, you were just in a crappy situation.'

'No, you're right,' I say in a small voice. 'I did do that to Idris, and I feel like shit about it.' I pause, my head hanging. 'I remember one time when he found some messages between Will and me, he asked me about it and I got angry. Or rather, I *pretended* to be angry – what kind of person does that? I threw it in his face that he shouldn't be reading my messages. I accused him of being some kind of jealous child snooping through my private computer. Then I accused him of getting upset because I was friends with a boy.' I sigh. 'It was just to buy time, to give me a minute to shove down my guilt and redirect the conversation. But the truth is I fucking *knew* I was crossing a line. I knew perfectly well that I was doing something wrong. But I didn't want to stop. I liked the ego boost and the fireworks I got from Will too much. I loved Idris, but flirting with a stranger like that was such a thrill.' I glance up at Lou, who looks shifty. 'At one point in that argument, he even said *sorry* to me, Lou. To *me*! I made him feel like he was mad. I can't deny it, I fully gaslit him and I'm deeply ashamed of it.'

She swallows hard but doesn't say anything, just rubs my arm kindly.

'I worry sometimes that I'm a bad person,' I say at last in a whisper.

'You're not,' she says in a quiet but fervent voice. 'You've done some bad things – we all have – but it doesn't make you a bad person.' She takes a long breath. 'Do you think it's a good idea to contact Idris? I mean, you went through so much together. I mean ...' She pauses. 'Maybe it's time to take a break from the mission altogether?'

Before I can answer, my phone vibrates and I snort when I see the message.

Will (Twitter)
Have you ever had to do a wee sample at the doctor's? How much do you think you're meant to fill the sample pot they give you? Any less than half feels stingy, but full feels like you're showing off, right?
4.21pm

I show Louise and she gives a slightly grossed-out half-smile. 'Well, if you're not going to quit, what *about* Will?' she says, taking the vase off me and scooping up the water. It's not her turn yet but I was doing a very poor job – there's water all over the floor. 'Are you ever going to meet up, or is it just set to be flirty messages until the end of time?'

I make a sort of groaning noise and perch on the bath, getting splashed a little as she empties. 'I'm just worried,' I admit. 'Last time we were so unbelievably great on messages – there was so much chemistry online – and then it was only *OK* when we finally met up.'

'But you dated for, like, five, six months, didn't you?'

'Yes, but that was a guilt relationship.'

'A guilt relationship?' She cocks her head at me curiously.

'You know, because I felt like I'd led him on. Like, I'd led everyone on. I made out like he was amazing and worth ruining things with Idris over. I couldn't end it two seconds later and come running back, tail between my legs. I had to pretend it was good for a while.'

She nods, understanding.

'But if he's that lame in real life, maybe it's not worth meeting up with him?' she suggests, and I sigh.

'That's the trouble though, Lou,' I say. 'He wasn't *lame* per se. He was just . . . fine. Like, it was all perfectly nice and perfectly ordinary between us. There was no real reason *not* to like him. And no real reason *to* like him.'

'Those are the worst!' she cries and I nod, knowing she's

been there. And we both know sometimes those relationships are the hardest to leave.

'But maybe Will's changed?' I sigh again. '*I've* changed in the last few years, haven't I? And that's the whole point of this exercise, isn't it? To see if any of my exes had anything I missed.' I pause, and put my hand out for the vase. She lets me take it. 'I was absolutely fucking heartbroken over what had happened with Iddy, and had to pretend I wasn't – because it was my fault we'd ended. It was my decision, so I felt like I wasn't allowed to grieve for him. That's the trouble with overlapping relationships, you're suddenly with someone new and having to pretend you're totally over the last person. So maybe I didn't give Will a fair shot in those five months we were together.'

'I guess that makes sense,' she nods, wiping her hands on the towel.

'Anyway, he suggested we FaceTime this week.' I feel nerves jangling in my stomach at my own words. 'So I might end up meeting up with him in real life after that. And y'know, if he's mega lame and boring, or repeating old *Seinfeld* jokes during the call, we can just leave it there.'

'*Seinfeld*?' Lou screws up her face and I wave her confusion away.

'He does that. I think most of his jokes are stolen from *Seinfeld*.'

We fall into companionable silence: filling, emptying, vaguely enjoying the sloshing noise as we up-end the vase into the bath. There's something kind of satisfying – something cathartic – about the process.

'This vase was a good idea,' Lou comments lightly. 'Much better than using a cup.'

I narrow my eyes at her. 'What cup were you using?' She looks guilty for a minute.

'Oh, er, definitely not yours.' She doesn't meet my gaze. 'Just one of Sven's old mugs, I swear.'

'Hmm.' I eyeball her too hard, missing the bath and emptying most of the toilet water on my own feet. Serves me right.

EX 6: WILL AKUFFO

AKA The Overlap

PART THREE

Will's house

His uncomfortable bed

12.47am

'That was great!' I smile over at Will, slightly breathless.
'Really great!'

Across the bed, he grins back. 'It really was! You're amazing! I'm so glad you're here.' He reaches over to kiss me on
the cheek. It's tender and sweet, and it makes my heart ache.
But not for him, for Idris.

But that will fade, I know it will. I've done the right
thing. Breaking up with Idris was the *right thing*. We had
a good time, a decent innings, as they say. Three years is a
long time to be with someone! And I'm only twenty-seven;

it's too young to be talking marriage and babies and all that forever stuff.

Plus, being with Will, it's worth all this drama. We have a real connection – something special. I definitely like him. A lot! Definitely.

He runs his forefinger along my collar bone and down, landing the tip on my nipple.

'Boop!' he says, flicking it lightly.

I wince. 'Please don't do that,' I whisper, wishing I could cover up my nakedness, but not wanting to seem shy.

'Sorry,' he says awkwardly. 'My ex liked it.'

I smile quickly to make up for any irritation in my voice. 'They're just a bit sensitive.' I pause. 'Because of the great sex we just had.'

He nods, self-satisfied, and I breathe out, relieved.

I mean, I probably won't have to fake it for long! Everyone has to fake it at the beginning anyway, don't they? It takes time, y'know, to get used to each other's bodies and quirks. And to having your nipple flicked for some reason. No way did his ex actually like that.

He rolls over, looking up at me. His used-up little penis flops onto his thigh and I try not to look.

OK, so being with Will has been … an adjustment. But adjusting doesn't have to be a bad thing! Life is all about change. He's not Idris, that's all. He has a different face and a different body and a different penis. I will get used to it – to *him* – and I will grow to love it. I mean him.

We've only been seeing each other for a few weeks now.

209

A few weeks since I broke up with Idris and went running into Will's arms. And so far it's all . . . fine! He's really nice, and very considerate. It's fine. It's good. Actually, it's great!

Will switches on the telly and a late-night repeat of *Everybody Loves Raymond* comes on. Yuck.

I snuggle into him, feeling and enjoying his warmth. He circles an arm around me and I breathe him in.

See, this is all definitely, definitely, *definitely* worth it.

CHAPTER TWENTY-THREE

'Do you think I' – puff puff puff – 'look like the type of person who would kidnap your child?'

'I don't have a child,' Bibi observes, barely breathing harder than usual.

'Thanks for the pedantry, Beelzebub.' I huff heavily some more. 'OK, do I look' – pant pant – 'like someone who would kidnap *a* child?'

'No, definitely not,' Louise manages to get out between gasps.

'WHAT ARE YOU SAYING?' At the end of the row, Alex shouts over the music in her headphones.

'That's a relief.' Puff puff puff. 'It's just that as we arrived here earlier' – I tap some buttons and slow the tread-mill down a few degrees so I can speak properly – 'some woman was leaving the gym with her little girl and she looked right at me in this really accusing way, you guys. And then she yanked her kid closer to her as I went by, eyeing me suspiciously the whole time. Like I was going to kidnap her daughter. And that's not even the first time it's happened. Parents are constantly pulling their kids away from me!'

'I saw that woman!' Bibi confirms. 'Her child wasn't even cute, why would you kidnap it? She *wishes* someone would want to kidnap it.'

'Who brings their child to the gym?' Louise joins me in slowing the pace down. She's sweating just as much as me, which is reassuring. I thought I was easily the most unfit of the four of us.

'WHAT HAPPENED?' Alex yells, still not taking out her headphones.

'But actually, I mean' – Bibi is still jogging; she looks a bit hot but she's not even sweating – 'you don't know what a kid kidnapper looks like these days, do you? And you *do* have quite starey eyes.' She regards me suspiciously from her treadmill and I glare back. Then I remember glaring will make my eyes even starier and stop.

'Why would starey eyes make you a criminal?' Louise is now sauntering on her machine.

'WHERE'S AN ANIMAL?' Alex yells, still chewing gum, even during workouts.

Bibi shrugs.

'So now I look like a child murderer *and* I have creepy eyes,' I muse. 'That's good to know.' I examine myself in the wall-sized mirrors in front of all the exercise machines. It is not a pretty sight. I'm not quite as red as Lou, but I'm still pretty disgusting. A big dark ring of sweat circles the neck of my t-shirt, and my hair has plastered itself in clumps around the edge of my face.

'No one said child *murderer*.' Bibi sounds exasperated. 'You only look like you'd *take* the child. But I reckon you'd just walk it to the park and give it ice cream. Then get bored when it whined and give it right back.'

'Aw, thank you, Bibi!' I give her a winning smile as I turn off the machine. It beeps in protest and I silently tell it to go fuck itself. 'I'm going to do some rowing – anyone want to join me?'

'IT'S SNOWING?' Alex shouts, looking baffled.

We go to the gym very much once in a blue moon, and only when we can all go together for support. Without peer pressure, I don't think I would ever exercise. We even invited Sofia today but she has another Tinder date. She seems to be having a great time since the hospital. She's having more dates than me, and I'm mostly happy for her. I'm really trying to get my jealousy thing under control.

'I'm coming!' Lou leaps off her machine, almost tripping over as she does, and then pokes at Alex. 'ROWING NOW,' she mouths, pointing at the nearby machines. Alex removes her headphones and joins us, wiping sweat off her brow.

'What did I miss?' she asks. 'Were we talking about Esther's mission? Have you met up with Will yet?'

'Obviously not,' Bibi snaps, rolling her eyes. Lou and I exchange glances, quickly taking the middle two rowing machines between them.

'Well, no,' I add swiftly. 'Will and I are still texting a lot, but a big part of me feels like that relationship is, and would always be – I dunno – *tainted*. I know it doesn't make a lot of sense, but every time I think about him, I feel these horrible stabs of guilt.' I pause. 'I never thought I'd be a cheater, never ever ever ever. But when it happened, it all felt way too inevitable. Like I had no control, no say in it.' I look down at the machine, ashamed of myself. 'I know that's just an excuse. But that night it happened, that's what I kept telling myself.'

'How did it actually happen?' Alex frowns, looking intrigued.

I sigh. 'Well, we'd been messaging for weeks and things were getting out of control flirty. He'd been asking to meet up for ages and I kept saying no. And then one night, I was out for some drinks with my assistant, Katie, who was brand new at the time. We'd had a week-long conference at the museum that had ended that day and we wanted to celebrate. I was sort of *determined* to get really drunk – forcing down glass after glass of Prosecco. It's pretty obvious now that I wanted an excuse to do what I did.'

I pick up my towel to dab at my sweaty forehead. It's an obvious excuse to wipe my eyes, which are starting to well up. Louise reaches over to stroke my back, getting a palm full of sweat for her trouble.

'Anyway,' I continue, trying to regain some composure, 'I *let* myself be drunk. I *let* myself get in an Uber to Will's house. I *let* myself kiss him when he opened the door. And I *let* myself fall into his bed right away. I kept telling myself it was all happening *to* me. I had no control, I was just some passive victim of fate and destiny.' I roll my eyes. 'And the shitty thing was that I had no control over the horrendous guilt that arrived afterwards, either. Which is why I went home right away and told Idris.'

'At least you told him,' Bibi says in something close to a comforting voice.

I nod slowly. 'But that's also why I was so determined to make it work with Will. I kept telling myself he was fantastic and everything was brilliant between us. Like, it had to work! Because it *had* to be worth all that pain. He had to be worth it.'

We fall silent. I reach forward to fiddle with the settings of my machine, avoiding their looks. I am afraid they will be accusing, or – worse – pitying.

'Well, so what about The Serious One, have you contacted him yet?' Alex tries to reset the mood.

I shake my head. 'I haven't contacted him, but to be fair to me, I actually don't have a number. I deleted it after we broke up.'

'Didn't you write it down somewhere?' Alex asks, pulling hard on her machine.

'Who writes down a phone number?' Bibi snarks, fiddling with her own row settings. We ignore her.

'He's not on social media,' I explain. 'He never was. And the only email address I have for him is an old work one. I know he doesn't work there anymore, so I'm not sure what to do.' I sneak a look at Lou. She's yanking on her machine, pointedly not involved in the chat.

'Wait, doesn't Sven have a number or an email?' Bibi suggests, leaning forward to look at Lou, who slows down. She doesn't say anything so I do.

'Um, yeah, Sven would do . . .' I feel very uncomfortable.

'Why would Sven have it?' Alex glances up as she reties a shoelace.

'He's still friends with Idris,' I explain carefully. 'They've been mates for a long time – since school. Idris and I actually set Sven and Louise up on their first date, back when we were together.'

'So?' Bibi looks over at Louise expectantly. Louise finally looks up.

'Ohhhhh, it's just so awkward, OK?!' she wails. 'Idris was so devastated when you ended things. Sven always says it took him ages to get over you. I feel baaaaaad!'

Shame washes over me. 'I'm sorry, Lou, I don't want to put you in the middle of things.'

'Honestly, Sven won't even talk to *me* about Idris!' She flicks her sweaty ponytail away from her shoulder. 'We haven't really ever discussed him since you guys split. I asked him about Iddy when you started this mission and he point-blank said he wasn't going to get involved and I shouldn't either. He said something about ethical firewalls.'

'Bit self-righteous,' Bibi sniffs.

'What about Alistair?' Lou clutches for something. 'He's still on the table, isn't he?'

'I'm seeing Alistair for another *friends* thing soon.' I resist the urge to roll my eyes. 'It's been a couple of months now and he hasn't confessed his undying love or anything. Plus, hullo, girlfriend, remember?'

'Apart from Idris' – Bibi pulls hard on her machine, still not breaking a sweat – 'you only have Carl the Work Mistake and Rich the Bastard left now, right?' She leans forward to look pointedly at Lou. 'Do we *really* want her to move onto Rich the Bastard already?'

'Oh fine!' Louise dramatically throws her rowing handle down. 'I'll give you Iddy's email address. Let's just do this.'

'Right now?!' My voice is panicked as I stop rowing too suddenly, almost falling off the seat.

'Why not?' Bibi says, picking my phone up from its dumped spot on my sweaty towel. 'Do it now or you might lose the nerve. Plus, we can crowdsource what to say.'

'Are you ladies actually using these rowing machines?' The shadow of some huge, muscle-bound monster coats us in darkness and we turn en masse to look up at him.

'Yes, we are,' Bibi replies calmly, unmoving on her machine. Louise starts half-heartedly pulling at her rower, while Alex stares Arnie out. I hide my face in my phone until he's gone, always the bravest.

He grunts and leaves, back to the weights corner from whence he came.

'Maybe we should get up?' Lou whispers and Alex poo-poos her.

'No way! We've paid the same to be here as him, and his lot always make us feel unwelcome in the weights section, so fuck him.'

I sneak a glance at Bibi, knowing she would agree, but she stays silent, fiddling again on her machine. It will take a lot for her to admit she's starting to like Alex, but I have faith it will happen. Eventually.

I open my emails and Lou reads out the address. Honestly, I could've guessed it annoyingly easily.

New Message
To: Idris.Abara@gmail.com
From: estherthechef98234@hotmail.co.uk
Subject: Entente Cordiale

Hey Iddy,

                                                    Sent from my iPhone

'Wait, is *Iddy* too personal?' I look up to three heads too close to mine.

'Yes,' they all confirm at once.

'Oh.' I feel silly already and we're only two words in. Maybe I should've waited to do this at home without all these eyes.

New Message
To: Idris.Abara@gmail.com
From: estherthechef98234@hotmail.co.uk
Subject: Entente Cordiale

Hey Idris,

I hope it's OK to email you out of the blue. I'm so
sorry if it isn't, I don't want to bring anything bad
up for you.

Sent from my iPhone

'That's a bit too much, I think,' Alex notes. 'We don't want
him to think you see him as some kind of broken mess, all
these years later.'

'I agree,' Lou nods, while Bibi grimaces.

'OK,' I sigh, deleting. This could take a while.

New Message
To: Idris.Abara@gmail.com
From: estherthechef98234@hotmail.co.uk
Subject: Entente Cordiale

Hey Idris,

I hope it's OK to email you out of the blue. I know it's
been a couple of years since we last spoke, and I
completely understand if you'd rather leave it like that.
But I was wondering how you are and how your life is
going. It would be really nice to meet up for a coffee
sometime and catch up. I'd love to see you.

Let me know what you think.

Love Esther x

Sent from my iPhone

'I think that's good!' Alex pronounces.

'Maybe take out the "I'd love to see you" part,' Bibi pouts. 'I'm worried it comes off as too keen. You don't want him to think you want to get back together or anything.'

'But what if she *does* want to get back with him?' Lou asks anxiously.

'Well, that's one of those bridges that can be crossed etc.,' Bibi says with a wave of her hand.

'It would genuinely be lovely to see him and talk to him,' I say a little dreamily. 'It's so strange when you break up with a long-term partner. You go from knowing every incon-sequential bit of information about their daily lives – their haemorrhoids are back! A cat looked at them funny! – to nothing at all. He could be married for all I know.'

'Surely Sven would've told you that much?' Alex looks to Lou a bit anxiously. Louise makes a face.

'I don't know.' She gives me a worried arm squeeze. 'I hope he would've. But he's very protective of his friends, I just don't know.'

'Well, he can't have changed *that* much,' I say, defiantly hitting send. 'He was always the nicest, kindest man, and I was an immature little brat who didn't deserve him. I wasn't ready for everything he was offering back then. But maybe I am now.'

'Really?' Bibi looks at me askance and I nod confidently. 'Really.'

EX 5: IDRIS ABARA

AKA The Serious One

PART ONE

St Albans Crematorium

Sixth row of the chapel

1.55pm

'What about this one?' I stage-whisper.

Lou squints, trying to see his face in the small blurry photo. 'Has he only got one picture? It's not very clear.'

I take the phone back and swipe. 'Only that one,' I confirm and she makes a face.

'Nah, sack him off. You can't trust only one picture.'

'Agreed.' I send his profile to the no pile. 'What about this guy? He has a few options and looks relatively normal.'

'So did Ted Bundy,' Bibi says too loudly, the other side of me.

'SHUSSSSSSHHHHH,' someone a few rows back hisses.

Lou takes my phone again to look closer. 'Oh, I think I dated him.' She flicks through the rest of the shots, nodding. 'Yep, definitely. He was a funny one. Brought Wotsits along on the date and sat there, crunching away and stinking of cheese.' She leans closer. 'Not just one little packet either. A full-on multi-pack of twelve, and he didn't even offer me one.'

'That is so rude!' Bibi declares too loudly again as the shusher gives us another spitty telling off.

'OK, he's a no then,' I sigh and retrieve my phone from Lou. 'Ooh, this one? He sounds very together.' I show them both a shot of a guy in his university graduate gown.

'Believe me,' Bibi rolls her eyes, 'finishing uni does not mean you have it together.'

'But *you* do!' I protest. 'You've got your awesome, cool marketing job and it's all going so well. You love it, don't you?'

'I do love it,' she says carefully. 'But I don't think the company is doing that well. They keep threatening redundancies – it doesn't make you feel very secure.'

'They wouldn't get rid of you!' Lou whispers, outraged. 'You're brilliant.'

'No one is indispensable,' Bibi says ominously, taking my phone. 'And this guy looks like a doofus. All he's put in his bio is that he's got two degrees and is studying for another. How tedious is that?'

'I think someone *too* clever might be a bit intimidating,' Lou adds anxiously.

Quite right. Bub-bye.

'What about this guy?' Lou is examining the phone over my shoulder. 'He's very handsome, and sounds nice enough. Plus, I haven't dated him!' She looks a bit put out for a minute. 'In fact, hey! Why hasn't he come up on my Tinder?'

'Yeahhhh.' I regard the picture lighting up my screen. 'I've seen him on my Hinge, my Bumble, on Match.com, on eHarmony, on Guardian Soulmates and now on Tinder. He seems nice but maybe ... I dunno, a bit basic? I know he's really handsome, but I'm not sure I actually fancy him, y'know?'

'Pleeeeeease be quiet!' the person behind us hisses again and Lou and I glance guiltily at each other. I put my phone away, while Bibi sighs aggressively.

We're here at my Great-Uncle Merton's funeral and I know we're being unbelievable dicks, but there's, like, six people here – including the vicar. My mum and dad are in front of us, and have been chatting to Great-Uncle Merton's next-door neighbour about *Bake Off* throughout the whole thing. The only other people here are carers from his home. Personally, I only met the guy once, when I was a teenager, and he called me 'Sonny' the whole time.

We are quiet for another few minutes, listening to the vicar talk about the years Merton spent living in Wales (where – from what Mum says – he used to shout at Welsh people the whole time, for daring to speak – you guessed it – Welsh). Oops, now the vicar is calling him Michael. That must be his next gig.

'I think you should give that guy a chance.' Louise leans

close, this time properly whispering. 'I mean, you never know and he seems like a decent choice. I know he's not your usual type, but your usual type hasn't exactly been working out.' She looks a bit bashful. 'Sorry to say that. I just mean – god! – we're getting on now. We'll both be *twenty-five* soon. We have to settle down if we want to get married at twenty-seven and have kids by thirty. Right? Our priorities have changed, haven't they? We shouldn't be messing about with dickheads anymore.'

'SHUSSSSSSSSSSSSSHHHHHH!'

Lou sits back in her seat, face red. I dig my phone out of my bag and look at it, taking in the guy's grown-up features. He really is handsome, and, more than that, he has a sort of *kind* energy to him. If that's possible to tell through a photo. He hasn't tried to be serious in his bio, but also hasn't tried too hard to be funny. I'd dismissed him so easily on so many different apps; it seemed obvious to keep doing it without considering why.

Lou's right. It's time to be an adult. It's time to try men outside my box. I need a boyfriend and Paul definitely doesn't want the job. Fucking *Celeste*. I can't believe he started dating someone just when I wanted to go out with him. It's so rude.

OK, Idris, you get a right swipe.

It's an instant match and something in my belly fizzes. The promise of something new and exciting.

I put my phone away and listen to the vicar as he espouses the many virtues of my great-uncle – now apparently named Martin.

CHAPTER TWENTY-FOUR

OK, so this isn't . . . terrible? I mean, it's not wonderful either but it's not bad exactly.

On the screen in front of me, Will doesn't look much different from the man I remember. His features are all still in the same place they were, he still has legs and arms. His eyes are still mediocre levels of sparkly.

And our chat is still . . . fine?

After a bit of small talk about how the world has changed since we once fucked, we have at least tried to recapture some of our online magic.

'What do you think of the word *mulch*?' he's pondering now. 'It's weird, isn't it? It feels weird in your mouth.'

'I quite enjoy it,' I nod. 'It's satisfying. The words I hate are the complicated extra syllabley words. Like – I don't know – *necessarily*. Why the absolute fuck does that word need so many changes in direction? Ness–sir–sare–ra–ley.' I taste the nonsense syllables, disdain in my voice.

'I just googled the word that has the most

syllables,' he says, looking away from the camera as he types. He attempts to pronounce the monstrous result: 'Pneumonoultramicroscopicsilicovolcanoconiosis.'

'Intense,' I agree and we fall into silence, trying to think of other words we hate.

It's not a *bad* chat. It's quite interesting, I guess. But I can't help thinking it would be more fun with someone like Alistair or even Collector Paul. At least he really made me laugh. If I could untangle the misleading flirting, I'd enjoy this kind of silly chat with Collector Paul.

No more backsliding, I scold myself. Just because this isn't going that well, I have to stop looking back to the last man who made me laugh or gave me a compliment.

'So I have to buy a present for a difficult aunt this week,' Will says, changing the subject after too much silence. 'What do you think I should get her?'

It takes all my mental strength not to yawn directly into the camera. I hate buying presents for difficult people, never mind coming up with ideas for someone else.

'Um, I don't know, a pony?' I suggest and he laughs nicely.

See, he *is* nice. There's no denying that. He's a nice, decent, OK guy.

And ugh, this is the problem with so many dates I've been on. What do you do when they're just . . . fine? Like, the man is nice and handsome *enough* and you can see he's a decent fellow, even though he does induce you to say things like *decent fellow*. I've been on sooo many dates like this. Dates where the bloke is OK and you can see you'd probably have an OK time together if you carried on going out. Sure, there wouldn't necessarily be fireworks, but maybe they'd come later. Or maybe life doesn't need fireworks? They're expensive and dangerous and they scare dogs. Fireworks are *bad* actually.

Depending on my mood, I can sometimes see a future with people like this. If I've recently been through a shitty old time with relationships, nice – decent – seems good enough. For example, when I'd just broken up with Rich last year, all I dreamed about was a decent, OK-looking man who would actually turn up to our dates and be nice to me.

Will makes a face. 'Got a hair in my mouth,' he says, smacking his lips. 'Ugh, hate it when that happens, isn't it annoying?'

'Yeah,' I nod slowly. 'That *is* annoying.' We fall back into silence as he tries to locate the offending intruder. I watch him for a few seconds as he goes cross-eyed trying to get it, then politely look away.

To be fair to Will, I've been pretty distracted during our FaceTime. I have a lot on my mind: Idris not replying to my email; Alistair's girlfriend; the fact that I only have two exes left to contact, and they're the worst; Bibi being distant; Louise up to something that I can't bring myself to say out loud; the fact that Katie's about to kick off at work and I'm totally going to be sacked; Instagram being full of gorgeous wedding pictures and cute, fat little babies. It's all too much.

'What do you think?' Will looks at me expectantly.

'Um . . .' Shit shit. He was talking and I wasn't listening. He looks quite serious. 'Well . . . um, what do *you* think?'

This works and he continues talking – something to do with his boss and HR. I'm so relieved I got away with not listening, that I – again – forget to listen.

I feel so weary all of a sudden. This call is reminding me how meh the whole thing with Will was for our few months together. I feel bad, but there's no point denying it now – he was just an excuse to leave Idris. I was too much of a coward to end it like a grown-up, so I cheated with the first guy who showed me a bit of interest. And then I let the relationship with Will drag on for a tiresome five months, just to prove to myself and everyone else around me that it was real and worth it. Thankfully, lockdown and Covid came along and gave me an excuse to end it.

I can't do it again. I don't have any real feelings for Will and we don't have anything in common. Plus, I'm pretty sure he's been reading conversation cue cards during this FaceTime call. He keeps glancing down and wildly veering into new subject topics.

'So, Esther.' He clears his throat and the change in tone is enough to make me focus. He's looking at me seriously. 'I'm having such a great time, I love chatting to you. Would you like to do it again sometime?' He sounds nervous. 'I mean IRL next time!' He laughs awkwardly. 'Like a proper date?'

I take a deep breath. This time around I will be an adult. This time I won't hedge or date someone I don't really like because I'm a pathetic coward. I will be honest and mature and tell him the truth. I'll tell Will that he's a lovely man and that it was fun catching up, but that I don't think we're a good fit. I'll wish him all the best and we'll say goodbye like adults.

'Will,' I begin sombrely. 'I want you to know' – oh fuck this is hard – 'errrrrm, that, er, the connection keeps cutting out and I didn't hear what you said.' I quickly freeze in place, as if the screen has frozen, giving it a few seconds, before frantically hitting the disconnect button. Will's face disappears.

Ah, feck it, I'll text him a Dear John later.

CHAPTER TWENTY-FIVE

It feels like ages since we were in The Swab, watching Bibi not work. So much has been happening recently, so many exhausting emotions, it's a genuine relief to find a bit of normalcy here, drinking gross wine and talking about nothing.

'Can you serve those people at the bar, Bibi?' Franco is asking her politely. She doesn't give him the courtesy of eye contact.

'Will do.'

He moves off awkwardly, knowing Bibi will not do.

Lou gives Bibi a little shove. 'Why are you so mean to him, Barbarella?'

'He deserves it.'

I roll my eyes and Lou laughs. 'No he doesn't! Really, you should be nicer.'

'No.' Bibi sighs aggressively. 'But OK, fine, I'll go serve some customers.' She angrily shoves her wine glass away and stomps off.

In the void she leaves, Lou stares down at her phone, looking a bit lost.

'Are you OK?' I whisper, nudging her. She looks up, eyes searching for something in mine.

'I keep dreaming about your great-uncle Michael – you know, the one who died? Whose funeral we went to all those years ago, when you first saw Idris on Tinder?'

'Martin,' I reply automatically, then quickly correct myself. 'Merton. Great-Uncle Merton.'

'Merton,' she nods. 'Ever since you started talking about Idris again, I've been dreaming about him.'

'Huh.' I don't know what to say.

'Yeah,' she nods, a sort of relief in her voice. 'I think it's because I feel so guilty about how disrespectful we were at his funeral.'

'You feel guilty about ... that?' I say it slowly. So she can hear how stupid it is. 'You feel guilty about something from five years ago? You feel bad about a ninety-six-year-old man I didn't know and you didn't know even more.'

'Yes,' she confirms. 'I don't know why, I just really, really do.'

'Lou ...' I begin slowly. 'Is there anything you want to talk about?' I search her face. 'Anything you want to tell me? Something *else* that you're maybe feeling guilty about? That maybe you're redirecting into the great-uncle funeral thing?'

There is a long silence between us and she is first to look away.

'No, I just feel guilty about Great-Uncle Mervyn.'

'Merton.'

'Right.'

Bibi returns, bringing with her a bottle. I smile gratefully up at her before checking my phone emails and sighing loudly for attention.

'Still nothing?' Bibi looks vaguely sympathetic.

'It's been over a week,' I complain.

'It's probably a big deal for him,' Lou says charitably. 'He's probably just having a big old think about it and is carefully composing his reply!'

'What if he doesn't reply, though?' My stomach explodes with anxiety. 'Should I just forget Idris and move onto Carl?' I pause to groan, throwing my arms across the table. 'But Iddy was such a big part of my romantic history! And he was ready to give me *everything*, y'know? He wanted the whole thing: marriage, babies, a big house in the country. And he had a good job that could provide all those things! He's a much more sensible option than my other six exes combined! He always had his shit together.'

'You could tell that.' Lou is nodding. 'He always wore such sensible jumpers.'

I sigh again. 'I was stupid to run away from it.'

'You were just young!' Bibi sounds defensive. 'You weren't ready and that's OK. Don't give yourself a hard time for not wanting to settle down back then. Wanting to be single isn't an illness that needs curing.'

'Do you think he'd actually be open to going back there with you?' Lou is wide-eyed.

I duck my head, a bit ashamed of what I will say next. 'To be honest,' I explain in a low voice, 'I think I've always kind of known Idris was still an option. He was so madly in love with me back then, that's why I had to be so strong when we split up – y'know, with deleting his number and everything – because I knew he'd come back to me in a heartbeat if I asked. He kept saying that when I ended things – that he'd always be there if I changed my mind. It was awful.' I pause. 'And now that I've thought about him so much, I really want to talk to him. I want to see him!'

'I knowwww.' Lou throws her body across the table next to me. 'It's like when you're up for a part in a show or you spot someone in a bar you fancy, and then you can't stop picturing the what-if of it.'

'Yeah, or you go for a job interview.' Bibi's voice is quiet. 'And you start imagining yourself there, doing the work, setting up your desk, making small talk with colleagues – all of it.' She glances over at Franco. 'And you think about telling your current boss to go fuck himself.' She turns back to us. 'It's hard to go back once you've crossed that line.'

'No more jobs around at the moment then?' I pout sympathetically.

She puts her head in her hands. 'I think I've now interviewed for every marketing firm in London. There are, like, a hundred applicants for every job posting and the recruiters all keep telling me how brilliantly I've done to get through to the interview stage. But then I'm not *quite* the right fit for the job.'

Lou reaches over and strokes Bibi's arm.

'I'm never going to find anything.' Bibi sounds so sad, I wish so much that I could help.

'Why don't you join me in my mission?' I suggest brightly. 'That would give you something to think about and focus on. You could retrace your romantic history to help you meet someone. It would be good for you, and – even better – it would be a distraction from this bloody job hunt! Why not, eh?'

Bibi sits up straighter. 'Because I'm not interested in dating right now, Esther, I've told you that a thousand times.'

I roll my eyes. 'Yeah, yeah, I know that, but I think you'll change your mind once you meet someone.'

Bibi eyeballs me. 'Don't say that.' There's something in her expression that makes my smile waver. 'I'm so sick of hearing that from everyone. My parents, my relations, fucking acquaintances I've met one time. I don't need it from my friends, too. I need you – my friends! – to believe me when I say I love being single.' She pauses. 'And also not judge me if I *do* change my mind. Because it's my prerogative! I'm not anti-relationships, and if I meet someone amazing, I'm open to it. I just don't want to date, dating is a horrible shitshow of disappointments. And I definitely don't need to force anything. Like *some people*.'

I hesitate for a moment, feeling the sting of her last comment. 'Sorry,' I tell her at last. 'I'll shut up about it. You're right of course, it's up to you.'

'Your dreams are not my dreams, Esther,' she says,

standing up and adding shortly, 'I better go serve some more customers. It's getting busy in here.'

She goes and I look to Lou a bit helplessly. Was I in the wrong there? I know Bibi *says* she's happy single, but she's lying, surely?

Lou looks back at me solemnly, before offering, 'Do you think there's any chance Great-Uncle Marvin is haunting me?'

'Morton,' I correct knowing it's wrong but not caring. Sighing, I turn away to check my phone again. 'Idris,' I mutter as I refresh my emails yet again. 'You *better* reply to me soon. All this nonsense you're bringing back up has to be worth it . . .'

EX 5: IDRIS ABARA

AKA The Serious One

PART TWO

Bella Italia in central London

The loos

8.52pm

'So???' My enthusiasm is without bounds. I've never been more invested in anything in my life, I cannot cope with the failure of this and I WILL NOT ACCEPT IT.

It's always the same when I set up two friends on a blind date.

Louise shrugs. 'Mehhh,' she says at last, as I gasp, horrified.

'MEHHH?' I repeat, super outraged. 'But ... but he's nice! And handsome! And he's friends with Iddy, so it means we could double date all the time, Lou! Think of it!'

She does and brightens a little. 'That would be super fun,'

she concedes but then slumps again. 'I don't know, I just don't think I'm feeling it.'

'Ugh,' I groan at her in the mirror as I reapply lipstick. 'For god's sake, Lou, you've been begging me for, like, two and a half years to set you up with one of Idris's friends. One finally becomes available and you're meh-ing me. I'm so cross.'

'Oh, please don't be cross.' She looks desperate. 'I'm sorry! I'm really grateful for Sven. I don't know what it is, I *should* like him. He seems nice and he loves unpretentious pasta, which is always a plus.'

'That was my number one criteria for you,' I note.

'Right!' she nods. 'I don't know what it is exactly.' She sighs and then stands up straighter. 'OK, maybe I'll snog him after dinner to see if sparks fly. It's worth investigating, isn't it?'

'Definitely!' I crow, checking my teeth for spinach ravioli. 'Let's get back out there.'

Outside the loos, Idris is simultaneously emerging from the gents'.

'I'll catch up with you.' I shoo Louise back towards our corner table where Sven is grinning happily.

'Let's just give them a second alone,' I whisper to Idris.

'Good idea,' he says agreeably. 'And it gives me a chance to do this.' He grabs me around the waist and I resist only minimally.

'Doooooon't.' I push against his wide chest. 'I just reapplied my lipstick.'

'Was it the last of your supplies?' he enquires cheekily and I laugh.

'No, not technically.'

'Then more can be applied!' He raises his finger in the air and I laugh, pulling him closer for a kiss. He smells familiar and warm, but also of garlic.

'Ow, my ulcer,' he winces, pulling away. 'Sorry, I forgot it's too sore for kissing. Can you see it, is it gross?' He pulls up his front lip and I move closer to inspect his gums.

'Yes, very sore-looking,' I pronounce sympathetically. 'We need to get you some more sleep and healthy food. Would you like me to Bonjela it for you later?'

'Yes please,' he beams. 'The tomato sauce on the pasta really aggravated it.'

'I have a back spot I need you to put cream on for me, while we're doing body admin,' I note, and he nods, adding it to the mental list.

'Isn't long-term romance grand?' he laughs and squeezes me.

'How do you think it's going between them?' I turn in the direction of Sven and Louise who are talking easily in the corner.

'Hmm.' From behind, he circles his arms around me. 'I think pretty good? Did Louise say much?'

'Er, nah, not really,' I hedge. 'What about Sven?'

'I forgot to ask,' he says mildly. Typical bloke, not asking important – vitally important – questions.

'Ugh, why do you think we left you alone?' I poke his forearm.

He chuckles, his body moving against mine.

'Sorry, baby, I needed a wee, too.' He touches my face, smiling widely. 'But it would be cool, wouldn't it? If they liked each other? I can just picture the four of us, a bunch of old-timers, all sitting together on some porch, watching our grandkids running around, being annoying.'

I smile, but there is a strange chill in my veins all of a sudden.

'We could have a double wedding,' he laughs and I pull him in for a hug so he can't see my expression. 'And be god-parents for each other's kids.'

Every word is stabbing in my chest and I am struggling to breathe properly. It's the hug, it's just too tight. I pull back a bit.

'You OK?' He's looking at me strangely now. 'You've gone a bit pale. Was it the kid stuff?' He laughs and I try to join in. 'Because obviously we don't have to do any of that yet. As long as we're on the same page.'

'Of course we are.' I choke it out, my voice sounding weird and forced.

But we are, aren't we? I've always thought I'd want to get married and have kids at around twenty-seven – and I'm only a few months away from that. That seemed so old when I was seventeen and mapping out my whole life. The trouble is, I still don't feel any older than seventeen. I'm not ready for any of this grown-up stuff. And this isn't the first time Idris has talked – very casually, I might add – about our future together.

I know he wants marriage, I know he wants babies. He's

also two years older than me, which means he'll be thirty in a year. Which feels *old*.

I can feel sweat prickling my armpits but the rest of me is cold.

Where has this come from? I love Idris, I *really* love him. We've had an amazing two and a half years together and he's everything I could ask for! What's wrong with me?

Idris kisses me again, lightly this time. 'Shall we head back to the table? Carry on the matchmaking?' He winks jokingly and I titter politely.

'Um, yes, you go ahead.' I wave him off. 'I just, er, remembered I forgot to actually go for a wee when I was in there! Too busy chatting to Lou, what an idiot!'

I run back into the ladies' before he has a chance to say anything else, diving into a cubicle. In there, sitting on the floor, I breathe hard as the room spins around me.

What's wrong with me?

CHAPTER TWENTY-SIX

Oh, the indignity.

I was just minding my own business, shopping in Zara, and I came face-to-face with a fucking mannequin wearing my entire outfit. It's so humiliating and I will be writing to head office to complain.

Worse still is that I can't leave yet. It's the middle of the day and I'm the only shopper in here, which means a sales assistant has been following me around offering to 'help' for ten solid minutes. Now, I have never participated in a war zone, but I cannot imagine it is worse than the social awkwardness of being tailed by a bored shop assistant.

'I'm fine, don't need help!' I tell her because she's looking at me again. Looking at me like I want her help. 'Ha-ha!' I say, pointing at my clothes and the matching mannequin – y'know, to make up for not wanting any help. She only looks confused by the gesture, though, so maybe the outfit looks very different on a headless, life-size Barbie?

'I'm here!' Alistair's out of breath as he joins me, throwing lanky arms around me for a hug. 'Sorry I'm late, the brown line was broken again.'

'Don't worry!' I let him catch his breath, taking him in. He looks undeniably great; bright-eyed and happy. He's dressed up again, today in smart trousers and a dark blue shirt, French-tucked. I mentally thank Tan France for bringing men everywhere this style.

'Oh hey, that mannequin looks like you!' Alistair points at the offending dummy.

'Shut up,' I mutter, embarrassed. 'I had it first, that bitch is always copying me.'

'What a cow.' He shakes his head, smiling. 'But you know what they say? Imitation is the sincerest form of flattery.'

'That is nonsense,' I scold. 'You know what the most sincere form of flattery is? *Flattery*.'

'OK,' he laughs, showing off his adorable teeth. 'In that case, Esther, may I just tell you that you look wayyyy better in that outfit than the mannequin.'

'Oh my god, you're so sweet,' I simper, side-eyeing my rival. It really *is* sweet because it's not true. That plastic bitch has the whole sexy model, swan-neck thing going on.

I have a random midweek day off, thanks to a massive weekend-long wedding at the museum. I'd been useless in the planning stages, letting Katie take care of everything while I doodled the names of my exes at my desk. So I wanted to make sure I was front and centre at the actual big day. It was exhausting, with a thousand last-minute crises that needed resolving. Half our agency waiting staff didn't show up and I ended up having to be a waitress myself at one point while simultaneously cueing up the musicians in the main hall. But that's the thing about events – everything can be falling apart behind the scenes as long as no one front of house can tell. And it was all worth it when the bride hugged me at the end and said thank you. It's such a buzz. I'd kind of forgotten how much I love my work. I have a renewed determination to stop being bad at it.

It also kept me distracted from waiting by my phone for yet another weekend, hoping for an email from Idris. I was grateful my boss gave me today off, but I also couldn't sit around at home all day, with only my own stupid company to keep me busy.

I'll be honest, I messaged Alistair as a bit of a last resort.

Usually my flatmates would join me for a distraction outing like this, but despite not working today, Bibi and Lou were both mysteriously unavailable. Lou hasn't even called me back and I tried ringing, like, three times. They've both been acting a bit strangely lately. I don't know what's going on and they keep brushing me off when I ask. I tried Alex next, but she was busy with work and Sofia wasn't answering her door either. I'm feeling a bit abandoned, truth be told.

So I messaged Alistair to see if he fancied a shopping trip. And he did.

We wander around, picking items up and throwing them carelessly back on the shelf. The bored shop assistant shoots us daggers, but at least we're giving her something to do.

Maybe I should email Idris again?

No, too much. Bibi would tell me off.

I guess I have to accept the fact that he might not ever reply. He might not want anything to do with me. And I have to be an adult about it and acknowledge that it's fair enough.

Except it's not. Fuck him to hell, the massive twat.

I glance over at Alistair, feeling a pulse of guilt at using him to distract myself from another man. But we're *friends*, aren't we?

He stops, picking up the most garish yellow shirt I've ever seen in my life.

'What do you think?' He holds it up against himself, straight-faced, and I nod emphatically.

'That shirt is going to change your life,' I tell him. 'The yellow really brings out your jaundice.' He checks the price. There's a big red discount sticker on the label.

'It's only £8,' he says, glancing up, full of delight. 'I'm genuinely going to buy it!'

'Your girlfriend is a lucky lady,' I say dryly, hoping I'm not going red right now.

He doesn't say anything to this, strolling away down the aisle instead, face turned away from me. I wonder briefly if they've had a fight.

Fuck, I definitely fancy him. I shouldn't be here. It's not right. I try to swallow down any trace of fancying or flirting.

'What about you, eh?' He turns back to me at last, moving closer to wrap an arm around my shoulders affectionately. 'What's going on with your love life?'

I clear my throat. Why shouldn't I tell him about Idris? Or about any of them? Or about the whole damned mission? There's no reason why not. We're friends, aren't we?

Friends friends friends.

'Friendssssss,' I find myself murmuring under my breath.

'Huh?' He looks confused, his big shaggy eyebrows furrowing. It makes me want to stroke his face.

'Erm, I said, er, friends!' I squeak as we head for the tills to pay for Alistair's hideous new shirt. 'I mean I've only got friends at the moment, no love life!'

He looks a bit befuddled. 'Oh, right!'

My phone vibrates in my pocket. It's Louise calling me back at last.

'Are you OK?' Her breathless voice is in my ear. She sounds worried.

'Yes, I'm fine,' I reassure her. 'I just missed you and wanted to hang out. Where have you been?'

'Oh.' She takes half a beat to answer. 'Just ... with Sven. What about you?'

'I'm actually shopping on Oxford Street with Alistair.' I laugh at the absurdity of it.

'Wow!' She sounds shocked. 'Is Nick Wilde with you guys?'

'What?' Why on earth is she bringing him up? 'Why would he be here, Lou? Him and Alistair aren't even really friends these days.'

'OK,' she replies neutrally.

I watch Alistair a few feet away as he pays for the

god-awful shirt. He grins at the assistant who is telling him how brave his fashion choices are. I feel myself aching to take his hand in mine and squeeze it tight.

To stop myself going mad, I need to move on. I need Idris to reply, or I need to message Carl or Rich.

'I better go,' I tell Louise. 'Will I see you at the flat later?'

'Um, maybe!' she replies enigmatically. 'Love you, bye.'

Alistair joins me, waving his bag happily. There is something so energizing about being around him; he's so full of positivity.

'Shall we go get some lunch now?' he suggests, and I beam before he adds, 'It's so much fun hanging out with you again, Esty. I love being mates.'

Oh god, fucking *mates*. I can't take this.

Idris, if you can somehow hear this, *please reply*.

EX 5: IDRIS ABARA

AKA The Serious One

PART THREE

My flat

My bedroom

3.45pm

Should I cry? I should probably cry. It's not that I *don't* feel like crying – I do! – and I probably would've cried in a few minutes anyway, so crying now isn't like fake crying.

I start crying.

He can't be quite so angry with me if I'm crying. He's always been so kind and lovely when I'm upset, he'll be nicer to me now.

'Oh baby, what is it?' Idris stands up, crossing the bedroom and wrapping me up tightly in his arms.

It makes it so much worse. Dammit, I shouldn't have cried.

Except now I've started, I'm not sure I can stop.

I keep crying, trying to find the words as he leads me to sit on the bed, stroking my hair the whole time. 'It's OK, baby, it's OK.'

It's not OK, he's wrong.

'I've fucked up, Iddy.' I get it out at last. 'I've really truly fucked up and you're never going to forgive me.' He gets super still, next to me on the bed. His back stiffens, but he doesn't let go.

'What is it?' he says eventually in a quiet voice. 'Just tell me. Just say it.'

But I can't. The words won't come and there are so many bloody tears in the way.

After a few minutes, he gently extracts himself so he can look at me. But the sight of his face is too much and I throw myself down on the bed now, sobbing uncontrollably. This time, he doesn't join me, or offer up a cuddle. He just waits.

My face in the pillow, I manage to get it out at last.

'I slept with someone else.'

Idris doesn't immediately react, but the air in the room seems to change. It gets colder and my tears are suddenly dry.

'I'm so, so, sorry – you have no idea how sorry, Iddy—' I sit up but he has turned away now. Hunched over on the end of the bed, he's staring at his lap. 'Can you please look at me for a second?' I plead but it's like he can't hear me.

'Who was it?' he says after another minute, in a voice unrecognizable as his.

'It doesn't matter who,' I say softly, knowing full well it matters a fucking lot.

'Was it Will?' he says in the same tone. 'Did you fuck that guy Will?'

I can't answer. Or, I should say, I'm too much of a coward to answer.

'I guess that's a yes,' he spits out, standing up and heading for the door.

'Please don't go,' I beg, the tears starting again.

He doesn't. He leans both hands against the closed door, trying to find something in himself. Some strength.

'How could you?' he says at last, his voice breaking almost imperceptibly on the final word. It sends me into another spiral and I press the duvet to my face to stop the tears. I don't deserve to cry right now. He does.

'I don't know,' I say lamely, when I can speak again. 'It happened, I was drunk, and I'm a fucking bitch. I know you must hate me, I'm so sorry. You have no idea how sorry.'

There is another silence before he turns to look at me, his eyes red and watery.

'I don't hate you,' he says in a low, sad voice. 'I couldn't ever hate you.'

I stand to pull him close and we hold onto each other for a very long time.

CHAPTER TWENTY-SEVEN

From: Idris.Abara@gmail.com
To: estherthechef98234@hotmail.co.uk
Re: Entente Cordiale

Dear Esther,

Firstly, sorry about the above 'dear', this message felt
like it called for some level of formality. But also hello!
It's nice to hear from you, I hope everything is good
and happy in your life.

I've thought a lot about your request to meet up and
I'm going to have to say no. Sorry. I'm not sure how
much Sven passes along to Louise about what's
going on with me and my life (probably not much, he's
always going on about an 'ethical firewall') but in case
he hasn't mentioned: I'm engaged now! Her name is
Amy and she's absolutely brilliant. We've been together

for just over a year and she makes me really happy.
Life is good.

If it matters, I did speak to her about your email, and
she encouraged me to see you. She thought it might
be nice for us to catch up. But ultimately, I didn't
feel right about it, and I'm not sure what it would
really achieve.

That's not to say I don't still care about you. I really
loved you a lot, our relationship was important to me –
I'm sure you know/knew that – and you will always
mean a lot to me. I don't feel any regret about what
happened, so I hope you don't either. I know it ended
in a pretty shitty way and was all a bit abrupt, but I feel
quite strongly now that even all the sad stuff was how
it had to happen. I know we were both hurt, but I'm OK
now, and I hope you are too. I really mean that. I hope
you've found all the happiness in the world, Esther. You
deserve it.

Best wishes,
Iddy x

PS. Nice subject line. I see your half a term of history at
uni didn't go entirely to waste . . .

CHAPTER TWENTY-EIGHT

Best wishes.

Best wishes.

Best FUCKING wishes!

That is a shitty sign-off when it comes from your boss, never mind the man you spent three years of your life in love with.

Ugh, I cannot believe the adultness. The *grown-up*, fucking maturity of that email. How *dare* he be so mature and so over it and so happy and so completely fine. HOW DARE HE!

UGH, and fucking *Amy*! All perfect and sweet and laid-back about her fiancé getting an email from the former love of his life. She encouraged him to meet up with me! Did she horseshit. Actually, I bet she did! I would have pretended to be fine with it, too.

'Ooh, yeah, baby, tewwwwwtally go meet up with your ex-girlfriend! I'm fiiiiiiine with it! I'm not like those other saddo women who feel insecure and threatened by exes. I'm chiiiiiiilled out! Why don't you kiss her and have sex with her as well, I'm cooooooool.'

What a load of monkey turd.

I stomp through the flat to Bibi's room, computer in hand.

'Can I come in?' I shout, banging on her door. 'I need you to look at this.'

'Hold on,' her half-asleep voice mumbles after a minute before she appears at the door. 'What is it?' She sounds annoyed.

Whoops, I've woken her up. I got up at six to head to work early because – let's face it – I have a lot of making up to do with my poor assistant Katie. She's been picking up my slack all over the place.

I hand over the computer with the open email on screen. 'Idris replied,' I pronounce furiously.

'Wow.' She rubs her eyes. 'He took his time.' She takes the laptop, scanning the contents before finally looking up. 'What a nice guy,' she says before taking in my thunderous face. 'Er, I mean, what a complete tosser! Um, who even says *best wishes*?'

'That's what I thought!' I wail, bringing a bleary-eyed Lou out of her bedroom next door.

'Idris is fucking *happy*!' I tell her.

'He's what?' she frowns, pulling her dressing gown tighter around herself. I catch a glimpse of a silky nightie underneath. Lucky Sven. I hope.

'He's HAPPY!' I shout, taking my computer from Bibi and shoving it in Lou's direction now.

She blinks for a minute, squinting at the screen.

'Aw, what a lovely email!' she says at last, smiling and

handing the laptop back to me. Her smile falters at my nose flare and she hesitantly adds, 'I mean . . . um, what a . . .' – she anxiously studies my face – ' . . . meanie?'

'Yes! Exactly!' My nostrils de-flare. 'He's so out of order! He can't wait to tell me how great his life is with this dickhead, *Amy*! What a smug twat. I bet they're having engagement photos done right this minute and he'll forward me a link so I can see them both up close, throwing each other up in the air and fake laughing. What a couple of bellends.'

'Oh dear.' Lou scrunches up her face. 'So, is that it then? You're not going to message him back? Or try to persuade him to talk?'

'I have more pride than that!' I sniff. She doesn't look convinced, so I add, '*Yes*, it's totally done, Lou! I never even really wanted to see him in the first place. I thought he'd want to see me, I was trying to do him a *favour*. I was being kind.'

'Er, right, *kind*,' Lou nods slowly.

'I'm going back to bed,' Bibi says abruptly, returning to her room and shutting the door firmly.

'Bit rude,' I mutter to Lou who looks surprised, too. 'Is it me, or she acting a bit secretive at the moment?'

Lou seems panicked at the suggestion. 'No!' she says too quickly. 'I mean, not particularly. Maybe?' she continues in a hushed voice. 'And if she is, that's fine! Secretive is allowed! Maybe she has a job interview coming up or something, but doesn't want us to know about it yet. She's had so many disappointments, it must get her down, telling us about each and every single one. And . . .' – she pauses – 'like, I dunno, sometimes we don't always want to share things with our best friends until they're a done deal, y'know?' I give her a weird look and she stares down at the floor, retying her dressing gown cord. 'Right, I might go back to bed now, too, actually. So sorry Idris has been such a . . . er, arse?' She says the insult like it's a question, so I nod. 'But at least you got an answer, right?'

'I guess so,' I reply begrudgingly. 'OK, yeah, go back to bed. Sorry to disturb your morning.' I wave in the direction of her room and the panicked look returns.

'You're not disturbing anything!' Her voice is high. 'I'm just tired and don't have any auditions today!' A beat of tense silence follows and I nod, quashing my follow-up questions.

'I better go track down Carl then,' I say at last, reluctantly.

She nods quickly. 'Yes, best to keep moving with it, I guess.' She opens her door just enough for her to slide her body through. 'See you later. Have a good day at work!'

She shuts the door, locking it, and I'm left alone, feeling a bit bereft. I really needed more from my two best friends. Idris was my whole world for such a long time. And I know it was my fault it ended but it still stings.

That night we broke up was one of the most painful of my life. After the initial apologies and a whole lot of crying, we spent all night talking. There was more crying, some sex, and so many horrible questions. He wanted to know everything; every nasty, weak, horrible detail.

I can still picture his angelic face now, all swollen and wet, his eyes so sore-looking. And then came the worst of it, as it started to get light outside, when he offered to forgive me.

When I came back from the loo and he was standing there, framed in the doorway looking at me with this gut-wrenching expression on his face. And he said, 'I think I can let it go, I don't want us to break up.' I wanted to say thank you and pull him close and marry him and have children and a life with him. I wanted to do all the things I knew would make him happy, forever.

But I also knew I couldn't. I'd damaged us too much. What I'd done would never go away. And the truth was I didn't want to be forgiven. I wanted him to push me away and end it. I wanted him to hate me. It's why I did it really, I know that now. I did that awful thing so he would dump me.

I needed Bibi and Louise to see all that. To comfort me and lie to me more convincingly about Idris. I needed enthusiastic advice on messaging Carl to help distract me from the rejection.

Maybe they're bored of this mission? It *has* been taking things over a bit lately. I've ignored the rest of my life to focus on this. I'm sacrificing so much at the altar of this fucking mission.

But I need them. After such a strong start, it feels like maybe the last couple of exes are both going to rebuff me. Maybe the last part of my romantic life is too recent to bring back up. Too raw. Too full of knobbers like Idris and his best wishes.

Sigh.

Of course, the better – more rational – part of me knows it was an incredibly kind email. Way more generous than I deserved. And somewhere in me I'm pleased that Idris has found happiness. This Amy woman certainly sounds like a much more decent person than I ever was. And it's all he ever wanted, isn't it? To meet someone sweet and get married. He deserves all that and so much more. He was a good person who always treated me so nicely. And I was awful to him in the end. His email was actually very lovely to a person who discarded him years ago and is now trying to shoulder-barge back into his life without even much of a reason or purpose. Would I really have wanted to get back with him? Let's face it, probably not. I should be grateful he's been so decent.

Ooh, I know, I'll message Alex. She never even knew Idris. If I tell her he was an arsehole, she'll believe me and slag him off with me.

Fucking *best wishes*, what a scumbag.

CHAPTER TWENTY-NINE

Have I been awake for hours, or have I only been dreaming that I've been awake for hours? It's that kind of dark, fuzzy point of the witching hours where I just can't tell.

I pull the thick duvet closer around my chin. I'd reach for the lamp on my bedside table but it's way too chilly out there. Also, it's that sort of spooky night where I'm fairly certain a monster would reach out and grab me if even an inch of skin were to exit the covers.

I can't sleep. Or, if I can, it's for hungrily snatched minutes where it's all anxiety, stress-ridden dreams chasing a faceless boy, screaming about weddings and babies. One minute it's Alistair I'm hunting, while he runs for the hills. The next it's Paul. Then it's the fuzzy avatar of Will's Twitter profile or Rich the Bastard grinning at me as he texts other women in front of me. In one really sweaty moment, Carl turns up.

I can't keep lying here, thinking, worrying. It's too much. OK, I will be brave. I will turn on the lamp. If the monsters get me, I've had a good life. I've loved and I've been loved.

I reach for the switch, flooding the room with light that hurts my eyes. I blink quickly, trying to acclimatize to the brightness as I take in every corner of the room, checking everything is normal.

All clear. Phew.

I check my phone. Fucking 4.52am. That is among the worst of times to be awake. I know there's only really a couple of hours until I have to get up for work, and yet, it's way too early to give up the ghost and just get up. Instead, it seems likely I will lie here thinking and worrying now until I have to drag myself, all zombie-like, into work.

OK, I have to admit this Seven Exes Mission is getting to me. There are only two exes left – Carl and Rich. And there are so many weird and complicated emotions tied up with both. Never mind the five I've already contacted.

Oh sod this, I'm done with just lying here – there's only so much fucking introspection any one person can take. I will get up and wear myself out, circling the flat. And if someone thinks I'm a burglar and the police get called, so much the better. If I'm in jail, I can't go into work looking like a zombie, can I? What better excuse to take the day off.

Ooh, warm milk is meant to help in this situation! I mean, technically, more than a teaspoon of milk gives me the shits, but that's OK because at least pooing out my internal organs means I won't just be lying in bed staring into space, thinking about the many dreadful people I've slept with.

I work myself up to a sitting position, still wrapped cocoon-like in my bedding. The next big question is: can I somehow reach my big, cosy dressing gown – currently hanging on the door – without having to leave my duvet? I can figure this out. I did get a B in GCSE maths after all.

I ditch the warmth and make a run for it, feeling the rush of cold enter my bones, even in those few seconds before I can re-wrap myself up.

Idris bought me this dressing gown.

It's the warmest, loveliest thing I've ever owned. I look around the dimly lit space of my bedroom. Does everything I own have some kind of link back or memory attached to a boy? How miserable. And how very depressingly like me.

I shuffle out into the corridor, yawning widely. Maybe I'll treat myself to a long, luxurious witching hour poo. When you live with other people and there's only one bathroom, you never really get to enjoy your poos. You're always tense, waiting for a bang on the door or worrying about a smell that might linger afterwards. Lou once went in there after me and I heard her mutter something about mackerel. A meal I'd had three days before.

Outside the bathroom door, I almost scream as a shapeless blob of human emerges out of nowhere.

'Jesus,' I hiss, trying to laugh away the fear still coursing through me. 'Sorry, dude. I didn't realize anyone else was up.' My eyes struggle to adjust to the dark after the lamplight of my bedroom, but I recognize Bibi's distinctive yellow dressing gown. It has a hood with bear ears, and if my dressing gown were not so brilliant, I would be very jealous of its coolness.

Bibi doesn't reply immediately and the fear returns to my stomach. Not really because I think someone has broken in to use the loo dressed as Bibi – more like, I don't know, something else undefined. It's like something big is about to happen. All my internal warning bells are sounding. The hairs on my neck are up.

'Beeb?' I whisper more carefully and step back, groping for the light switch. It floods the hallway with yellow light and we both blink hard.

It's Alex.

'Oh!' I laugh, relieved, but the Something is still there. 'What are you doing here? Are you and Lou having a sleepover without me? How dare you! I always bring the Milky Ways.'

'Um.' She stares down and I wonder if she is maybe sleepwalking.

From behind me, a door opens and a voice whispers, 'Alex?'

It's Bibi. She tiptoes towards us, stopping suddenly and noisily when she sees me.

For a moment, her face flushes with guilt. It only lasts seconds before it's replaced by a sort of complacency. A kind of resignation to whatever fate is about to befall her. I look between her and Alex. They have the same expression on their faces.

My first reaction is to laugh because how absurd! This

looks like I'm catching Bibi and Alex having a one-night stand! But how stupid, of course it's not that.

Ha. Ha. Ha.

Bibi wouldn't have sex with Alex! Alex wouldn't have sex with Bibi. They wouldn't do that to me. Bibi wouldn't sleep with my ex and my ex wouldn't sleep with my best friend!

Never mind that we've all only just survived and recovered from the last disastrous inter-circle sexing, it would also be the worst idea ever. It would ruin everything! They know I'd never forgive them! Plus, Bibi hates Alex!

Ha. Ha. Ha. How ridiculous and funny that it looks very, very, very much like these two are sneaking around, caught out in a lovers' tryst.

I search my brain for what else this could be. What else could explain this? Because they definitely, definitely, DEFINITELY are not having sex with each other.

'Um, Esther.' Alex is first to speak and she does so in a tone much like she would use with a five-year-old who has just hurt her knee. 'Listen, um . . .' she trails off and I fight the urge to laugh again.

Just explain it! I want to scream as I look expectantly between them. Just tell me the very plausible reason for all this. Did the toilet break again, soaking Alex's pyjamas, along with all of Lou's spare pairs? Did she accidentally take Bibi's bear dressing gown thinking it was Lou's or mine, and here Bibi is to demand it back? Or maybe both Alex *and* Bibi are sleepwalking and are just as confused about all this as me right now.

263

Why aren't they saying anything? I swallow hard as Bibi looks away. Bibi never looks away. She's always confronting, always honest – brutally so – and always, always looks you dead in the eye.

It hits me fully then and my chest catches, unable to pull in oxygen.

I run to Lou's room, flinging open the door. I just need to see for myself that Alex isn't in there. A part of me is still sure I'll find Lou passed out across the bed, the TV still playing *13 Going on 30*, surrounded by discarded sweet wrappers.

But no. Lou is alone, asleep in her bed. No chocolate remains, no nothing.

She opens her eyes, bleary and confused. 'Whasss—' she half forms the question and I tell her.

'Bibi and Alex fucked.' My voice is calm as Lou blinks harder, trying to understand my words. My hand still on Lou's door handle, I turn back to Alex and Bibi. They are standing stock-still, a foot apart, shame radiating off them. 'Or . . .' I pause politely, as if making small talk with strangers in a lift. 'Sorry, I shouldn't assume, should I? Are you fuck*ing*? Fucked or fuck*ing*? Has this been going on behind our backs for a while?' I wait patiently, looking between them. They still won't meet my eyes but the answer is clear.

'FuckING it is!' I declare and my voice is no longer calm or quiet. 'Hear that, Louise? My ex and my best friend are fuckING. Tonight is apparently not the first time. They've been lying and hiding it from us for probably ages!' I briefly consider Sofia upstairs and Ivan downstairs. But I am too angry to stop. I raise my voice louder. 'Bibi's been pretend-ing to barely tolerate Alex, all the while doing this.' I glance at Alex's face. She's ashen and blank. 'I don't even fucking KNOW you.' I notice my hands are trembling as I struggle to comprehend Alex and Bibi's lack of response.

Surely they're not? After so many years of lost friend-ship with my childhood best friend – all because I did this stupid thing – and Bibi goes right in and does the very same thing again. Without a word. Without giving a second shit about me.

'How *could* you?' I try again, my voice shaking. 'Are you seriously fucking telling me this is happening? That you'd lie and jeopardize everything?' I start to scream. '*EVERYTHING?* YOU'RE SERIOUS?'

It's Alex who tries to stop me first. She steps forward, reaching for me.

'Esther,' she begins slowly as if I don't know my name. 'Please don't be like this. I'm so sorry we didn't tell you or talk to you about this. I—'

'Get a-fucking-way from me.' I step back, hands raised to stop her. I'm so angry with Alex, but it's Bibi I can't believe. 'You have nothing to say then?' I direct my full fury at her and she shakes her head. 'You're not even going to say sorry or tell me you made a mistake and you won't do it again?' I am yelling again but she remains unmoved. I want to tell her – tell them both – to get the hell out of this house. But it's Bibi's house, too.

Fine then, I'll go!

But I have nowhere *to* go. No boyfriend or partner or husband to save me from this horrible, horrible situation.

'I can't believe you would do this to me.' I spit the last words in Bibi's direction before turning on my heel. I stomp down the hallway, slamming my bedroom door behind me and locking it, before collapsing on the bed. I feel the tears begin right away, coursing down my face and into the pillow like they'll never stop.

So much for sleep.

CHAPTER THIRTY

I've talked myself into thinking the knock won't come, so when it does, I forget myself.

'Yes?' I call out in a sing-song voice. Ugh. Idiot, it's only been twelve hours since the blow up, I meant to sound raging. 'What is it?' I add sharply.

'Can I come in?' It's Bibi, of course it's Bibi, and her voice sends a miserable shiver through me. There are so many important, brilliant moments and memories associated with that raspy voice. And she's ruined each and every one.

'No, get lost,' I shout, knowing I will use it as further ammunition if she really does get lost.

'Let me in.' She doesn't sound annoyed, which is annoying. I want to fight her.

'Why?' I am being churlish but I don't care.

'I want to talk to you,' she says in the same ever-patient tone. I sigh, waiting. After a moment she adds, 'I'm not going anywhere, so you might as well let me in.'

Sighing furiously again, I stomp across the room and flip the lock.

'What?' I say, yanking the door open and taking her in.

She looks like she hasn't slept much. But that's probably more about the all-night shagging sesh with my ex, rather than any guilt she might be feeling. She doesn't say anything for a moment, just looks me up and down. It makes me even crosser because I don't know if I want to look normal, so she doesn't get the satisfaction of knowing she's hurt me, or if I want to look dreadful so she feels guilty. If she's capable of such an emotion.

'You didn't go to work,' she says coolly. The observation is infuriating and I roll my eyes.

'I called in sick,' I say impatiently, feeling momentarily bad again about my put-upon assistant. Yet another day of projects she'll have to crack on with all alone. 'I found out my two best friends have been lying to me and I guess I couldn't sleep that well.'

I wait for Bibi to say something else but she doesn't. 'So?' I snap. 'What do you want to tell me? Are you going to tell me how Alex is The One and how you loooooove each other and couldn't resist betraying me? And how finding your soulmate meant I didn't matter to either of you and that I deserved to be lied to for ...' I pause. 'For how long? How long has it been going on, Bibi?'

She regards me carefully, assessing things before answering. 'A month. Five weeks, maybe.'

'Five weeks?' I am aghast. I thought she would say a couple

of weeks max. Five weeks is too long – that's way too many lies. I've seen them both countless times in five weeks. I see Bibi every day, Alex at least a couple of times a week. How many collective lies is that? Or lies of omission if I'm being extremely generous? Which I'm not.

My chest gets tight. I will *not* cry in front of this traitorous, deceitful cow.

Oh my god, was Alex just using me and my friendship so she could cop off with Bibi? How much of the last couple of months as friends again was a lie?

'I know we've hurt you,' she says slowly and the *we* hurts more than any of it. They are a team now; a pair. They're in it together. They've comforted each other over this and discussed how awful my reaction was. They've convinced each other that what they've done isn't that bad and told one another I'm being a dick. They've cuddled for hours and talked about how to move forward with this situation. They had each other. They chose each other over me.

All while I've been sitting here alone, crying my eyes out, wondering what to do.

'So what's all this bullshit been about, claiming you've been sooo super happily single then?' I spit out, wanting to hurt her. 'Clearly you weren't! You made out like I was some desperate loser, chasing this mission to meet someone. You looked down at me and acted like I was pathetic, and all the while you were chasing something too! You copped off with the first woman to walk in our front door!'

'It wasn't bullshit!' Her eyes flash. 'Don't you dare

start saying that! I have been very happy, being single has been great.' She sighs. 'I never expected to meet someone like Alex. Honestly, she blew me away from the moment I met her.'

I shake my head at her hollow words. 'And a bit of *lust* was more important to you than betraying me?'

She looks down and a tiny part of my fury gives way to sadness.

Don't cry. Not now, not yet, not again. She doesn't get to see me break.

'You know what you've done,' I say quietly now. 'You've chosen to sleep with someone who isn't just someone I cared about but someone I lost for *years*! I lost her because of this kind of situation and you've chosen to go ahead and casually do it again. You're going to end this fling eventually and I'll lose her again. Or you. Probably both of you.'

She looks broken and devastated, but says nothing.

It makes me angry again. 'You're not even going to fucking apologize, are you?' I can feel the tears welling up in spite of myself. 'Just get the fuck out of my face, OK, Bibi? Just get out, I don't want to talk to you again. Not ever. In fact, I'd really appreciate it if you could find somewhere else to stay for a while, while I look for a new place to live.' I walk over to the door and hold it open for her. 'I'm sure Alex will gladly have you stay with her. That way you don't have to sneak around here and lie. You poor things, it must've been so difficult, lying to everyone all this time.' My voice drips with sarcasm.

Bibi looks like she will say something, but instead she nods and walks out. I slam the door behind her as hard as possible. It sets Ivan off downstairs and I am grateful for his cover noise, because my tears – when they finally arrive – are loud and embarrassing.

It is half an hour before I stop weeping, and when I do, I instinctively reach for my phone. I need a distraction. Any distraction will do. And I find one.

I open Google and type: 'Chef Carl Hurst'.

EX 2: CARL HURST

AKA *The Work Mistake*

PART ONE

A'Diva Restaurant

The car park

10.35am

'Lou,' I hiss into the phone. 'You have to help me, I've tried everything.'

Someone walks by, glancing curiously at me standing so close to my car.

'Hey,' I nod over as nonchalantly as possible. They nod back awkwardly, walking away a little faster.

'What's wrong?' Lou asks down the line. She sounds worried.

'Where are you? Can you come to west London? Like, now? Immediately? How quickly could you get here?'

I can practically hear her bafflement. 'What? What are you talking about?' Actually, she sounds half asleep. Bloody actors. Half the day's gone.

Oh great, on top of everything, I'm now my dad.

'Look, I borrowed my mum's car for my interview today—' I begin.

'Why?' she interrupts and I reply impatiently.

'I thought it would make me look more professional! More hireable, y'know? More like a grown-up.'

'Oh crap.' The realization dawns on Lou. 'You've got your second interview for that fancy new restaurant, A'Diva, this morning, right? How did it go?'

'It hasn't *gone*,' I hiss, glancing down at the problem. 'I'm trapped and I'm late.' She doesn't reply, so I carry on frantically. 'I bought a pencil skirt because the model in the advert looked so powerful and cool, and I wanted to impress Carl Hurst.' I pause, because I *knew* Lou wasn't listening when I told her about Carl Hurst. 'The head chef?' I say into her silence, trying to keep the annoyance out of my voice. 'He's a huge fucking deal in the food world, Louise, and I've wanted to work for him ever since I started cooking. This was supposed to be my chance! I wanted to look like a sexy, capable woman, but this fucking pencil skirt is like wearing a corset around my legs. I thought the difficult part was getting *in* the car, but getting out was like trying to wiggle through an obstacle course backwards.' I sigh heavily. 'Basically, I fell out of the door, which launched the keys across the car park, and the door slammed shut and locked behind me – onto the back of my skirt.' My voice rises an octave. 'I'm fucking trapped, Lou! I'm attached to the car! I've tried pulling my skirt out but it's stuck fast. In fact, I think the zipper is on the inside of the door, which means the only way out is to rip off the whole back of my skirt. I can't even fully reach around because it's so tight and there's no way in hell I can reach the keys. I'm trapped. And my interview was meant to start five minutes ago!'

Down the phone, Lou makes a noise that I could swear was her trying not to laugh – except that would make her a total cow so it can't have been that.

'Lou?' I sound desperate. 'Can you help? Can you come?'

After more noises on the line, she finally replies. 'Can't you just ask someone passing by to hand you the keys?' she says at last in a strangled voice.

'I'm too embarrassed!' I wail. 'And only one person has come by in fifteen minutes anyway. This is so mortifying!' I cover my face, trying to reach around to the back of my skirt for another yank. Why don't I do more yoga? I'm sure I could've reached around properly if I did yoga. 'This was my big chance, Lou!' I tell her again, squeaking through my hands. 'I was finally going to have a proper chef job! No more cooking pasta for people who couldn't get into the Bella Italia around the corner. I had a shot at working in a *real* restaurant. I sailed through the cooking test last week – they loved me! This meeting was meant to be just a formality to meet Carl Hurst. I could've worked for *Carl Hurst*, Louise! But now I've ruined it.' Behind my fingers, I squeeze my eyes tightly shut.

'Esther Adams?' A voice pierces through my wails and I freeze.

Shit.

Slowly – very slowly indeed – I open my eyes and uncover my face. In my ear, Lou is asking if I'm OK and what is happening. I ignore her, quickly ending the call and throwing the phone into my bag. Oh my god.

'Mr Hurst,' I say in an unrecognizable voice, taking in the man I've studied on pages and pages of Google Image results. The renowned chef winking out at me every week from the pages of my favourite magazine's food pages. My idol, the man rumoured to be in talks for his own show on ITV2. The man I was supposed to meet inside ten minutes ago for a job interview.

If I wasn't attached to my mum's car.

And oh my god, he's the hottest guy I've ever seen.

'Did we . . .' he trails off, smiling magnanimously. 'Did we plan on meeting in the car park for our interview? One of my staff said he thought the applicant I was waiting for might be the woman leaning against her car outside. I thought I'd better investigate.' A smile plays on his lips. 'Did you want to speak out here?'

To tell or not to tell.

'Um,' I hedge, trying to appear casual, pinned though I am against my mum's car. 'Well, um, I just thought' – my eyes dart side to side – 'that it was such nice weather out here, maybe we could chat outside?' It starts to rain. 'Why not, eh?' I cough a little as cold, wet drops hit me in the face. 'Um, after all, us cooks, we're, er, we're cooped up inside all day every day, right? Let's take advantage of this lovely weather.' Somewhere a few miles away, thunder starts to roll.

Carl Hurst regards me solemnly and sweat breaks out on my brow. Luckily, the rain is starting to fall so hard, it's unlikely he'll notice.

He's unbelievably sexy, like, *unbelievably*. Older than me by maybe fifteen years, but the craggy edges around his eyes and mouth only add to his sex appeal. He's so talented, so knowledgeable. I don't know if I want to learn from him or fuck him.

Ideally both.

'OK, Esther Adams,' he says at last, his mouth curling at the edges, eyes dancing. 'My sous said you can cook and we need someone urgently.' He pauses, looking me up and down in the now-pouring rain. 'And I've got something like a good feeling about you.' My insides burn from happiness and lust as he adds, 'So you've got the job.'

'Oh my god, *thank you*!' I cry, no longer caring about my skirt or the rain streaming down my face. 'I promise you won't regret this, Mr Hurst, I swear it. I'll work so hard, you'll see. I'll do anything for you.'

He grins again and I force down a massive lump of longing in my throat.

'Please, call me Carl, Esther,' he says in a deep voice. 'Oh, and do you want me to hand you your car keys so you can get your skirt out of the car door?'

CHAPTER THIRTY-ONE

Google: ('Chef Carl Hurst')

All **News** **Images** **Maps** **Shopping** **More**

About 3,270,000 results (0.56 seconds)

Results for Chef Carl Hurst
DailyIndependent.co.uk

Celebrity chef loses top job at A'Diva

TV chef Carl Hurst has walked away from his exclusive
gig as head chef at celebrity hotspot A'Diva in west
London, we can exclusively reveal. While there's been
no official word on why or how it happened, insiders
say ... **Read more ...**

Two months ago

My heart beating fast, I click on the top link and study the accompanying picture. Carl looks old. It's been eight years since I saw him, and he must be about forty-five these days, I guess, but examining him now, I wonder if he'd lied about his age back then. He looks much closer to fifty-five. But maybe life in the kitchen used up all his collagen.

I read the full story, stopping several times to remind myself to breathe.

The news story is vague on details, with 'sources' reporting that Carl 'quit before he could be pushed'. There are several anecdotes included about his bullying tactics in kitchens. One unnamed former protégé describes how he once threw him across a countertop and another reveals Carl's thunderous, explosive temper tantrums where he would swear profusely at his staff.

It is damning and yet . . . confusing? Because surely everyone already knew all this about Carl Hurst? That was his schtick for eight years at A'Diva, and even longer at the restaurant before. Being vile and difficult just proves you're a genius, doesn't it? If you're a man, at least. When he broke a sous chef's arm, the ensuing hype is what secured him that weekly column in a celebrity magazine and a spot on morning TV. Plus, er, attacking people? Swearing at them? That's how Gordon Ramsay became a multi-millionaire, surely.

There is more to this. I can feel it.

I roll over in my bed, clicking back into the search results and reading the next link.

I need to know more.

CHAPTER THIRTY-TWO

There is something oddly comforting in being *this* disgusting.

And when I say disgusting, I'm not being self-effacing. What I mean is, that it's Sunday now and I haven't showered since Thursday morning. And even that was a fairly hasty wash, with the promise to myself of a more formal hose down later. But then later was when ... y'know, my best friends fucking betrayed me. Either way, that Thursday rinse certainly wasn't meant to hold everything together for a long period of time while I had a major friend-mergency.

But, like I say, it's kinda nice. There's something a bit familiar and safe in all of this festering in my own stink. Testing my own limits of health and safety. Matching my horrible outsides with my horrible insides. It feels right to be rank.

I briefly lift my duvet to reach for the TV remote and the waft of stank hits me. I wince. It reminds me suddenly of all the other days in my life that I've spent like this; unwashed and uncaring. All those miserable, boy-related days and weeks. After every break-up with every single one of those seven exes on the Dickhead Tree, I did this. I lay in my own filth, feeling sorry for myself, eating stale rice cakes out of the back of my bedside table and ignoring my sad, sorry life. Is it really worth it? Is *love* really worth it?

And this situation with Bibi feels even worse than a break-up.

I try to picture the world outside, continuing without me. With the curtains shut, it's hard to imagine. It seems more appropriate that everything will have stopped in solidarity. The PM has likely decreed that the shittiness of my life is worthy of a worldwide pause. The British people have all gone home to hide under their covers and feel sad for me and my situation. Out there is only an unbathed nation in their beds, ignoring calls and emails. A nation lying around, focusing all their sympathy on me and my crappy life.

Except I haven't *fully* ignored the world.

I've been googling Carl obsessively and thinking about him obsessively. I need to know what happened at A'Diva, I have to.

Maybe he'd just had enough, like me, of the working hours and conditions? Maybe he had an argument with the owner, Hugo? Maybe he was just done with never sleeping and always stinking of food.

I need to see him, or speak to him. I need answers. But I can't just message him, can I? I can't just call him up and go,

'Oh hey, Carl, what's up? How have the last eight years been? Heard you got shitcanned from the restaurant!'

I went to his house once – just once – during our seven-month relationship. I don't know if he still lives there but I could go. I could see. How would he react to seeing me after all this time? How would he feel? What if he didn't even recognize me?

I'm not brave enough to do it alone. Not without my back-up. Not without Bibi and Louise and Alex. But I don't think they've had my back for a while now.

I've always been pretty good at distracting myself from negative emotions. See, when there's something bad in your life, all you do is just quickly put all your energy into some-thing or someone else and never think about the bad thing. It's easy!

Except this time, bits of bad keep slipping through my denial net.

I keep having flashes of Bibi and Alex cuddled up in bed at Alex's house. Laughing together behind my back. Revelling in their lies. Kissing, having sex, barely caring what they've done to me. Deep in the darkest of these moments – even while knowing they wouldn't do this – I picture them whis-pering my secrets to each other. I pull the covers back again, ignoring the odour, and stare down at myself. My body is grotesque and shapeless in baggy mismatching pyjamas. Underneath them I feel ugly and rejected. In this moment, I am a monster. A monster that Bibi and Alex are laughing about in their love cocoon.

A massive wave of rice cake nausea passes over me and I grab for one of the fifty empty coffee cups by my bed. I dry heave but nothing comes up, so I hover there over the mug. I study the swirling brown stained bottom and listen for noises in the flat. I can hear Lou, moving about, clattering in the kitchen, but she's alone. From what I've gathered, Bibi has been gone since our fight. Louise has knocked a few times and I saw her once when I went to the loo but I haven't wanted to talk yet. Not about all this. Not about what I've lost.

But you know what? Maybe I haven't lost all that much. Maybe Bibi and I weren't even really very good friends anyway.

I mean, she's not even a very nice person! After all, she can be so cold and mean. She's so rude to people – like her boss, Franco! He's a decent person, sweet and unassuming. She's so cruel to him without any reason. I don't know why I haven't thought about this much before. She's a bitch! I don't need that kind of toxic negativity and meanness in my life. And clearly she's a disloyal liar, we know this now, too. Actually, now I'm thinking about it, she's *always* been secretive and cagey. I know we joke about wanting to find out her real name but why hasn't she ever told us? Lou and I share everything with her and she likes to have this sort of *power* over us by keeping us in the dark about her life. It's pathetic. I'm done with her, I really am. Even if we somehow get past all of this Alex shit, I don't think we can really be close mates ever again. She's a mess in my life that I'm Marie Kondo-ing.

I don't need Bibi or Alex. I don't need any of them. And I think I know what I'll do about Carl now.

I'll go to A'Diva.

EX 2: CARL HURST

AKA The Work Mistake

PART TWO

A'Diva Restaurant

The stockroom

1.12am

'We're missing a whole delivery of onions,' I yell from inside my cupboard. No one replies. I bet the fuckers have all gone home, while I've been stuck with stocktake, yet again.

I take a moment to perch on a shelf stacked with potatoes and close my eyes. I'm totally exhausted; totally drained. I've been here since 8am, and will have to be back – to do it all over again – in seven hours. I've never worked like this in my life.

But it's worth it. The things I'm learning, the range of food, the joy of making top-quality meals – it's all so worth it.

And, I can't lie, it's also worth it because of him.

I've felt his eyes on me all night. Watching me across the kitchen as I move from plate to plate. I *know* he feels it. I know it from the small, secret smiles we've shared, the moments of intense eye contact. It's close to being unbearable. It's been building for weeks now and I know something is about to break.

Of course I know it's a terrible idea and I definitely shouldn't do it. Having sex with my boss? With my hero? It's all a terrible, terrible, terrible idea and I definitely won't do it.

Not even if he begs.

OK, maybe if he begs.

Maybe I'll beg?

All my friends say I shouldn't do this. Shelley says I'll get sacked, Lou says I'll get hurt. But at this point I would gladly take both of those for one night with Carl.

I put my head in my hands and sink further, deeper into my daydream. I picture us kissing, us touching, us fucking. Carl flipping me around and over like I'm a tiny doll. Him inside me and us both finishing in a hailstorm of messy, filthy bodily fluids.

'Hello.' I jump at the greeting, opening my eyes to Carl's voice. I feel insanely guilty, like I've used him in my fantasies without his permission. Can he tell what I was just thinking? I know he can't, that's stupid. But the way he's looking at me, I'd swear he knew. I laugh nervously, taking in his outline in the dimly lit doorway.

'You're always sneaking up on me when I have my

eyes shut,' I point out, glad of the semi-darkness hiding my red face.

He smiles. 'Well, you have your eyes shut a lot.'

Oh god, I honestly don't know if I can survive this tension between us. It feels like I might die.

I gulp, looking away. 'Has everyone gone?' I ask in a husky whisper and he takes a step towards me.

'Yes.' His voice is deep and full of something. 'It's just you and me left. Just us, Little Esther Adams. The two of us alone, in the stockroom, in the dark.'

I can't resist looking up at him again. We stare at each other for a long ten seconds, the energy sparking between us in the dark silence.

It's too much. I will explode if I don't kiss him. I can't resist him any longer.

I launch forward, grabbing him by the scruff of his chef whites and pulling him in to me. His lips on mine, we kiss frantically, hands everywhere. Clothes are coming off in all directions and I vaguely note the thud of potatoes rolling off the shelf beside me. He deftly yanks my underwear off and lifts me by my butt, up onto him. I wrap my legs around his middle and feel him pressing against me.

'Oh my god, you're so fucking sexy.' His voice is urgent and low. 'How could anyone not be seduced by those eyes? You've seduced me from across the kitchen, you sexy fuck-ing bitch.'

Bitch? OK, no . . . no, that's fine. That's . . . it's *sexy*. I *want* to be his bitch.

'You're a sexy fucking ...' I can't think what the male equivalent of a bitch is? Prick? Tosser? I'm not sure if that would be OK to say to my boss. I try, 'Um, you're a sexy fucking ... chef.' Luckily, he's panting so hard he misses it.

As he finishes inside me – which I'm totally fine with because I can get the morning-after pill from the twenty-four-hour chemist near my flat – he calls me a whore and it lights something up in me. I've never felt so wanted or so used. And I know with every inch of me that I need more.

CHAPTER THIRTY-THREE

'Are you in the bath?' It's Lou's soft voice muffled through the door. 'Can I come in?'

I examine myself, moving thick bubbles strategically over nipples and bush.

'OK,' I call out, a little lacklustre. I'm finally washing myself properly, in preparation for a visit to my old workplace in the morning. I'm really not hugely in the mood for a Big Chat.

'I just wanted to check in with you.' She comes in wearing pyjamas and a worried expression on her face. It makes me feel worse; patronized and like I'm in this alone. 'Are you doing OK, Esther bear?'

'Sure,' I tell her easily, moving more bubbles around in the water. 'How about you?'

She perches on the edge of the bath and rubs her eyes a little sleepily.

'Lou,' I say, softening. 'We don't need to do this now. Go to bed, you're obviously exhausted.'

'No, no,' she yawns. 'I'm fine. Talk to me. Are you doing OK?'

'Fine,' I say robotically. 'I'm going to visit, um, Carl tomorrow. Y'know, my work mistake? I'm going to A'Diva, the restaurant where we worked together when I was twenty-one. When he was my head chef and I was a lowly trainee!' I don't fill in the blanks; that he no longer works there. That he's left under a mysterious cloud. 'Oh, plus, Alistair is still messaging a lot, so it really doesn't seem like he's *that* into this girlfriend.' I smile as brightly as I can manage. She looks dubious so I add quickly, 'It's all really great. I'm so glad all of this has happened! I have options at last. I haven't had options for years!' I tinkle and Lou attempts a smile.

'That's good,' she says kindly. 'I guess I ... I mean, yes, great, that's very good.' She pauses and I wait. We both wait silently.

I break first.

'Have you heard much from her?' There's no point pretending she doesn't know who I mean but she takes a second to answer, clearing her throat.

'A little,' she nods awkwardly. 'Not loads, to be honest. I don't think she wants you to feel like I'm taking sides.'

I look up so I can clearly watch her face. '*Are* you taking sides?'

'Of course not!' She looks appalled.

Fuck. I was really hoping she would take sides and that — obviously — it would be mine.

'She's, er . . .' Lou coughs again lightly. 'She's had a job offer!'

'Oh right.' I don't know how to react to this. I know Bibi's been job hunting for ages, but the one time I'm not rooting for her to get a job, it comes together. She gets to screw me over, steal my oldest friend, risk something I spent years hurting over – she even gets to have a relationship, something I've been desperately chasing for months with a full-on fucking *mission*. And now she's also got a brand new exciting job on top of everything. Good old Bibi, always landing on her feet. 'Well,' I add begrudgingly, 'that's nice for her, I suppose. Isn't she the lucky one.'

Louise looks uncomfortable and we fall back into silence. I wish she'd go away. I wish she'd just leave me alone. I know she's trying to be nice but this isn't the kind of nice I need right now. I need the kind of unconditional nice that tells me I'm a million per cent right in all this. The kind of nice that fully takes my side and tells me what a fucking bitch Bibi is being. I need a friend to slag her off with me and dissect her personality with. To point out all of Bibi's frostiness and rudeness I never particularly minded until all this.

I pick up a flannel and lay it across my face. Partly so Lou might take the hint and go, and partly because I want to stop any potential tears in their track.

She ignores the signal.

'Oh, so by the way,' she begins fairly cheerfully, changing tack, 'I still think Great-Uncle Merlin is haunting me. I fell over on stage in an audition earlier and I swear it was because some ghostly hands gave me a little shove!'

I really don't think I have the energy right now for Louise's misplaced guilt – or whatever it is.

'Oh dear,' I murmur from under my flannel. It actually smells pretty bad. I think someone must've left it out wet and scrunched up, it's all damp smelling. But if I remove it now, Lou will think I'm up for chatting about this shit. Must be polite, though. 'So you don't think you got the part?'

I feel her shake her head and silence descends again.

'I wish you would talk to Bibi,' she says at last, in a quiet voice. It hangs in the air for a minute, making my bathwater feel cold. Under the flannel I fight all kinds of emotions but say nothing.

After a couple of minutes, I feel her get up and quietly leave the bathroom, shutting the door gently on her way out.

I squeeze my eyes shut and sink down under the water. The flannel floats away and the water deafens my ears. Everything is black and silent.

See how easy it is to shut out the world?

EX 2: CARL HURST

AKA The Work Mistake

PART THREE

A'Diva Restaurant

The kitchen countertop

11.12pm

'I've been waiting to get you alone all night,' he growls in my
ear and my insides twinge, but not in a good way. Grabbing
me by the waist, he flips me around to face him, like I weigh
nothing. It used to make me feel wanted and sexy, now I
feel ... something else.

'Maybe we shouldn't ...' I begin, thinking about the other
woman I saw him holding close outside earlier. But he is
already kissing my neck and it feels rude to make him stop.

The truth is, I've been trying to avoid him tonight. Things
between us lately have been edged with something. I feel

increasingly ... not *used* but, well, yeah, used. It's harder to ignore the talk about us in the kitchen, and the way I'm regarded by everyone else with suspicion and pity. It's getting harder to ignore that Carl clearly has other women in his life. I've even heard awkward whisperings that he has someone at home. Which might explain why he's only let me visit him there once. But I can't ask him, can I? And either way, avoiding the man you're sleeping with isn't easy when that man happens to be your boss.

Tonight was busy in the restaurant and I was hoping to sneak away right after we closed, but Carl loudly instructed me to stay behind and help him clean the fridges. I saw the way my co-workers looked at each other as they filed out for the night. Even Paul couldn't look at me as he said goodbye.

'Get down on your knees,' he orders me now, already undoing his belt. It's been a busier than usual night, and we've been on our feet in a boiling hot kitchen for ten hours straight. He will not taste good.

This is sexy, I remind myself. I am sexy. I am a strong, empowered woman making an empowered choice.

He grabs the back of my head, ramming himself harder into my face. I gag, choking on it, unable to breathe.

I am a strong, empowered woman making an empowered choice to demean myself. To let him do this to me. He grunts, pushing harder against the back of my throat. When I start to gag again, he groans noisily, as if the sick, choking noises I'm making are hot for him.

My knees hurt. I have grazes that are still pink and raw

from the last time we did this. The fashionably tiled floor was not designed for kneeling.

I want to stop. I really want to stop. He tastes horrible, I'm covered in my own foul-tasting saliva and all I want is to go to bed and sleep for twelve straight hours. I'm exhausted – by the work and by him. I want to stop. All of it.

But I keep saying yes to him, so why would he listen to a no now?

'WHAT THE HELL IS GOING ON HERE?' The furious voice comes out of nowhere. Carl lets go of my head and I fall down forward across my own knees. I stay there, in a yoga child's pose – afraid to lift my head to see what's happened.

'GET UP!' I recognize the voice now. It's the restaurant owner Hugo's. He is my boss – he is Carl's boss – he's everyone's boss. 'GET UP NOW, RIGHT NOW!' He's screaming at me, at us both, and I try to find the strength to stand amid all this humiliation.

We've been caught. Caught by the one person Carl can't bully into keeping quiet. People have walked in on us before – kitchen porters, waiters, even a customer once – but Carl knows how to keep the others silent.

The danger – the horrible risk – even invigorated us.

It takes me several long seconds before I can move, and when I finally look, Carl is already back in his trousers and at Hugo's side, speaking in a low tone. I make out certain words though they're both already moving away, heading out of the kitchen.

'Seduced . . . Begged . . . You know what these young girls are like . . .'

I stand still, total fucking horror creeping over me. Caught out by someone I respect so much, doing something like that – there is nothing about this I could've imagined. But it's all my fault, all my doing. I started this, I wanted this.

I feel my insides turn over, trying to exit my body, never to return.

Instead, I get up, brush down my knees and leave out the back way, as quickly as possible. As I go – as I close that outside door – I know I won't be back.

I get a short, sharp text from Carl later that night, telling me it's best if I find work somewhere else. And then I get a dirty bank transfer that makes me feel worse than any other part of the last seven months. I don't see Carl or Hugo, or any of my old work colleagues – apart from one – ever again.

But Carl's words to Hugo stay with me for a long time. Because you see I *did* seduce him. I *did* beg him. Didn't he say those very words to me many times when we were having sex? And didn't I *like* it?

I am disgusting, and all of this was – and is – all my fault.

CHAPTER THIRTY-FOUR

I can already hear Louise shrieking as I put the key in the door.

'FUCKING TOILET!' she's screaming and I take a moment before entering to try to calm myself down. Looking down at my shaking hands, I instruct myself to stop, sucking in cool air for long breaths. I can react to the last few hours *later*.

I take a deep breath, paste on a rictus smile, and go in.

Louise is panting and red-faced as she appears in the hall-way. 'Help!' she says simply, waving a toilet brush uselessly in the air. 'Can you grab the vase?'

I nod, rushing into action.

In the bathroom, we settle into our new routine, empty-ing the overflowing water into the bath, and moaning about the landlord.

After a few minutes, Louise exclaims, 'Oh! Weren't you going to see your work mistake today? How did it go?'

I look down, watching the water swirling down the

plughole. I wasn't going to say anything, I didn't want to admit my latest devastating humiliation. But Louise has already seen and heard so much of that from me. Especially in these last few months. It's all such a mess.

'I've decided not to see Carl,' I tell her, clearing my throat. 'Not face-to-face anyway.' I pause and look up to meet her sweet eyes, curious and round. 'The truth is, I didn't go to see him today, I went to see A'Diva.'

'But he wasn't there?' she asks, sloshing water. 'Doesn't he work there anymore?'

I shake my head. 'No, because they got rid of him. He quit, but only to stop himself getting fired. What he did to me –' I exhale, sharply '– he did to loads of young women. Affair after affair. And he was very quietly married the whole time.'

'Oh my god,' she breathes, visibly shocked. 'That's horrendous. How do you know?'

'I spoke to someone who works there now,' I explain. 'She's front of house manager and I told her I used to work for Carl. We sat down, had a coffee and she told me how he'd been targeting junior female members of staff who worked for him for years. So many vulnerable young women who looked up to him. He'd always got away with it, but things have changed since MeToo. He couldn't escape by blaming his way out anymore. Plus, the last owner, Hugo, had retired and his daughter took over. She was much more savvy and knowledgeable about this kind of thing.' I grin, feeling marginally better for talking. 'Apparently she came in one day a few months ago, called the entire staff together and listed every grimy, disgusting, depraved thing Carl had done – that she knew of.' I glance down at my feet. 'Then she invited him to offer his resignation. Apparently it was glorious.'

'Wow!' Louise looks blown over. 'I bet he was furious.'

'Yep,' I confirm. 'The woman said he was simmering with rage – looked like he was ready to hit the new boss. A couple of his deputies stepped in and escorted him out of the building. They were more than happy to be kicking him out, it seems! Everyone had had enough of him.' I remember the other detail. 'Oh and someone told his wife, and she's divorcing him.'

Louise bites her lip. 'Do you think this woman you spoke to – this front of house manager – had been one of Carl's targets?'

I take the vase from her to give me something to do with my hands. 'I didn't ask, but I think so. She had a kind of look I recognize. But I don't really know.'

We're quiet for a minute, and then she asks, 'How do you feel?'

I shrug and then let my shoulders slump.

'Worse? Better? I don't totally know,' I admit. 'I never wanted to say out loud how horrible that relationship was. And how powerless I felt. I really wanted to believe it was all my choice. That I was a grown-up, making my own decisions. But in another way, it helps to know that what I felt underneath the surface – that he was an absolute monster – was actually right. And it's good that I got to see that. I guess I was just very naïve at twenty-one.' I shake my head at my previous self. 'I *really* thought he was sexy and cool back then. I thought the way he behaved was very adult, and that it made *me* an adult to go along with it. But actually he took the piss and messed with a young girl's head. Actually, not just a young head but his employee's head! It was all very wrong.' I pause. 'But I think that's why older men date younger women, isn't it? When we're young we don't know what's OK or what our boundaries are. We don't push back in the same way or disagree as much. I thought Carl must know better than me because he was older – he was my hero! – so I never said no to him.' I give her the vase now and squeeze my hands together. 'I don't think men like Carl can handle women on their level. Women who don't put up with their shitty behaviour.' I stop, thinking about just how much I did put up with. 'Anyway, the humiliation is all part of this process, isn't it? I have to go back over all these mistakes to see if I could've done anything differently, or learned anything.' I lift my chin. 'And I learned that I'll never go out with a sex pest again.'

'Well, that's a lesson well learned,' Louise laughs. The toilet makes a sudden angry, gurgling noise and we both jump away.

'Ugh, I wish Bibi were here,' I say loudly, annoyed. Lou stands up straighter, looking hopeful and I roll my eyes. 'Only because she has to take her turn at bailing out water!

It's not fair at all, us having to sort out the loo without her. She's meant to ring the landlord and shout about tenants' rights. I did it last time and I was rubbish.'

'I know.' Lou hangs her head. 'I did try before you got here, but I'm so hopeless at being stern when I speak to him. He swore he'd send a real plumber, though! He swore on his own grave!'

'I'm not sure swearing on your *own* grave is a thing?' I consider this. 'Because presumably you wouldn't *have* a grave if you're not dead.'

'Oh.' She looks confused again. 'Well, I'm sorry to be useless. Only Bibi is really good at telling him off. Remember when she called him a bitch-ass-bitch? Do you remember?'

I do remember but I'm not ready to think about it. It was too much fun; the three of us standing around Bibi's phone, while she screamed bloody murder at our landlord.

Louise is silent again, but watching me this time.

'What?' I say in a prickly voice.

'You know what,' she replies softly.

'Look, Bibi obviously doesn't want to talk to me anyway!' I wave my hand. 'I haven't heard from her since she's been staying at Alex's. And why would she need me anymore, eh? She's got everything she ever wanted out of this, right? The girlfriend, the perfect job—'

'She hasn't taken the job yet,' Lou interrupts. 'It's a bit more corporate-y than she's used to and she's not sure—'

I interrupt her right back. 'Oh I'm sure it'll turn out to be absolutely perfect in the end!' I spit, not really recognizing my own voice. 'Bibi doesn't even have to try for it to all fall into place. It's all come together for her, hasn't it? I'm sure the job will be a dream as well! Lucky old Bibi!' This isn't me. I know how hard Bibi's worked to find a job. I hate the person coming out of my mouth, but I am still too angry to be reasonable.

Lou looks confused. 'But you love your job, too, don't you? I thought you did?'

Oh great, another stab of guilt for me. As if I wasn't carrying enough of it.

Yes, I love my stupid fucking job. How brilliant to be reminded! Because I've been sabotaging that to fuck lately, too, along with everything else. I flush with shame, thinking about how little I've been trying these last few months at work. Katie has been rushed off her feet, taking on all my extra workload while I ignored my responsibilities.

I open my mouth and am saved by the doorbell.

It's – predictably – our landlord's useless son-in-law and Lou ushers him through, handing him the vase as she goes. We retreat to the living room where we talk in awkward whispers on the sofa.

'I'm bored. Shall we go to The Swab?'

I look at her, aghast. 'Bibi's pub?! Of course we can't go there, Bibi and Alex might be there!'

'Oh,' she laughs a little. 'No, they definitely won't be! Bibi's not working this week and they never went there anyway – Bibi said it made her sex drive die a thousand deaths seeing Franco.'

'When did she say ...' I frown as the realization dawns. 'Hold on ... Lou, did you know? Did you *know* about them? Did you fucking know about Alex and Bibi sleeping together?'

Her face goes white, realizing what she's said. And what it means.

She looks down at the cushions between us, shame-faced. 'Yes,' she replies simply. And suddenly it's not just Bibi's betrayal — not even just Lou's betrayal! — but the FOMO of it all. My three best friends had a secret together. Without me. Lou continues quickly, 'But look, it wasn't a conspiracy or anything. I just noticed something was up. It seemed kind of obvious to me — all that weird tension between them! All the awkwardness and Bibi's school playground pulling of Alex's hair. And Jesus, the longing glances all the time!'

'I thought they hated each other!' I cry. 'And I never saw any bloody longing glances.'

Lou takes a second before she replies. 'Well,' she begins hesitantly, 'you've been kind of distracted in the last few months with this Seven Exes Mission.'

There is a criticism in what she's saying but I don't understand it.

'But we were all in that together.' I sound defensive. 'I thought you guys were invested in the mission just as much as me. You knew how important it was to me.'

She nods. 'Of course! And we do support you. We talked about it *a lot*. But ...' She hesitates again. 'Sometimes it felt like it was *all* you were talking about. Bibi and I have our own stuff, too.'

'Don't make out like I never asked you guys about anything in your lives!' I search my memory banks but no specifics come to mind. I definitely talked to them about their lives, though; I'm not some selfish prick who only cares about herself. I *know* I asked them about things.

'No, no.' Lou is shaking her head. 'I'm sorry, that's not what I'm saying. You are a good friend, you really are. But me and Bibi have been going through similar things this past year – we've both been endlessly trying to get our careers off the ground, while you've got yours sorted. We've been to countless interviews and auditions, with nothing decent coming of it. And you've been really nice and sympathetic! But it gets boring to keep saying it. We know it's boring to hear, and believe me, it's boring for us, too. But it doesn't mean it's not hanging over everything we do. Everything revolves around whether I got an audition or Bibi got an interview. And then whether we got the job after all that work and emotional investment. It's draining and exhausting – *but boring*.' She pauses, looking pained. 'I guess it's brought us a bit closer in the last few months. We've got a sort of shared pain.'

'Right, so I couldn't understand your bond,' I say shortly, feeling jagged jabs of pain in my stomach. 'You know I didn't make Bibi redundant, and I didn't make you choose such a difficult career, Louise.'

She looks sad for a moment but nods at last. 'I know,

Esther. I'm just trying to explain a little bit.' Then she adds softly, 'It's just that you have your life together – sorted – and we felt so far behind.'

'I don't have everything together!' I explode, before remembering the guy in the bathroom and lowering my voice. 'Lou, that's ridiculous. You know my love life is a mess! That's the whole point of what I've been doing these last few months!'

'But you have a home, friends and a career that you love.' Her voice is pleading as she looks down into her lap. 'You have a stable, decent income and that gives you so much freedom. You have no idea the crushing fear Bibi and I go through every month wondering if we can afford the gas bill, as well as food. You have the important part of life sorted.' She adds hastily, 'And I understand you want to meet someone! But that's not vital, is it? You're only twenty-nine! Humans are all going to live to 150 soon, do you really want to be with someone for the next 120 years? Finding a relationship isn't the be-all and end-all, is it?'

I search her face, wondering if she's being serious. Of course it is! Surely it is? Isn't it? I thought it was?

We fall into an awkward silence. I'm angry – furious actually – but I can't fall out with Lou as well. Then it might start to look like *I'm* the one with the problem.

'So,' I say after another minute, 'you, Alex and Bibi all share everything because I have a good job. You knew about them all along and you think they're a brilliant, great couple, and you foresee no issues when they break up.' I know my tone is aggressive and sarcastic but I can't help it. Why can't she see this from my point of view?

Lou takes a deep breath. 'Well,' she begins carefully. 'I do think they're great together actually, yes.' She stops for a moment. 'And *if* they break up, yes, it will be awful and difficult and sad. It could really make things horrible again and I don't want to lose Alex again either, you know? But love is about taking big risks like this. And if Bibi and Alex have actually found someone who makes them happy, then they deserve to take that risk.' This is a strong speech for Lou. 'And, if I'm honest with you, Esther' – uh oh, I don't need honesty right now – 'I actually think you were much more foolish when you went into things with Alex all those years ago. I'm sorry to say it. But I think that's why you're reacting so strongly to all this – because you know you made a massive mistake back then and a part of you knew it was a bad idea from the beginning. But you ignored that warning sound in the back of your head. It *was* partly your fault that we lost Alex last time, so I think you feel responsible for these two and their decisions now. And you're angry because you don't have any control over what they're doing or what might happen.' She breathes out heavily. 'But, look, Alex and Bibi are much older than we were back then. They understand their choices better. And more than that – they've fallen in love. They *love* each other – already! That's why they kept going even though it might hurt you. And that's not a mistake. Whatever happens now between them – and between the four of us – that can't be a mistake.'

305

I'm fighting back tears. I want to argue and I want to tell her she's wrong. But she's not.

'Esther,' she starts again slowly, a change in her tone, 'don't hate me for saying this, but maybe it's time to stop this mission? It's been such a huge emotional drain for you. You've had such letdowns with Alistair, Paul and Idris. Then facing up to your history with the likes of lechy Carl! It must've been awful. It's been an interesting journey but you don't *have* to finish it. We both know Rich is a bastard, through and through. It's only going to be a terrible thing seeing him again. Especially when you're going through such a rubbish time with Bibi and Alex.'

I consider her words. I think about what a relief it would be to agree. To end this and get back to my life. To throw myself back into my job instead of sabotaging everything. To admit I'm wrong about Bibi and go find her for a hug. To say sorry to everyone for being a selfish dick these last few months – forcing everyone to join me on this rollercoaster mission. It would be so freeing, so liberating for it to be done with and over.

But I can't. I have to finish it. I've come too far with it all and put everyone through too much. I've waited too long for the night bus, I can't give up and walk away now.

But what if Lou is right? What if a relationship won't magically fix things? What if having someone at my side isn't worth ruining my friendships and my career over?

I shake my head regretfully.

'I'm going to finish it, Lou,' I tell her simply. 'I'm going to message Rich tonight.'

She looks alarmed. 'Are you serious?' Her voice is high. 'Please don't be serious. I never thought you would actually see Rich the Bastard. What if you get sucked into his charming bullshit again, Esther?' She looks frantic. 'Why not, er, make plans with Alistair and then see how you feel once you've ruled him in or out?'

I shake my head. 'Nah, I'm not waiting anymore. This mission has taken over my life and you're right about the emotional drain part. I need it done with. I should've been doubling up exes all along, it's taken too long.'

Lou goes a purplish-red colour before exploding. 'This is such a mistake! Can't you see that? That bastard has a power over you and you won't be able to resist him if you see him again! Don't you know enough about that relationship to skip him? It only ended, like, eight months ago! Can't you just picture how smug he'll be when you come running back?'

'I'm not *running back*!' I sit up straighter. 'And you clearly don't understand. I need to do this, Lou.'

'But *why*?' Her voice is desperate.

'You wouldn't understand,' I say again, pulling out my phone, renewed determination pulsing through my fingers.

Lou stands up. 'Well, I can't sit here and watch you do this.' She sounds a bit shaky. 'I'll leave you to it then.' She walks slowly to the door, as if waiting for me to call her back.

'See you later,' I tell her shortly and she gives me one last sad look before leaving. I hear her bedroom door slam just as the son-in-law pokes his head round.

'I think the toilet is completely fucked up now,' he laments.

'It's not the only one,' I mutter, determinedly typing my message to Rich.

EX 7: RICH LOWE

AKA The Bastard

PART ONE

Strawberry Moons

The bar

11.50pm

I feel his eyes on me before I see him. They're like lasers, hot on the back of my neck.

Or maybe that's just the tequila. After seven shots, a couple of bottles of wine and intense dancing for four hours straight, you'd be hard pressed to find any part of me that isn't boiling hot.

Wiping my sweaty face with the back of my sleeve, I turn around, searching for something, and find the sexiest fucking eyes I've ever seen in my life. And they're looking at me from across the room.

The man attached to the eyes is leaning against a pillar, watching me as I move to pay for yet more drinks. It has been hours since I cared what I looked like – hours of drinking and shouting 'woo' at my friends for no reason – with a blanket of booze blocking out how dumb we all looked to the revellers around us. Now, all that self-consciousness comes rushing back in. Suddenly I realize with harrowing self-awareness that I must look rancid. My clothes are mis-shapen on my body and my make-up has leaked everywhere. I suddenly – acutely – care about the fake tan on my arms that has migrated exclusively to my elbows, armpits and fingernail edges.

Carefully balancing the drinks I've just bought, I glance up again. He's still watching, examining me with an almost clinical eye. For a moment I wonder if he is a doctor who's noticed something wrong with me. Surely that's more likely than a man *that hot* fancying me? I'd struggle to believe a genuine fancy even when I look my best.

I stumble lightly – tipping the top inch of Bibi's drink onto someone's back. A large, burly man turns around, squaring up to me and roaring.

'Sorry,' I slur and he calls me a bitch.

'Watch it,' a stern voice warns him from behind me. 'Don't speak to girls like that.'

'Fucking white knights,' I mutter as I turn. 'I don't need your benevolent sexism, thank you. I'm perfectly capabl . . .' I trail off when I realize it's sexy eyes. 'Oh, it's you.'

'I've been watching you,' he says, moving nearer to

my face. Up close his gorgeousness is overwhelming. It's almost hard to breathe. Again, though, that might be all the tequila.

'I know you have,' I tell him with a level of confidence I don't feel. 'I just don't know why.' I feel so uncomfortable under his gaze. And so uncomfortable generally – my bra has somehow twisted itself around with one cup trying gallantly to support both boobs.

'Here, can you hold these for a sec?' I hand him the drinks I've bought for Bibi and Lou, wondering briefly if they're watching any of this. I hope so. Someone has to witness me talking to this sex god – it must be recorded for posterity because it's unlikely to happen again. He eyes my drinks as I fiddle with my bra.

'Can I taste one?' he asks, taking a large sip of Bibi's mojito.

Actually, I hope she's not watching, she'll be livid.

'Hmm, that's really good, I'll keep this one.' He doesn't wait for my permission but I've lost all my power of speech. 'I'm Rich, by the way. What's your name, hot stuff?'

'Who is this very obvious bastard?' Bibi is suddenly at my side. She gives Rich a bleary, but definitely disdainful, once-over.

'I'm Rich,' he grins, apparently delighted with the moniker.

'And I'm pissed off,' she replies coldly. 'Because you're drinking my cocktail.'

'It's delicious,' he grins, unapologetic.

'What's going on?' Louise has arrived too, alarmed at

having missed out. She still looks beautiful, even after the bottomless brunch that turned into an all-night sesh.

'She's got a boyfriend,' I tell Rich, pointing at Louise. He looks back at me, amused.

'And do you have a boyfriend?' He leans in, leering slightly. It does something to my insides.

'Esther's definitely single!' Louise eagerly jumps in. 'She's been single for ages! Like, forever basically! You should take her out!'

'Cheers, Lou,' I mutter.

'I think I should take you *home*,' he says, eyes still intently looking into mine.

OMG I am absolutely gone.

'Christ, Esther, you're not going to buy into that awful line, are you?' If I could tear myself away from Rich's eyes, I would no doubt see Bibi rolling hers in this moment.

Of course I'm buying into that line. He could've told me to put haemorrhoid cream on his penis, while offering me anal, and I would've said yes because oh god, he's *so hot*! How do normal grown-ups resist doing things they know are going to be bad for them? I'm twenty-eight now, I really should've figured this out.

OK, so it's very clear this man is another dickhead – a bastard even, as Bibi said. And I've met so many bastards. *So many*. I have been through a thousand of them on Tinder and Bumble and Hinge and every other space we allow men to continue to be fucking men. And I swore I was done with them. I *am* done with them. Bibi's right. Maybe – for once – I will be the grown-up here and say no when I know I should say no. I will not get suckered into being a sucker. I will be a mature, sensible person who is looking for kindness over abs.

'So?' Rich the Bastard smiles confidently at me. 'Can I take you home?'

Not this time. I'm not going to be another idiot who goes home with a sexy stranger just because he's sexy. I will not let myself fall for the undeniable charms of a bastard.

I make a decision then, taking Bibi's drink from him with determination and facing him with steel. 'Rich' – my voice is strong and my chin high – 'let me just finish this drink and then let's get a fucking Uber immediately.'

CHAPTER THIRTY-FIVE

At the sink, Lou is washing her hands, an intense look on her face. She glances up. 'Ugh, stupid lilies.' She wiggles her fingers at me. 'I look like I've been eating a curry with my bare hands.' I cock my head, noting the orange-stained nail beds.

'Lou, it's OK if you *have* been eating curry with your bare hands, you don't have to pretend flowers did it.'

She gestures at the table and I feel my eyes widen at the huge bouquet of pink lilies, arranged awkwardly in our toilet vase around some green foliage.

'Whoa,' I mutter, stepping closer to sniff them. We never have flowers or plants in the flat. No living things are allowed because we kill them. Idris once bought us a cactus because he said it was impossible to get wrong, but it turned yellow within a week.

'They're beautiful.' I turn to Lou, still scrubbing her hands at the kitchen sink with her back to me. 'From Sven?' I watch her visibly stiffen.

'Er, no,' she says quickly. 'They're from my agent.'

She's lying.

I move to the sink so I can see her face better. 'Your agent? Why would your agent send them? Did you get a job?'

Her side profile to me, she shakes her head. 'Nah, just a, er, yearly thing to make me feel special.'

'You'd probably feel more special if she ever took your calls,' I point out.

Her laugh is stilted.

Things have been super awkward in the flat since the other day, when I told her I was messaging Rich. I know she's annoyed with me, but the truth is I'm annoyed with *her*! We've been best friends for nearly twenty years and her refusal to take my side over Bibi's is bullshit. Never mind the fact that she knew what they were doing and kept it quiet.

But it's not even that.

It's this big secret she's so obviously keeping. And has been for ages. She has the romantic, wonderful thing I want more than anything – a great partner who adores her – and it's increasingly obvious she's fucking it up. I haven't wanted to admit it – and I'm still hoping I'm wrong – but I can't see another answer. I glance over again at the flowers.

I *told* her how awful it was to be a cheater! I told her how you carry it around forever, how much I still think about this unconscionable thing I did to Idris. How *could* she?

She moves to grab the tea towel, noticing my outfit at last. 'You look great!' she says, surprise in her voice. I'm wearing my nicest dress, but her shock is likely more because I've mostly been in pyjamas since BibiAlexGate.

315

'I'm going to see Rich,' I tell her spitefully, wanting a reaction.

She turns round to the sink again but I catch her back stiffening. 'OK,' she says simply and it makes me angrier.

'Yep.' My voice is tight. 'I really think he's probably changed. He sounded super excited to hear from me.'

She doesn't bite. 'Right,' she replies dispassionately.

The truth is Rich the Bastard's reply to my vague hello text wasn't particularly excited. It was enthused but neutral. He said he was happy to hear from me and that a drink would be great, but he gave nothing much else away. And the closer the hour gets until I see him, the more I'm getting this creeping, horrible feeling that Lou is right. I shouldn't be giving him the time of day.

The trouble is, I don't really know why I'm doing it. I *know* I don't want to go back there with him. I *know* he's a dick who would – did – make a terrible life partner. I know I should run a mile.

So why am I going? Why am I not cancelling? Do I actually enjoy self-flagellation?

I don't think it's that.

I think maybe this is about confronting him. Maybe that's really what's driving me to meet up with Rich. I need to finally tell him how much he hurt me, explain to his face how awful he was. To officially say into those sexy ears that he's a malignant narcissist – an armchair diagnosis I have many-a-time labelled him as when drinking heavily with clinical psychologists Bibi and Louise. Sure, I told him off when we were together, but they were all words said in anger, from a place of desperate and dysfunctional love. Maybe it'll get through now, if I tell him in calm tones, with the benefit of distance and much cooled feelings?

I mean, wouldn't that be great? To tell him what a prick he is, to his face, and have him actually *hear* me! Maybe he'd even apologize! Imagine the satisfaction! And the girls would be so proud of me for doing it. Louise would eat her words, after begging me not to see him. She'd be delighted that I ignored her words! She would tell me how brilliant I am for getting the closure and she'd tell Bibi what a selfish bitch she's being after all. Then she'd end whatever the hell she's doing behind Sven's back and tell me I was right all along.

Louise doesn't move.

'Bye then,' I say and get out before she can clock how close I am to crying.

EX 7: RICH LOWE

AKA The Bastard

PART TWO

The flat

Outside the front door, screaming into a phone

8.50pm

'Rich!' I hate the sound of my own voice, whiny and shrieky like it is now. 'Just fucking call me back, OK? Just call me back so I at least know you're not dead.' I hang up, furious, and then hit his name again.

Voicemail. Again.

'Look, you fucking bastard, you're two hours late for our date, what's going on? I won't keep putting up with this, y'know? I'm sick of it. I deserve better than your bullshit.' I hang up again but it's not enough. I have so much more to say. The anger in me isn't going away. It's boiling over again and again, overflowing onto the street like the fucking magic porridge that never stopped bubbling over.

Voicemail again.

'Rich, you can't keep doing this to me.' Sounding broken is even worse than sounding whiny. Who even am I? 'You can't keep claiming you're into me and that you love me and want to see me, then doing this crap. I can't handle the hot and cold! We're both nearly thirty for fuck's sake, not twenty-one.' I take a deep shaky breath. 'You treat me like shit. You're late for dates, you don't reply to my texts for hours – even though I can see the blue ticks, man! And I know you're still seeing other women. Why are you doing this to me?'

And why do I keep letting you? – I don't ask. Instead I hang up and sink down on the step. The stone is cold through my thick black tights and I pull my coat around me feeling foolish in my slinky dress. I thought tonight was going to be so lovely. He promised to take me to a nice restaurant. I got the night off work because he made such a big thing of it. This was meant to make up for the last time he treated me like shit with barely an explanation.

I have to hold onto the anger. If it goes away, I will cry. I can't cry, I hate crying. I've cried so much in the seven months since I've been seeing Rich. I know it isn't working with him, I know this is all so dysfunctional and miserable. But I can't leave. Why can't I walk away? What is wrong with me? I know this is wrong but I keep going back.

Focus on the anger.

Why do I keep getting seduced into thinking things will change? Why do I keep believing him when he says he wants me? The trouble is that he's so fucking charming when we're together. He is so beautiful and sexy and so persuasive.

I shouldn't have shouted on the phone just now. Something might have happened to him this time. What if he's lying by the roadside, having been hit by a bus, and when the police retrieve his phone, all they'll hear is me shouting and calling this poor accident victim a bastard?

I will just call him one last time. I should say I'm sorry.

Someone takes the phone from my hand, sitting down beside me.

'Hello, dear.' It's my elderly neighbour from upstairs. I think her name is Sophie? She's from France or some other sexy European place.

'Oh!' I am too surprised to respond properly. I don't know whether to be angry or confused that she's taken my phone. Especially when I watch her slide it into her coat pocket. 'Um, can I—' I begin but she lightly shushes me.

'I don't know that we've met properly,' she says and smiles sweetly. 'I live above your noisy flat? I am Sofia.' She offers me a gnarled hand and I take it, feeling foolish. It's soft as fuck. This is not someone who has worked hard.

'I'm Esther,' I tell her and my throat sounds dry. Dry from too much shrieking and crying into a phone. 'Sorry we didn't introduce ourselves when you moved in. Have you settled in OK?'

She nods cheerfully. 'Your friend Louise knocked,' she explains. 'She told me all your names and life stories. She brought me biscuits. I ate them but they were not very nice.'

'That sounds like Lou,' I sniff.

We sit quietly for a minute and I shiver in the cold.

'Are you cold?' she asks nicely and I nod.

'A little bit.' I glance over at the elderly woman beside me. 'Um, may I have my phone back, please?'

She ignores my request, leaning back on her hands.

'I have a policy,' she smiles at me. 'People who make you cold are not worth your time.' She looks up at the night sky. It's too cloudy to see much but I look too anyway. I want to see what she sees. 'You can be outside in December, wearing nothing but your pants' – she smiles again coyly – 'and believe me, Esther, I *have* – but if you're with someone kind and special, you won't be cold.' I stare down now.

Hold onto the anger, I tell myself sternly. No tears.

She continues in her soft voice, that French accent coming through more now.

'This man you have been shouting at down the phone, he is *très froid*.' She reaches across to take my hand. Her fingers are warm. 'He has left you out here in the cold. He has made you cold. You could be sitting by a fire in your woolliest of jumpers and you would feel *froid* with this man.'

I do feel so cold. I've felt cold for months.

'Are your friends inside?' she says after a moment. 'They are good girls. They will warm you up. Keep them close and they will make you warm, Esther.'

She stands up, her hand still in mine and together, we go inside.

Sofia doesn't give me back my phone for two days and when she does, there are no calls or messages waiting from Rich.

CHAPTER THIRTY-SIX

I almost don't recognize him when he walks in. He's the same dangerously gorgeous Rich I knew a year ago, but he's also completely unrecognizable. His demeanour is different, something in his eyes has changed and he's almost smaller for it.

Was this me? Did I do this to him? Surely not.

He spots me and shuffles closer, smiling weakly.

'Hey.' Even his voice is different.

'Hello.' I swallow. Some of my righteous anger has gone. Who is this man?

He sits slowly, like he's had flu, and we regard each other for a moment. I take a deep breath. Even if he's been ill, I still get to say the speech. He still did all the bad.

We sit in silence for a moment. I have lost my words. How was I going to start?

I clear my throat, trying to find a way to begin. It's then he leans forward. 'Er, um, before you say anything, Esther,' he stutters in a very un-Rich-like tone, 'I want to say thank you for messaging me. There's so much I've needed to say to you. It's weighed on me so heavily since we broke up.'

It's weighed on *him*?

He takes another ragged breath. 'I owe you an apology.' He leans in, looking haunted. 'A huge apology. I am so ashamed of the way I treated you.'

I feel my mouth open and close. Wait, what?

'I have felt so terrible about everything that happened and how I treated you. I was incredibly unfair and horrible to you.'

'Um.' I had been ready for these words, but from my mouth, not his. 'Yeah . . . you were.'

'It wasn't about you.' He rocks a little and I note the dark circles. 'It really wasn't. I was . . . going through some things.' He leans back away, distancing himself from the words. 'I've suffered for a long time with my mental health and the time we were together was one of my worst periods. I could keep it together for the odd evening, when I was seeing you, but mostly I was a mess. And I couldn't bring myself to open up or tell you.'

I wasn't expecting this at all. I had no inkling of anything like it during our year together. I don't know what to say, so I stay silent. But the sincerity in his words is crystal clear.

'I tried to reach out a few times, y'know after we'd split up, to say sorry and explain but—'

'I'd blocked you,' I confirm simply.

'Quite right,' he nods and falls silent.

'I'm sorry, I had no idea,' I say at last and he shakes his head fiercely.

'No, please don't say sorry.' He reaches across the table but doesn't quite take my hand. 'You have absolutely nothing to be sorry for. I know that if I'd actually talked to you – instead of punishing and torturing you – you would've been kind. You would've tried to help me. But I didn't want help at that point.' He shakes his head, remembering. 'But after you'd gone, I did reach a very bad place and it forced me to confront some things.'

I wanted him to confront things. But pettier things about being nicer to women and not ignoring WhatsApp messages, not this. I wouldn't have wished this on him.

He coughs weakly. 'I've been in therapy for a few months now, and I'm starting to get there with a couple of big things.' He looks away, scanning the pub. 'I'm speaking to someone brilliant – a psychotherapist – and I know she'll help me. I'm also working with my doctor to find medication that works best for me. It's going to be a long process but I'm ready to do the work.'

I nod, taking it in. I thought his behaviour back then was about me, but it was about him. Some of it becomes clearer; his regular disappearing act, where he'd go cold and silent for days or weeks, then come back all sweetness and apologies. His refusal to let me in properly or introduce me to his life. It makes some sense at last. I understand – as much as it's possible for me to.

'I'm just so sorry that you got caught up in my awful mental health crossfire.' He looks down at his hands. 'Depression is not an easy thing to admit to having, especially as a man.

None of my friends ever talked about anything like this. I felt like a freak.' He pauses. 'The stupid thing is, when I did finally speak to them about it, a few others were suffering with similar issues. We'd all kept it bottled up.'

'I wish you could've told me,' I murmur, knowing it's unhelpful.

'I'm sorry,' he says again, eyes searching mine. 'I'm so glad you were finally willing to speak to me so I could explain. I know you didn't think you meant anything to me, but you did and I really needed you to know that. All those nights . . .'

'You mean when I thought you were off with other women? When you turned off your phone and wouldn't answer . . .' There's still a hint of accusation in my voice.

'I can tell you now, I was actually in a very dark, black hole in my own room at home.' He stops, watching my face a little anxiously. 'I don't know if that helps or makes it worse. But I am truly sorry.'

'Stop it.' I shake my head. 'Don't say sorry anymore. I'm sorry I didn't know.'

'Well, if I'm not saying sorry anymore, you shouldn't either.' We exchange small, wary smiles, acknowledging a strange sort of truce between us.

My stomach pools with so many strange emotions. My heart aches for this man I never really knew anything about. I loved him, but I only knew the superficial layer Rich let me see. He didn't trust me with the rest of it and that hurts, but I also understand. It's scary – much scarier than love – to let people see all the broken bits of who you are.

He sits up a little straighter, like he's let go of something heavy. 'It's so good to see you, really, Esther.'

'Same,' I smile, taking in the new Rich. The Rich who has been brave enough to get help. The Rich who has started to take himself apart to make himself better.

It makes him even more attractive, to be honest. And now I know it wasn't me – or even the real him I was dating – maybe there's . . . No, I shouldn't think it. But . . . what if . . . I feel a crack of light piercing through that brick wall of hatred I'd built up. There's something like hope shining through.

What if all of this bullshit was leading me here? What if the last few horrible months were the path I had to follow to find this New Non-Rich the Bastard? What if I had to go through all of those other guys to re-find ex number seven, the final ex, the one I held out the least hope for? What if this was what was supposed to happen the whole time? What if I can help him now, when I couldn't a year ago?

I stare into Rich's big, luscious eyes and feel myself falling.

He reaches across the table and this time he does take my hands in his – and I melt into a puddle on the floor. Just like always.

EX 7: RICH LOWE

Aka The Bastard

PART THREE

Home

Crying over an iPad

1.12am

All men are the same. Cruel, mean, vicious, none of them care about any fucking thing. They feel nothing, they're just a bunch of cold, hard shells with penises. I hate men so much. I don't care if that's unfair and wahwah hashtag notallmen because YES ALL MEN. I fucking hate every single last one of them. None of them care how they treat people. They're all the same.

I sob and scroll. Another sob, another scroll.

'Shushhhh, honey, it'll be OK.' Lou rubs my back and Bibi presses me closer into the space between her head and shoulder.

'You're doing the right thing,' Bibi adds in a soft voice.

I'm deleting pictures of Rich and me, and every single dumb, blurry selfie from a drunken night out makes me cry harder. Every bit of me wants to pick up my phone and message him. I want to *beg* him to come over and see me. I need him to plead with me not to do this. He has to tell me that we have a love worth keeping. I want him to tell me not everyone understands our relationship – they don't understand *us* – but it's worth saving.

The only reason I'm not doing that is Bibi and Lou. They're literally and metaphorically holding me up right now and I can't let them down again. Not again. We've been through this so many times. Me saying I'm done with him – for good this time (every time) – and then letting him wheedle his way back in. But not anymore. He's treated me badly one too many times.

This is the right thing, it's the only thing. He's destroying me and I can't take it anymore. And yet. And yet. And yet.

It makes no sense; he's the one making me cry like this, and I still feel like he's the only one I want to come and comfort me. Why is love so nonsensical?! Surely evolution should've weeded out this flaw in love. This stupid bloody *hope* love forces us to cling onto.

I take a deep breath and keep scrolling through photos. Somewhere inside, I'm finding the strength because I know I can't keep doing this anymore. I can't take the lying and the cruelty. I can't handle the unkindness and the thoughtlessness and the broken dates and the ignored messages. Most of all I can't take the monster it turns *me* into! I am at the end of my patience. I am beyond the end of my patience. I'm through patience, out the other side into pure hatred. And it's the only thing keeping me together as I scroll, sob, delete.

'Should you block him on social media, too?' Louise asks hesitantly. She's being careful, knowing I've done this before. I've tricked her into slagging Rich off, only to go back to him. Bibi doesn't care for subtlety, though.

'Of course we're blocking him!' she says furiously. 'It's the only way to get him out of your life.' She pauses. 'And out of your head, Esther.'

'Right.' I sniff loudly, and one of them hands me a tissue. I wipe my snot first, then my cheeks. I use my sleeves for my eyes.

'Black tears are so disturbing, aren't they?' Lou observes, studying my face. 'It's like you're leaking tar or something. Makes me think of *The X-Files*.'

'Cheers,' I mutter and she grabs my hand.

'Sorry, no, not you. You look unbelievably great with mascara everywhere. It actually *suits* you.'

I pull up Rich's Facebook profile. We're not even 'friends'. He wouldn't accept my request, even after dating for nearly a year. But it didn't stop me stalking his profile obsessively, day after day. Most of his pictures are viewable, and I would spend hours at my desk clicking through them, wondering who that woman was and when that party happened. When you're in a toxic relationship, social media is a troll in itself, goading you into self-torture.

'Well done.' Bibi nods her head firmly as I click the block button.

We fall silent and I stare at the happy smiling face of Rich on the computer screen. You would never, ever guess that he was an irredeemable bastard. An unfeeling monster with no compassion, no guilt and definitely no kindness. And he will never be capable of any of it.

UGHHHHH. All men are the same. And I'm never dating bastards – which is ALL MEN – again.

CHAPTER THIRTY-SEVEN

Holding my hands in his, I feel such a surge of affection for this fragile, broken man.

He's been through so much. If he'd talked to me a year ago, I would've understood. I would've done anything for him, to help him survive. None of us are immune to shitty mental health, and I would've understood.

Rich pulls away after a moment.

'Of course, I'm not here to try to win you back or anything!' He laughs a tiny bit too enthusiastically and my heart sinks. '*Obviously* I'm in absolutely no state at all to be starting – or restarting – any relationships,' he titters again. 'Even if there were anything still between us – which there isn't, right' – he doesn't wait for me to answer – 'it wouldn't be a good time. Love and lust were distraction tools for me, for a long time. A coping mechanism. Until they stopped working.' He pauses. 'My therapist says I won't be ready for a really healthy, loving relationship for a loooong time.' He looks enormously cheerful as he says this. 'Probably years!' he grins, before patting the back of my hand playfully. 'I've got to figure out how to be nice to myself before I can be nice to someone else. At this rate, I'll probably be single forever!' he laughs.

Oh right. Yeah, fair enough. Makes sense.

But for fuck's sake, seriously. So much for my destiny theories.

He sits back in his chair looking contemplative. 'Anyway, Esther, I hope you know you truly deserve more than a man who's only ever treated you like a bastard.'

I nod slowly. 'I'm getting there,' I say quietly.

He smiles. 'Enough about me and my stuff! Talk to me, Esther. It's so lovely to see you looking so well and happy.'

Well and happy! What a load of horse turd. I've never been less well or happy in my entire life.

'Yeah!' I swallow down the lump forming in my throat. 'Um, yeah, it's all . . . good.'

He examines my face silently for a moment, and when he next speaks it's in a kind voice. One I've never heard from Rich before. 'Esther, really, are you OK? What made you get in touch after all these months?'

I stare down at the table unable to speak, but he lets it hang, knowing I'll get there if he gives me the space.

'I don't know,' I say at last, my voice a little trembly. 'Things have just been a bit weird lately.' I hesitate. 'No, not weird, *crappy*.' I meet his eyes and he's nodding ever so slightly, encouraging me to continue. 'I've had a, er' – I take a deep breath – 'quite a big fight with a couple of my best friends. I don't know how to get past it.'

He takes a second before he responds. 'I'm really sorry.' He sounds it. 'I know how much your friends mean to you. Is this Lou? Bibi?'

I shake my head, slightly in wonder that he remembered my flatmates' names. He seemed so disinterested in me and my life while we were together. But I know why now. 'Bibi mainly, yes. And a friend called Alex.' I add quickly, 'You never met Alex, but we were best friends at school.'

He nods patiently and all of a sudden I urgently need to tell him everything. Not because he's Rich, and not even because he's a person I once loved. But just because I can't keep it inside anymore. I need to talk to someone. Someone outside of this whole fucking nonsense. I need some perspective and some kindness from a stranger. And Rich is basically a stranger to me. I never met *this* Rich before.

Huh, I guess this is why everyone loves therapy so much?

And so I tell him everything. I tell him how life was good – how I loved my work and my friends and my life. But how something was missing. I tell him about my Seven Exes Mission and how he's the last of the trips down memory lane. And how good and bad and miserable and brilliant the whole thing has been. I tell him how cathartic and harrowing some parts were, and I tell him how many things I've worked through. I explain how I've revisited my old self and forgiven myself a whole lot and given myself a slap and a laugh. And how it resulted in this huge, horrible betrayal from Bibi and Alex. A betrayal I don't know how to come back from, even though I miss them both so fucking much I want to cry every minute of every day.

And it helps.

Rich is *so* nice. He's kind and non-judgemental. He asks me follow-up questions in a non-pushy way that helps me see things a little more clearly, but he doesn't tell me what I should do or think.

He smiles a big catlike grin when I'm finished. 'So the big question is: has the mission been a success? I know you've learned a lot about yourself and all that, but what about love? Have any of your exes been more or greater than you expected? Is there hope for a soulmate out of all this?'

I inhale slowly. Because I've been thinking a lot about this question in the last week or so. Lying in bed, staring at the ceiling, ignoring my friends, pushing others away, trying to force something with Paul or Will – even trying desperately to feel something with Rich tonight when I could see very clearly that he wouldn't be ready for anything like a relationship for a long time – throughout all of it, there has still been that one person.

'Maybe.' I give him my own coy smile.

'Well,' he laughs happily, 'I hope you do find love, if it's what you want.' He stands up and engulfs me in a big bear hug. When he lets go, he gives me a long comforting look. 'You deserve to be happy,' he says. 'You're a good person, Esther, don't ever feel like you're not. We all make mistakes, and sometimes we're bastards.' He coughs lightly, acknowledging his own bastardy era. 'But it doesn't necessarily mean we *are* bastards. It's too easy to lose yourself and take your stuff out on other people. But everyone's going through their own thing, or coming from some kind of darkness, and we're all just trying to do our best in a tough world.'

I nod and he gives me another hug – this time a goodbye. 'Remember, we all make mistakes,' he tells me in my ear. 'Your friends make mistakes, you do – we're all at it. It's part of being human, and it definitely doesn't have to mean an end. There's always more to the story.'

He kisses me lightly on the cheek and smiles as he turns to leave.

I watch him go, feeling all kinds of emotions and affection for our ups and downs. Hmmm. Now *that* is a guy who will make someone happy one day. And I am delighted to realize I don't want that person to be me. We've been through so much, and I'm really glad Rich is doing better, but he's right, I deserve much more than to wait for someone who only ever treated me badly. I do want to find a partner one day, but it's better to be on my own – surrounded by friends – than to be with someone who takes anything away from my happiness.

On a whim, I pull out my phone to text someone who has always been kind to me, throughout all of it. Even when *I* wasn't being especially kind.

Alistair Morris (school)
I'm so glad we've become friends xx
10.22pm

CHAPTER THIRTY-EIGHT

'There's someone here to see you.' I look up to see Katie in my office doorway. She looks perplexed.

'To see me?' I ask absent-mindedly, but my mind is racing. I've been half expecting a call from Neima in HR for weeks. Y'know, to discuss my recent absences and seriously shit work ethic. And she is the kind of person who will use those words.

But – I check the wall clock – it's 5.10pm on a Friday. Surely they wouldn't wait until the last moment of the week to sack me?

Oh shit, of course they would. No questions asked when I disappeared with my stuff – and fewer questions when I failed to reappear on Monday. Fucking Neima. That clever bitch. She's too good at her job.

Katie shifts her weight from foot to foot. 'Yeah ...' She looks weird. 'It's a bloke. He seems a bit het up. A bit sweaty. You weren't expecting him, right? There's nothing in the diary.'

Of course there's nothing in the diary! It's Friday afternoon. Even if I wasn't currently in a period of being extra shit at work, I wouldn't schedule any meetings for this time of the week. You'd have to be a monster.

I shake my head.

'Shall I call security?' Katie is almost hopping now.

'That seems like a slight overreaction,' I tell her nicely, but I'm thinking: MAYBE WE SHOULD. MAYBE WE SHOULD JUST CALL 999 RIGHT NOW FOR THE LOVE OF GOD. 'Let's just go see who it is and then see if the authorities need to be alerted?' I tinkle a little, trying to ease her fears BUT OH MY GOD I'M ALREADY DIALLING THE NINES ON THE PHONE IN MY HAND WHAT IF IT'S A MANIAC.

It's Alistair.

I blink at the sight of him, standing in my reception, looking at a nothingy framed picture on the wall. He's so out of place here, so incongruous with this world. He reaches to touch the frame and it falls. He catches it, juggling with the corporate art for a second and quickly replacing it on the wall, looking guilty. Clumsy old Alistair.

'Hello,' I say as normally as possible. He turns to me and his whole face lights up into a huge grin, cute snaggle tooth on show.

'Esther!' he says, and I sense Katie hovering nervously at my shoulder.

I turn to hiss at her, 'It's fine. He's an old friend, I know him. You can go back to your desk now. No security necessary.' I'm also not sure what security she was planning to call. Ninety-five-year-old Barnaby on the front desk downstairs?

She looks a little disappointed by the lack of maniacs but does as she's told, still glancing back curiously as she leaves.

'What are you doing here?' I ask, my voice bewildered as Alistair pulls me in for a hug. 'I mean, it's lovely to see you but—' He pulls away, but his face is still close to mine.

Oh that Alistair smell. Jesus, it makes me go weak at the knees.

'I need to talk to you,' he says in an urgent tone, and up close I notice that he does look a bit sweaty – more so than normal – and freaked out.

'What's wrong?' I'm worried now. Has something happened?

'Can we' – he lets go of me fully now, pacing a little in front of me – 'can we maybe, um, I don't know, go somewhere? To talk? I really need to talk to you.'

'Er . . .' I have no idea what to make of this. 'I don't finish until six . . .' I gesture helplessly and he grabs me by the hands.

'Please?' he says, looking deep into my soul and I can resist him nothing.

'OK!' I whisper, checking behind me to see who's about. No one. 'Go go go!' I say urgently. 'I'll meet you outside in two minutes.' He runs for the lifts and I hesitate. Am I really going to leave without a word? Is this important enough? Is he going to say what I think he's going to say? If so, isn't it worth it?

Sod it. I dash inside, grabbing my bag and coat, then running out the door before Katie has a chance to say anything. I feel a pang of something but ignore it, focusing instead on Alistair, waiting for me down there.

He is leaning against the wall outside, and gives me the crooked smile when he sees me. My heart thumps at the sight of him. He's so handsome, just like always. I picture him now in the playground, his curtains flying in the wind as he kicked the football to Nick and the other lads.

He was so good at football.

'Esther.' He says my name again as he closes the gap between us and I'm so sure he will kiss me.

But girlfriend.

I step back and he looks at his feet.

'Can we walk?' I ask, checking over my shoulder for anyone from work who might've chased me out. 'I might get in trouble if I'm seen here.'

He nods and we start moving aimlessly.

'Look,' he begins, sounding breathless. 'I just have to say this thing to you after your text last night. And I feel like an absolute idiot for lying in the first place but I was so overwhelmed and freaked out by seeing you again ... I don't know.' He sighs and I feel my brow furrow. 'OK, I'm just going to say it, and I understand if you never want to see me again.' He takes a deep inhale before continuing. 'I don't have a girlfriend. My last relationship ended over a year ago. I made her up because I was scared of how I felt about seeing you. I was scared of getting back into anything or what it

340

might mean. I was scared of how seeing you was making me feel. I was scared of how much it made me realize nothing had really changed for me.' He side-eyes me coyly. 'And maybe I wanted to make you a bit jealous, too, I don't know.'

I don't look up, I just keep walking, my heart racing.

I have no idea how I feel about this. He lied? Another person who lied to me. But this lie doesn't feel like a betrayal. It feels ... flattering? Sweet? Endearing? I mentally pat myself down. I am pleased by what he's saying. I'm relieved he doesn't have a girlfriend waiting in the wings. Nothing's happened between us but the emotional affair element has concerned me. Seeing him and knowing how I felt about him made me feel awful.

I can feel his anxiety beside me as he starts talking again. 'But then we saw each other again, and then again ... And my lie seemed more and more foolish. And embarrassing. What an idiot to do something like that! I felt like such a dickhead! I've wanted to tell you so many times but I couldn't.'

'So, why are you telling me this *now*?' I try to keep my voice even.

He pauses, stopping me with a hand and turning me to look up at him. 'Isn't it obvious?' he says and my heartbeat notches up from fast to nuclear meltdown.

We say nothing for another minute, just staring at one another, before Alistair continues casually, 'Shall we head down to the South Bank?' He smiles, taking my hand in his, and begins to walk again. 'It's getting dark and it would be romantic to stroll down there, along the river, don't you think?'

'Fucking romantic,' I say, my whole body filling with warmth as he intertwines his fingers with mine.

CHAPTER THIRTY-NINE

Are you my person, Alistair?

Are you him? Are you the person I will finally, somehow, be fully *me* with?

Imagine if you were that person after all these years! Imagine if you were someone I could just *let go* with. Someone I could stop worrying about holding it all together in front of. Imagine if I could be all of the *me* I hate so much; if you were the one person in the world who wouldn't judge me for it. Imagine if I didn't have to say sorry when I let those parts I don't like leak out of me. If you just held me close when I was anxious for no reason. If you stroked my head through hangovers without judgement, if you brought me coffee with three sugars in the morning without being asked, if you left the towels in the specific way I like them. Imagine if you were someone I could show my saggy stomach and boobs to, and you only fancied me *more*. Imagine if you giggled when I farted in my sleep, or bought more chocolate without saying anything when I ate all our supplies for breakfast a week before my period. Imagine if you were him.

Are you the person I'll be able to talk to about all the things I feel sad about? Will I be able to cry in front of you about everything that's happened, without feeling embarrassed and ashamed of myself? Can I get too drunk with you and talk nonsense too loudly, and obsess about that girl I hated at school who has her own cake business on Facebook that seems to be doing annoyingly well now – and *not* wake up at 2am, heart thudding with horror that I have alienated and disgusted you with the real me? Are you him?

I look into those big eyes, examining his long, dark eyelashes – so much nicer than mine – and wonder silently: are you The One?

He takes my hand, kissing the throbby, veiny bit on the inside of my wrist and moves closer to kiss me on the mouth.

Fuck. I think you might be.

As Alistair moves closer, the river shiny and dark behind him, I think about how it will feel to finally touch his lips to mine. To finally unleash the feelings I've been burying for months. The feelings I've kept buried for *years*. Everything seems to move in slow motion as his eyes burn into mine. I can't believe this is happening. He's so sexy. I've wanted this for so long, it's hard to believe it's really happening at last.

No more searching, no more pointless swiping on dating apps, no more exhausting messages with strangers, no more endlessly disappointing dates. Just me and my first love, Alistair Morris. Alistair Morris from the football team, who will be mine forever. Just mine. My first and my last.

As our lips finally touch, a flash image of us getting married crosses my vision. Me in a white dress, laughing as he tears up watching me walk towards him down the aisle. I see us freaking out over a pregnancy test as it turns positive. I see us bickering over who's going to do bedtime with the kids tonight. I see us getting old and teasing each other about our wrinkles. I see us still holding hands, like we are now, as we sit in our medium-sized garden, watching the grandchildren and our dogs chasing pigeons away. I see us reaching across the gap between us and kissing, just like we are now and—

Oh.

Oh no.

Oh no, what's happening here? What is this? He's jabbing his tongue at me, his lips pecking on and off mine. This is less a kiss than it is an overzealous, overworked dentist mining for cavities. Oh Christ, what's going on now? He seems to be gnawing on my bottom lip. It fucking hurts, honestly. Oh, now the peck-jab is back. What is – oh fuck this is bad.

All that awful teen sex we used to have suddenly comes flooding back, triggered by his woodpecker embrace.

He was good at football, I remember thinking back then, but shit at sex. And as a teenager, I was OK with that balance. Now? Probably not so much. And, if this kiss is anything to go by, he hasn't improved much in the intimate areas across these intervening years.

'Um—' I pull away a little, though he jabs me with his

mouth one more time as I lean out. 'I mean, *hmmmmm!*' I add quickly. 'That was soooooo good! But, er, maybe we could, um, just go a little bit more softly?' I venture. He deserves at least a little bit of coaching. Maybe this could still be OK. I owe our grandchildren that much.

He nods eagerly. 'God, it's so good to kiss you at last!' he says, closing the gap between us again. This time he doesn't jab, he mashes. He smushes his lips against mine, lapping at my tongue with an intensity previously known only by dogs on arseholes.

I pull away again when his hand reaches to – and this is the only word for it – *honk* my right boob. I wince in pain and regard him with panic.

This is catastrophic.

Because it's not just bad kissing and bad groping. Those things, you might be able to work with in the end – if a person were open to careful instruction – but this is bad *everything*. There is absolutely no chemistry there between us. Nothing is firing anywhere in me. If anything, my vagina is shrinking further inside my body, husk-like. I can feel it dry-coughing inside me, desperate for a drop of liquid to quench its desert-like thirst.

Jesus. How has this happened? Have I mistaken nostalgia for sexiness? I examine him again now and he looks back at me, eyes half closed, pupils black.

Oh no. I don't fancy him at all.

I mean, I can see he's handsome, and I feel an intense fondness for him and for our memories together. But that's it.

Oh my god, oh my god, oh my god. Am I sure?

I regard him again, begging my body for some kind of spark to ignite. For some kind of flicker to catch inside me. Nothing.

Oh no. FUCK. This isn't my One. Not even close.

And oh my god, I've led him on so much! I've completely led him on. Look at us, romantically kissing by a river in the moonlight. This is a fucking *film set*! He's going to think I love him madly. He's even dumped a fake girlfriend for me. What can I do?

'Shall we walk for a bit?' I swallow a clump of – what I hope is – my own saliva, turning for the path. Tourists continue to pass by, smiling sweetly in our direction, unaware that all my romantic notions have just been crushed to smithereens.

He takes my hand again, sighing happily. It feels nice enough. His hands are warm and it's quite cold, but there's no more to it.

As we walk in apparently contented silence, I realize all those images I had flashing through my brain before we kissed, they could've been with anyone. They weren't really about Alistair himself. They were big, romantic ideals a lot of people hope for from their future. It's OK that I have them, but I can't use him to achieve them. Not when he's all wrong for me.

With my other hand, I fish inside my mouth for something in my teeth. It's a bit of what looks like orange Wotsit. Did I ...? No, I've had nothing like that today. It's come from Alistair's mouth. I almost retch but don't.

'I'm so happy,' Alistair says blissfully, swinging our arms between us as we walk.

Oh god. I feel *so* unbelievably awful.

Louise was right, I shouldn't have done this. I should've quit this mission – this experiment – before it went too far. I've been so caught up in what this project might do for me, I forgot that I could really seriously hurt people in the process. I've hurt Bibi, I've hurt Alex, I've hurt Lou, I've hurt Katie at work. And now I'm going to hurt Alistair.

But I have to.

'Alistair . . .' I take a deep breath and stop walking. For a second, I take one last long look behind him at the view. It's so beautiful here, along the water. If I was walking with the right person, this would be totally magical and wonderful. But he's not the right person, I know that for sure. None of these seven exes have turned out to be the right person. That's why they were exes! And, if anything, this mission has left me more alone than I ever was before. This stupid obsession has taken so much from me.

'Yes?' He looks at me with his lovely crooked smile, eager for another genuinely horrendous kiss, and I tell him the truth.

I watch his face fall, slowly, bit by bit, but as the words come out of my mouth, I feel stronger and stronger. I'm doing the right thing.

And I still have time to fix things. I can fix all of this.

CHAPTER FORTY

I decide to walk home.

The theory was that it would give me time to think and understand where my head is now. To try to see a purpose in these last few months. To think about my seven ex partners and whether any of them meant anything. To figure out a way to not get sacked at work on Monday. To decide once and for all what to do about Bibi and Alex.

But also because it felt a bit dramatic and cool? A bit movie-esque to walk for a solitary two hours in the evening dark. But it isn't movie-esque at all. Unless you're thinking of maybe a depressing sitcom? It's fucking cold and I stood in a puddle within the first ten minutes, which meant I walked the entire rest of the way with a soggy right foot. Then my left foot started aching a bit, so instead of thinking about my romantic situation, I was mostly thinking about how unfit I am and that I should go to the gym more.

At one point I passed a tube station, but told myself, 'No, you've committed to this, you decided to walk.' Then chided myself for the next half an hour for being such a stubborn, prideful prick, forcing myself to stay the course when there's no one even around to judge my backtrack.

I mean, just because you decide to do a thing doesn't mean you always have to fucking do it! You can try things and if they don't work – or you get a soaking wet sock early on – you can stop. Sure, it's good to try new things and push your own limits, but if those limits push back and you find yourself miserable, just don't do that thing anymore!

Ugh. My whole life is a wet foot.

About ten minutes away from home, I spot our lovely gross local pub in the distance.

God, I could do with a drink. I need to chase away the disappointment of this evening, and warm my bones after my not-the-least-bit-movie-esque walk.

But I can't go in, can I? Because Bibi might be working. And I'm not ready to see her.

Am I?

What if I am?

Sigh. Why *am* I still angry anyway?! If I'm really so scared of this new relationship of theirs ruining my friendship with them, why am I going out of my way to actively ruin it myself? Wouldn't it be better to stay their friend and let what will be, be? Either I cut them out now on the off-chance the situation will end with me being cut off, or I stay their friend and hope for the best. And if it's jealousy that's keeping me away, then I need to STFU.

Honestly, I think it's only really my ego preventing me

being OK with this. The idea of my ex and my friend. The idea of them choosing each other over me. That is a hard pill to swallow.

But you know what's really easy to swallow? A drink.

My need for booze trumps my fragile little ego. I'm going into The Swab.

My stomach is in bits as I enter, but the slightly plasticky smell of warm air blasting out of the heaters immediately soothes my many ills. It's relatively busy, I note, a bit surprised. Although – I check my watch – it's gone eleven and it's a Friday night. We tend to be more *off-peak* pub users, when it's quieter. They really should give us a discount.

I scan the room, frantically. No sign of Bibi. Maybe she's out the back, or – god forbid   actually serving customers?! I take a tentative seat at the bar and wait to be served, my back complaining about all that stupid walking.

A woman sitting a couple of stools away leans in my direction, nearly toppling over as she does.

'Hey.' She is a bit slurry. 'You wanna shot? I just bought some shots, you want one?' She waves at the barman. 'Another apple sour!'

I like it when drunk people insist on buying you shots. If I was given a choice, I'd probably say no thanks, but when they insist, it's great! You have no power, you *must* have the shot.

He dumps the small green liquid in front of me and I grimace, unsure how well I can handle an apple sour tonight. We cheers and I thank her, downing the shot in one and ordering a large House of Virtue gin as a chaser.

'Bad night?' she says and I laugh a short, sharp acknowledgement.

'Very, very bad.'

'Please tell me about it.' She turns on her stool, nearly falling again. 'I need to hear someone else's pain – I got made redundant today. It's the third time it's happened to me.'

I gasp. 'Jesus, that's horrendous, I'm so sorry. My friend got made redundant last year and it's been so—' I stop myself. 'Well, anyway, I'm sorry.'

'Not your fault,' she shrugs, waving down the bartender for another green shot. 'It's my own bad choices that got me here. I work in a dying industry. Every time I start a new job, six months later, the place bloody shuts down.'

I nod sympathetically. 'The world keeps changing,' I comment, aiming for wise and sounding grandfatherly. I add quickly, 'I'm Esther.'

'Demi.' She offers a floppy hand to shake. 'Nice to meet you, Esther. So? Tell me why you've had a shit day.'

'Well . . .' I take a long, deep breath, deciding she's drunk enough not to remember anything I tell her. 'I've been on this rather stupid mission lately. Hunting down all my exes to see if I'd let anyone really brilliant pass me by.'

'Wow, exes,' she laughs lightly, leaning her stool back on two legs. It's very difficult to focus when I'm constantly worried she's about to crack her head open. I try to distract her with my life story.

'I know!' I nod. 'It's been an absolute rollercoaster. Anyway, it's mostly been a shitshow of bad choices and embarrassing rejections.' I pause. 'But tonight, I thought my first love might really turn out to be The One.' I look down. 'He isn't, though. He's a really nice guy – really handsome and optimistic and kind and sweet – but it's just not there between us. There's no chemistry. It was like kissing the back of my hand.'

'Give him my number, I don't mind kissing hands.' Demi slumps forward a bit.

I ignore her comment. 'So now I don't know what to do. I've kind of thrown everything I had into this project and not one of the exes was really a decent option.'

'Everything?' she blinks and I nod.

'Seriously! It started off well. I re-found an old friend, which was so lovely and I even put some ghosts to bed. But everything seems to have gone to hell lately, and I've re-lost that friend, plus another one.'

Demi blinks some more. 'Oh no!' She swigs her drink. 'That's the problem with exes. They bring nothing but trouble.'

I huff. 'That's true enough!' I wave at Franco for a wine. 'I just panicked, thinking I'd never meet anyone. I read this old article that said you only really get seven relationships in your life, and one of them is your soulmate.'

Demi lurches forward. 'Wait.' She's looking at me with more sober eyes. 'Not in *Cosmour*? From *years* ago?'

'Er, yes actually,' I frown. 'Did you read it, too?'

She laughs heartily, head thrown back, hair long past the stool. 'I sure did!' she laughs some more. 'And I wrote it!

"The seven relationships every woman has before she finds the one." Right? I was going through my cuts book in this very pub a few months ago and pulled out that copy of *Cosmour*. I think I left it here actually.'

'Oh my GOD!' I shout and Franco looks over, worried. I wave at him reassuringly and turn back to Demi. 'You're Demi Doris?'

'That's me!' she giggles.

'Well then, I need to buy *you* a shot!' I declare, delighted. 'It was probably your copy of the magazine we found. That article changed everything for me.'

She frowns again. 'But not for the better, by the sounds of it.' She pauses. 'I'm sorry.'

I give her a small smile. 'Oh, I don't know, really.' I study the wood of the bar for a moment. 'I think it's been more good than bad. It feels better to know than to *not* know, if that makes sense? And now it feels like I can just move on, knowing that's it for me when it comes to love. I'm done.'

She snorts. 'What?'

'None of them are The One,' I say slowly. 'So I guess that's it. The article said research confirmed it, remember?'

This time – as she leans forward to me – she actually does fall off her stool. I catch her in my lap, and she can't stop laughing as she rights herself. 'Oh my god, don't be ridiculous, Esther! Didn't I just say *I* wrote that article?! Me! Stupid, clueless, perpetually single me! It was just another feature assignment between mass redundancies. Bloody magazines, dying all over the place. The whole thing made no sense really anyway. It was only meant to be a fun, fluffy piece, y'know? Something to lighten the mood between Taliban features and sex trafficking.'

'What are you talking about? It was exactly right about me!' I am outraged.

'Was it, though?' She peers across the space between us as she tries to get back on the stool. 'Or did you just see what you wanted to see?'

I shake my head, furious. 'No, no, I've had all of them – The First Love, The Work Mistake, The Friend With Benefits, The Missed Chance, The Serious One, The Overlap, The Bastard . . .' I recite them so easily. They've been looping through my brain ever since I read her article.

'It's like psychic readings or horoscopes,' she says, waving her hand. 'People read or hear what they want to in them. I mean, like, if you've ever been a teenager, you've got a first love! Even if it was unrequited or – I don't know – a Jonas Brother.' I screw up my nose at this but she ignores my reaction. 'We've all been in love for a first time, haven't we? And as for the rest, they're just obvious.' She pauses, sloshing her drink on the bar a little. 'And I bet your exes could've been described in a thousand other ways, and you still would've recognized them.' She thinks for a second. 'Like, I bet if I'd included a category called The Messy Break-Up' – Idris flashes through my head – 'or The Secret One' – Carl now – 'or The One With All The Ups And Downs' – that would be Rich – 'or, I dunno, The Guy Who Was Almost Good Enough' – Will – 'every relationship can be described in a thousand different ways.'

Back on her stool, she seems to have sobered up a little more now as she continues. 'We're human beings, and we're a little bit of everything. So every relationship has its good and bad moments. I was writing a feature with a very strict word count – the sub editors shouted at me a lot – and you can't include nuance in everything. But life is *fucking* nuanced, Esther. I promise you, you will definitely fall in love again one day, if it's what you want. Maybe you'll find a soulmate of some kind, maybe you'll just find a good guy you can share a family with. Maybe you'll find friends or a job you have that kind of passion for, and a relationship won't matter so much—'

I interrupt her then. 'I *do* have a job and friends I feel passionate about!' I shout this a little too loudly and Franco glances over again. 'I absolutely love my work, and I love my friends!'

Demi regards me solemnly. 'Then why was this mission so important to you?'

Her words stump me.

I have absolutely no idea.

Why *is* having a relationship so important? Before all this, my life was rich and full and *fun*! Me, Lou and Bibi sharing and giggling in this pub every weekend. Me and Katie killing it at the Norris Museum during the week. I was really, truly happy. The only part that dragged me down – the part that made me think I *had* to find someone – was dating. Dating was the only thing that made me miserable.

So maybe that's the problem. Dating. Chasing a mythical great love that may or may not make me happy – that's the real problem here. Not my life – my life is great! Or it was. Before I fucked it.

Suddenly it all fully hits me. I've ruined everything. I've ignored Lou and pushed her away. I've told Bibi and Alex to get out of my life. I've barely made any effort with work in months. If they weren't already going to fire me soon, they're certainly thinking about it after I abandoned my post without a word today. Who could blame them?

'Right.' Demi scrambles for her bag. 'I'm off, babe. Nice chatting to you.' She staggers away towards the exit and I sit for a moment, feeling the full weight of everything.

It's too much and I run for the disabled loo just off the kitchen, tears already running down my face. I've only been in it once before – several years ago – and I dive in, thanking my lucky stars it's unlocked. I couldn't face sweet drunk women in the ladies' offering me tissues and lipsticks. I slam the door shut and turn around, leaping five feet in the air when I realize it's already in use. By Franco.

'Oh my god, I'm so sorry, Franco!' I shriek, grabbing for the door, and wailing slightly, as tears stream down my cheeks.

'Whoa, whoa!' He's waving his hands and flecks of liquid are spraying everywhere. 'It's OK! Esther! I was just washing my hands!' He shows me and I calm down ever so slightly. 'Are you all right?' He peers at me worriedly. 'You're crying – what's wrong?'

He puts a hand on my arm and I inhale a big, shuddery breath.

'It's nothing!' I try to say but my voice comes out as a squeak.

'Just sit down for a minute,' he instructs in a firm, nice voice. 'Here, I'll take the baby changing table.' He perches, waving me towards the loo. 'And you have a sit there.'

I nod, following his instructions. I'm too weak and drained to protest.

'Do you want to talk about it?' he asks after a moment and I hesitate.

'Not really,' I say honestly. I'm done with talking. Telling Rich and then Demi about this whole experience has put a few things in perspective. I know what I have to do next; it's just all too big and too much right now. 'I'm fine, I just needed a minute on my own.'

'Do you need a hug then?' He smiles and it's a little lechy.

'Um, no thanks,' I say, suddenly wondering why he stayed. I was a crying girl in a loo, clearly looking to be alone. We're not friends and I said I didn't want to talk. He was under no obligation to stay. In fact, it was weird to stay.

'Come here, let me give you a cuddle.' He stands, reaching for me, and I draw back, a bit alarmed. 'It'll make you feel better, I promise.' He grabs me and bundles me into his arms. I pull away but he's strong. What's happening here?

'Let go of me, Franco, seriously,' I say in an embarrassed whisper. Why am I not shouting? Why am I *embarrassed*?

His hands move down to my arse and something in me loosens. I bring my foot up as high as I can and stamp it down on his with my full force. Then, with the other leg, I knee him squarely in the balls. He yelps, falling away, and I dash for the door.

I'm free seconds later and running for the pub exit. I don't stop until I find myself outside our front door, breathing hard.

Shit, Bibi was right about Franco. This must be why she hates him so much! Why she's always telling him to get lost and trying to keep us away from him. He's a fucking creepy assaulting scumbag monster.

I have to talk to her.

CHAPTER FORTY-ONE

My furious stomp through the front door and down the hallway is loud enough to bring Louise out of her room.

'Er, are you OK?' She unsubtly pulls her door shut behind her. She never used to do that.

'Sorry,' I stammer. 'I just had to dump Alistair and then fight Franco.'

Her face falls and then rights itself into one of pure confusion. 'What? Sorry what? Wait . . .' She tries to comprehend my words. 'You . . . when were you with Alistair? Why . . . did you say *dump*? And what did you say about Franco? As in Bibi's Franco? Were you in the pub? What is—'

'It's a long story,' I say and sail on past her, towards the kitchen. 'Do you want a drink? I'm having one. Or fifty-five. Does your secret bedroom pal want one, too?'

I don't turn around but there is guilt in her voice when she replies. 'What do you mean *bedroom pal*? It's just, er, Sven!'

'Sure it is.' I roll my eyes, hands already deep in the fridge fishing out wine. Hmm, pretty sure we opened this bottle two months ago. But that's fine, right? Wine is like cheese, it just gets better with age. Sometimes you just have to scrape off the mould.

Grabbing a large glass, I pour liberally and take a swig, ignoring the luminous film of stagnant liquid swimming on top. Louise joins me and I pour her one, too. She frowns at it but says nothing, following me to the sofa where I collapse.

'Talk to me,' she says after a disgusting sip. 'What's happened? You saw Alistair?'

'Yep,' I nod, taking another long drink. 'He lied about the girlfriend and wanted us to be together. But it turns out kissing Alistair is like climbing inside a working mine and having someone with a pickaxe attack your face.'

She gasps and then gasps again. 'Hold on.' She brings up a finger. 'Yes, that's right. He was always a bad kisser when you were together at school, wasn't he? But *surely* he's improved since then. We were all bad kissers at school.'

I sigh. 'It's not his fault.' I put down the glass on the coffee table and flop back into the sofa cushions. 'It's mine. Or no one's, I don't know. We just have zero chemistry, it was awful. I'm so sad and I feel terrible that I had to hurt him like that.'

Lou leans back and into me, trapping my arm. I release it, circling it around her shoulders instead.

'Well,' she says slowly. 'I know I was all for Alistair, but I was also a bit worried about you getting back with him.'

'You were?'

'Yeah!' She nods against my shoulder. 'I mean, I got the impression he hasn't changed much since school. He's still mates with loads of people from school – organizing reunions and that. He's still obsessed with his school girlfriend. He still wears Lynx Africa like when he was fifteen. And have you talked to him about his flat? His parents pay his rent! He told me at those reunion drinks!' She looks agog. 'He hasn't really matured much, has he? He had that tantrum when you first met him up with him – storming off to punish you for saying something really not even that bad!'

'You never said that at the time!' I sit up a bit straighter. 'I thought I was really out of order, and that's why he abandoned me like that.'

She shrugs. 'Well, you were *a bit* out of order, too. But adults can't deal with stuff by storming off into the night all the time, can we? That was lame. And how immature was it for him to lie about having a girlfriend to – what? – make you jealous?' She throws her hands up, spilling the old wine on me. 'I mean, come on, that's not cool! How would a long-term relationship work out with him if he lies or throws tantrums when he's not getting his own way?'

I consider this. Louise has hardly spent any time with Alistair these last few months, and yet she sees him so much better than I do. Maybe I never really wanted to get to know him as a grown-up; as the Alistair he is now. I wanted to relive the glory days with the football captain from school. Maybe it never would've worked because I didn't let myself get to know him *now*.

'Perhaps you're right,' I say slowly, the guilt and regret I feel over Alistair easing off.

'With a long-term relationship,' she continues authoritatively, 'you have to be really honest and open.'

Huh.

I ease her off my shoulder and turn to face her. I can't keep pretending. I want her to talk to me. I want her to tell me the truth – whatever that might be. And whatever it means for her poor boyfriend, who I'm actually really fond of.

'Er, like you are with Sven?' I say it softly, as kindly as I can manage. I don't want her to feel judged.

She looks down at her drink. 'OK, yeah, so I haven't always been, but we're working on that. I'm getting better.'

'You *are*?!' I am incredulous. 'You mean apart from the' – I'm going to say it, I'm totally going to say it – 'cheating?'

Louise looks up, her face suddenly unreadable. 'What?'

'Come on, Lou,' I sigh. 'Who's really in your bedroom right now? And who have you been secretly texting the last couple of months? You're cheating on Sven, aren't you? It's pretty obvious. Talk to me.'

Something crosses her face and for a moment I think she will start crying. She puts her head in her hands and her body shakes. But no, she is . . . laughing. Laughing laughing laughing, until she's vaguely hysterical. I watch, bemused.

I mean . . . I guess it must be quite a relief to be confronted with it? This is relief, I suppose? She must've been dying to tell someone. To confess.

'I'm not *cheating* on Sven!' she finally chokes out through her laughter. 'It *is* Sven in my room right now, you can go check!' She calms down a little. 'Although, please don't, he'd be very embarrassed in his costume.'

'*Costume?*' I am truly confused now.

'Yeah!' she nods enthusiastically. 'We've been doing a lot of roleplay stuff lately. Dressing up and getting into character. It's a bit embarrassing but it's really helped our sex life. I feel closer to him than I've ever felt. We're really, truly great.'

'But what about all the misplaced guilt you were feeling?' I cry and she looks baffled. 'Y'know! About my great-uncle Merton? You were obviously feeling bad about something. I thought it was because you were cheating on Sven and were feeling a bit haunted because of it.'

'No!' She shakes her head seriously. 'I genuinely feel really bad about your great-uncle Merton. We were so disrespectful at his funeral.'

'Really?' I'm still sceptical.

'Honestly!' She's nodding a lot. 'And I actually do think he's haunting me, for the record. I feel haunted. But not emotionally – legitimately!'

I shake my head, trying to understand. 'But what's changed?' I ask. 'You and Sven have had rubbish sex for years. Where has all this renewed effort come from?'

She looks sombre for a second before answering. 'It was that thing you said ages ago – at the start of all this.' She turns away, suddenly shy. 'You'd just met up with Alistair and I asked if you really thought it was possible to have a different kind of relationship with someone you'd already tried to love once. You said yes, and it got me thinking that maybe things could be even better with Sven.' She laughs lightly. 'You were trying it seven times, why couldn't I try it once? Y'know, *try* having a different kind of relationship with Sven that actually includes the physical intimacy I've been missing. And it turns out I could. So easily. He's such a kind, wonderful person, Esther, and he was so up for trying this with me.' Lou turns back to me, looking moony. 'We still have our moments, y'know – nothing is perfect! – but I'm lucky to have Sven, and I'm really grateful for him. We've been having so much fun trying out new things and giving each other our undivided attention. It turns out' – she looks surprised even as she says it – 'I am completely mad about him *and* his penis.'

'Wow!' I breathe.

She hangs her head. 'I'm sorry I didn't share any of this sooner. And sorry I've been so cagey, but I felt silly. It was all a bit too embarrassing to explain the cosplay stuff.'

'Oh my god, that's wonderful!' I shout, giving Louise a huge hug. 'I'm so happy for you. Go get him dressed – I honestly do not want to see Sven in a sexy costume – and we'll get drunk together.'

She laughs again, hugging me for an extra minute. 'I'm sorry about Alistair,' she whispers into my hair. 'I'm sorry about the others, too.'

'It's OK,' I tell her and I really do mean it.

She runs to fetch Sven and I realize my phone is buzzing. Shit.

It's Katie, and her name sends terrible pulses of guilt

through me. I want to ignore it so badly. I want to continue pretending nothing is wrong and that I haven't been behaving like a twat at work lately.

But I have to start growing the fuck up and taking responsibility for my actions. If I'm going to get sacked, Katie doesn't deserve to as well. I can't take her down with me. She's brilliant and I've let her down.

'Hi,' I answer solemnly. There is no immediate reply. 'Hello?' I try again and this time Katie heaves a huge sigh of relief down the line.

'Oh thank god you're OK!' she says, her voice a little shaky. 'I was so worried. I've texted you, like, five times to ask what happened earlier. I was about to call the police. I thought that sweaty maniac had kidnapped you.'

'I'm really sorry, Katie,' I say, meaning it. 'I had a . . . thing and I had to run out. I'm sorry, I know I've been letting you down big time lately.' I realize as I say it how much I've missed throwing myself into work the last couple of months. The truth is, I love working for the Norris, I love planning events! And before all this, Katie and I have been such a great team. I've ruined it with my tunnel vision on this silly mission. 'I swear I'm getting my shit back together,' I tell her. 'From Monday I'm back in the game.' I pause. 'Unless HR have already decided to let me go. Honestly, I couldn't blame them, I'm really so sorry.'

'Let you *go*?' Katie sounds aghast. 'Why the hell would they let you go? They love you, I love you – everyone loves you!'

I wince at her niceness. 'Katie, that's really generous, but I know I've been useless lately. Missing days, ignoring events, handing off all my work on you. And then running out of the office like that earlier.'

She is silent for a few seconds. 'I mean,' she begins, 'leaving the office half an hour early on a Friday is officially *not* the end of the world. Especially when we don't even have an event booked in. Most of the team do it, haven't you noticed that?'

Oh.

Oh, right, I guess that's true. Now I think about it, Katie and I were probably the only ones left there when I ran off earlier. Us two and ninety-five-year-old Barnaby the security guard. Even Danielle on reception had buggered off, that's why Katie had to tell me Alistair was in our office. It's probably why she was so scared of him, too. We were pretty much all alone on our floor.

'And as for the rest' – she sounds a bit sad – 'I actually thought you were giving me more to do and more control over our events because I was doing so well. I was delighted! You're an amazing boss and so great at what you do, but sometimes you forget to delegate. I thought you were finally trusting me to get on with things by myself.'

'Oh Katie!' I rush to interject, feeling terrible. 'I *do* trust you, I promise I do. And you've done so brilliantly on everything I've given you.' God, have I been an absolute control freak? 'I promise I'll keep delegating, I'll keep skiving so you can do more.' I pause. 'But what about all the days off and holiday I've been taking?'

She laughs again. 'Esther, I think you've forgotten you don't work in kitchens anymore. You're *allowed* to take time off, you know? Nobody minds that. In fact, the only time anyone ever says anything negative about you is to moan that you make the rest of us look bad by not taking your full holiday allocation. You work – or you were working – way too much and far too long hours.' She pauses. 'In fact, I was so glad you were finally prioritizing your life outside of work a bit.'

Her words fully sink in. 'You mean, you haven't reported me to Neima in HR? Or to the bosses?' I ask hesitantly.

'Reported you?' She sounds horrified now. 'Esther, I would never do that! Even if I did think you were a big old skiver. Which I don't! You're the best boss I've ever had. The other places I've worked at were so stressful and I got shouted at so much. You're really patient with me. I've learned a huge amount working under you. I mean it, Esther, you're a great boss.'

I swallow down the lump forming in my throat.

I haven't fucked things up with my job. Seriously, thank god. I don't know what I would've done if I had. Thank god.

'Thanks, Katie,' I say quietly. 'I hear everything you're saying.' I smile. 'Now stop sucking up to your boss and go enjoy your weekend. It's bloody late, you know.'

We say goodbye and I make a mental note to talk to my boss about a promotion for Katie on Monday. She more than deserves it. I head to the kitchen to find the years-old bottle of whisky I resort to in emergencies. I make another mental note to buy some new alcohol for this flat, but for now, it's all we've got and I need to celebrate.

And I also require some Dutch courage for what I need to do next.

Despite what I just said to Katie, I don't care how late it is. I'm going to see Bibi.

CHAPTER FORTY-TWO

With Louise in tow, I fling open the front door of our building, the cold air slapping me wide awake and readying me for a whole new mission.

This one isn't about exes, but it *is* about love. But a much better love than stupid romantic love. It's about my friends.

Lou is breathless at my shoulder, moving too close to me, but we're both too excited to slow down. Which is how we end up bowling over a couple on our doorstep as we leave.

'Sorryyyyy,' Louise and I both shout, picking ourselves up, as I add, 'Sorry, we were rushing. Are you guys OK?'

We reach down to help up the pair, who are still entangled, and realize that it's Ivan and Sofia.

Louise gasps. 'You were kissing!' she says, pointing out the obvious, which is handy because I still hadn't fully comprehended what we were seeing.

'At last!' I squeak. 'You took your time.'

'Yes, indeed!' Sofia announces, looking decidedly delighted. 'And it was really very good.'

'Lucky you,' I mutter, my lips still a bit sore from the earlier gnawing.

'This is our third date,' Ivan explains, grinning cheekily. 'I'm hoping to get lucky tonight.'

Sofia elbows him. 'You're already lucky to be dating me, young man.'

'I sure am,' he beams, pulling her in close to his side.

'But ... but ...' Lou can't get her words straight. 'Who's Pearl then?'

'Pearl?' Ivan looks perplexed but Sofia starts laughing. She whispers something to him and his face clears. 'Oh right, that's what I call my teeth.' He flashes us his giant veneers. 'I have to take good care of my Pearlies.'

Louise makes a weird noise and goes red. 'Oh,' she stutters. 'Well, that's good then.'

'But how did this happen?' I ask, feeling emotional despite myself. It's all too much. This is just too, too nice.

'We matched on Tinder!' Sofia declares, clearly thrilled.

'We did,' Ivan confirms seriously. 'I had to set my distance settings to the bare minimum to make sure I found her on there!'

'But if you were so keen, why did you keep saying no when Sofia invited you in for tea?' Louise is still fighting to understand.

He huffs. 'Oh, I can't get up those bloody stairs! I'm seventy-two don't you know.'

'I'm seventy-*seven*,' Sofia teases and he smiles at her, looking up at her with such adoring eyes. 'And you could've invited me down for tea instead.'

He looks alarmed. 'That seemed a very impertinent thing to do! I didn't want to make you uncomfortable, Ms Dove. I don't know, the very idea of it! Inviting you into my bachelor pad, what would people say about you and your reputation if I did that?'

'I know you're in your seventies, Ivan,' I say nicely, 'but this is not 1953.'

He nods slowly. 'Maybe I've been watching too much *Downton Abbey*,' he admits thoughtfully.

'Well then, you really shouldn't be getting *lucky* without a proposal,' Louise reminds him and the new couple both look at each other shyly. Ivan takes a deep breath, turning to Sofia and bending down on one knee.

Louise fully screams, 'OH MY GOD HE'S DOING IT!' just as Ivan and Sofia both start laughing. She helps him back up.

'Just joking, love,' Ivan says. 'You youngsters are far too caught up with your silly romantic notions of fairytale endings.'

Guilty.

'Oh.' Louise looks disappointed. 'But fairytale endings are really nice!'

Sofia gives her a comforting pat. 'Maybe we will do that one day, but we're not in any rush,' she says gently. 'We've got plenty of time. I'm only seventy-seven!'

With that, they start snogging again and we tiptoe away, me struggling not to cry and Lou muttering something about baking them love cookies.

I pull myself together – no tears, not yet. I have a feeling there will be a lot of crying on its way and I don't want to get too dehydrated.

CHAPTER FORTY-THREE

Standing on Alex's doorstep, I am suddenly very hot. Too hot. I need to take this coat off.

'What are you doing?' Louise hisses. 'Ring the doorbell!'

'I'm trying to get this coat off!' I wave at her, annoyed. 'I'm too hot to see Alex and Bibi yet. I need to cool down. How can I say sorry properly when I'm TOO HOT?'

The coat zip sticks halfway down and I yank at it several times. It doesn't move.

'Do you need a hand?' Lou offers helpfully.

'Of course I don't need a hand!' I snap. 'It's a ZIP, Lou, I am familiar with zips, I have used zips before in my life. It's stuck, that's all!'

'Maybe a bit of fabric is caught in it?' she suggests and I turn to face her.

'Obviously a bit of fabric is caught in it, *obviously*, Louise,' I say crossly. 'Zips throughout time have got stuck for that very reason, I'm familiar with that situation. I *know* it's probably a bit of fabric that's stuck in the zip. I KNOW THAT, LOUISE.'

She shrugs. 'Just trying to help.'

'I KNOW YOU'RE TRYING TO HELP,' I yell at her, too hot to keep my voice down. 'BUT HELP OF THIS KIND IS ACTUALLY KIND OF UNHELPFUL, ISN'T IT? WE ALL KNOW THAT ZIPS GET STUCK, WE ALL KNOW HOW ZIPS ARE SUPPOSED TO WORK AND WE ALL KNOW STUPID BITS OF FABRIC CAN BREAK THEM VERY EASILY. HONESTLY, IT'S SO WEIRD THAT WE'VE INVENTED DRONES AND NUCLEAR WEAPONS BUT WE HAVEN'T FIGURED OUT SOMETHING BETTER THAN ZIPS THAT BREAK THIS EASILY—'

'Um, guys?' A sleepy-eyed Alex has opened the door. 'Why are you shouting about zips on my doorstep?'

'BECAUSE I'M HOT, ALEX!' I stop short when I realize she is actually here, in front of me. A person I came to say sorry to – who I am now shouting at.

'They came up with Velcro,' Louise mutters from behind me.

'Sorry,' I lower my voice, giving up on the coat. 'I'm sorry for waking you up and' – I burst into tears right there on her doorstep in my hot coat, half pulled off – 'I'm really sorry about everything, Shelley.'

She steps outside, gathering me up into her arms and hugging me close.

'I've been such a dick,' I sob into her shoulder, my eyes pressed shut. I suddenly feel another set of arms close around me. I don't need to open my eyes to know who it is – I can smell Bibi's perfume.

'Sorry, Bibi,' I wail, enclosed by arms and bodies. I'm hotter than ever but I couldn't care less.

'I'm sorry, too,' she wails back with emotion I've never really heard from Bibi before. 'I'm *so* sorry. I feel so terrible about everything. I wanted to say that right away but I couldn't get the words out.'

'*You* feel terrible?!' I sob. '*I* feel terrible! It's all my fault. You did nothing wrong. I made it all about me when it wasn't anything to do with me.' I draw back slightly so I can look at them both. We're all tear-stained and red-faced, despite the cold night air. 'It should've been about you two! I should've listened to you guys and been excited for you. I hate that you felt you had to hide it from me! But that's down to me, I know, because you knew how badly I'd react! I didn't give you the space to tell me or reason to trust me with your secret. I'm so ashamed of myself.'

'We shouldn't have hidden it!' Alex cries. 'We were just so shocked when it happened between us. It was so unexpected, but' – shame crosses her face – 'also so amazing. And then I think we just wanted to make sure it was real before we made a big thing of it and risked upsetting everyone.' She looks at Bibi with an expression I never saw when we were together. 'It *is* real, right, Beeb? And,' her old Aussie nature leaks out and she grins as she adds, 'it's also *unreal*.'

Bibi nods, smiling this ethereal smile. She tries to look back at me but can barely drag her eyes away from Alex's visage. 'It's absolutely the real and unreal deal.' She beams, finally turning back to me. 'It's so real, Esther. We wouldn't have done this to you if it wasn't.'

'You haven't done anything *to* me.' I sniff loudly. 'I shouldn't have made any of this about me. It's about you guys. And I'm really, honestly so happy for you both.'

'SHUT THE ABSOLUTE FUCK UP,' someone screams from the window of a neighbouring house. 'IT IS TWO IN THE FUCKING MORNING.'

We snigger and then all start crying again when Louise throws her arms around the group.

'I'm so glad we're all friends again,' she murmurs, cuddling us hard. 'I wish you'd all stop falling out with each other.'

'I'M CALLING THE FUCKING POLICE,' the neighbour yells.

'We should probably go in . . .' Inside the four-way hug, Alex looks worried.

'Yes, everyone come in!' Bibi sounds exuberant as she lets go, and I notice for the first time that she's in her pyjamas. They're really a couple. 'I need to hear about everything I've missed. You need to fill me in! What's happening with the mission?!'

She doesn't wait for an answer before herding us all inside. Louise and I have just a half second to glance over at one another. There's so much to tell her, I don't even know where to begin.

CHAPTER FORTY-FOUR

'Guess what!' I settle into Alex's big corner sofa, eyeballing Bibi. 'Louise *isn't* cheating on Sven!'

Bibi sits up straight, looking fascinated. 'She's not?' She turns to Lou, who looks affronted. 'I thought for sure you were!'

'No,' I shake my head delightedly. 'She's just having great sex with her boyfriend!'

'With Sven?' Alex looks interested. 'I thought it was rubbish, Lou?'

'It was,' she says defensively. 'But now it's not.'

'What the fuck!' Bibi shouts with shock and delight.

Lou huffs. 'See, this is exactly why I took ages to talk to you guys about it, because I knew I'd get the piss taken. It's not easy to try something new, you know? I'm basically super brave.'

Bibi and I laugh, united in our teasing of Louise once again. 'No, you actually really are,' I say sincerely. 'And I'm so happy for you two, Lou. It's brilliant. You and Sven deserve all the happiness in the world. He's a good bloke.'

She softens, looking gooey-eyed. 'He is amazing.'

'Sven is great,' Bibi smiles warmly. 'And we're really pleased for you.' Alex places a tender hand on her girlfriend's and I roll my eyes.

'Ugh,' I moan, only half joking. 'Am I going to have to deal with you three being all cute and loved up from here on out?' Bibi and Alex grin at one another. 'I thought the last few months were meant to be about finding *me* my happily ever after. Stupid Seven Exes Mission.'

'Is that it then?' Bibi looks a little sad. 'The end of your mission? And none of them were right? None of your exes?'

'Nah,' I sigh. 'I guess I ended all of those relationships for a reason after all. Who knew Younger Esther actually had some sense?' I hesitate. 'And, surprisingly, I feel pretty good! I have a new perspective on things, y'know? I have a job I really love' – I pause, thinking about my chat with Katie – 'that I have somehow – miraculously – managed to not fuck up. I have some pretty great friendships that I also haven't fucked up *too* badly.' I grin around the room at my three best friends. 'And, believe it or not, after everything, I do still actually have faith someone nice will probably come along to marry me at some point. I don't know why I was in such a rush, there's plenty of time! I've got my whole thirties!'

'And then the divorce circuit kicks in, when a whole load of great new options get unleashed onto the market,' Bibi points out helpfully. 'You won't think twice about your seven exes!'

'Technically I think it was only ever six exes anyway,' I

muse. 'Clearly Paul never counted as an ex. He never was a Missed Chance. He was an idiot.'

'But what about your other Missed Chance?' Lou asks, her brow furrowed. 'He counts as a seventh ex.'

'What seventh ex?' Alex leans forward a little, intrigued.

'You know! Her *other* ex!' Lou looks from me to the others expectantly. 'You know?' She rolls her eyes. 'Nick!'

Everyone looks at me.

Lou stamps her foot a little impatiently. 'I know you didn't include him in your Seven Exes Mission, Esther, but I thought that was just because he didn't work with the magazine article thing. It was such a perfect fit for all your other exes, I thought you'd deliberately left him out because you wanted it to – I dunno – fit the narrative. He didn't make sense with the others.'

'Oh my god, there's a secret eighth ex?!' Alex gasps. 'Nick who?'

'No, no!' I laugh nervously. 'He wasn't – he isn't! – an ex.'

Louise scoffs. 'Of course he was!'

'Wait,' Alex moves in closer. 'Not Nick from school? Nick Wilde?'

'No!' I say again, firmer this time. 'We never actually dated – Lou is being mad. We never even went out on a date together! He's *not* my ex, shut up, Lou!'

She gives me a firm stare and I watch as she straightens her back and lowers her voice.

'Do not tell me to shut up, Esther.' She says it softly but with purpose. This secret sex mission she and Sven have been on has clearly given her bonus confidence. 'And you know I'm right.' She turns to an open-mouthed Bibi and Alex, who – I note – are holding hands excitedly.

'They had a one-time thing at uni and then met up again a few years ago.' She glances back at me. 'Just because it hasn't gone any further doesn't mean it wasn't real between you.'

Fuck. I never should've told her anything. Why did I tell her? I knew I couldn't trust her. I mean, er, I couldn't trust her beyond these, like, ten years she's kept all this a secret.

Bibi is goggle-eyed. 'Come on, tell us! What happened between you at uni?'

I take a deep breath. Fuck it.

SECRET EX 8: NICK WILDE

AKA *The Ex That Wasn't An Ex*

PART ONE

Durham University

The student bar

2.31am

'I always had a crush on you at school, you know?' Nick is
lying next to me, on a bench covered in penis doodles. We
university students might technically be adults, but we're not
grown-ups. Especially when working with a toxic combination of marker pens and alcohol.

'No you didn't, shut up,' I laugh.

He turns to face me, looking serious. 'I did, I really did.
But then Alistair said it out loud first and I knew he'd be
annoyed if I said I did too. Or maybe I was worried he
might think I was copying him or something. So I became

your matchmaker instead, shouting at you across the play-ground!' He laughs a little cynically. 'Such an immature thing to do.'

I'm silent for a minute, wondering. Picturing what might have been. How school might've been different if it was Esther and Nick, instead of Esther and Alistair.

I sit up on my penis bench and look at him properly, trying to get my head around this weird night.

To be honest, when our eyes met across the student bar earlier, my first reaction was to go home.

I've actively avoided Nick since starting at uni a couple of months ago. Firstly, because we were totally *not* friends at school. He was a mouthy little idiot who only hung out with the other boys and seemed to think girls were icky. Secondly, he was Alistair's mate, and I just broke up with Alistair so I didn't want Nick reporting back any of my drunken, snoggy behaviour.

But mostly, I'd avoided Nick because he was a reminder of the old ways. The old me. He knew me as *Fanny Adams*, the loser I'd left behind at school. I'm a university student now! I've reinvented myself into sexy, cool Esther. A person who actually fits in with these awesome, clever, *together* people. As far as these new friends I bought with booze know, I'm brilliant. And I don't want them finding out I'm actually not. I don't want anybody who knew the old me – the real me – to be here, reminding everyone what a gross loser I really am. I don't want Nick telling everyone I spent my school years hiding behind the bike sheds.

The problem is that he's the student bar's newest member of staff.

Completely unavoidable.

I mean, what am I going to do? Go to a different bar and pay real prices?! When I've already spent all my money in a matter of weeks? That's just foolish.

So I stayed. And I found, as the night went on, that I was looking over at him more and more. Seeing him in something like a new light. And when he came over to say hi, he was nothing like the annoying schoolboy I remembered. He was sweet, funny, polite, thoughtful, silly, kind. Everything you'd want.

I realized then that he was probably doing the same thing as me. He'd reinvented himself, too. In fact, he was probably just as scared as me about getting rumbled by his new mates.

'You're so different here,' I say now, switching benches to join him, lying down so we're face-to-face.

He looks thoughtful. 'I don't know if I'm different really. I think, if anything, I'm more *me* here than I was at school. At school there was so much pressure to be a certain thing. Or – I guess more accurately – *not* be a certain thing. To fit in, you have all these rules you're supposed to abide by. I don't mean school rules. I mean, like, *social* rules. I spent so much time and energy trying to be the boy everyone thought I should be back then. It feels like I've been released from prison, coming here.'

'So you like uni so far?' I smile, watching his mouth move.

He nods, laughing. 'I love it. And this new bar job is the bomb! I get free booze and I get to have a little two-person lock-in after hours every now and again.' He makes bold eye contact and my stomach leaps a little.

This is so wrong.

But it feels oddly right. Hanging out here with Nick Wilde in the emptied-out university bar, no one else left but me, him, and a thousand half-drunk pink cocktails in plastic pint cups, waiting to be collected. 'What about you?' he asks earnestly. 'Do you like it here?'

I consider lying and don't. 'No, not really.' I sigh. 'It's fun in some ways but I don't get anything they're saying to me in lectures. I find it boring and confusing. Honestly, I don't really know why I'm here. I feel a bit like I just went along with my parents' suggestions that I "make something of myself". Mostly I just wanted to get away.' I make a face as I wonder if I should tell him the next part. He looks at me, waiting patiently – like he knows there's more to it.

God, he's so much more intuitive than I would ever have guessed. Nick Wilde, the empath! Who would have seen that coming? Shelley and Lou are going to shit their pants when I tell them about this. Maybe I won't tell them.

'So' – I take a deep breath – 'I just started working at this Italian restaurant – just as a dish washer! – but I weirdly really love it. I've always really enjoyed cooking, but never thought I could do anything with it. And watching the chefs at work is amazing.' I look down at my hands. 'Honestly, I really, like, *itch* to be doing it with them. One of them let me help with starters the other day and I was buzzing for hours afterwards.' I look away, embarrassed. 'It's silly.'

'Do you think it's what you want to do?' His voice is serious. 'Like, for real? With your life, I mean?'

I think about this, still looking away. 'I kinda do,' I hedge at last, feeling something fluttering in my belly. 'I want to move to London with Shelley and Lou, and get a fancy job in a glamorous restaurant! But obviously I have to finish university first. Then I guess I'll see what happens.'

'But why?' He looks confused. 'If you know what you want to do, and you're not particularly enjoying uni, why waste these three years? It's not like you're studying anything to do with food, and it's not a career path that demands a degree.'

I frown. 'Because—' I can't think of a reason. The only answer I have is: because my parents told me I should go to university. Instead, I offer: 'Because I already spent all of my student overdraft?'

He laughs at this. Why did I never notice what a great laugh he has? It makes you want to join in and never stop. 'Well, we're only going to spend a fuck ton more money in the next few years.' He pauses. 'Look, I totally selfishly want you to stay' – our eyes meet again and something like a heat pulse flashes between us – 'but university isn't the right thing for everyone. Despite what got drummed into us as kids. If you really do want to be a chef, you should go for it. I think it's a terrific idea, and if you already love it, that's really special.'

God, I want to kiss him.

There is a silence between us as I bite my lip and sit up,

trying not to look down at his long, lean mid-section. His polo shirt – complete with the bar's logo emblazoned across its front – is tight against him. There surely can't be abs under there? None of the boys I've ever met or been with have had abs. Going to the gym wasn't cool at school. You just played football. Football doesn't give you a sixpack, does it? Alistair didn't have one – he had a boy's body. What if Nick Wilde has a man's body?

'All I will say,' he continues after a minute, oblivious to the filth running through my head, 'is that I have an uncle who's a chef. He loves it but he says it's one of the most intense jobs *ever*. He works the longest hours of anyone I know. We never really see him. Plus, he says it can be pretty male-dominated and sweary – you need a thick skin.'

I puff up. 'I can handle it,' I grin. 'I love swearing.'

He smiles at me again and the tension between us is suddenly so thick, I can taste it. He awkwardly pushes his hair off his face and I resist an impulse to grab his hand and lick it. I want to lick every bit of him. I want his fingers on me and in me, I want his man-body pressed against mine. Everything aches for him.

And even though I've never wanted something more in my life – never craved a person like this, never silently begged for a thing so much – I almost don't see it coming when he kisses me.

His lips find mine and it's like some kind of explosion. I've never been kissed like this before. It's hungry and passionate and there's tongue and lips and hands everywhere.

It's unlike anything I've felt before. I've spent the last week kissing every random person I could grab a hold of and the years before that endlessly kissing Alistair – and none of it could compare to this.

The thought of Alistair brings me back to reality. 'We can't do this.' I'm first to pull away but I don't know how I do it. My head is swimming and my vision is blurry. And when I see the lust on Nick's face I nearly dive back in again. I want him so much.

But I can't. It's not right.

'I only just broke up with Alistair,' I say, my voice low and throaty. 'And you're his friend, we can't.'

He regards me intensely.

'You're right,' he says at last. 'I know you're right.' We draw apart properly, both breathing like we ran here. When he speaks again, his voice is determined. 'OK, we'll pretend this didn't happen. We won't tell anyone. Alist— *he* doesn't have to know.' He gives me one more long look and my legs feel weak underneath me. 'But' – he stares at me – 'I don't know if I'll be able to keep away from you, being at university together for the next three years . . .'

CHAPTER FORTY-FIVE

'God, I can't believe you snogged Nick Wilde from the school football team!' Alex looks agog and I feel a stab of irritation.

'I did *not* snog Nick Wilde from the school football team,' I say, giving her a stern look. 'I snogged sexy university student and bartender Nick Wilde, thank you. Totally different people. He grew up and reinvented himself. I kissed sensitive and kind Nick Wilde, who had stubble and feelings even at eighteen.'

'You know what?' Louise looks contemplative. 'Men are really complicated, y'know? Like, *just* as complicated as women.'

'I think you're right!' I nod at her. 'I've been thinking the same lately. I've always dismissed men as dickheads who don't care about anything, but I think men might have *layers*. I think they might be struggling with difficult things and life problems, same as us. I mean, look at Rich the Bastard who it turns out wasn't a bastard at all. He was just a man in a really bad place. And he got help! That's fucking brave, it really is. Especially when we tell men they're not allowed to be vulnerable or sad ever.'

'Exactly,' Lou says. 'We're all in it together. Women don't get the money, but men don't get the emotions! We need equal crying just as much as we need equal pay.'

'Man up, have some balls, don't be such a girl.' Bibi shakes her head sadly. 'The things we say to boys are pathetic, they really are.'

'Although I do quite enjoy *big girl's blouse*,' I ponder. 'That's so evocative. Maybe we could reclaim it, y'know? Make it a good thing? Like, everyone wants to be a big girl's blouse! How fun to be a big girl's blouse!'

'*Blouse* is a weird word,' Alex murmurs.

'We're all equally blousey!' Louise responds with passion. 'Everyone is a blouse.'

'I think men and women are all just as messed up as each other,' Bibi says solemnly. 'It's not as simple as saying an entire gender are dickheads. We're all just people; all lonely and scared and trying to survive.' Alex squeezes her hand tighter.

I nod. 'That.' Something occurs to me. 'I mean, there are definitely exceptions on both sides. Like, Franco is definitely not a blouse. He's a scumbag.'

Bibi sits up straighter, her face dark. 'What happened? What did he do?'

'Huh?' Alex and Lou lean in, looking confused.

'He, well, he sort of tried to force himself on me,' I admit, feeling stupidly ashamed even while knowing I have no reason to feel that way. Lou gasps and puts her arm around me.

'Fuck,' Bibi says in a low voice. 'I'm so sorry, Esther. It's my fault. I did my best to keep you guys away from him. I've been trying to get him fired for months.'

'Has he done it to you?' I ask, suddenly afraid. What if I hadn't got away earlier? What would he have done? What might he have done to Bibi?

Thankfully, she shakes her head. 'No, but only because he knows I would take a rusty kitchen knife to his testicles.' She pauses. 'I already did a bit.' She looks between us all and sighs. 'He's been doing that shit to all the other women who work at the bar. Since long before I started working there. In fact, I was warned about Franco on my first day, but didn't take it seriously until I walked in on him grabbing one of the women's arses. She was so upset.'

'Why didn't you say anything to us?' Louise looks horrified.

Bibi casts her eyes down. 'Because I knew you'd try to get me to quit or do something about him. And, to begin with, I couldn't afford to lose that job. When I told him to get away from my colleague that time, he cornered me later and said he'd get me sacked if I said a word. I couldn't have paid my rent without that job and – as you all know – I couldn't find anything else, despite all my best efforts.'

I reach for her hand and she looks at me gratefully.

'Then, when I caught him doing it again, I went to see him after hours – holding a knife.'

Oh my god, Bibi is a fucking *badass*.

'I was just holding it casually,' she adds quickly when Lou gasps in alarm. 'Y'know, I *am* a bartender, it was legitimate that I would be carrying one. Sometimes I have to chop a lime or a lemon! But I didn't tell him that. I told him if he ever went near any of the other women in the bar, I would come for him. I think he's genuinely terrified of me now.'

I think of all the times we've been in there and Franco slinked past looking scared, or refused to push Bibi when she was rude to him. I thought he was terrified of her because she's generally quite a scary person, not because she'd threatened him.

'You were protecting the women you work with,' I breathe out, in awe of Bibi and her strength. 'You are incredible.'

She looks a bit bashful. 'Well, it was stupid and I very easily could've been hurt or . . . worse. I don't think it's something I'd recommend. But he did leave everyone alone after that.' A pained expression crosses her face and she looks directly over at me. 'Until now, that is. Esther, I'm so sorry. The worst of it is that I've been working with the HR department at head office. They had me documenting anything and everything he's done, and he's about to get fired.'

'He should be fucking *arrested*!' Alex yells, furious. 'He's the Harvey Weinstein of shit bars.'

'Well, that's next on the list,' Bibi nods. 'They're speaking to the police, too, and a few of the women I work with are going to give statements.'

'Woah,' I say in a low voice. 'I will too, if they need?' I

shake my head. 'I thought he was just a pathetic, harmless little man. I can't believe how wrong I was. What's wrong with me – do I give out a signal to predators like Carl and Franco?' I look around, feeling shaken.

'It's them, not you,' Bibi says quietly. 'And we'll all been there multiple times. The world needs to change, not you.'

Alex shakes her head, turning to her new girlfriend with awe. 'You're amazing, baby, so brave.'

'I cannot *wait* to tell that prick where to stick his job,' Bibi replies through gritted teeth.

'Oh,' I perk up, excitedly. 'Have you accepted that job offer then?'

Bibi smiles a bit sheepishly. 'Actually . . . no.' She glances over at Alex, who gives her an encouraging grin. 'I've turned it down. It wasn't really what I wanted to do in the long term and I've decided to go it alone! I've registered myself as self-employed and I'm starting my own little marketing and consulting firm. Alex is going to help me with my website.'

'Oh my god!' I shout delightedly. 'That is perfect! And absolutely fantastic! I'm so proud of you.'

She shrugs, clearly deliriously pleased. 'Plus, I've met so many talented other marketing execs on the job-hunting circuit. We could work together, form a company, make it all a bit more legit. And I can keep working at the bar part time, while we make a go of things. Now Franco's leaving, it might even be quite fun. The rest of the bar staff are nice and I think they'll all like me a lot more if I start doing some actual bartending.'

'I just *know* my bosses will put some work your way,' I throw in happily. 'It turns out,' I tell them shyly, 'that I'm actually pretty well respected and liked by my team. Who knew!'

'Duh.' Bibi rolls her eyes. 'Of course you are. You are so weird the way you doubt yourself all the time. You're brilliant.'

'And speaking of Esther's brilliance' – Alex turns back to me, looking excited – 'tell us about when you next saw Nick after your frustratingly sexless night together at uni.'

I look down at my hands. 'OK,' I reply in a small voice, feeling strange. 'So I was twenty-four, and it was a few months before I met Idris . . .'

The group nods excitedly.

SECRET EX 8: NICK WILDE

AKA The Ex That Wasn't An Ex

PART TWO

The ~~Swan~~ Swab

The exit

7.15pm

We're just leaving when I see him.

'Um, I'll see you at home,' I tell Louise. 'I just spotted someone I know.' She nods, barely glancing back.

'I'm knackered, babe,' she yawns. 'I'm going straight to bed for an early night, I'll see you in the morning.' She goes and I turn my attention back to the pub. Much as I love Lou, I don't want to share this person with her.

We've only been to this pub a couple of times before, despite it being minutes from our flat. It's pretty grubby and old man–y, but we're starting to quite like it. We might even make it our regular.

I cross the room and tap his shoulder lightly. He turns and my stomach melts at the sight of his face.

'Esther?' Nick sounds incredulous like he can't believe it's me. 'It's been years! Jesus, how are you?' He wraps his arms around me and I instantly wish he hadn't. His smell is too much, it lights something up inside me.

'What are you doing here?' I laugh, drinking in his beautiful face, so happy to see me. He has more stubble than the last time I saw him in the student bar, and he's wearing glasses now – they suit him. Otherwise, he's much the same.

'Pub crawl with the work mates,' he answers with an eye roll. 'Actually, they were about to head to the next place. Are you going? Will you stay and have a drink with me?'

He nods his goodbyes to the rowdy group and leads me to a table in the corner. We sit down and regard one another shyly.

'It's nice around here,' he begins hesitantly, glancing about. 'I even like this grotty pub! I've never been to this area before. I've been thinking of moving, maybe I'll move around here?' We make direct eye contact and my mouth is suddenly dry.

'Can I have a sip?' I nod at his beer and he shakes himself.

'Of course, but let me get you one. Sorry, I wasn't thinking.'

I put my hands up. 'No, no, I've probably had enough. I've been in the pub all day with Louise – remember Louise Hickman from school?'

He laughs. 'How could I ever forget Louise? Is she doing OK?'

I nod as we exchange catch-up pleasantries. The small talk feels strangely intimate; natural and warm. Like I could reach over and touch him without it being weird. I could scratch his stubble with my fingernails and kiss his neck.

Hold on, maybe that *would* be weird.

He gestures at the room. 'Do you remember when I worked in the student bar at uni?'

I laugh. 'Obviously! Although I was only at uni for a couple more weeks after, er, *that night*.'

'Yes,' he smiles a little sadly. 'We didn't get any more secret lock-ins.' He pauses. 'Although that one was definitely memorable . . .' Images of the evening hang in the air between us and I cough awkwardly.

'So,' he asks, 'did you end up as a chef? Are you set to be the next Gordon Ramsay?'

I make a face. 'I hope not. But yes, I am working as a chef!'

He looks pleased before catching my expression. 'Oh. Is it not as fun as you hoped?'

'Ahhh,' I sigh. 'I don't know, Nick. I absolutely love it in so many ways. But the hours really are killing me. Today has been my first day off in six months, hence drinking all day with Lou!' He laughs sympathetically, lifting his chin, and I stare at the stubble again.

Maybe just a quick scratch? Maybe he wouldn't mind?

'And some of the people aren't that great,' I add quietly, thinking of all the horribleness with Carl. Leaving that job so suddenly was intensely humiliating, not to mention how many people in the industry seem to know what happened. I got a new job in a kitchen eventually, but some of my co-workers still make comments about Carl as if the situation was all on me – all my fault.

'We're still young,' Nick says kindly. 'Twenty-four is nothing! There's still plenty of time to change your mind about what you want to do. Your dreams are allowed to adapt and change direction.' He nods, almost to himself. 'One minute I'm dreaming about zombies, the next I'm dreaming about wearing the wrong pants to work. Dreams are bananas.'

I snort. God, he's so nice. And so hot.

'I bet you're really good at what you do,' he continues. 'I went to a work party the other week where the food was so terrible.' He makes a face. 'It can spoil your night so easily. Maybe you should get into planning events so you can always make sure the food is decent?' He laughs and I join in but . . .

But . . .

Huh, events. That's something to consider. Events . . . Because I do love the process of creating something special for people. Making something from nothing that people remember. I love being involved in the creation of a special night that brings a whole lot of joy to a group. Huh.

'What about you?' I say quickly, changing the subject. 'Are you happy? How's life going for you as we enter our mid-twenties?'

'Pretty good,' he smiles. 'I'm considering getting a dog. Do you think that would be mad? It's a lot of responsibility, isn't it?'

I reach across and take another cheeky sip of his beer. He doesn't answer immediately, just watches me do it. And I catch his pupils change colour.

'Oh god.' He puts his head in his hands. 'Esther, I don't want to make small talk with you. I mean, it's fun and lovely, but all I'm thinking about is kissing you. I still really, really fancy you.' He pauses, then grins. 'Are you single? Can we, like, go out on a real date?'

I swallow down the instant yes. It can't be as easy as just saying yes. 'Um, are you still friends with Alistair?' I ask at last. He regards me for a few seconds.

'Kind of,' he admits. 'We're not close mates these days, not like we were at school. But we still hang out in a group occasionally.'

I tear my eyes away from his. 'It's too complicated,' I say softly, staring at my hands. 'There's Alistair and ...' I consider how hurt my first love would be. And then I think of Paul. We're just mates at the moment, but increasingly I think something might happen between us now we're both finally single at the same time. We have unfinished business that will get in the way if I go for it with Nick Wilde. Just because I have this weird chemical reaction to him doesn't mean it's the right thing to do.

I try to steady my breathing. 'Sorry, Nick, I don't think we should see each other again. I can't ... It's too much, too intense.'

He gazes at me and then breathes out dejectedly. 'If that's your decision, I guess I have to accept it.' He pauses. 'But I think you're wrong. There's something really fucking cool here, between us. And I think you feel it too.' He reaches out to take my hand and chills pulse through me. He leans closer and whispers urgently, 'Look, can we just have one night together? Tonight? Right now! To get it out of our systems? I feel like I'll never want anyone like this again. Just one night?' He takes my other hand and fireworks explode in me.

I can't, I shouldn't. There's other things to consider. This isn't sensible.

Oh Jesus, he's going to kiss me.

He does, reaching for me across the table, and it's just like last time, but even better. I taste him in my mouth and want more.

'Can we go back to yours?' He is breathless in my ear.

'I really, really want to.' I gulp. 'But Louise is there, and I have a mean old downstairs neighbour who whacks on the ceiling every time we make any noise. I bloody hate him.'

Nick looks crestfallen and it somehow makes him even sexier.

God, I want him.

When people talk about not being able to resist a person, I've always internally scoffed. Like, *of course* you can resist! That's so stupid. You're just saying it as an excuse to behave badly or have unprotected sex or whatever.

But honestly, if Nick asked me to get pregnant right now, I would do it.

'Follow me,' I say in a quiet voice and he does as he's told. We walk with purpose towards the bathrooms.

Ah, there it is. I knew there would be a disabled loo around here somewhere. Right by the kitchen.

With Nick close at my heels, we slip in, shutting the door behind us and waiting for a possible knock and a scolding. When it doesn't come, we launch at one another. Kissing and grabbing and fumbling. Clothes are coming off, my bra pings open, I run my hands over his taut, toned stomach, my insides aching. I want him so badly. More than I've ever wanted someone.

Both naked now and still frantically kissing, I feel him lift me up by my hips, the pressure of his dick against me. I want it so much, *so much*. As I feel him enter me, a bang on the door almost knocks us both off our feet.

'Fuck fuck!' he exclaims, pulling away.

The door is flung open and a nervous-looking man with a name tag that says 'Franco' stands there, a horrified look on his face as he takes in the scene: us in flagrante.

'Get out right now!' he shrieks and we throw clothes on, too ashamed to look up at any point.

'He had a real twat energy,' Nick mutters as we hasten for the pub exit, staring at the ground the whole time.

CHAPTER FORTY-SIX

'So,' I say triumphantly, 'it doesn't count, does it!' Lou's mouth is open and she seems too turned on to reply.

Bibi scowls. 'What do you mean it doesn't count?'

'I mean' – I roll my eyes dramatically – 'that the tip only went in a bit, so it doesn't count. I've never counted Nick as one of my sex partners.'

'Well, you are a lying little strumpet then,' Alex says, looking amused. 'Tip went in, it counts, mate.'

'What would you know about penises,' I mutter and she tuts at me. 'Either way, he's not an ex,' I pout. 'It was just those two encounters until I saw him again at those drinks with Alistair.'

'And how did you feel then?' Bibi asks and three sets of eyes stare at me intently, waiting.

How did I feel?

How did I tell myself I felt, or how did I *actually* feel, deep down in the place I mostly refuse to look?

I'm saved by Lou's phone vibrating and I glance at it.

Upside down I spot a name flash up. The same name that appeared that night we took Bibi to the hospital. The same fucking name! I grab her phone. I can't have been right all along, surely? Was all this I-love-Sven stuff total bullshit after all? What the absolute fuck?

'What are you doing?' she cries, trying to take her phone back.

'Why is Nick texting you?' I shout. 'Why are you making me talk about him? Is it just because you want to check if I'm still interested? What's really going on here, Lou?'

Her face screws up in confusion and then clears. 'Nick?' She sounds like she wants to laugh. 'You think Nick is texting *me*? Why would he be texting me?' She snorts and waves at the phone in my hand. 'Have another look.'

I turn the phone up the right way and read the screen slowly. 'Nikar . . .? Er, um, what?' I look back at her, any anger draining away, replaced by embarrassment.

She looks embarrassed, too. 'It's Sven's alter ego,' she explains in a whisper. 'Nikar the magician. We tried a few scenarios, and this was the character we both fancied the most.'

Bibi and Alex squeak and she turns on them. 'What? You better not be laughing! I've heard some of your sexy talk through the wall, you haven't got a leg to stand on!'

Alex shuts up but Bibi still has the audacity to look amused.

'You want to watch it, *Bibi*!' Louise warns. 'Or I'll call your mum and find out your real name once and for all. I bet it's worse than Nikar the magician.'

The smirk disappears.

'Oh god,' I stutter. 'Sorry, Lou ... that was completely out of line. I thought it said ... well, I don't know! You kept going on about him when we saw him at Alistair's drinks that time. You were staring over and saying how hot he was. Drooling over his sexy beard and everything ... It seemed like you were flirting with him all the time and invited him along to the hospital ...'

She giggles. 'Yeah, no duh! I was trying to get you to admit you still fancied him. I thought you would agree with me about how hot he was, and we could go chase after him for *you*. I was trying to get you to see there were other options outside of these seven exes.' She tuts and then adds as an afterthought, 'Plus, his beard *is* excellent.'

'What about the flowers you were so weird about the other day?' The memory flashes through me. 'That you claimed were from your agent!'

She frowns. 'Oh, they really were from Sven, but you were being so intense about this love mission, I felt bad shoving his romantic gestures in your face.'

I open my mouth to deny this, but close it again. She's right, I got way too intense. I let my head fall into my hands. 'Sorry,' I mutter. 'I guess I care more about Nick than I realized.'

'So we *can* call him an ex?' Alex crows.

I shrug, trying not to smile. Louise looks at me sternly. 'So, for the official record, I haven't been texting Nick, but you know who *should* be? Who should've texted Nick a long time ago?'

This time I do smile. Widely. Because yes, I know. And I think I'm ready now.

NOT SECRET ANYMORE
EX 8: NICK WILDE

AKA The Ex That Wasn't An Ex But Is Now Officially Classed As An Ex

PART THREE

Alex Shelley's house

Esther's phone

2.32am

Nick Wilde (school)

Hey Nick, sorry about the message out
of the blue.

I wanted to say how great it was seeing
you recently and how much more I've really

406

wanted to say to you. I think about you a
lot, and our couple of evenings together all
those years ago. I never forgot about it or
about you.

I've had a weird few months, to be honest,
but today I got to see two of my best friends
fall in love, which was the best thing in the
universe and it's made me want to be braver
than I am. I know this all feels a little strange
and over the top, but if I don't ask, I think
I'll regret it and always wonder. So – deep
breath! – would you like to go out on a real
date with me next week? Jackie Weaver is
obviously invited too.

Esther x

2.33am

Oh fuck yes.
2.35am

EPILOGUE

ONE MONTH LATER

'I can't believe it's really happening.' Lou dabs her eyes. 'I really never thought this day would come.' She laughs shakily and I hug her, trying not to crease her dress.

'Me neither.' I steal a tissue to wipe my face, too. 'I didn't think I'd be this emotional. It's so pathetic, I hate crying! I always promised myself I wouldn't cry.'

'Well' – Lou takes a deep breath – 'today is a big day. A really special day. I think it's OK to feel emotional. It's been such a long time coming.'

I give her another hug, and when we pull away, we look at each other, smiling brightly, our eyes shiny and wet.

'Love you, Esther,' she says softly and another tear rolls down my cheek.

'You, too, Louise,' I whisper.

'OK, SHITTER'S DONE,' the plumber yells from inside the bathroom and we shout a simultaneous 'HURRAH'.

Neither of us can believe it's taken all these years to get the loo fixed properly. By a real professional plumber and not by the landlord's incompetent son-in-law. No wonder we're both so emotional.

'Can we see?' The two of us cram into the doorway and coo as the plumber stares at the ceiling, looking bored. 'It's amazing! There's no water around the rim!' I speak in awed tones. 'Can I flush it? It won't overflow?' The plumber screws up his face at my question.

'Of course it won't overflow, what am I, a fucking idiot? It was an easy fix.'

'Wowwwww!' I say, stepping forward to test the handle.

'Hold on!' Lou sounds fearful. 'I'm going to step back. I don't want to mess up my dress if it does spray water or something.'

'Good idea,' I agree reverentially. Louise has got a new job as a – wait for it – magician's assistant. Perfect, right? She absolutely loves it and has an incred outfit to wear. She reckons Great-Uncle Merton helped her get the job, but I think she's confusing ghosts with magic. It's a year-long contract and she'll be touring all over the country with the show. She's thrilled. She gets all the buzz of being on stage in front of an audience, and doesn't actually have to act. Which is handy really, because it turns out she is pretty shit at acting. She finally got a one-line job on *Casualty* recently and when it aired, they'd cut her face out. You could just hear her off-screen, shouting, 'Someone ring 999!' And even off-screen she somehow managed to be utterly unconvincing. Either way, she's happy and the new job is giving her loads of role-play fodder for bedroom time with Sven.

The plumber huffs angrily and crosses his arms. 'It won't fucking spray water. What toilet sprays water across the room?'

We both eye him. 'We've been through a hell of a lot with this toilet, mate,' I tell him calmly. He has no idea.

The door bangs. 'Girls?' Sofia's voice echoes in from the hallway.

'We're in the toilet!' I yell back. 'With the plumber.'

'Filming pornography, are we?' She peers round the door and nods at the gruff plumber.

'Oh, I've never heard that one before,' he says, rolling his eyes. 'Now, who's paying me?' the loo-saver grunts as Lou and I exchange looks. The landlord is not going to screw us again, is he? He promised he'd be here to sort out the invoice.

'He's outside.' Sofia catches our worried glance. 'I just passed him. He's screaming at someone on the phone.' I raise my eyebrows. Of course he is. He'll be punishing another poor tenant who pays the earth to live in one of his many London hovels.

'I'll go,' I volunteer bravely, giving Sofia a quick smile as I pass. She's here a lot these days, it's nice. Especially with Bibi gone.

I fling open the front door. 'Mr Whittle?' I enquire, nervously.

'WAIT!' One hand is on the phone and the other comes up in front of my face, palm up. He continues shrieking into the phone for a minute while I hop from foot to foot, freezing my butt off out here without my coat.

After a minute, I try again. 'Mr Whittle, the plumber is inside and he's waiting to—'

'Just SHUT UP,' he spits in my face, yellow teeth flashing. 'I'm speaking to a tenant and you're being disrespectful.'

I'm being disrespectful? I AM?

'You're *shouting* at a tenant actually,' I say furiously. 'Just like you do with all of us. You're a *bully*, Mr Whittle, and I've really had enough of it.' I'm yelling all of a sudden. 'Just because you're the landlord, you think you have all the power. But we have rights, y'know? We've put up with a lot of shit from you over the years, and we've always been good tenants. We pay our rent – the rent you put up every year! – and we pay the bills. You don't get to treat us with such disdain! I bet if we called up all your tenants, they'd say the same.'

'How DARE y—' Mr Whittle's chest expands to twice its usual size as he steps into my personal space. But his rant is stopped in its tracks by Sofia and Ivan appearing from nowhere. With a dancer's light step, Sofia is suddenly in front of me. 'Step back, *monsieur*!' She draws herself up to her full five-ten, towering over the puffed-up Mr Whittle. He quivers. 'We will find not only all your other tenants,' she threatens, her eyes flashing as she gets in his face, 'but Ivan and I will both join the complaint. There are rules in place to stop tiny pricks like you taking advantage of the housing crisis. You will face sanctions, sir! We all know the roof is full

411

of asbestos and we say nothing. If we choose to complain, it will cost you thousands.'

Ivan joins her, another body between us. 'And we know the electrics aren't up to code. Or the pipes. You'd be buggered, mate. Better start getting your act together around here.'

Whittle looks shocked at this. Tenants uniting together to help one another? This is his worst nightmare. The horror!

I step forward. 'Go pay our plumber for finally fixing the toilet, Mr Whittle. Oh, and that bloody yellow damp on my bedroom ceiling is going to be sorted as well, isn't it?' His face darkens so I add a killer blow. 'Because' – I pause super dramatically – 'Bibi might be moving out, but I *will* send her after you if I need to. Believe me when I say she has taken down bigger pricks than you.' I don't mention the time she threatened a man with a knife. We currently have the higher ground; I wouldn't want to blow it.

He pales at the mention of Bibi's name – as he should.

'Fine,' he snaps. 'I will go in and pay the man. And I will sort out your stupid stain. Even though I'm sure you caused it.' He narrows his eyes at me furiously as if I really am penetrating damp. 'Here.' He hands me some documents. 'Give these to your friend moving out. It's her paperwork.'

I take them, eyeballing him as he heads inside.

'Thanks, guys,' I smile brightly at Ivan and Sofia. 'I'm glad you've stayed friends.'

They beam at each other. 'Us too!'

A part of me is sad Ivan and Sofia didn't make it past their fourth date, but there's no bad blood there. Sofia was the one who ended it, explaining how she had too many other options on Tinder to just settle for one man. She said she'd finally realized how much she loves being single. She loves the freedom and the adventure and the spontaneity it offers. Plus, the on-demand peen on dating apps. Either way, I can understand what she means now. Being single can be amazing if you're in the right headspace for it.

I take the documents inside and leave them on Bibi's old bed. She can pick them up when she and Alex come over for dinner later.

Out in the hallway, I can hear the plumber arguing with Whittle about money, and Louise laughing on the phone to Sven – Nikar – in the living room. But I stay in here for another minute, looking around, taking it all in. It's so weird seeing Bibi's room empty like this. All her lovely stuff, gone. Well, not gone, just moved over to Alex's. Not even that far away. Only three stops up the Northern Line.

I sigh.

Change is weird, isn't it? I try not to resist it – I even try to embrace the good changes – but it's still weird. And it feels like the last few months have been all change.

Me turning thirty, Bibi moving out, Sven moving in. Bibi starting her new company and us getting to work together on some fun events. Actually, that's been fantastic. My bosses have been blown away by her work ethic. So have I, given what I'd seen at The Swab. They're even talking about taking her little company on in some kind of formal capacity. Like, with a financial retainer of some kind. It's brilliant and I know Bibi's having the time of her life. Plus, it makes me look good that I brought her in.

What else, what else? Oh yeah.

Nick.

'Helloooooo?' a familiar voice shouts down the hallway, accompanied by the scrambling sound of doggy nails on wood floors.

Jackie Weaver appears from nowhere in the doorway, breaking into the biggest doggy-grin when she sees me. Bounding towards me, tongue out, she leaps into the air, knocking me backwards onto Bibi's old mattress and covering my face with delirious licks.

'Do I get a kiss, too?' Nick leans on the door frame, grinning at the sight of me and Jackie wrestling.

Like I said, some change is good. Very very good.

It's early days but I know what it is me and Nick have. It's the first time there haven't been any games or messing about. He texts me right back, he turns up on time, he tells me I'm beautiful without me dropping heavy-handed hints. I'm not in any rush to get serious or define it – not like I was before – but we have the best time together. We get on so well and the sex is amazing. Especially since we were able to get more than just the tip in.

'Get over here and help me,' I laugh as Jackie licks my eyeball. Nick obliges, fighting his way through, to gather me up and into his arms for a proper hello.

God, his kisses still make me dizzy.

'You ready for our dog walk in the park?' he murmurs into my neck and I'm suddenly not ready at all. In fact, I might have to just take him over to my room and—

'Jackie!' I exclaim, pulling away from Nick, as she knocks over Bibi's paperwork from Mr Whittle, scattering it across the floor.

'Sorry.' Nick grabs for Jackie's collar. 'I'll get her out of your way. Meet you outside in a minute?' I nod as he leans over for another kiss before exiting.

As I gather up all the papers and stack them back in a pile, I stop short.

Oh my god.

No way no way no way.

It's her name. Bibi's full, proper name. It's right there, in the documents. In black and white.

Holy crap.

Birgit Morag Colmer.

BIRGIT. That is fucking brilliant.

I hear the door slam as the plumber and landlord leave together, still arguing loudly.

I pull out my phone to text Bibi – sorry, Birgit – to tell her I finally know her secret. But then I stop.

She doesn't want us to know and she likes teasing us about it. I can let her have that. And if she wants to tell us the truth one day, I can always act surprised. I can give her that much. She gives *me* so much. Her, Alex, Louise. They're the very best of people and I want to hang out with them for all my life.

415

I'm excited about Nick, I really am. I'm excited for what adventures we might have, but I know what's important now. He isn't the *everything* I needed from a man, and I understand that. He adds something to my life; he makes me smile and laugh and it *is* fun having someone on my team, to do fun things with. But he adds loveliness to what is already wonderful. I don't need a partner to make things good because it already is good. I'm so, so glad I finally understand that; understand how lucky I am. It's the best thing to realize. And I'm weirdly grateful to every single one of my seven exes for teaching me that. They helped me understand myself and helped build me into the person I am. They all led me here, to the place I am now, with my best friends at my side and a job I love that doesn't take over everything in my life. And they led me to Nick.

I'm grateful.

Louise pokes her head in. Her new magician stage dress is soaked and she looks stressed out.

'Toilet's broken again, babe. I've put out the vase, it's your turn.'

Acknowledgements

Hello you strange and sexy readers who look at these back pages. I want to firstly say my biggest thank you to YOU. Because they would not allow me to write books at all if you didn't read them and say kind things about them. You are honestly the best people in the world and I LOVE YOU.

My next biggest thank you has to go to my gorgeous (she really is gorgeous – Google her) editor, Molly Crawford and my wonderful publisher Simon & Schuster. Thank you all SO much. You guys have been absolute rockstars throughout this whole process and I can't thank you enough. Thank you SO MUCH Sabah, you beautiful publicity magician, you really blow me away. To SJV for organising the best parties and for writing out my jokes so you can quote them back to me. And mostly for the House of Virtue gin! I mean, WOW. Thank you a million to Clare for bringing me into the S&S fold, to Amy Fulwood for your amazing marketing prowess, to Jess for having cool hair, to Pip for her beautiful cover, and ermagahd, to the glorious rights team, Amy, Ben and Maud, who did so much work to get this book sold around the world in so many exciting places. I'm sorry I keep sending you gushy messages and weird-hugging you.

I also really want to thank Olivia Barber, who helped me hugely in the early stages of brainstorming with this book and who is a truly lovely, talented human.

Diana Beaumont – as queenly as that sexy name would imply – I love you very much. Thank you for all the support and love you send my way. I can't believe I still haven't seen The Dress, what the hell.

An infinity thank you to all the generous and kind authors who have been so lovely and nice to me. I had no idea when I started writing books, that I would find such a warm, inclusive community of talented women who would shout nice things from the rooftops to help each other. It makes me want to cry how GOOD you all are. There are so many people I should thank, so if you are an author pal and your name isn't here, know that there were many close friends and family members I literally forgot to invite to my wedding party. That's the brain level we're working with.

Thank you to the glorious Lindsey Kelk, Daisy Buchanan, Lauren Bravo, Beth O'Leary, Holly Bourne, Caroline Corcaran, Paige Toon, Ayisha Malik, Isabelle Broom, Rosie Walsh, Cesca Major, Kate Riordan, Caroline Hulse, Marian Keyes, Milly Johnson (Johnny), Mhairi McFarlane, Salma El-Wardany, Louise O'Neill, Lia Louis, Justin Myers, Lizzy

Dent, Beth Reekles, Hannah Doyle, Poorna Bell, Kate Weston — and oh god, so so so many others who've been so ridiculously lovely and supportive, cheerleading my books now and in the past. Thank you to the moon and back.

A massive — probably boozy — cheers to my friends and family; you are all amazing and I'm so grateful for all the support you continually give me. Thank you for always listening nicely whenever I moan about spending all day in bed crying about procrastinating. I finished this book, OK?

I also want to thank David H–HH. Between writing *Seven Exes* and it coming out, we ran off to Vegas together — along with my CAFCs Sarah and Fred — to get married, which was nice. David is a very cool dude who has been so enormously brilliant to me in the last few years, especially while I was trying and failing to write words on a page. Thank you for making me laugh every single day. Let's have purple drinks until I suffocate you.

Thanks again, all you gorgeous humans. I should probably go now because the next book is due with Molly in a matter of weeks and I've only written about 10k words — please don't tell her. The main reason these acknowledgements are as long as they are is because it's another excuse not to get on with the new book. Lalalalalalalala. Right, Imma go hug my dogs for half an hour. Bye.

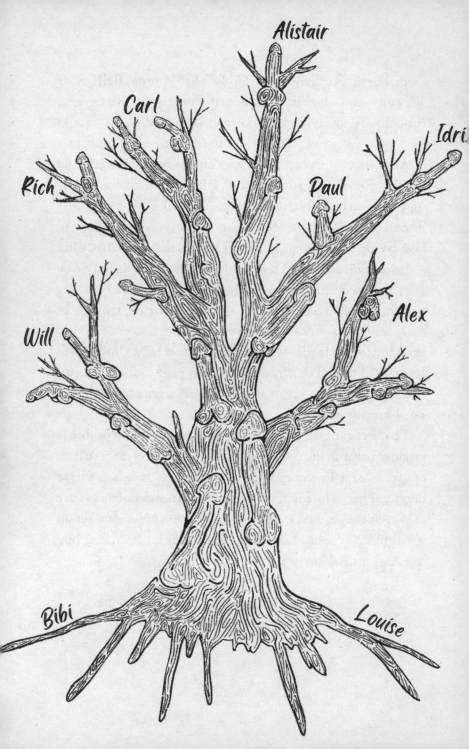

Esther's Dickhead Tree

The Bastard
RICH
- Stupid hot
- Never answered texts
- 10/10 Dickhead

The Overlap
WILL
- Big ears but they worked
- Only funny online
- 5/10 Dickhead

The Serious One
IDRIS
- Very serious
- Nice jumpers
- 4/10 Dickhead

The Missed Chance
PAUL
- Lovely
- I'm the idiot
- 1/10 Dickhead

The Work Mistake
CARL
- Required constant blowjobs, ugh
- Exhausting but sexy
- 9/10 Dickhead

The Friend with Benefits
ALEX
- Super fun
- Many orgasms
- 2/10 Dickhead

The First Love
ALISTAIR
- Good at football
- Shit at sex
- 6/10 Dickhead

Esther
- Petty
- Good tits
- (Unintentionally) funny
- 10/10 Dickhead

Louise
- Sweet
- Basic AF
- 3/10 Dickhead

Bibi
- Sexy bitch
- Cooler than me
- 7/10 dickhead